SIMPLY IRRESISTIBLE

Abruptly, he closed the door, forced her up against it, and kissed her, his hands buried in her thick hair. It was a fiery, undisciplined kiss, his tongue leaping wildly as he discovered her openness. Juliet welcomed it, her heart beating wildly as again and again his mouth closed over hers. When he was finished, he reluctantly released her but leaned his hands against the door on either side of her head.

She reached up very deliberately and kissed his mouth. Unlike his kiss, hers was gentle, savoring, sweet. She touched his lips with the tip of her tongue. "There is not the least need for restraint with me," she whispered. "I'm yours if you want me."

The weakness she saw in his eyes made her feel all-powerful, irresistible. Slowly, she pulled the laces of her ombre dress and shrugged out of it. As he watched, stunned, the silk crumpled at her feet, and she stood before him wearing only her white silk drawers, stockings, and satin slippers. Her hair covered her breasts, but almost defiantly, she pushed the long, dark curls aside . . .

Simply Scandalous

Tamara Lejeune

ZEBRA BOOKS
Kensington Publishing Corp.
www.kensingtonbooks.com

ZEBRA BOOKS are published by

Kensington Publishing Corp.
850 Third Avenue
New York, NY 10022

All Kensington titles, imprints, and distributed lines are available at special quantity discounts for bulk purchases for sales promotion, premiums, fund-raising, educational, or institutional use.

Special book excerpts or customized printings can also be created to fit specific needs. For details, write or phone the office of the Kensington Special Sales Manager: Attn. Special Sales Department. Kensington Publishing Corp., 850 Third Avenue, New York, NY 10022. Phone: 1-800-221-2647.

Zebra and the Z logo Reg. U.S. Pat. & TM Off.

ISBN 0-8217-7973-7

First Printing: December 2005
10 9 8 7 6 5 4 3 2 1

Printed in the United States of America

Chapter 1

Even on the foggiest of London nights, there could be no mistaking Mr. Cary Wayborn for any other gentleman about town. In addition to a heliotrope greatcoat with numerous capes and buttons the size of copper pennies, Mr. Wayborn was known to wear spectacles filled with lavender glass, high-topped boots with silver tassels, and, most regrettably, an aubergine tricorn hat twenty years out of fashion, which even Miss Juliet Wayborn, his affectionate sister, could not look upon without wincing.

It was, therefore, easy work for two shadowy underworld figures to follow that young gentleman from his club on St. James's Street; wait until he parted company with Mr. Eustace Calverstock, his friend from the City; then attack him from behind with short, heavy clubs. Piccadilly was a silent trench of fog as they dragged him into an alley and went to work.

Their victim, who was more than a bit tipsy when the first blow cracked his skull, was unable to do anything to stop the rain of abuse that followed, being sprawled facedown upon the cobbles in a semiconscious state. Cary's walking stick was kicked from his hand to join his hat a few feet away. His left arm was very quickly broken, and it was only the unexpected return of Eustace Calverstock that saved his friend's right arm.

Screaming for the Night Watch, Mr. Calverstock ran back into the thick, woolly fog. As he approached the scene, he heard one of the attackers unburdening himself of a few words, delivered in a rough Cockney accent: "There now, your honor! A present, if you like, from my Lord Swale, and sure you'll not be driving them chestnuts of yours to Southend in the morning!" Giving Cary a final kick in the ribs, he followed his cohort back into the misty stews of London, his leisurely pace demonstrating a long familiarity with the inefficiency of the Watch.

"Did you hear that, Stacy?" Cary cried from the ground. Up until the moment his attacker had spoken, Cary naturally had assumed that he had met with a pair of footpads intent on stealing his purse and watch. "Swale has done this! *Swale!*"

"He'll pay for it," Stacy Calverstock said grimly as he helped his friend to a sitting position. The amount of blood pouring from his friend's head was incredible. "Don't try to talk," he advised. "Your arm is broken, old man," he added, averting his eyes as blood always had a most disquieting effect upon his digestion.

"I know it," Cary rasped, his jaw clenched against the pain. With his right hand, he began clawing at his cravat. Stacy, who had questioned his friend's wisdom, if not his sanity, at the time this purple-spotted neck-cloth had been purchased, nonetheless saw its usefulness as a sling or a bandage, but before he could help Cary unravel its knot, they heard the Watchman's bell.

Stacy froze. When he had called for the Watch, he had never supposed that anyone would actually answer. It was deuced embarrassing. He saw his friend's hat and stick lying in the street and hurriedly scooped them up.

"Help me to my feet, for God's sake!" cried Cary. With sheer force of will, he beat down the pain and climbed to his feet. "Get me away from here before the Watch—"

He broke off as a figure emerged from the fog, and a lantern swung before their eyes. "'Ere now!" cried a lusty voice not unlike that of Cary's attacker. "What's all this then?"

The Watchman, despite the unusual diligence he had shown in responding to their cries, had arrived too late to intercept the miscreants, but he was just in time to embarrass the Gentry.

"Nothing to concern you, Watchman," Stacy Calverstock said coldly. "You may go."

"This gentleman don't appear well," the Watchman observed with less concern than satisfaction. "I'd be remiss in my duty—"

"Quite right," Stacy said crisply. "My friend is ill. He fell down and broke his head, as you see. I am taking him home. Good night." With Cary leaning heavily on his arm, he turned to go.

"Just a minute, guv!"

Stacy swore under his breath, but his injured friend managed a wan smile. "Yes, Watchman?"

"Would these be your eyeglasses, sir?"

Cary gingerly accepted the miraculously unbroken spectacles with his right hand. "Thank you, Watchman," he said, his voice faint but steady. "Sorry to trouble you on such a cold night. Heaven knows you should be safe in your box with a hot cup of tea."

The Watchman stiffened. "I'd be remiss in my duty, sir—"

"Yes, yes!" Stacy said impatiently and tossed the man a silver coin. Then, half-carrying, half-dragging his friend, he turned into an alley leading back toward Piccadilly. "You need a bloody doctor," he told Cary, panting.

Cary sagged in his arms. "I may need a doctor, but when I have done with Swale, he will be needful of the undertaker!" The bravado cost him; his legs gave way, and he sank to the ground.

"Where do I take you?" Stacy demanded. "Not back to White's—"

"Lord, no!" Cary forced his eyes open. "Take me to my sister, to Julie," he managed just before fainting for the first time in his life.

Miss Juliet Wayborn, Stacy knew, was currently lodged with her aunt, Lady Elkins, at Number 17 Park Lane. Indeed, he had often taken tea at that excellent address, sometimes as late as eight o'clock in the evening, and had reason to believe he was a favorite of both the young lady and her aunt. All the same, Lady Elkins was unlikely to welcome the sight of his white-topped boots on the Axminster carpet in her front hall at half-past two in the morning.

The Apricot Salon, so named for the pattern on the silk panels adorning its lofty walls, was soon bathed in the light of a hundred candles as curious servants brought their bedroom tapers down from the attics. Mr. Calverstock had never seen so many nightshirts and lace caps in all his life, and it seemed to him that every servant in all of Mayfair had joined the throng in Lady Elkins's salon before Huddle, her ladyship's maid, abruptly made the executive decision to wake Miss Juliet. Lady Elkins should not be disturbed, of course, for she was a lady of advancing years, much celebrated for her authentic tremors, megrims, and palpitations, but her niece was a young lady of stout constitution and steady nerves. Miss Juliet would best know what to do.

As Cary was brought in, Mademoiselle Huppert, Miss Wayborn's very dashing French maid, wept single-mindedly into the curtains. The footmen formed a grave cabal at the mantelpiece, while Parker, the butler, regarded Stacy Calverstock with open hostility.

"Not *that* sofa, if you please!" Parker exclaimed coldly, having mistaken Mr. Wayborn's deplorable condition for a drunken stupor. "It has just been recovered by Mr. Soho!"

Another sofa untouched by the famous Mr. Soho was made available, and a footman brought a branch of candles. Cary's face was white as cotton wool, and streaked with blood.

"He's been murdered, Mr. Parker!" cried a footman.

Parker, shocked into civility, at once sent Tom for her ladyship's cognac.

Huddle, meanwhile, had tiptoed past Lady Elkins's room to the smaller chamber currently occupied by her ladyship's niece and was approaching the bed.

Miss Juliet Wayborn was by no means the ranking beauty of the Season, but the servants were proud of her all the same. She was a tall, dark-haired young lady whose intelligent gray eyes and patrician good looks tended to intimidate rather than attract the opposite sex.

"She's not pretty," Huddle was fond of saying. "She's *handsome.*" It was Huddle's considered opinion, based upon years of study, that serious young ladies like Miss Juliet tended to make better marriages than the more sensational beauties the society columns raved about. A quiet, elegant, dignified young lady like Miss Julie would appeal to men of sense, education, and property, and she would not be bothered by the rakes, wastrels, and frivolous young gentlemen with more hair than brains.

A draft from the open door awakened Juliet, and she sat up, shivering. "Huddle?" she murmured, squinting at the figure holding a candlestick in one hand. In the next moment, she had thrown back the covers. "Is my aunt unwell?" she asked anxiously, reaching for her purple dressing gown.

Huddle, usually such a sensible woman, lost no time in telling Juliet that Master Cary had been brought home to die. According to Lady Elkins's maid, there was neither a drop of blood left in his veins nor a bone in his body that hadn't been broken. To send for surgeons seemed futile, but perhaps there was still time to fetch a priest?

Fearing the worst, her heart pounding, Juliet fastened her dressing gown and ran down the steps in her bare feet.

Stacy Calverstock jumped as she entered the salon and discovered, to his surprise, that he could not take his eyes from her. He had always regarded Juliet as a well-behaved, feminine version of his friend Cary, and on those occasions when he found himself in her company, he had willingly accepted her as an amiable substitute for his friend, but never before had it struck him so forcefully that she was a desirable young woman of nineteen. He had always understood her to be seven years Cary's junior, and the mathematics of the situation were not beyond him, but seeing her in a silk and lace dressing gown with her rich dark hair unbound unaccountably threw him into confusion. Her wide gray eyes, usually so steady, were wild and fearful. He had never seen her looking so vulnerable or, he was forced to admit, so appealing.

She made him wish that he were taller, handsomer, and, above all, richer.

"Stacy!" she cried, rushing past the servants to take his hands. "What has happened to Cary?"

Before he could answer, she caught sight of her brother. Cary, who was still bleeding freely from the head and clutching his left arm, was trying to sit up. "Don't worry, Julie," he croaked. "Don't . . . make a fuss. Not as bad as it looks."

She was at his side in an instant. "You priceless ass!" she remonstrated with all the fury of a devoted sister who has been given a bad fright. "What have you done to yourself? Lie down! You'll only make it worse."

Her words proved true. Cary fell back onto the sofa and could not be roused again.

"Has anyone sent for Mr. Norton?" his sister demanded.

"No, Miss Julie," Parker said. "That is, Master Cary has just arrived."

"Right!" said Juliet, recognizing that they were all looking to her for guidance. In just a few moments, she had the situation in hand. Tom was sent to fetch Mr. Norton, the surgeon, and the female servants were instructed to boil water and prepare bandages. Huddle was dispatched to her ladyship's medicine box for laudanum and antiseptic. Stacy and the second footman were enlisted to carry the injured man up to his sister's room, there being no fire lit in any other bedroom, with the exception of that of Lady Elkins. Juliet's clearheaded command of the situation impressed Mr. Calverstock greatly, and the servants seemed relieved to be given something to do.

Stacy saw his friend laid on the bed, then hastened to assist Juliet in lighting a branch of candles. "Why do you stare at me as though you've never seen me before?" she asked him suddenly, frowning.

"I beg your pardon!" he exclaimed, blushing. "Was I?"

"Help me get his boots off, for heaven's sake," she ordered him, hurrying over to the bed. When this task was accomplished, she calmly handed the footwear to the manservant. "Take them away and give them a good polish, Arthur," she instructed, as though her brother's prized high-topped boots were spattered with mud rather than blood. It was not to be doubted that the Wayborns knew how to carry on in the face of adversity. "Do what you can with his coat and hat."

"Yes, Miss Julie."

"Now then, Stacy," she said, turning to her brother's friend. "Come with me." Leaving Cary in the care of Huddle and Mademoiselle Huppert for the moment, she led her brother's friend down to the first floor.

In the Apricot Salon, she spied the brandy on the tea tray. "Put the cognac away, Parker," she angrily commanded the butler. "You know perfectly well that's only for emergencies!"

Mr. Calverstock, who could have done with a cognac at the moment, made as though to follow the butler from the room, but Julie rounded on him furiously. "I should very much like to know what you mean by bringing my brother home in this condition!" she said sharply.

"My dear Miss Wayborn," he said feebly, acutely aware that he was addressing an attractive young female dressed for bed, "I feel certain that Cary would prefer to tell you himself when he is recovered."

"Sit down at once, and tell me what happened," said Juliet in a tone that a rhinoceros would have obeyed. Stacy sat on the sofa recently recovered by the famed Mr. Soho and gave her a very spare and sanitized version of the evening's events. "I ran back as soon as I heard the noise," he finished. "By the time I got there, the damage was done, I'm sorry to say."

Juliet exploded. "These murderous thieves must be captured and hanged! I shall write to Benedict at once."

"No, don't!" Stacy cried, alarmed. It was said in Parliament that Sir Benedict Wayborn could shear the flesh from a man's body with a glance, and Stacy had reason to believe it was true. "On the whole, I'd say that Sir Benedict would rather not know."

"You're right, of course," she agreed as Parker left the room. "And now, I think," she went on coldly, "I should like to hear the truth."

His cheeks burned. "I assure you, Miss Wayborn—"

"Nonsense!" she interrupted. "I know you are lying because you are calling me Miss Wayborn. Very odd, don't you agree, since we have been Christian-naming each other since you were ten and I was five? Of course, if you want me to call you Mr. Calverstock—"

"No!" he exclaimed. Suddenly, it was very important that he forever remain Stacy to her.

"Very well then, Stacy," she said gently, "if Cary is in trouble, you must tell me. I'm smarter than both of you put together, though I admit that isn't saying much. I'll be able to tell you what to do."

He could not help but smile at the notion that even so accomplished a young lady as Juliet might have anything to teach Mr. Cary Wayborn and Mr. Eustace Calverstock, two experienced men of the world. "The situation is well in hand," he assured her. "I know who is responsible for this night's work, and he will be held accountable."

"Stacy!" she cried, her eyes lighting up with so much admiration he felt his heart begin to thud. "You caught the man who did this?"

"Er . . . no," he said.

The admiration was replaced by annoyance. "You let him get away?" she cried in disgust. "Never mind! Who is he? Who is responsible for this outrage?"

Suspicion suddenly entered her range of expressions. "Is it—is it gambling debts? Does Cary owe insane amounts of money?"

"Certainly not!" he protested, his pale skin turning bright pink.

She shook her head impatiently. "There is something you're not telling me. They did not even take his watch! And footpads and cutpurses do not typically beat their . . . their victims with Turkish brutality, you know."

"No, I didn't know," he said, attempting a lofty tone. "Are you very well acquainted with the criminal class?"

The lofty tone, never easy, became impossible as Juliet's hand flashed out and took a very firm hold on his nose. "I am holding your nose, Mr. Calverstock," she informed him. "I shall go on holding your nose until you tell me what happened. You'll look pretty silly going back to your rooms at the Albany with Miss Wayborn attached to your nose. Better tell me," she added kindly, while tightening her hold. "Uncle?"

"Uncle!" he agreed.

She gave the Calverstock beak a vicious twist before releasing it.

"The brutal Thuggee of India could learn from your methods," he complained, rubbing his nose. "All right! All right," he cried as she lifted her hand again. "I don't think they *were* footpads."

She glared at him. "Well? What were they, Stacy? Jealous husbands?"

He blushed. "Don't be silly!"

"Not jealous husbands, not footpads," she murmured thoughtfully. "Not gambling debts. What then, hired assassins?" She laughed briefly at the absurdity of the idea.

"Well . . . "

"Hired assassins!" Juliet cried. "Are you mad? Why would you say such a thing?"

"I didn't say it, in point of fact," he said, beginning to babble. "In point of fact, I haven't said anything. You can't say I've told you anything because I haven't."

Juliet jumped to her feet. "And yet I heard you quite distinctly! Someone has hired *assassins* to kill my brother. And you say you know who is responsible? His assailants must have said something when they were beating him. What did they say?"

"Something about the broken arm being a gift from Lord Swale," Stacy mumbled unhappily.

"Swale? I've never heard of him," she declared, tossing her head. "He must be new. Ring for Parker, will you?"

Since at that moment the butler was listening at the door, he was not long in arriving.

"Parker, go and fetch the Peerage from her lady-ship's sewing basket," the young lady commanded him. "I want the history, if any, of a creature called Lord Swale."

Parker was astonished. Obviously, Miss Juliet was not thinking clearly. Fortunately, Mr. Calverstock spared him the embarrassment of having to tell the young lady that butlers do not fiddle with ladies' sewing baskets.

"It's a courtesy title," Stacy explained. "Swale's father is the Duke of Auckland."

Juliet gasped. "The Duke of Auckland! I danced with his Grace twice last week at Almack's! An amiable old gentleman. Indeed, I was terrified he might make me an offer. Some older gentlemen do seem to prefer the plainer girls, you know, especially when they are in the market for a second wife. Well, perhaps they don't prefer us exactly." She smiled ruefully. "Perhaps it's just that they have learned not to trust the really pretty ones!"

Stacy, who ought to have been accustomed to such frank talk from his best friend's sister, found himself blushing. "My dear Juliet," he stammered, "you are anything but plain."

"Thank you for your gallantry," she answered with a faint smile. "But I know very well I am not a beauty like your cousin Serena. All the same, I expect I shall manage to find a nice, quiet, respectable husband. Don't look so shocked," she teased him. "Someday, someone will make me an offer, despite what you might think, *Mister* Calverstock. I just hope it won't be his Grace of Auckland—I absolutely refuse to marry a man old enough to be my grandfather! I must say," she continued in a more serious tone, "I can scarcely believe that Auckland has a son capable of such outrageous conduct! Why on earth would Lord Swale want to harm my brother? Has . . . has Cary done something terrible to Lord Swale?"

Stacy snorted. "On the contrary, Cary has honored his lordship too much by challenging him to a curricle race. Cary's chestnuts against his lordship's grays. If it is any consolation, I . . . I don't think Swale wanted Cary dead."

"Just out of commission for the race," she retorted. "The shameful coward! Someone should teach this Swale a valuable lesson about good Ton and bad Ton."

"I intend to," said Stacy resolutely, inspired by her flashing eyes and heightened color. "Tomorrow . . ." A glance at the pretty ormolu clock on the mantel forced him to correct himself. "In a few hours, I shall ride down to the yard of the Black Lantern Inn, where everyone will be assembled for the race at the ungodly hour of seven o'clock. My dear Julie, I mean to call him out!"

"Call him out?" she scoffed. "Is that the best revenge your feeble brain can invent? What good is a duel to us? There will always be people who say that *my brother* was the coward for forfeiting the race. And if you were to shoot his lordship, you would have to leave England forever, and I would miss you, Stacy." She regarded him intently, her eyes dark with feeling.

"Would you—would you really miss me, Julie?" he cried, the pain in his nose forgotten.

"Of course," she said briskly. "Quite awfully. What a pity you never learned to drive properly! If you had, you might take Cary's place and beat Lord Swale at his own game."

"I'm afraid I would only disgrace myself," he said ruefully. "Worse yet, I might damage your brother's chestnuts. Then *my* crime would throw Swale's perfidy quite into the shade!"

Juliet smiled thinly. "Cary will owe a great deal of money, I suppose. What was the wager?"

"Now, look here," he protested. "Leave all that to me."

"How much?" she said, tapping her foot. "How much, or I swear I shall never call you Stacy again!"

"Five hundred pounds," he said weakly.

"Good Lord!" she whispered, horrified. "Why are men such fools? For five hundred pounds, I could have a gown encrusted with diamonds and pearls. Encrusted, I tell you!"

"I should be happy to pay Lord Swale," he said uncertainly.

"Indeed?" she murmured. "You must have a stomach lined with copper! The thought of paying him a farthing, let alone a monkey, makes me positively ill. Still, we must pay him his money, the nasty cheat." She stood up abruptly, and he correctly interpreted this as his dismissal. She extended her hand to him, and, to her surprise, he bent over it and kissed it. They had always shaken hands before.

"I think you are quite fuddled, Stacy," she remarked as she walked with him as far as the stairs. "Go home and go to bed. And you needn't trouble yourself about the money. I'll send Bernard 'round with it. The Black Lantern Inn, you said? Seven o'clock? You can see yourself out, can't you?"

Before he could answer, she was already dashing toward the staircase that led to the third story of the town house, where the bedrooms were located, leaving him to make his way down to the front door on his own. "Good night, Julie," he called after her.

"'Night, Stacy," she called back carelessly, and Stacy realized that, whatever had happened to his own heart that night, her feelings for him remained unchanged.

When the surgeon arrived shortly thereafter, he found that not only was Cary's arm broken in two places, but several ribs were cracked as well. "Mr. Calverstock thinks they weren't trying to kill him, Mr. Norton," Juliet told him, blinking back tears. "What do you think?"

"I've seen better looking corpses, Miss Wayborn," the surgeon replied grimly. "But Mr. Cary won't give in so easily," he added with an encouraging smile. "He's a Wayborn, isn't he?"

When he had gone, Juliet dried her eyes and instructed the footman to ask Bernard, Cary's groom, to come up from the stables.

Tom was shocked. "Oh, he wouldn't come into the house, Miss Julie! He'd have to be dragged in chains, and even then, he'd say it wasn't right for a stableboy to set foot in the house."

"Nonsense," said Juliet. "Tell Bernard if he doesn't

come to me at once, I shall be forced to go down to the stables in my nightgown and bare feet."

This threat was enough to bring the reluctant groom not only into the house, but up the stairs to Miss Juliet's bedroom, where the young lady showed him the battered body of his unconscious master.

"Good God almighty!" the Irishman breathed, crossing himself. "I never thought I'd live to see the young master lying so still and the breath of him rattling like the wind through the trees."

"Listen to me carefully, Bernard," she said. "A foul insect called Lord Swale has done this to Master Cary."

"You don't say, Miss—and he a lordship!"

"There was to have been a curricle race tomorrow. Our chestnuts, Bernard, against his lordship's grays. Swale must have known he'd never beat my brother honorably, so he hired two lowborn curs to cripple him the night before the race. Now, would you say that Lord Swale is a coward?"

"I would so, Miss Julie!" said Bernard stoutly. "And a damned dirty coward besides, begging your pardon for the strong language."

"Bernard," she said, her eyes gleaming, "I am going to teach this dishonorable wretch a lesson about the Wayborns that he will never forget. And you're going to help me."

"Well now, Miss Julie," he said, scratching his shiny bald head. "Sure I'd not advise a wee lass to be going up against the likes of himself, and he the devil's own limb."

"I don't care if he's Satan's hound," responded the wee lass. "He's grist for the mill now, and I'm the miller."

"More grist to his lordship than you'd think, Miss Julie," said Bernard coolly. "Seven foot high, if he's an inch, with a blacker heart than Henry Tudor. Sure, it's your own darling neck he'd be after breaking, Miss Julie, and never a pang of conscience."

"It's very simple, Bernard," Juliet said firmly, cutting through this Gaelic digression. "If Cary doesn't show up for that race tomorrow, he'll be the laughing-stock of London."

Bernard sighed. "Faith, Miss Julie. Sure, it's only a race."

"Only a race! Bernard Corcoran, I want you to look at your master lying there bandaged from head to toe, and then tell me it's only a race! He could very well be crippled for life. He *could* die!" She shook her head vehemently. "No, Bernard. It was only a race, but now it's a matter of honor. I may be a wee lass, but I'm still a Wayborn; Lord Swale will rue the day he ever wronged my family."

Bernard accepted the inevitability of trouble and sorrow with a shrug. "Right you are, Miss Julie. But what's to be done, short of murder?"

"There's only one thing that can be done, Bernard. Cary has to show up for the race tomorrow, and he has to win."

"Are you wise, Miss?" Bernard spluttered. "Begging your pardon, Miss Julie, but could it be that you've taken leave of your senses? Sure, your brother's half-killed with a broken arm."

"I shall have to go in his place, of course. Thank you for pointing that out to me."

"Oh, now, Miss," Bernard protested. "His lordship the Marquess would never consent to such a thing as that, racing against a female. He's not what you'd call modern."

"So," Juliet said, smiling calmly, "you would advise me not to tell his lordship that I'm a mere female? I should let him think that I'm Master Cary? What an excellent plan. Bernard, you are an absolute mastermind."

Bernard guffawed. "Begging your pardon, Miss Julie, but there's no mistaking your shape for the young master's."

"They'll think I'm Cary indeed," said Juliet reasonably, "if I have his hat, his coat, his spectacles, his curricle, his horses . . . and his groom."

"Oh, now, Miss," Bernard said softly, his eyes glowing, "that'd be a raking grand humiliation for his lordship, and no mistake. Though to be honest, I don't know how you'd beat them grays atall."

Juliet stiffened. "I drive just as well as Cary. Indeed, I've beaten him dozens of times when we've raced in the country, thank you very much, Mr. Bernard Corcoran."

Bernard shook his head regretfully. "Aye, but—"

"And Lord Swale obviously knew himself outmatched," she interrupted him to point out. "Why else would he hire mercenaries to break Cary's arm? I will win that race tomorrow, Bernard. I will win it because I have to. I will win it because the honor of the Wayborns is at stake. I shall be like one of the Furies of ancient myth."

"You'd not be content to roast him alive with your eyes then?" he asked hopefully.

"No, Bernard, I wouldn't," she said firmly. "Like all swine, his lordship deserves to be roasted properly—in a fire with the sharp end of a skewer up his backside!" She cleared her throat delicately. "Begging your pardon for the strong language," she added without a hint of contrition.

Chapter 2

Geoffrey Ambler, Marquess of Swale, could not help his looks, but even the Honorable Mr. Alexander Devize, Swale's closest friend, was forced to admit that the Duke of Auckland's heir had done much to deserve his reputation as a brutish lout. His lordship's palate could discern no appreciable difference between claret and Madeira; he stubbornly maintained in the face of all evidence to the contrary that Shakespeare was the horse that had won the Lincolnshire in the year '03; and he had the uncanny habit of knocking flat anyone who irritated him, though to his credit, his abuse had never yet extended to servants, animals, children, or females.

While admitting to his friend's many faults, Mr. Devize steadfastly maintained that deep inside the rough exterior of this undisciplined brawler, beat the heart of an English gentleman. True, Swale was ignorant, obstinate, and completely unable to control his fiery temper, but this was entirely due to the fact that his lordship had been cursed at birth with a head of bright red hair. As a child, his natural cheerfulness and easy generosity of spirit had been crushed by constant teasing, and almost through no fault of his own, the young Marquess had become that old cliché, a redhead with a foul temper.

The Swale–Devize alliance had begun at Eton College, where they had roomed together. For many months, Alexander Devize had regarded this arrangement as one of life's unfortunate incidents, but in the Michaelmas Term of 1805, his opinion changed abruptly when an upperclassman had attempted, innocently enough, to attach the nickname of Ginger to the red-haired Marquess. Despite being half the boy's size and three years younger, Swale had knocked him flat. No one had ever dared to Ginger his lordship after that, and Alex Devize began to find him an interesting object.

Because of their friendship and despite the certainty of Swale losing this morning's race to Cary Wayborn's magnificent chestnuts, Alex had bet Stacy Calverstock five hundred pounds that his friend would be victorious.

Swale, who had bet the same amount on himself, likewise was under no illusion that he would win. "I don't say I'll win, Alex," he kept saying as they waited for Cary Wayborn to appear in the yard of the Black Lantern Inn, "but, by God, I shall make a damned fine showing!"

"It was a great compliment to be challenged this year," Alex reminded him, holding his bay mare steady next to his friend's curricle. "Win or lose, old man, you are now one of the Select."

Swale reddened with pleasure. High spirits had made his face tolerably pleasant this morning, but even his friends agreed that under no circumstances, was the Swale countenance ever worth looking at. There was too much of the bulldog in his short nose and fighting chin for him ever to be called handsome, and more often than not, he was not in high spirits anyway. He was usually found with an ugly scowl on his face, as though being born rich and titled were an injustice he could scarcely bear.

"I'm betting on you, Geoffrey," Alex said, slapping the Marquess on his broad, strong back. "If any man in England can beat Wayborn, it's you."

Swale grinned. "You like my chances then?"

"He's won eight races in a row," Alex pointed out. "No one can win all the time, not even Cary Wayborn. Today he falls."

"Damned peculiar, ain't it, that he never bets more than five hundred pounds? Fellow could be rich as Midas if he'd learn to lay a proper wager."

"Apparently, there was a vow to his Mamma on her deathbed," Alex explained with a shrug. "Can't be helped. Economy seems to be catching on with younger sons in this our Silver Age. My own brother never bets at all."

Swale was appalled. "What, never?"

"We're all thoroughly ashamed of him. You don't have a brother, do you?"

"No."

"Bloody nuisances," Alex said with the air of a learned doctor establishing an absolute fact. "Mine's *raison d'être* seems to be pointing out all my flaws to our father. He rather breathes down my neck, if you see what I mean. Really, younger sons ought to be strangled at birth."

"I'm rather fond of my sister," said Swale a little stiffly, not being an advocate of strangling one's relatives at birth or, indeed, at any time thereafter. Abruptly, he took out his watch again. "I just hope I acquit myself creditably in the next two hours. God knows I don't expect to win."

"My dear Geoffrey, we've all lost to him. There's no shame in it. But, by God, I hope you beat him!" Alex added with feeling.

Swale grinned irrepressibly. "By God, so do I. I should dearly love to fling that hideous purple hat of his into the dust."

Alex took out his timepiece and studied it carefully. "My watch must be losing time," he remarked, frowning. "Wayborn is never late."

"There's Calverstock," said Swale, catching sight of his opponent's friend arriving mounted on a tall roan. "Where the devil is Wayborn?" he called irritably as Stacy Calverstock approached his curricle. "Not going to be late, I hope?"

"Why should my friend be late?" Stacy demanded in cold fury. Unfortunately, cold fury made his voice high and wavering, almost shrill. "Why should my friend, Mr. Cary Wayborn, be late, my lord? Is there some *particular* reason why your lordship would think Mr. Wayborn should be late?"

Swale scowled at him. The fellow was talking nonsense. Swale had little enough patience for people who talked sense. For a man of his temperament, there could be no enduring people who talked nonsense. "What the devil are you blathering on about, Calverstock?" he bellowed, his gingery brows coming together in a fierce scowl. "He bloody well had better *not* be late; that's all I have to say!"

"Your lordship seems certain that my friend *will* be late," Stacy shrilled at him. "Pray, why is that, my lord?"

Swale was unable to put a finger on what it was exactly, but something in Calverstock's address made him want to pull the other man off his horse and knock him flat.

But before he could act on his impulse, a cheer rose from the assembly. Cary Wayborn's chestnuts cut through the yard just as the bells of St. Martin's began to peal. Stacy gave a start and swung his horse around to get a better look at the tall, slim figure in the curricle. It wore the bizarre purple tricorn; the purple greatcoat, still damp from Tom's not entirely successful efforts to remove the bloodstains; and the lavender spectacles, but there was no evidence of a broken arm.

Stacy's mouth fell open. "What the devil—" he murmured.

Juliet Wayborn had never been so frightened in her life, and that she would, at some point very soon, disgorge her breakfast of tea and toast seemed inevitable. Gentlemen, many of whom she knew at least slightly, were wedged into the yard in startling numbers, and all of them seemed to be drinking ale from hideous pewter tankards. Drunken laughter and the odor of tobacco filled the air. **Men, she decided**, should never be permitted out of **doors without** the supervision of some respectable female. Away from their mothers, wives, sisters, and daughters, they apparently threw off all the restraints of civilized society and became no better than the savages of Borneo. It depressed her spirits beyond description to know that her future husband—her nice, quiet, respectable husband—very likely was among the crowd assembled in the yard of the Black Lantern Inn, for these gentlemen were, she was to understand, the cream of English manhood. Many of the drunken brutes were on horseback and clearly intended to follow the two curricles all the way to—

A wave of fresh fear washed over her, and she felt

a burst of cold perspiration in her armpits. For the love of God, she had no idea where they were racing to! This tidbit of information, which she had never bothered her head about before, now seemed rather a necessity, and her failure to procure it was a glaring flaw in an otherwise magnificent plan. Brighton, she knew, was her brother's favorite destination, but the Black Lantern Inn was on the Colchester Road, which ran northeast out of London into Essex. Could they actually be racing to Colchester?

"Bernard!" she croaked to the groom standing on the board behind her seat, brandishing his whip like any good *petit tigre.* "Bernard, where do I go?"

The Irishman misunderstood the question. "Just you line up alongside himself the lordship there, Miss Julie," he called over her shoulder in a low voice that made the chestnuts prick up their ears attentively. Before she could ask him again, he had already turned to the crowd and begun employing his whip to keep the chestnuts' heads clear of the traffic, and there was nothing she could do but bring her brother's curricle alongside his lordship's grays.

She forced her nerves to steady. Of course, Bernard would be with her to handle the exchanges at the turnpikes. He would be able to guide her to the finish.

She took her first look at Lord Swale, the man she hated above all else on earth. Her acquaintance with the Duke of Auckland ill-prepared her for the appearance of his son. The Marquess had the most exceptional hair she had ever seen, so exceptional, in fact, that she could not quite believe she was seeing it now. The fiery red stuff hung shaggy and unkempt almost to his shoulders, and, with equally red sideburns lining his cheeks, he looked rather like a cartoon of a lion, she thought. And his clothes—! Rumpled, ill-fitting *homespun* unless she was mistaken. His coat was so dusty she could only guess at its color. Indeed, his general appearance might lead one to believe he had just *finished* the long, grueling race.

As she drew alongside him, he grinned at her. Despite the smile being lopsided and rather too full of crooked teeth, it was not without boyish charm.

At the sight of him, her courage, which could have withstood the fiery gaze of a mad monk or even the sneers of the most supercilious aristocrat, faltered in a manner inconsistent with the code of the Wayborns. Could this grinning mistake of Nature really be the sinister Lord Swale, mastermind of the cowardly attack upon her brother? It seemed impossible. The man looked like a country bumpkin!

But then she remembered her Shakespeare, as many an English soul does in a moment of crisis: "There's no art to find the mind's construction in the face." Undoubtedly, Lord Swale had deceived many with his idiotic grin, but he would not deceive Miss Wayborn. Miss Wayborn's eye pierced the unprepossessing façade and saw the black soul of the man.

Stacy approached, crying indiscreetly, "Cary! Good God, man!"

Juliet put a finger to her lips. As he drew alongside the curricle on his roan, she was able to speak to him in a low voice. "Stacy, it is I, Juliet. Please don't give me away."

His pale eyes started from his head. "Juliet! Have you gone mad?" he gargled.

"Probably. Do not betray me," she pleaded, all the while attempting to appear shrug-shouldered and nonchalant. It was difficult as her stomach seemed ready to convulse at any minute. The tricorn, fixed to her head with no less than six hatpins, still felt wobbly to her, and she feared that at any moment it would fall, exposing her coiffure of tightly braided hair.

"You'll break your neck, you little fool," Stacy said through gritted teeth.

"If I do, remember me kindly," she said, laughing nervously.

"I was just on the verge of calling him out, you half-wit," he hissed at her.

"Well, it's done now!" she snapped back at him.

"It certainly is!"

"Quickly, Stacy," she whispered urgently, "you must tell me where—"

"Hurry!" he said. "The bells—the last toll of the bells is the signal!"

Stacy was absorbed by the excited crowd, and Juliet heard the boisterous voices counting all around her as the bells of a nearby church tolled the hour. "Four! Five! Six!"

Bernard suddenly jumped down from the back of the curricle, and the way before her magically cleared. Juliet's heart was in her mouth as she saw Lord Swale's groom jump down from his curricle as well. They were to race without grooms then, and she had no idea where they were going.

Incredibly, the abominable Lord Swale shouted to her, "Good luck, Wayborn!"

She gave him a curt nod and pushed the lavender spectacles back up the bridge of her nose.

"Seven!" roared the crowd, and Cary's chestnuts leaped forward, two lengths ahead of his lordship's grays, their eyes alight with love of the race. This would never do, Juliet quickly realized. With no idea of the race's destination, she would have no hope of choosing the correct road when they came to a crossing or a fork. She would have to amend her plan to win the race, she supposed. Lord Swale would have to take the lead so that she could follow him to the proper destination. She would have to lose, but, she reflected, as long as she acquitted herself creditably and got away without being discovered, Cary would not be disgraced.

It required all her strength to slow the chestnuts even a little. After the first shock, when they understood that they actually were being asked to *slow down*, they hardened their crests angrily and, it seemed to her, redoubled their speed. They, at least, had no intention of losing. Her muscles could not sustain the effort, and she was forced to give them their way. She would simply stay on the Colchester Road, she decided, until they reached a fork in the road, and then she would figure out what to do.

She had often teased her brother about the mirrors he had placed facing backwards on either side of his curricle, but now she saw that they were actually quite practical for racing. In them, she could see that Lord Swale had pulled within a length of her and that he was obviously maneuvering to pass. She could take steps to prevent him or not, exactly as she chose. She chose to prevent him. She would be forced to give him the race in the end, but she saw no reason for him to annihilate her. She would give him the lead at the fork in the road. In the meantime, she would save her strength—she would need every ounce of it to slow the chestnuts enough to let his lordship pass.

The wind battered her face, making her grateful for the protection afforded her eyes by her brother's lavender spectacles. Her mouth and nostrils were soon caked with dust. Her back ached from the constant pull of the reins. The prospect of continuing in this manner for several miles did not appeal to her at all.

Swale, on the other hand, was having the time of his life. It seemed to him that every moment of his twenty-five years had been preparing him for this day. He was racing the great Cary Wayborn on a beautiful morning late in March, and he was acquitting himself creditably. He even began to feel that he might surpass the famed chestnuts if he could only find an advantage. Wayborn moved continuously from one side of the road to the other like a demon, anticipating his every move and cutting him off mercilessly.

Juliet had never known the chestnuts to go more than six miles an hour, but now it seemed to her as if they were going ten. One moment, they were leaving North London, and the next, or so it seemed to her, they were nearing the great fork at Brentwood. At this point, one might continue northeast to Colchester or turn right onto the Southend Road. It suddenly occurred to her as she approached the fork that Lord Swale almost certainly would attempt to gain the inside advantage. If their destination was Southend, he would try to shoot inside on her right; if Colchester, he would veer to her left. She would be able to see his move in the rear-facing mirrors.

Wrapping the reins around her wrists, she bore down with all her strength, nearly sitting on the floor of the car. The chestnuts naturally objected, and one of them forgot his manners to the extent that he reared up and pawed the air before coming to his senses. Juliet's arms were nearly wrenched from their sockets, but the chestnuts skidded to a stop. One twisted its neck around to look at her reproachfully. The other snorted and pawed the ground.

Swale could not believe his good fortune. He had once shot and killed a six-point stag at a distance of thirty yards, an impossible shot everyone in the hunting-box that year had agreed, but pulling ahead of Cary Wayborn's chestnuts on the road to South-end would undoubtedly surpass even that sublime moment. He drew a deep breath, a man on the brink of history, and urged his horses to the right, the better to take the inside of the turn.

Juliet saw the move and instantly released the chest-nuts, turning them onto the Southend Road and cutting off Swale's advantage so swiftly that Swale, who was in danger of driving off the road entirely, over-compensated to the left, grazed her back wheels, and nearly overturned.

The curricle righted itself, and Swale, cursing vo-ciferously, backed his grays and turned them toward Southend. But there was now no chance of him over-taking the chestnuts, let alone passing them. All that could be seen of Wayborn and his chestnuts was a cloud of dust. It was to his credit that he arrived in Southend only five minutes after Juliet did.

Her back was aching, and her throat was full of dust. A crowd had gathered in the seaside town of Southend to see the finish of the race, and more were arriving from London every moment. There could be no quiet escape for the victor, she realized, almost too tired to care. Undoubtedly, her deception would be discovered, and she would be disgraced; however, Lord Swale would also be exposed and humiliated, and that was her main object. When his part in the shame-ful attack on Cary became known, every respectable family in England would give him the cut. Marquess or not, he would feel the wrath of the English Ton.

That would come later. What mattered now was that she not be dragged bodily from the curricle and carried away upon the shoulders of a half-dozen admiring young men to the nearest tavern, as several in the crowd were threatening to do. The moment the curricle was opened, her skirts would be seen, and her secret would be out. On the whole, she preferred to expose herself in a more dignified manner.

Lord Swale himself provided her with the opportunity. Upon arriving in Southend, his lordship leaped from his curricle, screaming, "You, sir, ought to be horsewhipped! You damned near killed my horses, you bloody cheat!"

The favorable impression he had made before the race was gone entirely. *Here,* she thought smugly, *is the real Lord Swale.* No friendly lion, no simple country lad with a lopsided, innocent smile. Rather, an ugly, villainous barbarian—a Viking raider, in fact, hell-bent on mayhem and bloody slaughter for all the world to see.

Alexander Devize tried to hold him back, but Swale could not be held. His green eyes were blazing, and his complexion, always ruddy, now appeared to be covered with a particularly nasty case of nettlerash.

"Wayborn! What the devil do you mean by coming to a full stop in the middle of the road like bloody Balaam's ass?" he roared. "I call it devious and underhanded, and by God, sir, you will bloody well answer for it!"

At first shocked to hear such language, Juliet was fortified by the sudden appearance of Bernard and Mr. Calverstock, who had both ridden hard from London, arriving just behind Lord Swale. Both men gathered around her protectively. "How dare you, sir?" Stacy shrieked back, and, despite the fact that he sounded a bit like her aunt, Lady Elkins, Juliet was quite proud of him.

Lord Swale seemed ready to drag Stacy Calverstock from his horse and beat him with his fists, but Mr. Devize intervened. "Just give Wayborn his money, old man," he said reasonably, and it pained Juliet to see that such a fine young gentleman from such an impeccable old Suffolk family had been so completely taken in by a monster like Swale.

"Bloody cheat!" reiterated Lord Swale, shaking his fist at the purple tricorn. "If there is so much as a *scratch* on my grays, I shall rip your bloody arm off, by God! So this is how you win your races, Wayborn! I expect no one else has had the courage to accuse you, but by God, I will!"

"Dammit, Geoffrey," said Mr. Devize in a tight, embarrassed voice. "Pay the man his money and have done. You are making an ass of yourself."

Swale looked around. The crowd had fallen silent, but here and there, he detected a lip curled in scorn. The consensus seemed to be that he, Lord Swale, was a poor loser!

"Swale is right," said a lone voice.

Swale, looking around for his supporter, was astounded to find that it was Wayborn himself.

"I *did* cheat," said the figure in the purple greatcoat. "Swale wins by default."

A roar of shocked disbelief went up from the crowd.

Swale turned dark red with embarrassment. "I say, old man," he protested. "I never meant to say you cheated—dammit, I never meant to say—that is, rotten temper! Rotten temper, old man! There is no denying I've got a rotten temper."

Juliet coughed to clear her throat of dust. "Not at all, old man," she croaked in her best imitation of a man's voice. "Indeed, I owe your lordship five hundred pounds and a broken arm!" So saying, she flung the purse containing five hundred pounds in the direction of the Duke's son. Her arm, weakened from the strain of managing a pair of strong and willful horses, was inaccurate. Mr. Devize was struck in the shoulder but did manage to catch the purse.

He looked at her, his eyebrows raised almost to his hairline.

Swale's face was now the color and texture of blood pudding. Recovered of his embarrassment, his lordship yielded again to rage. "You won the race, damn you!" he roared. "Though I can't say I admire your methods!"

"I did win, didn't I?" she said clearly. "You were beaten fairly, Swale, whatever you complain. But you were not been beaten by Mr. Cary Wayborn. You were beaten by his *sister!*"

The return journey to London, despite the fact that Juliet was resting comfortably in a well-sprung chaise hired by Stacy Calverstock, proved more grueling to her than the race to Southend. Every mounted swank in Southend guessed at the chaise's interesting contents and accompanied its progress with hoots, wild yells, and occasionally, the ill-advised discharge of a pistol. Added to this was the incessant drone of Mr. Eustace Calverstock lecturing her on proper female behavior. He seemed to think that no one would ever marry her now and that he should be obliged to do it himself.

"Don't be such a gudgeon, Stacy," she said irritably, rubbing first one sore shoulder, then the other. "Really, there is no need for you to make such a sacrifice. You know I have no more than ten thousand pounds."

"I assure you, my dear Juliet," he said gallantly, "it is no sacrifice."

"Then, pray do not make a cake of yourself!" she snapped, for her head was aching.

"You do not understand the way of the world," he

told her sadly. "My dear girl, I am afraid this must put you beyond the pale. No respectable lady of the Ton will receive you now. That being so, you cannot hope to make a respectable marriage."

"You talk as though I'd eloped with an Italian dancing master or . . . or tied my garter in public! Anyone but an idiot can see I did exactly right, and I don't choose to marry an idiot, I assure you."

"How can you call it right," he objected, "when it destroys all hope of a felicitous marriage?"

"Then, if I were to marry you, it would not be felicitous?" she countered. "Perhaps you are right, and it is well for me that I don't wish to marry you."

"And you were such a favorite with the Patronesses of Almack's," Stacy lamented. "Your name and reputation were such that other young ladies looked to you for an example. What evils will proceed from this childish stunt, I don't know."

"Perhaps curricle races will become the fashion," Juliet said, laughing it off.

"I assure you, it is not in the least comical!" he snapped. "What will Cary say?"

"Cary will understand that at times, one must be a Wayborn first and a female second!" she answered smartly. "If I were a man, you would not be talking such fustian to me!"

"Well, you're not a man," he said sharply. "And it is not fustian! You'll see that soon enough when you are given the cut! It will be bitter for you, Juliet. You were so well liked before. Your manners were admired! But this dreadful, *unladylike* behavior—what will Sir Benedict say to this?"

Juliet, who had reason to dread her older brother's reaction, remained silent, hoping Stacy would do the same. But, no, he buried her beneath the weight of a thousand sermons on feminine decorum, and, by the time the chaise reached Park Lane, Juliet was so richly annoyed with him that she did not even thank him for his excellent generalship in extricating her from Southend.

Lady Elkins was in the Apricot Salon wringing her hands. "Oh, my dearest love," she cried weakly at the sight of Juliet. "I have been so worried. I was so frightened you had eloped!"

Juliet responded with a scorn unworthy of her. "Elope!" she scoffed, flinging her brother's tricorn onto a table. "I? After what I have seen today, Aunt Elinor, there is not a man in England that an Act of Parliament could induce me to marry!"

Her ladyship, already naturally pale, became ashen. "Why, my love?" she wailed. "Why, what have you seen? Why are you wearing my nephew's coat? Why are you so dusty? What has happened? Mr. Calverstock, what has happened?"

"I beg your pardon, Aunt Elinor!" Juliet cried, giving her excitable aunt a quick, reassuring kiss. "I've the most dreadful headache, that's all. Will you entertain Mr. Calverstock while I go and wash?"

As Juliet faded from the room, Stacy bowed correctly over his hostess's hand. "Mr. Calverstock!" Lady Elkins said fondly. "If my niece was in your care, I have no more worries."

Stacy was scarcely gratified by the compliment.

"I won't ask you to sit," Lady Elkins said nervously. "Indeed, I must ask you *not* to sit. Parker informs me that my nephew's clothes left a black mark on one of the sofas. No one must sit until I have heard from Mr. Soho. Pray, don't be angry."

Stacy smiled warmly. "Indeed, my lady, I prefer to stand."

"He was brought home last night in a state of collapse!" cried her ladyship.

"Mr. Soho?" Stacy asked hopefully.

"My nephew! My poor, dear Cary. But you are not to worry—I know you are his friend, but you are not to worry. Mr. Norton tells me it is only a touch of influenza."

"Ah," said Stacy.

"Do you think it will be necessary for us to remove to the country?" her ladyship inquired anxiously. "Mr. Norton tells me it is a very mild case—very mild. But I am no longer young, you know, and even a mild case of influenza might carry me off. I had better retire to Surrey. Still, I do hate to take Juliet away from London at the top of the Season. Did she tell you she danced twice with the Duke of Auckland?" A spark of vicarious ecstasy entered Lady Elkins's watery eye. "The Duke of Auckland! Only think if his Grace were to marry my niece!"

Stacy thought but found the notion unpalatable. "Perhaps," he said cautiously, "it would be a very good thing for Miss Juliet to accompany your ladyship to Wayborn Hall."

"I will ask my nephew when he comes. Dear Sir Benedict always knows what is right and best."

Stacy swallowed hard. "Is Sir Benedict coming *here*, Lady Elkins?"

"Why yes," she replied innocently. "He is coming tomorrow. He will know what to do about dear Juliet. I shall put it to him."

Juliet, still smarting from Stacy's reproaches, had crept into her brother's room, and dismissing the nurse, she availed herself of his sympathetic ear. Cary did not open his eyes once throughout her version of the morning's events, but she would swear his eyelids fluttered and a smile touched his pale lips as she related Lord Swale's humiliation.

"He is the laughingstock of the world," she told him proudly. "A duel with Stacy would have been too good for him, don't you think? But now he has been beaten by a female and exposed as a coward. I could tell his lordship dearly wanted to strangle me, but what could he do? The world was watching." She took his hand and kissed it. "When you are better, you may shoot him if you like, but I hardly think it necessary now."

"Well done, Julie," Cary whispered. "You're so clever—I knew I could count on you."

"At least someone appreciates me," she murmured, stroking his dark hair. "Stacy has been dunning me all the way home. He thinks that no one will marry me now and that he must do it himself or I shall die an old maid. How would you like him for a brother?"

She laughed softly, but Cary had slipped away again.

Chapter 3

Like his brother and sister, Sir Benedict had been born with patrician features; rich, dark hair; and wide gray eyes, but as a boy, he had been maimed by one of his father's mastiffs. His lean face bore terrible scars, and the tendons of his right arm had been so badly damaged that the doctors had been forced to amputate just above the elbow. He had never married, and, since the death of his father, his sole purpose had been the restoration of the Wayborn family seat, which lay just ten miles west of London in Surrey. Considerably older than his siblings, Sir Benedict was, in fact, a half-brother to Cary and Juliet, and to that lively pair, he seemed more of an uncle than a brother. He had no taste for fashionable Society, and, therefore, he came to London only to attend Parliament, of which he was a Member.

When her half-brother arrived in Park Lane the next morning, Juliet reluctantly left Cary with his nurse and went down to meet him, confident that, once Benedict knew all, he would take her part. Certainly, Benedict would scold her—her behavior was not to be wished for in a sister—but he must see that she had done the only thing possible under the circumstances. No one was more jealous of the family's honor than Sir Benedict.

In the Apricot Salon, she found that he was not so much his usual sober self as a thundercloud of disapproval. She had never seen his feelings so exposed; of all the Wayborns, Sir Benedict knew best how to wear the mask, and she had often been frustrated by his evenhanded temper. Now he looked at her in a way that shocked her. His gray eyes, never warm, were hard and brilliant. It seemed almost as though she disgusted him. In very short order, she found that she could not meet his gaze. Her limbs began to tremble, not with fear exactly, but with mortification. She had not expected to be congratulated for her courage, not by Benedict, but she had not expected *this*. Before he had even spoken a word, she was a shrinking vessel of guilt.

"They say you cut your hair for this notorious prank," he said abruptly. "I'm pleased to see it isn't so."

He sounded anything but pleased. His tone was awful, and its effect on her was made worse by the fact that he so very rarely rebuked her and because their father never had. If Papa had thought her his angel, the more critical Benedict at least had found her above reproach, and she would have preferred to have been horsewhipped by Lord Swale than to feel Benedict's disappointment. To her dismay, she felt hot tears welling up in her eyes.

"They say you wore breeches," said Benedict in the same awful tone.

"That is a lie!" she cried, almost choking on a sob. Angrily, she ground the tears from her eyes with the heel of her hand. "I most certainly did not! I wore Cary's coat over my dress."

"You greatly relieve my mind," said Benedict with bitter sarcasm.

The tears threatened again. "How c-could you b-b-believe such a thing?"

"Forgive me," he said harshly. "I am not accustomed to hearing my sister's name bandied about in the street! I am not accustomed to being slapped on the back by young men who I do not know and do not want to know as they congratulate me on my sister's high-flying exploits!"

"I beg your pardon, Benedict, but—"

"Really, Juliet!" he brutally interrupted. "I am accustomed to such reports of Cary as to make my hair turn white, but I had thought you had more conduct. They are saying you wore breeches, and they are saying a great deal worse than that."

Juliet flung herself into a nearby chair and shamelessly began to cry. "What could I do?" she choked, aware that she was blubbering like a baby but unable to stop. "Cary could not go!" She became unintelligible after that, and all he could make out were the words "family honor."

"I should have thought that even Cary would have more sense," said Benedict, "than to put his sister up to such behavior as must make her the object of universal disgust and ridicule."

She flung up her head. "Do not blame Cary!" she cried. "It was my own idea to go in his place. What else could I do?"

"My dear child," he said, exasperated by her display of raw emotion. "Don't tell me you sacrificed yourself merely to spare Cary the slight embarrassment of having missed a horse race?"

"Slight embarrassment! He would have been ruined!"

"Is that what my brother told you?"

"You have always been hard on Cary, but this ill becomes you, Benedict," she said sharply. "Naturally, he said no such thing! Indeed, he could barely speak when Stacy brought him home."

"Bah!" said Sir Benedict dispassionately. "A touch of influenza. I had not thought you capable of running into hysterics, my girl."

"Influenza!" Her eyes widened, and she felt, for the first time, a bit of hope. "Then you do not know the truth."

He frowned. "I think I do. My aunt was so obliging as to tell me. She has asked to retire to Wayborn Hall, and I see no reason why she should not go and take you with her, too."

"Naturally, we could not tell Aunt Elinor the truth. How is it you know all about me, but you have heard nothing about Lord Swale?"

Benedict arched a brow. "I take it his lordship was your opponent in this infamous race. He certainly will not thank you for handing him the greatest humiliation of his life. But tell me why a well-bred young lady should be unable to tell her aunt the truth. What has Cary done now?"

"Cary has done nothing," she retorted hotly. "It is this odious, pestilential Lord Swale! I wish you had attended less to the lies told about me and more to the truths told about *him*. Cary don't have influenza. He was attacked! He was brutally attacked, and by Lord Swale's hirelings! Furthermore, if Stacy hadn't been there to frighten the villains away, they would have killed him! So there!"

Sir Benedict paled at this news, but his expression became very guarded. "Cary? Attacked? I can hardly credit it."

"I'm not such a fool as to lie to you, Benedict," she

retorted. "You may see for yourself. He is resting upstairs now. His arm is broken in two places, and Mr. Norton is very fearful of an infection. He could lose his arm!"

Benedict rose as if he meant to go upstairs at once, but instead, he began to pace the floor. "Cary?" he murmured in a bleak voice. "My brother attacked?"

"If you had only seen him, Benedict, you would not blame me for what I did! If I were a man, I should have killed Lord Swale on the spot, and no one on earth would have blamed me if I had!"

"It is a very bad thing," said Benedict slowly, "to accuse his lordship without proof. I hope—"

"I have all the proof I need!" she flung at him. "Stacy *heard* the villains talking, and so did Cary! They were sent by Lord Swale to keep him from racing. They *named* their benefactor."

"And you thought you must take your brother's curricle and go in his place?"

She stared at him, her eyes red. "Do you think I did it to disoblige you, sir?"

"I have never known you to do anything to disoblige me," he said gently, and she instantly was ashamed. "Who helped you? Mr. Calverstock, I suppose? I should like to box his ears!"

"You must not blame Stacy," she said quickly. "He did not know until he saw me in Cary's clothes at the Black Lantern Inn, and he could not have exposed me there, you know."

"The Black Lantern Inn! My God, Juliet! I expect Bernard helped you as well."

"Don't be cross with Bernard," she begged. "He saw right away what had to be done."

"Indeed! And I daresay Mr. Calverstock covered your brother's losses?"

"Certainly not," she said. "I paid Lord Swale on the

spot. I flung it in his face, Benedict. You would have been proud. Well," she amended, biting her lip, "if I were your brother instead of your sister, you would have been quite proud."

"But you are not my brother," he snapped. "I expect Cary wagered his customary five hundred pounds?"

"Yes, indeed!"

"And where," demanded Sir Benedict, "did *you* get five hundred pounds?"

Juliet lifted her chin defiantly. "From Bernard, of course," she said.

"It is worse than I had thought," Benedict exclaimed. "Can it be that my sister has stooped to borrowing money from the servants?"

"Bernard is rather a special case," she said dryly. "He does not know what to do with his fortune. Indeed, I sometimes wish that Papa had not been so generous; it embarrasses him so."

"Generous!" said Benedict furiously. "That Sir Anthony Wayborn saw fit to leave his groom a sum equal to his own daughter's dower portion, I should think was rather more than *generous* of him!"

Juliet flushed. "No one thinks of it in that vulgar way except you. Papa liked him, that's all. I am sure I've never begrudged Bernard a penny of it!"

"No, indeed! If he is always willing, as I suspect he is, to frank your follies!"

"Well, what else could I do?" she demanded. "Tell me that! The race was forfeited; the odious Swale saw to that! And he must be paid, the scaly fiend!"

"You might have sent for me," he said quietly.

"You were in Surrey," she said resentfully. "You are always at Wayborn Hall."

"Yes, looking after our tenants and managing the estate."

"Hiding from life," she insisted. "Oh, Benedict, can't you see that what *I* have done is so much better than anything you could have done?"

"With but one arm, I should not have been of much use in a curricle race," he wearily agreed.

The color drained from Juliet's face. "I did not mean *that,*" she cried in dismay. "Why must you take the worst possible meaning of all that I say?"

He shrugged. "Very well, Juliet," he said. "You have humiliated Lord Swale. You have pricked him deeply, I daresay, but you have destroyed yourself in the process. You must know you will be shunned by all respectable society now."

She tossed her head. "I do not care two straws for that, I assure you," she said. "Pray do not lecture me on that head for I have had all I can take from Stacy Calverstock."

"No lectures," he agreed. "But you will have to leave London at once."

"You cannot ask me to leave Cary!" she objected. "Anyway, I won't. Why should I? I know very well I am in disgrace. No one will visit me, and I shan't be asked anywhere. I shall be left alone, which is precisely what I like. And when Cary is better, he will defend my honor, and anyway, if it comes to it, Stacy has offered to marry me."

"How very obliging of him," murmured Benedict. "You are certainly in disgrace, my dear, but you are quite wrong if you think you will be left alone. I daresay you will receive a great deal of attention, and not of the best kind."

Juliet shuddered, remembering those high-spirited rattles that had accompanied her chaise from Southend to her aunt's house. Undoubtedly, her company would be much in demand with *them.* "I don't care! You cannot induce me to leave Cary," she said stubbornly.

"If I cannot induce you," he replied, "I will take you by the scruff of the neck and drag you."

Juliet swallowed hard. It seemed to her that Benedict meant it.

"Cary will be well looked after," he said in a more reassuring voice. "And it will scarcely speed his recovery to be having to defend your honor against every bold young ass who insults you."

Though it chafed, Juliet could see the wisdom of this. Benedict was always maddeningly wise. "Very well, Benedict," she said. "Only tell me you are not angry with me," she pleaded. "Tell me you understand why I did it. I did not do it for my own amusement."

"You must have been frightened and angry when you saw Cary," he said with more gentleness than before. "You lost your head, and you did something very foolish."

"Benedict!"

"You want me to tell you what you did was right and sensible. It wasn't," he said flatly. "You're very brave and very loyal but not very wise, my dear Juliet. I hope you won't be made too unhappy."

"You mistake the matter," she said defiantly. "I shall be very happy. When you marry Cynthia, I'll live with you at Wayborn Hall, and you won't need to hire a governess for I shall teach my nephews and nieces very well!"

"When I marry Cynthia!" he said, coloring up. "What nonsense."

"Never mind," said Juliet, smiling. His admiration for her cousin Miss Cynthia Cary was well-known to her, and she enjoyed teasing him about it. "Cynthia is content to wait. Benedict!" she cried suddenly.

"Would you not let me go to Cynthia instead? Tanglewood is only a little farther away than Wayborn, and I should like it better to be exiled there. Aunt Elkins is well enough in town with all its diversions, but at Wayborn, with nothing to occupy her mind, I should be obliged to hear all about her many acquaintances who have died of influenza. I had much rather dispense with all that and go to my cousins. I should be more than adequately chaperoned, I think, at the Vicarage. The Reverend Dr. Cary will not let me go far wrong, and you know it has been almost a year since I was among them, and Cary neither visits nor writes our Hertfordshire relations."

"I have no objection to the scheme," said Benedict after some thought. "But at present, I am unable to escort you there—"

"There is nothing easier in the world!" she assured him. "My cousin Captain Cary has been in London all this week. He told me himself he meant to go to Tanglewood Tuesday next. He won't mind going a few days sooner."

Benedict did not like the idea. Horatio Cary, Cynthia's brother, was a very handsome young officer of the Royal Navy. With her reputation already in shreds, his sister could ill afford the ugly gossip that undoubtedly would attend her traveling alone with Captain Cary.

"I shall have my maid with me in the chaise," said Juliet persuasively. "And Horatio can ride alongside for he has just bought the most splendid white mare!"

Benedict, whose lack of a right arm prevented him from enjoying riding, had not considered that Captain Cary might do anything but ride in the chaise with Juliet. Naturally, if the Captain meant to ride his own horse, that put quite a different complexion on things. "I will write to Dr. Cary directly," he said. "If the Captain is in London, no doubt he has heard of our . . . predicament."

"Horatio will be anxious to assist me," she said confidently. "He has been most attentive since he came to London. He has even taken me aboard his ship, the *Monarch*."

Benedict looked at her sharply. "Indeed?"

Juliet went on in her lively manner. "She is docked at Tilbury, you know, and Cary and I dined there like real sailors, with our plates shuffling back and forth with the tide."

He smiled faintly. "Astonishing!"

"Horatio is much admired in London. He goes everywhere, and everyone is talking of him. In the last month of the war, he captured no less than five French frigates, and there is talk of elevating him to the knighthood. Serena Calverstock has dubbed him Phoebus and likes to think he is dangling after her, but, of course, I have warned him about *her*."

Upon writing to the Captain at his rooms in the Grillon, Benedict discovered that Juliet was right. Horatio was more than glad to assist his cousin, and the departure was fixed for the following morning after breakfast, which Benedict invited the Captain to take with them in Park Lane.

When Captain Cary arrived, Benedict was again dismayed by his good looks. The Captain wore his dark gold hair cropped short in the latest fashion; his eyes were bright cornflower blue; and though he wore small whiskers, one felt it was not in order to hide any defect of his features. Beyond that, he was tall and trim; he had new clothes; and he carried himself like a gentleman.

Juliet greeted him a little doubtfully. She had asked

to go to Hertfordshire impetuously, thinking only of her own preferences. But perhaps she had been wrong to impose on her cousin and cause him to change his plans.

Horatio at once put her scruples to rest. "You will not credit it, perhaps," he said as they sat down to breakfast, "but I was on the verge of calling to offer my assistance."

Juliet, seated opposite him, forced a smile. "It's very good of you not to abandon me in my disgrace, Cousin. Benedict thinks I've damaged myself beyond all hope of repair."

"I am sorry for you, Cousin," he said, shaking his head. "But I don't think it so black as that, Sir Benedict. After all, from what I understand, Lord Swale quite deserved his humiliation. Of course, some very old-fashioned tiresome people—"

"Like Benedict!" said Juliet. "Like Stacy Calverstock."

Horatio lifted a brow. "Calverstock? What had he to say?"

"He was chivalrous enough to ask for my hand!" she told him, laughing. "Did you ever hear anything so paltry?"

Horatio's eyes twinkled at her. "And shall I wish you joy, Cousin?"

"I wouldn't marry a man who offers for me out of some misguided pity," Juliet replied in scorn.

"Even if you loved him?" Horatio teased her.

"Especially not if I loved him," she said promptly. "That would be agony for me. In any case, I do *not* love Stacy Calverstock, I assure you."

Benedict watched this exchange thoughtfully. He had seen the look on the Captain's face when Juliet had spoken of Calverstock's offer. The Captain had recovered quickly and had made a joke, but his first reaction had been intense displeasure. Could it be that Captain Cary was in love with Juliet? It seemed so, and, what was more, Juliet seemed to return his admiration. In many ways, Benedict reflected, it would be an ideal match, especially if the Captain had grown rich in the war. Such a circumstance would not be likely to move Juliet's heart, of course, but it went a long way toward making Benedict easy in his mind. He began to think of the Tanglewood scheme with greater complacency.

"There, you see, Benedict," Juliet startled him by saying, "I've had two firm offers of marriage!"

"What?" he said sharply.

"Were you not listening? Cousin Horatio was just telling me the most amusing story. Completely apocryphal, I do believe, but apparently, when the Prince Regent heard about the race, he declared that *he* would marry me as soon as he is divorced from the Princess of Wales!"

Benedict was not amused. He had no great opinion of the Carlton House set, and he had no desire to see his sister drawn into its incessant absurdities, freaks, and scandals.

"You will be pleased to know, Sir Benedict, that the members of White's have taken action against Swale. No gentleman with a wager on yesterday's race has any intention of collecting. Including Mr. Alexander Devize and my own patron Lord Redfylde," Horatio added.

"There!" said Juliet, pleased. "Even his club is on my side."

After breakfast, she went upstairs to kiss Cary goodbye, and Captain Cary went with her. To her surprise, her brother was awake. With her help, he was able to sit up and drink a little water.

He greeted Horatio fondly but had not the strength to shake hands.

Horatio was plainly shocked at the sight of his cousin. Cary's arm was in a splint, his head was bandaged, and his lean, handsome face was haggard. Deep violet shadows stood under his gray eyes. But his sense of humor had not been quenched. "I like the fungus better and better each time I see it," he told Horatio with a faint smile. "Perhaps I shall take this opportunity to grow whiskers too."

Cary was pleased to learn that Juliet was going to Tanglewood. "I can't bear her clucking over me like a hen! I'll dictate a letter to you every day, Julie," he promised. "Do not bother your head about me. If you were to stay here, you would be bored to sobs."

"I do hate leaving you, Cary, but if I am to be sent away, I had much rather go to my cousins."

"Look after her, Horatio," Cary said. "Indeed, she is not the willful hellion you may think! She was always quite tame before. And, if no other harm comes to me, I expect she will be a good girl all the days of her life. Your father needn't worry she will lead Cynthia astray!"

"No, indeed," Horatio scoffed. "Only I wish she had called upon me to take your place, Cousin. Though I very much doubt I should have contrived to win the race."

"Tell your father I shall visit Tanglewood as soon as I am able," said Cary. "I know the Manor has been sadly neglected. I thank you for bringing it to my attention. Somehow, I never think of it, though it is my mother's birthplace and my grandmamma was kind enough to leave it to me when she died. I can't think why she didn't leave it to you."

"Perhaps it is because I was at sea when she died," Horatio said with just a hint of reproach. "You are very much looked for at Tanglewood and very much missed, Cary."

"Yes," Juliet chimed in. "Whenever I go there, the people talk of nothing else but the absentee landlord. You must do better, Cary."

Cary chuckled softly. "Very well," he said. "I shall! There is one favor I should like to ask of you before you go, Julie. Would you please inform Lady Serena Calverstock of my condition? Perhaps I flatter myself, but I believe her ladyship may be worried about me."

Horatio gallantly agreed to stop at Lord Redfylde's house in Grosvenor Square, where Serena, who was the sister of Lady Redfylde as well as the cousin of Stacy Calverstock, resided.

"You do not much care for the lady," Horatio said as he handed Juliet into the chaise.

"I don't believe she cares a button for my brother," Juliet declared. "She is false to her toes."

"But, my dear cousin," he protested, "they are seen everywhere together! Cary even allows her ladyship to drive his chestnuts."

Juliet flushed angrily. There had been a time when *she* had been the only female allowed to drive her brother's famous chestnuts, and she could not give way graciously to the beautiful Serena. "You do not know her as I do, Cousin," she told him. "You have been away fighting. You have not seen how coldly she conducted herself to my brother in the months before you returned. It was quite sudden that she began to take notice of him, I assure you, and I don't believe for an instant she is sincere. Before my brother, she was equally enchanted by Mr. Alexander Devize! I believe she enjoys having men dangle after her. Why else would she have had seven Seasons in London but have accepted no offers?"

"Has she had offers?" Horatio inquired, apparently amused.

"Several," Juliet replied. "No one is rich enough or high enough for her, it seems. My poor brother was on the verge of making her an offer, but I convinced him that Tanglewood Manor is not sufficiently grand to tempt her! I persuaded him it would be foolish to ask for her and that it would only cause them both great embarrassment."

"You did, did you?" Horatio's blue eyes twinkled. "What an excellent sister you are. Perhaps," he added with mock seriousness, "you would allow me to deliver your brother's message to the lady—*I* cannot be in danger for I have neither titles nor estates."

Juliet looked down at her hands. "It had occurred to me, Cousin, that Lady Serena might not be at home to Miss Wayborn today. Would you mind awfully—?"

"I am Miss Wayborn's servant," he replied so gravely that she laughed.

Horatio was not twenty minutes in Lord Redfylde's house. "I think you are right about the lady, Cousin," he reported to Juliet. "She seemed not to care in the least for your brother's injuries nor for your own predicament, my dear Juliet. Her ladyship was quite cold on both subjects."

"Indeed, I am heartily sorry to have been right about her insincerity," said Juliet, biting her lip. "Cary will be hurt, and I expect I am to blame, but at least, he is free of her now."

The peaceful village of Tanglewood Green lay twenty miles north of London in Hertfordshire, and travel was easy along the Great North Road. Juliet, her maid, and Captain Cary arrived at the Vicarage no later than one o'clock to the great surprise of Dr. Cary and his wife, who had expected to see their son the following week and Juliet not at all.

The Vicar's house was a large and stately stone building that at one time had held as many as seven children and their parents, as well as a full contingent of servants. The eldest of the Carys' seven children was Horatio, but the next five children had been named simply and safely George, Tom, Mary, James, and Edward. Then, quite unexpectedly, at the age of forty, Mrs. Cary had given birth to a second girl. Her surprise was so great that she had named the baby Cynthia. Now seventeen and a beauty, Miss Cary was the only child left at home.

When Juliet arrived, Cynthia and her mother were preparing to visit an elderly woman in the parish. They instantly offered to revise their plans, while Juliet suggested that she take Mrs. Cary's place.

"But, my dear, you must be tired from your journey," Mrs. Cary protested weakly. She was a large, comfortable woman who did not care for walking, and it had already occurred to her that, if Juliet went with Cynthia, it would give her time to make arrangements for her unexpected guest. The Carys considered themselves very humble country people, and the arrival of their smart London cousin, who had been presented to Queen Charlotte in the state drawing room of St. James's Palace, was sufficient to frighten Mrs. Cary into taking her very best linens out of the lavender-scented tissue in which they were stored.

Juliet insisted. After the confinement of the carriage, a long, healthy walk was just what she liked. Mrs. Cary's half-hearted objections were easily overcome

while Sailor, the family's spaniel, ran up to Juliet and
shoved his nose under her hand in a bid for her attention. It was soon decided that Sailor would accompany the girls on their errand.

Alighting from the vehicle, Mademoiselle Huppert
gazed up at the Vicarage with an expression of Gallic
scorn. If her mistress delighted in scampering about
the countryside with dogs and baskets of food, she,
Mademoiselle, had better ideas. Approaching Mrs.
Cary, she rather coldly asked for the housekeeper.

Juliet, meanwhile, took the basket from Cynthia,
and, arm and arm, the pair started down the lane.
Like her brother, Cynthia was fair-haired and blue-
eyed, but while her brother was bronzed from his time
at sea, Cynthia was pale, an almost ethereal-looking
beauty. Besides being quite the loveliest girl Juliet had
ever seen, Cynthia held a place of honor in her
cousin's heart, for Cynthia had been kind to Benedict
the summer before when he had visited Tanglewood
with his half-sister for the first time. Hampered by his
missing limb and scarred face, Benedict was usually
painfully awkward around the fair sex, and Juliet
would always be grateful to Cynthia for making him
feel so comfortable on that occasion. Indeed, she
was determined to make a match between the pair.

She lost no time in acquainting Cynthia with her own
disgrace, and her cousin, whose dull life in the country had ill-prepared her for tales of midnight muggings
and curricle races, listened in rapt fascination, horrified to learn that Cary had been attacked. "But, surely,
it was an accident?" she said nervously.

"Accident!" Juliet's color rose, and her eyes snapped
dangerously. "He was attacked from behind and
beaten mercilessly."

"Oh," said Cynthia, anxious to calm her fiery cousin.

"I did not mean an accident, of course. But a mistake. Could it have been a mistake?"

"A mistake?" Juliet scoffed. "They knew exactly what they were about. They were *sent* to do their work. Lord Swale paid them to make sure Cary could not drive his chestnuts in the race."

"Lord Swale!" Cynthia shivered, picturing a tall, dark, foreign-looking nobleman with a streak of silver in his hair and perhaps, a monocle, if not an eyepatch. "Even his name is sinister."

"I expect if we were to look him up in the Peerage, we would find that he is descended of a demon, like the Plantagenets," said Juliet.

"Shall we look him up then?" suggested Cynthia.

Juliet shrugged but expressed a slight curiosity in knowing who the mother of the monster might be. "A brewer's daughter, I should think," she said nastily. "The Duke is so refined."

"You said in your letter he wore more powder and paint than Her Majesty," Cynthia objected.

"Well, yes, dear," replied Juliet. "But he is quite old, you know. It must have been the fashion of his youth. At least his Grace does not try to look like a young man. That would be absurd!"

They reached the cottage of the invalid and completed their errand. Cynthia did not forget about the Peerage, and when they returned home, she smuggled it out of her father's study and up to Juliet's room.

"The family seat is at Auckland," Juliet said helpfully. "Auckland Palace. From all his Grace told me, it is very grand. There is an Amber drawing room and a room set aside for his Grace's porcelain collection. The Auckland Collection must make your father's china cabinets look ridiculous."

"Is he handsome?" asked Cynthia, searching the pages of the thick volume.

"His Grace?" Juliet shrugged. "I expect he was so in his youth. His manners are very pleasing. He was kind, but without that insufferable air of condescension which so many gentlemen of rank assume when they are meeting little nobodies like Miss Wayborn."

Cynthia glanced up, her eyes round with fear. "If Miss Wayborn is nobody, I expect I shall be *nothing* if I go to London next Season! I wish Horatio would not think of putting up so much money on my account. I am certain to fail. Besides—"

"Are you to go to London next Season?" cried Juliet. With a pang, she realized that she had very likely forfeited her own chances for another London Season, but she suppressed her feelings. "Oh, Cynthia, that is famous! It will bring Benedict up to scratch, I daresay," she added with a laugh. "He will not like to see you dancing with the handsome young gentlemen of Almack's!"

Two bright spots of red appeared in Cynthia's cheeks. "Almack's! Sir Benedict! Pray, don't be so absurd." She bent her fair head over the book and quickly changed the subject. "When I asked if he were handsome, I really meant Lord Swale, you know."

Juliet snorted. "He has horrid red hair and a snub nose," she said scornfully. "You would not *believe* his sideburns—they actually appear to be burning. He looked rather like a stableboy, I thought. A stableboy with nettlerash," she added contemptuously, recalling Swale's blotchy face as he jumped from his curricle, cursing furiously at her. "A big, hulking brute with no refinement," she concluded.

Cynthia frowned. She had never been to London, and she thought it must be filled with nothing but the most delightful ladies and gentlemen. She knew perfectly well what a marquess should look like. Even the most sinister marquess should be tall, elegant, and darkly handsome. They should *not* resemble stableboys with nettlerash. "I expect," she said doubtfully, "his friends call him Carrots."

"A scaly monster like Swale has no friends," Juliet declared, conveniently forgetting Mr. Alexander Devize. "He has henchmen, that is all. I daresay, when his back is turned, they must call him Ginger, for not only does he have the most appalling red hair, but he must also have the most beastly temper that can be imagined. Cynthia, when he found he had lost the race to me, he could do nothing more than accuse me of cheating and threaten to horsewhip me!"

Cynthia gasped. "H-horsewhip you!" she cried in terror. "But Juliet—!"

"He thought I was Cary, you see." She paused and frowned suddenly. "Though how he should have thought I *was* Cary I shall never know!"

Cynthia was puzzled. "You said you wore his coat and his hat and his spectacles."

"I mean," said Juliet patiently, "his mercenaries must have reported their success in eliminating my brother from the competition. Swale ought to have been *quite* surprised to see me! Instead, he was grinning at me. He even wished me luck. Never mind," she said quickly, burying the tiny seed of doubt in righteous indignation. "I expect he covered his amazement with that idiotic grin. Have you found Auckland yet?"

Cynthia handed her the book silently, too overwhelmed by the imposing list of titles, patents, and lands to speak.

"Why, his name is nothing more than Geoffrey Ambler!" cried Juliet indignantly. "Look! One son, Geoffrey, Marquess of Swale, and one d. Maria. The slimy snake has a sister. Since I did not hear of her this Season, we can assume her ladyship has married since this printing."

"Why, that sounds almost human," Cynthia remarked. "There is something stalwart about a Geoffrey, don't you think, Julie? And a Geoffrey with a sister can not be all bad, surely. She probably calls him Geoff or Geoffie."

"It is the name of a soulless swine," Juliet declared. "I expect Geoffrey Ambler, swine, has fled to Auckland. I expect London is no longer pleasant for him. I expect I shall never see him again."

"But Juliet!" Cynthia cried. "You do not wish to, surely."

"No, indeed," said Juliet. "No one who has ever seen him ever wishes to see him again. But if I ever do, I shan't call him Geoffie, I promise you. I shall call him *Ginger.*"

Chapter 4

Geoffrey, Lord Swale, was not greatly surprised to find a summons to Auckland House awaiting him at his rooms in Pall Mall when he returned to them after the race. The Wayborn Excrescence had done her damage with amazing speed. She had sown her miserable lies, broadcast them, like so much demon seed, and all of London was convinced of his guilt. Doubtless, his concerned parent wanted to console his beloved son. The following day he found Everard Ambler, the sixth Duke of Auckland, in his book room at the back of the London mansion that stood in Berkeley Square.

"Geoffrey, you mutt!" The Duke greeted him without any trace of paternal affection. The resemblance between father and son was not very pronounced. His Grace was one of the pale, slender aristocrats flawlessly turned out by his valet in wig and maquillage, while his son's burly physique, pugnacious face, and ruddy complexion were such that no valet or tailor could render them elegant. His clothes always looked rumpled; his hair was wild. His square chin regularly bore cuts from a clumsy razor, and his boots always looked as though they'd been left out in the rain.

"I take it, sir, you have dismissed your valet at last?"

Swale scowled, further distinguishing himself from the family portraits in the picture gallery at Auckland House. Stern looks, yes, but never that menacing glare a barman gives the bosky at last call. "Why should I dismiss my valet, sir?" he said belligerently. "Bowditch is as good as any other."

"Ha!" said his parent. "I don't say I want a dandy for a son, but you might at least be neat in your person. I also was cursed with red hair—"

"Were you, by God?" Swale exclaimed in astonishment.

The Duke smiled smugly. "Didn't know that, did you, sir? That is because I have always been properly ashamed of my head. I always cut as much of it off as possible and put the rest under a wig so as not to offend anyone. Good God! Look at you. It nearly touches your shoulders."

"I am," said Swale expansively, "what I am."

"I have always been told," his father said coldly, "first by your mother and then by your sister, that there are hidden depths to your character and that one day I shall be proud to call you my son! That day has not yet arrived. I have heard things, things which put me to the blush."

Swale's scowl deepened. It was only the Fifth Commandment that held his tongue in check.

"You have nothing to say to me, sirrah?"

"Sirrah!" cried Swale, unable to contain himself any longer. "You sirrah me? My own father! You don't mean to say you believe all this nonsense?"

The Duke raised one of the two slender brows painted on that morning by the steady hand of his valet. "I am told by creditable sources that you were involved in a curricle race yesterday morning?"

"Yes, obviously, I was," said Swale sullenly. "The whole world knows it."

The Duke brought his fingertips together. "And who was your opponent?"

"I had rather not say," Swale replied with a touch of hauteur.

"Did you or did you not compete against a female?" his father demanded. "A female called Miss Juliet Wayborn?"

"I hardly call that a female," said Swale, rather surprised that the creature in question possessed a Christian name. "More of a fiend in human shape."

"Is it true, sirrah, that you have been beaten by a mere female?"

"Dammed unnatural female if you ask me," Swale muttered, the nettlerash returning to his face. "A damned, dirty trick is what I call it! What does Wayborn mean, sending his sister out in his clothes?"

"It is popularly believed," said the Duke dryly, "that you hired two men to break his arm."

"I don't believe his arm is broken at all. *I* heard the man was put to bed suffering from nothing more than a touch of influenza. That is precisely what I said in my note."

The Duke's frown was very stern. "What note?"

"The note I sent 'round with the monkey that the bloody female threw at me."

"You damned fool!" said his father, and a bit of nettlerash peeped through the powder and paint so carefully applied by his valet.

"You don't expect me to keep his beastly money," said Swale, shocked. "By strict rules, I was the winner, but, really, after all . . . I sent a note to Wayborn, wishing him a swift recovery from the influenza. Naturally, as soon as he *is* recovered, I intend to shoot him. I daresay he thought it a pretty fine joke, sneaking his sister past me, but I don't go in for that shabby sort of thing."

"I have had speech of Mr. Norton, the surgeon," said the Duke in an icy voice, "and I am satisfied that Mr. Wayborn's arm is broken. There is also a head injury."

"And I expect you believe that I hired the ruffians who injured him too," Swale said bitterly. "My own father! Why the devil would I do such a thing? I was looking forward to racing Cary Wayborn. I had as good a chance as any man in England of beating him."

"You!" scoffed his parent. "You couldn't beat Cary Wayborn's baby sister, and you expect me to believe you entertained hopes of triumphing over the man himself?"

"That's hard," Swale observed belligerently. "And anyway, the Wayborn doxy bloody well cheated. She bloody well came to a full stop in the middle of the bloody road. To keep from ramming her, I had to swerve around. Bloody devious! I ought to have known *then* I was racing a damned, interfering bloody female!"

"Do you swear to me that you had nothing to do with the attack on Mr. Wayborn?"

Swale was incensed. "Do I swear?"

"Yes, sir," said his father. "Do you swear?"

"You are asking me," said Swale. He paused to gain control of his temper. "Let me be clear, sir. You are asking your only son to swear to his innocence?"

"That is what I am asking," the Duke said coldly.

"Well, I do *not* swear," said Swale defiantly. "Believe what you will, sir, and be damned."

"Very well," said the Duke, much relieved. "I believe you."

"I should bloody well hope so," growled his son. "My

own father asking me to swear like a common criminal. I like that! That pleases me like nothing else. I should rather be the son of a costermonger than of a father who entertains such doubts about me."

The Duke held up his slim hand. "I never doubted you for a moment, Geoffrey. I am merely trying to prepare you for the harsh reality of life. From now on, everywhere you go, you will be questioned. Your ferocious temper is well-known. On the whole, I think it would be best if you were to leave London for a while."

"Why should I leave London?" Swale growled. "Let the Wayborns leave. They have cast aspersions against me. By that I mean they have told bold-faced lies!"

"But why would they lie?" asked his Grace.

Swale exploded. "You said you believed me!"

"Mr. Calverstock apparently heard the villains say 'Compliments of Lord Swale' or some such thing. I don't think Mr. Calverstock is lying. His grandfather was the Fourth Earl of Ludham!"

"'Compliments of Lord Swale!' As though I would!"

"Your name must be cleared, Geoffrey. It is the Ambler name, after all. Someone has attacked Mr. Wayborn and has taken a deal of trouble to implicate us in this dishonorable business."

Swale frowned in concentration. "Depend upon it, I will! I will discover who has done this to me, and, by God, I'll make him pay!"

The Duke smiled thinly. In matters of raw courage and brute strength, his heir undoubtedly was one of the best, but the Wayborn Affair, his Grace was certain, would require cunning and intelligence to unravel. To that end, he had already put the entire affair before his man of business and the Bow Street Runners. "Very well, Geoffrey," he said quite disingenuously. "I leave it to you. In the meantime, you are under a cloud. What do you propose to do about it?"

Swale snorted. "Do? I shall do nothing. Why should I do anything? I have been falsely accused. When the facts are known, all London shall be begging my forgiveness. But I shan't forgive them! Why should I?"

The Duke was less sanguine. "Let us be reasonable, Geoffrey. You will be living under a cloud until the culprit is found, and it may be years. Indeed, you may never be cleared entirely."

"A fortnight at the most," Swale protested. "I tell you, sir, I am on the case."

"Even if you were to beard the villain in his lair," said the Duke impatiently, "it is highly unlikely he'd admit to his foul misdeeds! It is highly unlikely that he should have been so obliging as to leave us enough evidence of his guilt as will convince our friends!"

"*My* friends require no evidence," Lord Swale declared. "I am sorry to hear that yours *do*. Do you think that Devize has asked me for evidence?"

"I daresay there always will be men willing to give their daughters to Lord Swale," said the Duke exactly as if his son had not spoken, "but I should not care to connect my family with any of *them*, I assure you!"

"Never mind that!" said Swale. "*That* is the silver lining to this black cloud of mine. I have no wish to marry any of their hen-witted daughters, let me tell you."

"You will be allowed back into Society after some time has passed, of course," his father said. "But, amongst the best families . . ." He shook his head. "You will always be anathema."

Swale was not certain what anathema was, but clearly his father thought it very serious. "What do I care for all that?" he said, attempting the cavalier approach. "If they do not believe me, they may go to the devil."

"There is one family whose assistance in this matter would be most beneficial."

"You refer to the Devizes," Swale said wisely. "As I have already indicated, Mr. Devize's confidence in me remains unshaken. We may depend upon him at least."

"Yes, the name Devize is not contemptible," the Duke said absently. "But I was thinking of quite another family. A family whose influence in this matter would be of the highest order. If they were to embrace you, the rest of Society should follow its lead."

Swale cudgeled his brains. "Not the Royal Family!" he exclaimed after a moment. "But, sir, you despise the Royal Family."

"I refer, of course, to the Wayborn family," said the Duke patiently.

"The Wayborns!" said Swale, abandoning the cavalier approach. "Have you run mad? It is the Wayborns who have accused me!"

"Precisely. And if the Wayborns were to indicate by some public action that they no longer believe you guilty, would that not go a long way toward lifting the clouds?"

"The clouds would undoubtedly lift," said Swale with a short, bitter laugh. "The sun would shine, and the birds would sing. But it ain't going to happen!"

"If we could convince them—"

"If I was to go to them with my tail between my legs and swear to my innocence, you mean?" Swale scoffed. "Abandon all hope of that, dear Father."

"Then there is the question of Miss Wayborn."

"I think the question of Miss Wayborn is better left to her Maker!"

"You don't like her," his father guessed. "Too spirited, I suppose."

"Spirited! I should describe my own excellent sister

as spirited, sir. The Wayborn is a man-eating tigress, an amazon. Indeed, that's what they're calling her—the Amazon."

"I'm sorry you don't like her, Geoffrey. I like her *very* well. Though, I must say, I had not thought her capable of *this*."

Swale stared at him. "Do you mean to say you're acquainted with the Wayborns?"

"I am acquainted with Miss Wayborn. I danced with her at Almack's only last week. I found her quite charming."

"Charming!" Swale's guffaw was instantly replaced by a scowl. "I say! What the devil were you doing at Almack's? The place is nothing but a marriage mart. I avoid it like the plague. Good God, you're not thinking of making a fool of yourself with some young chit? At your age, it's positively indecent! What does my sister say?"

"It doesn't signify in the least what Maria says," said his Grace, considerably nettled by the unflattering reference to his age. "I've no intention of making a fool of myself, as you so kindly put it. Your own excellent mother provided me with an heir. I have no need of a wife."

Swale's green eyes narrowed. "Don't say you were browsing on my behalf!"

"You'll be glad to know that my efforts have borne fruit. I had already narrowed the field to three when this business of the curricle race burst in upon my reflections. Miss Coralie Price—"

Swale shuddered. "No bosom, sir. And no brain either. I absolutely insist on one or the other. I don't ask for both—I know it ain't possible."

"Lady Serena Calverstock. I knew her father, the Earl of Ludham, when he was alive."

"She, at least, has some beauty," Swale said grudgingly. "I suppose I could marry good old Serena, though she is older than I."

The Duke looked at him gravely. "She has violet eyes, Geoffrey."

"Does she?"

"What if your son should inherit his father's hair and his mother's eyes? Violet eyes, Geoffrey, and red hair. Hardly a desirable combination. Why, the child would be a freak! The idea is to *improve* the Auckland countenance through careful breeding."

"Is it?"

"In case you hadn't noticed, what our bloodline really needs is a truly fine nose. The Calverstock nose turns up at the end."

"What do I care if her nose turns up?" Swale wanted to know. "She's far and away the prettiest woman in London."

"If you had a creditable nose, which you don't, or unexceptional hair, which you don't, I shouldn't mind in the least if you married her," replied his father. "But, unfortunately, you have the nose of a prize-fighter, and only half of it at that."

"I got it from you, sir," Swale reminded him. "Along with my hair."

"That is no excuse," said the Duke. "Over the centuries, the Ambler family has accumulated land and wealth and titles. Now, it is our turn to enrich future generations of Amblers."

"We're going to accumulate a nose?"

The Duke nodded. "The moment I saw this nose, Geoffrey, I knew we had to have it. It had the most astonishing effect on me."

"Did it make you sneeze, Father?"

"I am perfectly serious, sir," the Duke said coldly.

"The Ambler profile is profoundly weakened by this snub nose of ours. Yours, at least, has a high, sturdy bridge—Maria's is positively a pug! I want my grandson to have a nose worthy of our position in Society."

"I can't say I've spent much time looking at ladies' noses," Swale said, trying not to snicker, "but let me venture to guess. Miss Cheeveley? Or is it to be Laura Ogilvie? Now *there* is a nose!"

"I should think it highly doubtful," said the Duke with a touch of asperity, "that either Mrs. Cheevely or Lord Ogilvie would encourage an alliance between their daughters and one who stands accused of such ungentlemanlike conduct."

"Well, it don't signify," said Swale stubbornly, "for I don't wish to marry *them*, I can tell you. What clings to a man like a limpet ought to be a limpet, not a female."

"Bravo, Geoffrey," the Duke said without applause. "I put it to you plainly. If you do not marry the young lady I have chosen, I will."

Swale thought it a good joke. He hooted with irreverent laughter. "You marry? Why, you're fifty if you're a day! What about the nose? How's it to end up on your grandson's face if you marry her? But perhaps you mean to do away with me and make my little half-brother your heir."

His father continued as though there had been no interruption. "I am confident that when the young lady discovers you are not guilty of this crime, you will suit very well. She is courageous and loyal. She will stand by you come hell or high water, as the expression goes."

Swale snorted in derision. "I don't want a wife to stand by me. I want her to lie down for a few moments and then go away. I never met a female yet whose company I could bear above five minutes," he declared.

"Don't think I don't know what you do in those five minutes!" snapped his Grace. "In my day—!" He paused to gain control of his temper. "I need hardly remind you that it is your duty to marry."

"Not, surely, at the tender age of twenty-five, your Grace! Why, there are bachelors twice my age whose duty it is to marry," Swale pointed out. "It doesn't do, you know, to run a fox to earth before it's had a fair run of the country."

"You are not a fox, sir," his parent informed him acidly. "You are my son, and you are in a devilish scrape, though you pretend not to know it. Geoffrey, I had rather you were fifty thousand pounds in debt than this! Do you think I care to hear the Ambler name maligned, or my only son labeled a coward? A despicable, cheating coward?"

"It is most unfair," Swale agreed. "And if you think," he added magnanimously, "that my marriage will put an end to the scandal . . . " He shrugged as one does who has resigned himself to his fate. "Then I expect there is nothing for it. I always meant to do my duty and carry on the Ambler name and all that sort of thing."

"That is gratifying," said his parent, "considering you cost me twenty thousand a year!"

Swale smiled. "I'll need more than that if I'm to maintain a nose, I mean, a wife. I trust you to be fair, sir. Indeed, I leave all the arrangements to you. Solicit her hand—or nose—and I agree to meet her in due time at St. George's altar like the good son I am."

The Duke's eyes were veiled, and for the first time, he seemed apologetic. "I'm afraid I would be unequal to the task of soliciting her hand, dear boy. It was all I could do to claim two dances with her at Almack's."

* * *

Much later in his rooms at the Albany, Swale related every detail of the interview with his father to his friend Alexander Devize. When he had reached this point in his narrative, he paused to allow the significance of the Duke's clue to sink in. "I leave you to imagine my reaction, Alex. It is the Wayborn he means, you see! Hers is the nose he wants on his grandson's face!"

Unlike his friend, Alex was neither stunned nor indignant. "Indeed," he said calmly. "I always said your father was a sensible old bird. And the nose in question *is* quite remarkable."

Swale was almost purple in the face with rage, and he did not hear his friend. "Of all the creatures in London, my father would have me throw myself away on that transvestite freak! Something about her being ruined and how no respectable man will marry her now, as if that is my fault! Naturally, no decent man will marry her. Frankly, the thought of the Wayborn bearing the offspring of a Christian man chills me to the bone! I should rather . . . I should much rather marry the Calverstock!"

"My dear Swale, you cannot mean it!" said Alex, laughing. "Serena is beautiful, but she is heartless man, heartless. If she marries you, 'twill be for your rank and your fortune. You deserve better than that."

"At least she is female," said Swale, "which is more than the Wayborn can say."

Alex frowned. "They are saying worse things about her in the clubs, you know."

"She deserves to have worse said about her," said Swale furiously. "Damned unnatural is what she is. What does she mean by grinding to a halt like that?"

"They are saying she gave birth on the road to Southend and still had time to beat you."

Swale stared at him. "They are saying *what*? No,

don't repeat it. No gentleman would say such a thing. It's too sick-making."

"Quite," said Alex. "It is Lord Dulwich saying it, and not a gentleman, as you say. Dulwich is such a notorious duelist that even Stacy Calverstock will not call him out, though anyone can see he dearly wants to."

"Calverstock," Swale scoffed, "is an ass. If he were not the friend of Cary Wayborn, no one would regard him at all."

"Two younger sons," Devize said dismissively. "They console one another."

"Oh, the Wayborn has *two* brothers, does she?" Swale said. "Why does Wayborn the Elder not put a stop to this wild behavior?"

"She has two brothers," Alex responded, "and between them, they now have two good arms. Sir Benedict's right arm was cut off, poor man."

"Sir Benedict," Swale repeated, trying to place the name. "What was he knighted for?"

"Why, nothing," said Alex, amused. "He's a baronet. The Wayborns are Old County."

"How is it you know so much about them?" Swale asked suspiciously. "Mr. Cary Wayborn and his chestnuts are famous, of course, but I never heard of any Sir Benedict."

"My sister," Alex said apologetically. "Lady Cheviot thinks I should marry sooner rather than later. It will amuse you to know she had fastened her eye on Miss Wayborn this Season."

Swale barked with laughter. "What is it about this wretched female that so attracts a man's relatives yet so repels the man himself?"

"I did not say she repelled me," Alex said reproachfully. "As a gentleman, I should refrain from criticizing a lady, but, if anything, I thought her rather too mild for my taste."

Swale stared at him. "Mild!" he said incredulously. "That hell-born termagant!"

"She seemed to me a quiet young lady with a well-ordered mind," Alex said, laughing. "Very grave and dignified. Bookish. I thought her well-suited to marry a bishop."

Swale glared at him. "That damned race has made me the laughingstock of all London, and her cursed accusations have made me . . . anathema!"

"My dear Geoffrey," said Alex, "you do realize that the foolish girl has damaged herself more than she could ever damage you? Your troubles will soon pass. Hers never will."

"That is her own doing," Swale said stubbornly.

"Come, come!" said Alex, losing patience. "Not only would such a marriage exonerate you in the matter of her brother's injuries, but it would place the very female that humiliated you in your power. You could revenge yourself upon her quite freely, I imagine."

"Revenge myself on her!" Swale cried, startled by the idea. "Beat her, I suppose!" he said, scowling. "That is what you think of me."

"I beg your pardon," said Alex contritely. "If you will but check your temper, you'll see that there's a great deal of sense in what your father says."

Swale stared at him in mute horror.

"Some do believe you did it, Geoffrey," Alex told him, "but most don't care whether or not it's true, only that it's made life interesting to have something so sensational to talk about! To absolutely kill the rumor, you need the Wayborns on your side. And if Miss Wayborn is ever to return to Society, she will need a husband of some considerable rank."

"They may all go to the devil," said Swale. "Society ought to be thanking me for getting rid of Miss Wayborn instead of curling its lip at me in scorn."

At that moment, Bowditch, his lordship's valet, entered the room. He was dressed to go out, and he was carrying a satchel packed with, one assumed, all his worldly possessions. "Bowditch?" said Swale, rather surprised. "What the devil are you about?"

"I am leaving, my lord," the valet announced.

"Not now? I expect your mother is ill or some such thing?"

"No, my lord," said Bowditch, drawing himself up to his full height. "I could not remain another day in the service of my Lord Swale. I have my reputation to consider."

How anyone should care two straws for a servant's opinion, particularly when the servant sent one out into the world looking like an unmade bed, was beyond Alex Devize's comprehension, but apparently Swale was attached to his man. "Surely you do not believe this nonsense!" Swale said incredulously. "Bowditch?"

Bowditch shook his head. "I do not wish to believe it, my lord, but Mademoiselle Huppert has issued me an ultimatum."

"Who the devil is Mademoiselle Huppert?" Swale demanded. Alex, who was less interested in the mademoiselle's identity, poured himself another glass of his friend's execrable Madeira.

"Mademoiselle and I," said Bowditch with dignity, "have an understanding, my lord. She is Miss Wayborn's *femme de chambre*, your lordship collects."

"No, I don't collect! Let me tell you, old man, unless your mother is sick, you are going exactly nowhere. Consorting with the enemy, by God." Swale ground his fist into his open palm. "I expect this Mademoiselle, with whom you have an understanding, has painted *me* very black indeed."

Bowditch appeared abashed. "It's not so much that, my lord, as Mademoiselle telling me that if I remain in the service of my Lord Swale, our friendship is at an end. I expect I shall find a place elsewhere."

Alex seriously doubted it and thought his friend well rid of the odious Bowditch. "Never mind," he said callously. "What you want, Geoffrey, is a Frenchman like my Laval."

Bowditch's face fell, and Alex almost expected tears, but Swale forestalled them. "No, no!" he cried. "A Frenchman! That would never do. Bowditch has known me all my life—he was a footman at Auckland when I was a boy."

Bowditch looked at his lord, and his watery eyes spoke of nothing but gratitude and adoration.

"Go upstairs at once and unpack," said Swale. "Leave it all to me."

"Yes, my lord," Bowditch said. "Thank you, my lord."

"Geoffrey, you astonish me," said Alex. "I should have sent him packing. Mademoiselle Huppert indeed!"

Swale waved him off. "But you don't understand, old man. When I was twelve, I stole the key to the cellar at Auckland, and . . . well, I drank rather a lot of the governor's best, I'm afraid. Bowditch—he was only a pageboy then—swore he'd broken the bottles and put up with no end of abuse on my behalf, I can tell you."

"No doubt," said Alex, unimpressed. "But I can't help but wonder why you would undertake for a servant something you wouldn't do for either your father or your friend."

Swale flushed. "I'll speak to Cary Wayborn, that's all. If he takes my word as a gentleman, so much the better. If not, he may go to the devil, and I'll tell him so to his head. But I don't think it necessary, even for Mademoiselle's sake, to pay my addresses to the Amazon!"

"If you will but attend me with as much courtesy as you showed your man," said Alex, "I would tell you that there's no need for you to marry Miss Wayborn."

"I am glad you think so."

"*If* you have made up your mind to call her Mamma."

"What?"

"You say your father means to ask for her hand if you do not. Let her take your mother's place in the Index as her Grace of Auckland. Let her preside at Auckland Palace. Sit in your mother's place. Sleep in your mother's bed. Who knows? She might even provide you with a few brothers and sisters. How would you like that, old man?"

"If my excellent father wishes to make a cake of himself, it's nothing to me," Swale said stubbornly, but he was very red in the face, and his fists were clenched.

"No?" said Alex. "Very well. Only consider this: make her an offer, and Miss Wayborn will very likely fling it back in your teeth. Your father would not be such a damn fool as to ask for a lady that has refused his son. End of dilemma."

"I always used to admire your brain, Alex," Swale said haughtily. "But I think you have gone slack! Of course she would snatch me up if I made her an offer. How could she resist? I am what is known by these grasping females as a matrimonial prize!"

Alex shook his head. "Have you learned nothing about Miss Wayborn?"

Swale snorted. "On the contrary, I know her like the back of my hand. The harpy would accept me if only to make the rest of my life a living hell."

Alex smiled faintly. "Perhaps," he admitted. "But you needn't apply to her in person. That could be disastrous and anyway, improper, for you have never been introduced to Miss Wayborn."

"God willing, I never shall be."

"But Sir Benedict Wayborn can be relied upon to decline your very fine offer of marriage. He is very proud. He will absolutely forbid you to pay your addresses to her. Rely upon it. I daresay you will find him a formidable ally."

"An ally!" cried Swale incredulously.

"Dear boy," Alex said dryly. "He must have some little interest in who, if it was not my Lord Swale, has done this to his brother."

As a matter of fact, Sir Benedict's interest in the matter was greater than Alex anticipated, and it was not much later that, as Swale was dressing to go out, Bowditch scratched at his lordship's door and told him in a hushed voice that Sir Benedict Wayborn had sent up his card.

Chapter 5

Swale scowled at his man. "But the fellow's got only one good arm! I can't shoot a man with one arm, Bowditch."

Bowditch appeared startled. "My lord?"

"Obviously, the damn fool has come to throw down the gauntlet, knowing I can no more fight him than I could his sister," Swale explained. "Tell him to go away and not be an ass."

Bowditch returned a few minutes later with a note on a tray.

"Bloody hell!" said Swale. He was at his mirror attempting to tie his neckcloth in a new style that his friend Mr. Devize had shown him. The attempt was not an unqualified success. "Read it to me, will you, Bowditch? It won't hurt you to practice your reading."

"Thank you, my lord," said Bowditch, placing a monocle in one eye and reading slowly and ponderously. "Sir Benedict Wayborn sends his compliments to his lordship, the Marquess of Swale, and—"

"Ha!" said Swale. "Compliments!"

Bowditch checked the word again, but it seemed to him really to be 'compliments.' "He begs the favor of your lordship's company," Bowditch went on, choosing to summarize.

"At dawn, I suppose, in Hyde Park near the Serpentine?"

Bowditch scanned the lines again. "No, my lord," he said regretfully. "He wishes to dine with you at his club, that is all."

"What?" cried Swale, abandoning his neckcloth and snatching the letter from his man. "He awaits me downstairs?" he said incredulously. "Well, if the damn fool challenges me at the front door of my hotel, missing arm or no missing arm—" He broke off and irritably completed his toilette.

Sir Benedict awaited him in a small private parlor downstairs. Seated in an armchair near the fire, he was enjoying a glass of claret, and his profile, Swale sourly observed, was that of a Greek god. The nose was particularly fine, long, but not too long; perfectly straight, with just the tiniest aquiline cast to its bridge. Swale was shocked to see that the baronet was not alone. Mr. Devize was with him. Alex appeared amused.

"What the devil do you want, Wayborn?" Swale demanded.

Sir Benedict set his glass down, rose from his chair, and surveyed the Marquess with neither praise nor censure, his gray eyes cold and hard. He made no attempt to hide the scars that disfigured the right half of his face. His empty right sleeve had been sewn shut and neatly pinned at the elbow.

Swale felt himself weighed and found wanting, but he was pleased to see that even when standing, the baronet had to tilt his head back to look the taller man in the eye.

"Good evening, my lord," said Benedict, resting his

left hand on the head of his cane and making a slight bow. "May I propose that we walk to my club?"

Swale did not like Sir Benedict's high-handed manner. "I am dining with Mr. Devize at White's," he said shortly.

Sir Benedict smiled amiably. "Splendid, my lord. I am also a member of White's."

Swale eyed him suspiciously. "What do you want?" he said bluntly.

The baronet raised a brow, but otherwise he remained undisturbed. "I wish to dine with your lordship at White's, in the window, if possible."

Swale became contemptuous. "You wish to dine with me, do you? I am accused of hiring mercenaries to break your brother's arm, and you wish to dine with me? You, sir, are a shabby, grasping creature. I have no patience to spare toadeaters."

"I daresay your lordship has little patience to spare anyone," said Benedict, unruffled. "You strike me as rather extraordinarily hotheaded, my lord."

Swale's temper blazed. He did not care for remarks involving either the color or temperature of his head. "If you were a man—like your sister—you would be calling me out, sir, one arm or no one arm! Instead, you invite me to dinner. Are you a worm?"

"I should find it difficult, indeed, to shoot your lordship with one arm," said Benedict with a faint smile, "which I am sure you would see, my lord, if you could only think it through."

"By God, sir!" said Swale, his face blotched with red. "It is well for you that you have only one arm, or I should flatten you. Why, Miss Wayborn is worth ten of you!"

"I expect that is true," said Benedict pleasantly. "Your lordship seems agitated. Shall we walk, my lord? The evening is fine. Perhaps the cool air will soothe you, my lord." With perfect equanimity, he took his hat from the attendant and left the room.

The faint chuckle that escaped the Honorable Mr. Alexander Devize at this point did nothing to improve Swale's temper.

The dining room at White's was full to capacity, but Sir Benedict commanded a table at the bow window without difficulty. The conversation in the room fell away, and startled looks greeted Swale and Devize as they entered the room on Sir Benedict's heels.

Apparently oblivious to the attention, Sir Benedict sat down and ordered dinner for himself and his guests. He then asked the attendant for the betting book.

"What do you want the betting book for?" asked Swale, curiosity overcoming his annoyance.

"It seems to me a good place to start," Benedict replied, "if I am to discover who is behind this attack upon my brother."

Swale blinked in surprise. "You mean to say you don't think *I* did it?"

"You, my lord?" said Benedict. "Do you mean to say you *did* do it?"

Swale glowered at him. "Are you accusing me?"

"Ought I to accuse you, my lord?" Benedict asked patiently.

"No!"

"Very well then," said Benedict. "And yet it seems undeniable that someone *has* plotted to harm my brother. Cary's attackers spoke of being sent on their errand by your lordship. To me, that is the most curious fact of the business. Apparently, our man hates my brother enough to wish him harm, but he also went to the trouble of blaming Lord Swale. I should not have thought this last part necessary if Cary's missing the race was all that mattered to him. Cary would have been forced to forfeit the race, but there it would have ended. Does it not strike you as curious that this was done in your name, my lord?"

"No," Swale retorted. "It strikes me as bloody impertinent!"

At White's, Swale's tastes were well-known. While the others were brought watercress soup, his lordship received his customary steak and kidney pie. He did not touch it, however. Now that Sir Benedict had laid the facts out, it did seem rather curious that his name had been brought into it.

"Needlessly elaborate," he postulated, "in addition to being bloody impertinent."

Sir Benedict, meanwhile, surveyed the ledger the attendant had brought along with the soup. "There are no less than eight bets recorded here concerning the race between Lord Swale and Mr. Wayborn," he said. "I expect any one of the parties might be cherishing a grudge against my brother."

Swale's astonishment showed plainly on his face. "But your brother is universally admired! He is the favorite of all London."

"Is that so?" said Benedict, smiling faintly. "It seems to me he has made fools of half of London with those pretty chestnuts of his. Yet you tell me he has no enemies. . ."

"He hasn't," said Swale. "Everyone likes him."

"Cary can be impetuous," said Sir Benedict. "He does not always guard his tongue."

Swale looked over the list of bets, frowning thoughtfully. "Bosher and Leighton—that's bound to be all right. I have known Bosher my whole life, and Leighton is his cousin. Devize and Calverstock. Obviously all right. Lord Alastair Hungerford and Lord

Meadowsweet. Lord Alastair is the Duke of Ram-
furline's son, you know. Charlie and Mr. Cammer-
leigh. Lord Redfylde and Lord Dulwich. Myself and
Mr. Wayborn, obviously. Sir Adam Osbert and Lord
Emsworth. Budgie St. John–Jones and Old Partridge—
Budgie wouldn't dare pull a mean trick like that. I
rather think he's afraid of Mr. Wayborn. I know he's
afraid of me."

"An excellent reason for hiring proxies," Sir Benedict pointed out.

Swale's eyes bulged. "Budgie! Are you mad? Besides,
he bet on Wayborn—your brother, I mean. Budgie
can't afford to lose even the trifling sum of five hundred pounds."

Devize said, "Really, Sir Benedict, there is no one
at White's capable of such a thing. Why, it would be
cheating!"

"It is possible our quarry placed no bet on the
race," Sir Benedict agreed thoughtfully.

"But if he did, he would have put his money on me,"
said Swale, his brow wrinkled with concentration,
"knowing that Mr. Wayborn would be forced to forfeit."

"You assume his motive was simple greed," Benedict
pointed out. "But if he merely wished to collect on a
bet, why implicate my Lord Swale? Why not simply let
it be known that my brother was attacked by footpads? Such attacks are woefully commonplace."

Swale attacked his pie. "I would dearly like to know
how my name came to be in the mouths of these
criminals."

"Perhaps our man impersonated you when he hired
his thugs," said Alex.

"The bloody cheek of him," said Swale. "I'll teach
him to impersonate me."

"Forgive me, my lord," said Benedict, "but if I

meant to impersonate a Peer, you would not be my first choice. Why then were you his?"

Swale frowned. "Eh?"

"He did not pluck your name from thin air. The attack on my brother may have been motivated by greed, but the attack on you must be personal, I think."

"But I was not attacked," said Swale, puzzled.

"Not physically," Benedict said patiently. "But your good name has been attacked, if you see what I mean."

"I don't care a damn about that," said Swale. "But my father is sick as a cat. And my sister . . ." He pushed his plate away. "Maria's a little high-strung when it comes to me. Like a mother lioness with her cub. This will cause her pain."

"It is difficult," Benedict agreed, "to see one's sister afflicted."

Swale blew out his breath. "Do you mean to say, Sir Benedict, that while this fellow broke your brother's arm, his true target was . . . was my good name? Bloody devious! Bloody convoluted, if that's the word I want. If he wants to harm me, why don't he say so, like a man? Why go after Mr. Wayborn?"

"It is possible he dislikes both of you," Benedict pointed out. "My brother's injuries do not begin and end with his arm. He was nearly killed. I was quite shocked when I saw him. That was not the work of a disinterested man. Can you think of anyone who might hate you, my lord?"

"Why should anyone hate me?" Swale demanded, scowling.

"I myself find it difficult to like you, my lord," said Sir Benedict apologetically. "Forgive me, but yours is a personality that seems almost to invite animosity."

"But anyone who hated Swale would want your brother to humiliate him," Alex pointed out.

"I tell you no one hates me," said Swale, considerably annoyed by Sir Benedict's reflections on his personality.

"Redfylde hates you, Swale," said Alex thoughtfully, consulting the ledger.

"Nonsense," said Swale. "Why should he?"

"When we were at school together, Redfylde tried calling you Ginger," said Alex. "You may recall knocking him to the ground. He's hated you ever since."

"He deserved it," said Swale, shrugging. "In the end, he admitted as much, and we shook hands. My name," he explained to Sir Benedict, "is not Ginger, but Geoffrey."

"Quite," said Benedict, hiding a smile. "I should say Lord Redfylde hates you more than the average man who is acquainted with you, and what is more, Lord Redfylde placed rather a large wager on Lord Swale to win."

"Did he?" Swale was flattered. "Good old Reddy. School ties and all that."

"Rather suspicious, wouldn't you say?" said Alex slyly.

"What do you mean? Oh, you mean to imply that Redfylde knew Mr. Wayborn would not be able to drive that day?" Swale snorted. "Perhaps he thought I had a chance."

"My dear Geoffrey," said Alex, "I am your friend, and I bet only five hundred pounds. My Lord Redfylde bet *ten thousand* pounds. He is very rich, I know, but he doesn't throw money away."

"I tell you, I had as good a chance as anyone else," Swale snarled. "My grays—"

"Never mind your grays," said Sir Benedict. "Had Lord Redfylde any reason to hate my brother?"

"Redfylde took it rather hard when Mr. Wayborn beat him," Alex told him.

"Another race?" Benedict guessed.

Alex nodded. "Redfylde overturned, and, as I recall, Wayborn teased him about it."

Benedict sighed. "I would say that Lord Redfylde makes an excellent suspect."

"If Reddy has done this," said Swale, "I will flatten him again, and this time, he won't get up to shake hands."

"My dear Swale," said Alex mildly, "we shall never be able to prove it."

"I daresay you are right, Mr. Devize," said Sir Benedict. "And even if we could, what would it cost us to prosecute a Peer of the Realm? A nasty business. No good can come of it and a great deal of harm. We have only just managed to return the King of France to his throne. We should do nothing to undermine our own British nobility. Think of the scandal. We must satisfy ourselves that my brother will recover and that no lasting harm has come to Lord Swale's honor."

"That's the lump sum of it," said Alex gloomily. "Reddy gets away with it."

"You've already convicted him then?" said Benedict. "Now that is hardly fair, Mr. Devize."

"There's one good thing," said Swale. "It must be killing Lord Redfylde not to collect his ten thousand pounds. But, thanks to your sister, Sir Benedict, no one is collecting on their wagers."

"Quite," Benedict murmured. "And now, my lord, I must ask you to step outside with me. There is something particular I wish to say to you, and it is of an intensely private nature."

Swale looked up, surprised. Sir Benedict was on his feet.

"You don't mean you want me to step outside with

you," he said. "We were having such a pleasant time. I was starting to like you."

"I should be obliged to you, my lord," replied Benedict, moving smoothly away.

"He don't mean to fight you, Geoffrey," Alex explained.

"What does he want then?"

"Go and find out," Alex advised. "I confess, I am curious myself."

Geoffrey tore the napkin from his neck and stood up. "Tiresome fellow," he observed. "Stiff-necked and shirty, if you see what I mean."

Outside, he found Sir Benedict in conference with that ass, Eustace Calverstock. His temper boiled over at the sight. So the stiff-necked Sir Benedict was not above trying two on one, was he? Well, they would find Lord Swale equal to both of them.

"Ah," Benedict said mildly as he advanced on them, his fists clenched and murder in his eye. "There you are, my lord. I believe you are acquainted with Mr. Calverstock? Mr. Calverstock, would you be good enough to leave us? I would speak to his lordship in private."

"I heard," said Stacy, his thin face red with anger. "I heard but did not believe that you were dining with the fellow, Sir Benedict! I should not have thought you capable of such toadeating as this. You know what his lordship did to Cary! Your own brother, man!"

"I am properly addressed as Sir Benedict, Mr. Calverstock," the baronet said icily.

"You mean to accuse me?" cried Swale, his face mottled. "You insolent puppy!"

"Mean to?" cried Stacy, his own mild face contorting. "I *do* accuse you, sir! You are a coward and a villain. If you were not the Duke of Auckland's heir, you would have been barred from White's long ago. You are unfit for respectable society! I advise you to take yourself to America where your madness will go unnoticed amongst the savages."

Lord Swale did not even think of honoring Mr. Calverstock with an invitation to a dawn meeting. Instead, he planted his fist in the man's face. There was a sickening crunch of bone, and Stacy doubled over in pain, his fingers clutching his nose. Blood spattered the cobbles outside of White's.

"You hit me!" Stacy exclaimed in disbelief.

"If you prefer to be shot," Swale replied, "you have only to name your second."

Such an event could not escape the notice of White's members. They came pouring out of the club, and to a man, they sided with Calverstock. Whatever transpires between two gentlemen, it is never excusable for one to bludgeon the other with his fists. Even Alexander Devize shook his head at the sight.

Benedict turned away with a sigh. He seemed to regard the unpleasant incident as closed. So did Swale until Stacy Calverstock flung up his head. "The only gentleman whom I would care to name as my second lies in his bed with a broken arm, thanks to you, my lord. You, sir, are an uncivilized baboon!"

A cool man such as Sir Benedict or even Mr. Devize might have pointed out that there is no such thing as a civilized baboon. Lord Swale was not a cool man. Before no less than fifty members of his club, he kicked Mr. Calverstock in the ribs. He would have done it again if Sir Benedict had not intervened by stepping into the fray.

The baronet's empty sleeve worked on Swale like the Medusa's gaze, which turns men to stone. "That is quite enough of that, my lord!" Benedict said sharply. "I beg you to remember that this gentleman is half your size."

Swale was breathing heavily. "He should have grown," he said through gritted teeth. "He should have grown before he called *me* a coward!"

"The man has no conduct," said someone in the crowd. "No more conduct than a fishmonger."

"You insult the fishmongers," someone else replied.

Swale angrily jammed his fists in his pockets and strode away at a sharp clip.

"My lord."

He turned and saw that Sir Benedict was attempting to keep up. "You had better see to your friend's nose," he growled at the baronet.

"There is something I wish to say to you," Benedict called to him. "It concerns the letter I received this morning from my lord Duke, his Grace of Auckland."

Swale stopped in his tracks. "Are you acquainted with my father, sir?"

"Not at all," Benedict replied. "Indeed, I was all astonishment when I realized his Grace was proposing an alliance between my family and his. It seemed rather too spontaneous."

Swale scowled. "Don't tell me the old fool has offered to marry your sister!"

"Why, no," said Sir Benedict. "He has offered for *you* to marry my sister."

"Bloody hell!"

"Naturally, I was pleased to entertain such a handsome offer on my dear sister's behalf."

"Naturally," said Swale bitterly.

"Unfortunately," Benedict continued, "your rank and fortune are all that recommend the match. Having met your lordship and spent an hour in your company, I fear I must regretfully decline the honor.

I have known Barbary apes with better conduct. You would never suit my sister. I would rather see her married to a penniless clerk than to you."

Swale laughed. "*I* would not suit *her?* Let me tell you, sir—your sister would not suit me, and I would not ask for her hand if my life depended on it! My father had no right to suggest such a thing. He must have run mad."

"Indeed, it does not surprise me to learn that madness runs in your family."

Swale's eyes narrowed. "You think I will not knock you down because of your arm?"

"I am sure you would not scruple to do so," returned Benedict, "for you have not one scrap of self-control. You are a bully," he went on as Swale silently glowered at him. "It sickens me to think of any gently bred girl being forced to become your wife. I say *forced* because that seems to be the only way your lordship will ever acquire a wife."

"Is that so?" sneered Swale. "I will have you know, Sir Benedict, that I am considered a matrimonial prize. I can go to Almack's on any given night and snap my fingers for a wife."

"Can it be," said Sir Benedict, "that your lordship is unaware that yours is a face designed to repel, rather than attract, the fair sex? If you were not a Duke's son, I expect no one would take any notice of you whatsoever."

"You mince words, Sir Benedict!"

"That will never do. Let me speak plainly, my lord. You have the face and deportment of a baboon. A lady prefers a gentleman to be handsome and graceful, but she may be willing to overlook defects in these areas if the man underneath is a gentle soul. In your case, I fear the unwholesome crust hides something even more unpalatable. You have an evil temper, my lord. When active, you are enraged; when in repose, sullen and resentful. I would not see my sister marry a man so singularly lacking in self-control. Also, your brain has not impressed me this evening. My sister has a lively intelligence. You would certainly bore her to sobs."

"Your sister—" Swale began harshly.

Benedict held up his hand. "Listen to me, you young fool. The Wayborns are an unusual breed. Consider yourself lucky. In other families, the elder statesman would not hesitate to sacrifice a sister or daughter for the sake of such a favorable alliance. I, however, do not choose to see my beloved sister chained for life to an animal."

"I am of age," Swale said, mustering his dignity. "My father can't go about the place arranging marriages for me. I will choose my own wife, sir, and I assure you, your sister will not be among the candidates."

"Candidates?" Sir Benedict's scarred face contorted violently, then composed itself. "Oh, you do see yourself as a prize! Undoubtedly, when the time comes, you will choose a wife. She will not love you—how could she? Even if she can bear your looks, she will shrink from your vile personality. Her family will sell her to you, and in a matter of weeks, your abuse will break her spirit, if indeed she possesses any spirit. You will both be miserable, but it will be Lady Swale whom the world pities. Good night, my lord."

The baronet turned on his heel and left Swale where he stood.

It took the Honorable Alexander Devize nearly four hours to find his friend in the stews of London. He had known Swale for many years, but he was ill-prepared to find his friend in the back of what appeared to be a rag-and-bone shop, drinking gin and ginger beer. The half-naked girl on his lordship's lap was pockmarked, and the smell in the air was of general unwashed decay.

"Good God, Geoffrey!" Alex cried, holding his handkerchief to his nose. "What have you done to yourself?"

Swale's bloodshot eyes fastened on him. "Sally thinks me handsome, don't you, Sally?" he said blearily, the words born aloft by a long, malodorous belch.

The pockmarked girl agreed wholeheartedly, having been well-paid by his lordship. To her surprise, she was promptly dislodged from her patron's lap. If she had been clever enough to say, "It's not such a bad face," she might have retained her seat. Swale knew he was not handsome. He did not believe he had the face of a baboon, but he knew he was not handsome.

"Liar!" he said bitterly and poured his gin and ginger beer over her head.

The girl started up angrily, but Alex forestalled her with a few coins and the gift of his scented handkerchief. "My friend is discomposed, my dear," he said suavely. "When he is sober, I don't doubt he will beg your forgiveness."

"Ha!" said Swale.

The girl flushed. For a girl with pockmarks, she was surprisingly pretty. Indeed, were it not for the scars of smallpox, she might have graced one of the exclusive establishments near St. James's Street. "You're a true gentleman, you are, sir," she told Alex, "and a true friend."

"I must be," Alex replied, struggling to get his bulky friend out the door.

It required three footmen to carry his lordship up to his room.

In the morning, Alex gave him the bad news. "You have been barred from White's for a year."

Swale blinked at him. "Do you know what he said?"

"Yes, I heard," said Alex. "But you can't go about the place knocking a chap's head off, even if it is attached to a worm like Calverstock."

"I could murder him!" Swale said weakly, letting his aching head fall into his hands.

"I shouldn't have thought Stacy Calverstock worth the trouble," Alex observed dryly.

"Calverstock!" Swale sat up straight. "It is Sir Benedict I mean."

"Sir Benedict," Alex said gravely, "is the best of gentlemen. In the space of an hour, with no great effort, he silenced a thousand tongues. Simply by having dinner with you, he laid to rest the worst of the gossip. If you had kept your temper with Calverstock—"

"The best of gentlemen!" Swale laughed unpleasantly. "He had the insufferable impertinence to say that if I were not a duke's son, no one would take any notice of me. He said that the only way I could get a gently bred girl to marry me would be by force! He said I had the face and manners of a baboon!"

"I daresay Sir Benedict did not admire you for your dealings with Mr. Calverstock."

"My suit to marry his willful chit of a sister has withered," said Swale.

"You asked for her!" exclaimed Alex. "After all you said, you asked for her?"

"Why would I ask to marry a girl who has exposed me to ridicule?"

"Come, come, Geoffrey! You must pity her a little."

"No! She is a hoyden, and a cheat besides. By God, if she beat me, she bloody well knows it was by that trick she served me—stopping dead in the middle of the road!"

"And yet you asked her brother for her hand."

"No, indeed. He can keep her bloody hand, and all the rest of her, too. My fool father has been matchmaking. *He* offered me up like the sacrificial lamb, and what did Sir Benedict do? Was he sensible to the honor being done his wretched sister? No! He said he would rather see her married to a penniless clerk than my Lord Swale! He said that I would not suit his beloved—*beloved!*—sister. He will pay dearly for this insult."

"Geoffrey, you *cannot* call out Sir Benedict," Alex said sharply. "The man is a cripple."

"I don't mean to call him out," said Swale, his green eyes gleaming. "I've a much better idea. And he said my brain did not impress him! My brain is bursting with brilliant ideas."

"What do you mean to do?" Alex asked anxiously.

"I cannot attack Sir Benedict," said Swale. "The man's short an arm. But there's nothing to stop me attacking that sister of his!"

Alex was appalled. "What the devil do you mean—there's nothing to stop you from attacking his sister? She's his bloody sister! That would be enough to stop any gentleman from attacking her."

"I don't mean I shall attack her," said Swale impatiently. "I am a gentleman after all. What I mean to do is make her fall in love with me."

Alex stared at him. "Have you gone mad? The girl detests you."

"I shall make her love me," Swale said stubbornly. "I shall wind my way into her heart like a serpent, and then, when I have that coal-black article in my possession, I shall tear it out of her manly chest and grind it under my heel!"

"Rather harsh," Alex said, relaxing a little. An indulgent smile played on his lips. "But, as you say, perfectly consistent with the actions of a gentleman."

Swale was impervious to sarcasm. "Wayborn the elder said no woman could ever love me. I shall prove him wrong with his own sister, by God. He will come to me one day soon and beg me to marry the harpy. I will not do it. I shall remind him of all my bad qualities and excuse myself. Let his sister's tears flow freely onto her mustache. That will be my revenge upon this pompous ass."

Alex vainly tried to hide a smile. "Yes, but, my dear fellow, how do you propose to make the Wayborn fall in love with you?"

"I assure you I do not lack charm!" Swale growled. "And contrary to what Sir Benedict may think, I do not have feathers for brains. I tell you I am a matrimonial prize, and I should be a matrimonial prize even if I were not the Duke of Auckland's heir!"

"Of course you are charming," Alex said soothingly. "On any *natural* female your charm would work its magic. But the Wayborn—"

"Leave the Wayborn to me," said Swale confidently. "You will see, Alex. A few posies, a box of diamonds, and the girl's heart will jump into my hand like a tame bullfinch! By God," he added, smiting his open palm with his fist. "I don't care if she bloody well *keeps* the diamonds, as long as I blast a hole in her heart!"

Alex smiled indulgently, confident that when his friend was entirely sober, the unworthiness, if not the hopelessness, of this notion would impress itself upon him and he would hear no more of it.

And it might have been so if not for Bowditch.

Chapter 6

When his lordship laid out his idea to Bowditch, the valet's admiration was very gratifying. He seemed to have none of Mr. Devize's reservations. His views were unmixed.

"Very good, my lord," were his exact words.

"Yes, yes," Swale said, impatiently brushing off the exuberant praise. "It is a magnificent idea. What I lack is a plan. How is it to be done, Bowditch? I can't think of a way of getting at her. If I am to break her heart, I must be able to get at her."

"Quite so, my lord."

"She's left London. I should say, her deplorable conduct has made London too hot for her! Undoubtedly, her brother has shut her up at the family estate, right under his nose, so to speak."

"No, my lord."

Swale cast his valet a sharp look, suspicious of dissent.

"Mademoiselle Huppert and I—" Bowditch began delicately. "That is, I had occasion to speak to Miss Wayborn's maid before they left London. She hasn't gone to Wayborn Hall, my lord. She's gone into

Hertfordshire. Mademoiselle was very sorry to leave London."

"Herts? Why, that is an easy distance," said Swale, pleased. "What is in Herts, Bowditch? A gruesome, old maiden aunt, I expect?"

"Cousins, my lord. Miss Wayborn is staying with cousins at Tanglewood Vicarage."

Swale faltered. "Vicarage! Bloody hell! These cousins are clergymen, I take it?"

"The Reverend Dr. Wilfred Cary is Miss Wayborn's mother's cousin, I believe," Bowditch answered. "Mademoiselle was uncertain about the rest of the household," he added apologetically.

Though a little shaken to learn that his quarry was under the protection of the Church, his lordship ordered Bowditch to pack for an extended stay in the country.

"Have I got an old aunt or a cousin languishing in Herts?" he asked hopefully.

"No, my lord."

The fact that he knew no one in the neighborhood did not deter his lordship; he was not too fastidious to stay in a local inn. If, as he could scarcely believe, the Wayborn fortress withstood his siege for more than a week, he might impose upon the local squire for accommodation until the thing was done.

The next morning saw him driving his curricle onto the Great North Road, his manservant in the seat behind him, for Bowditch, though officially his lordship's valet, was not above assuming the chores of a groom. Indeed, in many ways he was more suited to groom horses than a marquess, but to Swale, he was an indispensable factotum. He would cook breakfast if the cook were incapacitated or if his lordship had neglected to bring one to the hunting box; he would tend wounds and prepare baths; and he would even oversee the pruning of the shrubbery, if required. That he did none of those things more than adequately had never troubled him or his master.

The green, rolling farm country of Hertfordshire presented itself to the eye as they left Middlesex. It was a blazingly glorious day in early March. "Good English country," Swale remarked, looking around him approvingly. "Not too grand, not too pretty. Just what I like! The breadbasket of England!"

"Yes, my lord," Bowditch said expansively.

A scant two hours later, they came upon the sleepy, almost indolent village of Tanglewood Green. Of the three inns on the High Street, Geoffrey chose the Tudor Rose, a thatched box of the Elizabethan type, with black beams holding up its white plaster walls. A quiet, unassuming place, he thought, decked with ivy as old as England itself, and its back door was not twenty yards from the banks of a sparkling brook.

The landlord recognized the quality of his lordship's perfectly matched grays and set down the driver of the curricle, a burly, red-haired giant, as a man of wealth, though perhaps not a gentleman. Mr. Sprigge was never more surprised in his life than when he heard the manservant utter the words, "Very good, my lord," but he was not so shocked that he could not act. The best of food and drink was offered, and the private parlor was at his lordship's disposal, but nothing would please Swale more than to sit down in the common room and enjoy a tankard of Mr. Sprigge's ale and a slice of Mrs. Sprigge's rabbit pie.

The arrival of such greatness cast a pall over the usual good-natured liveliness of Mr. Sprigge's rustic customers. *Who is this Lord Swale?* they all asked themselves. *What does he want with Tanglewood Green?* Uneasy looks were exchanged, but no one spoke. Even Mr. Sprigge, whose lively tongue and easy manners made him well-suited to his duties as a host, fell silent, though he could not help but approve of his lordship's appetite. Swale himself seemed to desire more food and drink and less conversation.

Suddenly, the door opened, and a grizzled man in gaiters and breeches strode in. Over one arm was a broken rifle, and as he took what anyone could see was his customary seat near the fire, he dropped to the floor a handsome collection of dead rabbits tied with string. He took no notice of the illustrious Lord Swale, and therefore, his tongue was not shy. "I seen the Captain and Miss Julie riding together as far as the Manor," he announced with the air of one describing a particularly risky maneuver on a battlefield. "It would have been better for us all if old Mrs. Cary had left the estate to the Captain in the first place, as much interest as *he* takes in the place."

This intelligence meant nothing to Swale, but he welcomed the rabbits.

Mr. Sprigge, seeing that his lordship showed no signs of disapproval, ventured to speak. "Will they marry, do you suppose, Mr. Teal?"

The grizzled hunter drained his tankard. "Will they marry?" he repeated. "And why wouldn't they? His fortune he made fighting old Boney. Rich as you can speak, Mr. Sprigge!"

"I heard," said another man, emboldened by the effusions of Mr. Teal and Mr. Sprigge, "that Captain Cary went down to London to ask his cousin Mr. Wayborn if he would sell him the place."

Swale glanced up at the mention of the Wayborn name.

"Aye, and well he might," said Mr. Teal, "for he's rich enough, begad, to buy Tanglewood Manor five times over if he likes! Mr. Wayborn has let the place fall to rack and ruin. I'd not pay a farthing above a thousand pounds for it myself."

This last statement amused Mr. Sprigge. "You would not pay more than a thousand pounds, Mr. Teal? And where would *you* get a thousand pounds? You're only the gamekeeper!"

Mr. Teal flushed a dark red, and Swale was afraid he might storm out, taking his rabbits with him. This must not be allowed, of course; Mrs. Sprigge would need the rabbits for her pies. The situation called for prompt action.

"Is the Manor for sale, Mr. Sprigge?" he inquired.

Mr. Sprigge and Mr. Teal forgot one another and looked at him. Mr. Teal had not seen his lordship's spectacular grays and had no reason to think he was observing anything but an ordinary traveler with objectionable red hair.

"Is the place comfortable?" Swale asked, looking back at them innocently. "I have no objection to a comfortable place at this easy distance to London." While Swale did not often concern himself with the opinions of simple folk, he realized that his position might become awkward if the inhabitants of Tanglewood Green formed the impression he was up to no good vis-à-vis Miss Wayborn. Country bumpkins were prone to insanity, he knew; they might take it into their heads to form a mob and lynch him. House hunting seemed as good an excuse as any for skulking in the neighborhood. "In fact," he added, "I am traveling through Hertfordshire in search of just such a property."

"And who might you be?" demanded Mr. Teal, eyeing him with dislike.

"Be quiet, you old fool," Mr. Sprigge said roughly. "That is my Lord Swale from London. Don't you mind him, milord. He's only Squire Mickleby's gamekeeper."

"I collect it must be Mr. Cary Wayborn who owns the place—the Manor?"

Mr. Teal seemed embarrassed.

"Oh, is your lordship acquainted with Mr. Wayborn?" Mr. Sprigge asked nervously. "I daresay Mr. Teal did not mean to imply any disrespect for Mr. Wayborn—"

"Yes, I'm a little acquainted with the family," Swale replied with an ironic smile. "You say . . . did I hear you say that Miss Wayborn is in the neighborhood? How odd. I thought she was in London. Visiting her cousins, I suppose? The Reverend Dr. Cary?"

"Yes, milord," said Mr. Sprigge, impressed by the stranger's knowledge.

"And this Captain of hers with whom she rides and whom she may or may not marry, that would be Captain . . . ?"

"Her cousin Captain Horatio Cary, milord. The Vicar's son and a fine young gentleman. He's to be knighted, they say."

Swale frowned. He had not expected to find a rival on the scene, much less a Naval officer with a sizable fortune. But what, he reasoned, would a man like that want with the Wayborn? He suspected that the villagers were merely exaggerating for their own amusement the relationship between the cousins. "I expect I must pay my respects to this young lady," he told Mr. Sprigge. "Would you be good enough to direct me to the Vicarage?"

Mrs. Cary, who was meeting with her housekeeper, turned white as a sheet when the Marquess's card was brought to her. Men of rank did not often come to visit her husband, and she knew she was not equal to the encounter. Indeed, Dr. Cary had often blamed her timidity for the fact that despite his own merits, no bishopric had been thrown his way. In a state almost of terror, she attended his lordship in the small drawing room where her husband displayed the better part of his porcelain collection in several cabinets that were much too large for the cramped space.

When she had left her little drawing room the night before, she had not noticed the superfluity of ribbons, feathers, paper flowers, and balls of yarn scattered about, but as the nobleman stood looking about him like a Viking invader, she could see nothing else.

How *could* Cynthia and Juliet leave the place so untidy? she fretted silently.

To her dismay, the information that Dr. Cary was not home failed to repel the large, angry-looking man with bristling red hair. "I have come to see Miss Wayborn," he announced, declining the seat she offered.

"Juliet?" she repeated blankly. "Your lordship has come to see Juliet?"

"I have something very particular I wish to say to her," he explained.

"Oh!" cried Mrs. Cary, coloring up like a schoolgirl. It had been more than thirty years since Dr. Cary had had something particular to say to her, but she had not forgotten the fateful words that had changed her life forever. It seemed to her she had been mistaken in thinking his lordship an angry man. Rather, he was a man in the grips of the divine passion. Her fear of him gave way almost to pity. It must be difficult for such a proud, disagreeable man to admit that his heart was no longer his own, she thought sympathetically.

"I'm very sorry, my lord. Miss Wayborn is not at home. She has walked to the church with her cousin."

"Captain Cary, I collect? She walks alone with him, does she?"

Mrs. Cary detected definite signs of a passionate jealousy and hastened to correct his lordship. "No, my lord. She is with my daughter. As for my son, they are second cousins, nothing more. They have known one another their whole lives. Why, they are like brother and sister, so your lordship must not be discouraged."

Swale grunted, pleased.

"They will be returning very soon," said Mrs. Cary. "Or . . . . shall I send Mary to fetch them back, my lord? I know Miss Wayborn would not wish to inconvenience your lordship."

Heaven knows, she thought, if he does not propose now, he might lose his courage, go away, and never come again!

"Mary!" she cried. "Go and fetch Miss Juliet at once. She has an important visitor!"

Twenty minutes later, a nymph-like young lady with soft blue eyes and golden ringlets was performing a curtsey in the little drawing room. Swale stared at her in amazement.

He had not, of course, expected to find a dust-caked Miss Wayborn still dressed in a man's purple greatcoat and a man's purple tricorn hat, but a gauzy concoction of sprig muslin seemed rather outside the range of possible alternatives. As for the adorable heart-shaped face, the milk-and-roses skin, and the golden ringlets—he could only stare at the vision in disbelief. He had supposed Miss Juliet Wayborn to be something drawn along the lines of Michelangelo's Sistine Sibyls, brawny and mannish, perhaps with a budding mustache and the sinews of a prizefighter—in short, the type of female likely to be surprised by and grateful for any sort of masculine attention. Instead, she was the belle of the county!

"My daughter, Miss Cynthia Cary," said Mrs. Cary, and Swale nearly laughed. Of course this angelic creature with the speaking blue eyes was not the loathsome Wayborn!

"Miss Cary," he said, giving her a sketch of a bow.

A second young female entered the room, and again in defiance of his preconceived notions, she was no musclebound amazon. This must be Miss Wayborn, he decided glumly. While it was true she lacked her cousin's soft, vulnerable beauty, her clear-cut patrician features and flawless complexion were undeniable. The feminine version of the Wayborn nose was straight; thin; and, without calling too much attention to itself, wonderfully precise. He could readily understand his father's desire to add it to the Ambler profile. Unfortunately her wide-set eyes were as gray, cold, and inhospitable as the frozen steppes of Russia. She seemed to have few pretensions to fashion, but her dark brown hair was curled over her ears and knotted at the nape of her neck in the Grecian style. Dressed quietly and simply in a dark blue dress trimmed in black ribbons, she appeared anything but grateful to find herself the object of his attentions. At the sight of this imposing female, all thoughts of making her fall in love with him vanished in a puff of smoke.

He recognized the type: a Parthenon goddess of the

cruel variety. He'd have better luck with the exquisite Miss Cary—she at least could be made to pity him.

"Come, Cynthia," Mrs. Cary said, bubbling with girlish excitement. "His lordship has something particular to say to your cousin!"

Cynthia protested against leaving her cousin alone with the infamous Swale, but Mrs. Cary prevailed, closing the door behind them.

Juliet regarded her visitor with the coldness he deserved. He was larger than she had realized; at least, he seemed larger in the small drawing room, with shoulders fully as wide as the bow window. She had only gotten a fleeting look at him on the day of the race, but a closer scrutiny did nothing to improve his looks. His nose was too short, his mouth too wide, his chin too square. And that hair! A shade of red more often seen in nightmares than in nature, and he *would* wear it long, hanging in his eyes, tangled in his collar, and polluting the sides of his face with the most revolting sideburns she had ever seen. His eyes, however, were an interesting grayish green, and they were fixed on her with an intensity that a less spirited girl might have found disconcerting.

"Well, Swale? Have you come to break my arm?" she asked rudely.

The nettlerash sprang instantly to his cheeks, and he was heartily sorry she was not a man. "Cheat!" he growled at her, his teeth gritted.

This unseemly display of emotion seemed to amuse her. She sat down calmly upon the settee and rather languidly began winding some loose yarn into a ball. "I beg your pardon, Swale? I did not quite catch your remarks?"

"You know damn well you won that bloody race by

cheating! That was a mean trick you served me, and you are a damned, unnatural female *freak* besides!"

She smiled, observing his massive fists opening and closing. *How difficult it must be for him to use words instead of those enormous fists of his!* she thought contemptuously. "In what way have I cheated?" she inquired pleasantly. "Besides by taking my brother's place, I mean."

"Well, what the devil do you call coming to a full stop just as I was about to pass you?"

"You, Swale?" she said mockingly. "About to pass *me?* I'm afraid I don't recall that. In any case, is it against the rules to come to a full stop?"

He glared at her, seething with anger, but no cutting rejoinder occurred to him immediately. It was not, strictly speaking, illegal to come to a full stop during a race, but it was damned irregular. "Damned irregular, that's what it was!"

With perfect composure, she completed one ball of yarn, placed it into a basket, and reached for another that had come unraveled. "Well, Swale?" she said presently. "You told Mrs. Cary you had something to say to me. If you have finished saying it, I wish you would go. I am excessively busy at the moment, as you see. It is of the utmost importance that I wind this yarn."

"I am addressed properly as Lord Swale," he informed her sullenly.

"Yes," she sniffed. "I expect you are."

"You may address me as my Lord Marquess, your lordship, or simply, my lord."

"And so I would," she replied, "if I had any intention of addressing you properly."

He glared at her almost in disbelief. No one had ever spoken to him with such impertinence. Most people were afraid of rousing his anger. Even her

insufferable brother Sir Benedict had shown deference to his rank, if not to his person.

"It is a courtesy title, or so I understand," she said,
calmly winding her yarn. "I have decided you deserve no such courtesy. I shall call you Swale if I like.
I shall call you *Ginger* if I like—"

"Will you, by God!" he said violently. "Ginger, by
God! If you were a man, madam, I would make you
sorry for that remark!"

"Indeed, I shall call you Ginger until you are dead,"
she said, smiling. "It will be good for you. Well, *perhaps* it will be good for you, Ginger," she amended.
"Either you will learn to control your temper, Ginger,
or you will die of apoplexy."

"I should dearly like to break your neck," he said
bitterly. "If you dare call me Ginger again, I *shall*
break your neck! You should know I flattened the last
fellow who tried to call me Ginger."

"Would you prefer Carrots?" she inquired.

"Now look here, you harpy!" he said forcefully, if not
eloquently. "If you wish to trade insults, you must
allow me to tell you that you have the conduct of a
Barbary ape!"

"How dare you!" she said, her eyes flashing and a
crimson stain appearing in her cheeks.

"Quiet!" he growled.

"Don't you tell me to be quiet," she snapped. "You
orangutan!"

"Shut up then, if you prefer," he said roughly. "You
obviously have not communicated with your brother
Sir Benedict. If you had, he would have told you I am
innocent. Which I am."

Juliet recoiled. "You, Ginger? Innocent? Ha!"

"Ha, yourself!" he wittily rejoined. "All this nonsense
about a broken arm. When I want a man's arm

broken, I shall break it myself, my girl. I don't go about hiring people to do my dirty work."

"Is that so?" she said sharply. "If it was not you who hired them, then who?"

"Ask your brother," he returned. "Sir Benedict will tell you it was Lord Redfylde."

"Lord Redfylde! That is . . . that is vile slander," she said, flinging a ball of yarn at him.

He caught it and threw it back at her.

"Lady Redfylde," she said, catching the yarn and throwing it back as hard as she could, "happens to be the cousin of a dear friend of mine. How dare you accuse her husband!"

"He hates me," Swale explained, dodging the yarn.

"I expect everyone hates you," she answered. "*I* certainly do."

"Your brother Cary beat him in a race."

"Cary beats everyone," she scoffed. "Except you, you snake!" She snatched up another ball of yarn and prepared to pitch it at him.

"Redfylde wagered ten thousand pounds that I would beat your brother's chestnuts."

Juliet's arm froze in midair. "What did you say?"

"You heard me right," said Swale.

"But that's as good as throwing money away," she protested. "Ten thousand pounds! Unless—" She sat down abruptly, and her hand fluttered up to her mouth, which had fallen open.

"Unless he knew somehow that your brother would have to forfeit." Swale scooped up the ball of yarn she had flung at him earlier and returned it to her. It struck her on the tip of her patrician nose, but she did not notice.

"But—but he is a marquess!" she protested.

"So am I," he reminded her. "You had no trouble believing it of me."

"But they *said* you sent them," she wailed.

"Heaven forfend a murderous brute should *lie*," he scoffed.

Juliet was shattered. Bad enough if she were wrong, but to be obliged to make an apology to this redhaired, snub-nosed maniac—! Her soul withered at the thought.

She narrowed her eyes and studied him for a long moment. Except for his rumpled clothing, he might have just stepped off a Viking ship a thousand years ago, his face as hideous as any emblem those barbarians used to paint on their shields to frighten peaceful English farmers. "Do you swear you had nothing to do with the crime?" she demanded.

"You'd like me to swear, wouldn't you, Miss Harpy? Well, I wouldn't swear to my own father. I see no reason I should swear to someone whose good opinion means so little to me."

Her cheeks were bright red. "*If* I have wronged you, Ginger," she said slowly with a little toss of her head, "I am sure I am sorry."

"If!" He seized upon the insulting word. "*If* you have wronged me! Why, I ought to—!"

He advanced on her, his eye gleaming, and involuntarily, she shrank back. He tore the basket of yarn from her hands and flung it with all his strength across the room. The crash that followed burst upon the ears like an enemy cannonade. Whirling around, he saw that the basket had smashed the glass of a large, handsome display cabinet. Its contents, which appeared to be nothing more than useless bits of china, were likewise ruined. Yarn dangled from the shelves, and the basket fell to the floor with a shuddering crash, pulling something large and brightly painted with it.

Juliet gasped in horror, her eyes almost starting from her head.

Swale had imagined the situation could be rectified by little more than the sum of thirty pounds, but now he saw it was more serious. Juliet's face went from crimson to ashen, and for several moments, she could not speak.

"That was Cousin Wilfred's shepherdess collection," she finally gasped in disbelief. "He's very fond of those shepherdesses!"

Swale groaned. His own father collected porcelain and was excessively attached to his china bits.

"Cousin Wilfred," said Juliet with satisfaction, not to mention glee, "is going to murder you, Ginger!"

Chapter 7

The sound of an enemy cannonade cannot go unnoticed in a well-ordered house, and it was not long before Swale and Juliet were joined by other members of the household. Mrs. Cary's hysterical shrieks and Cynthia's tears convinced Swale he had destroyed the most treasured icons of the Vicar's collection. The Vicar himself confirmed this a few moments later.

He had been strolling in his garden and practicing his sermon on Brotherly Love, when he heard the crash. It did not sound to him like an enemy cannonade. It sounded to him like a clap of thunder. Eyeing the innocent blue sky nervously, he headed for his shelter. There he was greeted by the lamentations of his wife. He feared the worst.

"What is it, my dear?" he cried, rushing into the hall. "Is it one of the children?"

Mrs. Cary was unable to speak. She could only shriek and point.

Dr. Cary peered curiously into the little drawing room. He saw Juliet and his daughter, pale and round-eyed. He saw a big, strange man with hair like an unkempt fire. Stepping into the room, he saw the ruins of his collection. He gaped at it in utter disbelief. "No," he cried bleakly. "Not my Dresden shepherdess! Oh, my sweet Chlorinda!"

Swale cleared his throat nervously. His temper had landed him in many a tight spot, but none so tight as this. Being banned from White's for breaking Stacy Calverstock's nose had been a pleasant experience next to this agony. The little, round clergyman with the spectacles obviously was broken with shock. The demise of his Chlorinda had affected him as profoundly as the sudden death of a child.

"I beg your pardon, sir. I will gladly pay for the damage," Swale began contritely in a voice so diminished that Juliet was astonished. He seemed genuinely to understand the Vicar's anguish.

Dr. Cary turned on him, his eyes glittering with unshed tears. "Who the devil are you, sir?" he demanded. "Is this your doing? So you will gladly pay for the damage, will you? By God! Do you think money will compensate me? This collection represents for me the work of a lifetime! Only the Duke of Auckland has a finer collection of china shepherdesses!"

The name of Auckland had the effect of a powerful tonic on Mrs. Cary. "But, my dear," she interjected, "this is the Duke's son! It is Lord Swale himself, come to see Juliet."

"The Duke of Auckland!" The Vicar's eyes glowed. "The Duke of Auckland!"

"Yes," said Swale modestly. "He is my father. So you see, my dear fellow, I enter into your feelings on this tragic occasion. No one loves a porcelain shepherdess as much as his Grace of Auckland."

"So much so," Dr. Cary said grimly, "that he sends *you* here to smash my Chlorinda! It is infamous, sir! I shall take steps, sir! *Steps!*" He made as though to pound his pulpit and seemed rather surprised to find he was not in church.

All traces of contrition disappeared from Swale's face instantly. "What?" he growled. "You dare to accuse my father of . . . of sending me about the place smashing Chlorindas? Say what you like about me, sir, but I defy you to speak ill of my father!"

"I don't speak ill of him!" snapped the Reverend. "Indeed, now that my shepherdesses are smashed, I should send my compliments to his Grace—he now is undisputedly in possession of the finest collection of china shepherdesses in all England!"

A less volatile man might have withstood this remark with the exercise of stringent self-control. He might have told himself that Dr. Cary's pain had temporarily driven him mad or some such thing. Swale made a fist instead, a big fist the size of a small ham. It was only Juliet's swift action that saved the Vicar from a very thorough flattening.

"Indeed, it is all my fault, Cousin Wilfred!" she said quickly.

"You, Juliet?"

"Yes," she said nervously, unable to meet either his lordship's baleful glare or the Vicar's bewildered disappointment. "I'm afraid I playfully tossed my basket to his lordship, thinking he would catch it. But he did not," she concluded in almost a whisper.

"You tossed your basket to him, Cousin Juliet?" Dr. Cary said incredulously.

"Playfully, yes," said Juliet, looking down at her hands. She was not an accomplished liar, and her cheeks were pink with embarrassment.

"Playfully," he repeated dully. "Playfully, yes. But what is his lordship doing here? If he has not come to . . . to view my collection?" he added, choosing his words tactfully.

"I told you, my dear," Mrs. Cary whispered, tugging at his arm. "His lordship has come to see Juliet. He has something *particular* to say to her."

"He has something particular to say to her, does he?"

"Yes, my dear," said Mrs. Cary with speaking looks.

"Oh!" cried Dr. Cary, blushing like a girl as comprehension dawned. "Oh, I see! His lordship has something *particular* he wishes to say to Cousin Juliet, does he? And she playfully tossed her basket to him? Well, well! Let us put all this unpleasantness behind us, my lord," he said, thrusting out his hand.

Swale shook it reluctantly. Somehow, he had liked the little fellow better when he was shouting.

"Take her out into the shrubbery," the Vicar advised. "This room is not a fit place to—"

He broke off, blushing again. "All this broken glass. Juliet, take his lordship into the shrubbery. And you must come to dinner, my lord! Come to dinner. I insist."

Swale was ready to decline when it occurred to him how much Miss Wayborn must wish for him to decline also. *That* lady he would never willingly oblige. "You honor me, sir," he said instead. "I thank you." He faced Juliet's frown with one of his own.

"This way to the shrubbery," she said curtly, laying her hand on his arm. "You great, priceless ass," she added under her breath.

With self-control he had not known he possessed, he managed not to shake her hand from his arm until they reached the Vicar's garden.

"I expect you would like to finish your tantrum by uprooting the rhododendrons," she remarked airily.

"I wish you would not. If anything, Cousin Wilfred is fonder of them than he is of china shepherdesses."

"I expect *you* think I ought to thank you," he retorted. "Rest assured, I don't care to be under your protection, and if it didn't mean exposing a lady for a liar, I would not hesitate to tell your cousin the truth!"

She flushed. "So now I'm a lady, am I? I thought I was a harpy."

He shrugged. "You know best what you are."

Juliet folded her arms and faced him with a scowl. "If you think I did it to protect you, Ginger, you are mad as well as rude," she said. "I was only thinking of your poor father!"

He glared back at her. "You like my father, do you? An old man in a powdered wig with scarcely a drop of red blood left in him? Hold him in high esteem, do you?"

"Why shouldn't I? Don't *you* hold him in high esteem?"

"Whether or not I hold my father in high esteem is none of your business," he informed her. "If you think the old fool is going to marry you, you are sadly deceived."

She laughed shortly. "Is that why you're here, Ginger? You needn't have troubled yourself. Any alliance between the Aucklands and the Wayborns clearly is impossible."

He drew in a smoldering breath. "You persist in your accusations against me?"

She did not answer for a moment. The crow she had been forced to eat was sticking in her throat. "I expect, if you say you are innocent—"

"I say nothing of the kind!" he responded antagonistically.

"Very well!" she said impatiently. "I am satisfied

that if you had wanted my brother's arm broken, you would have done it yourself. I don't doubt you are a thorough villain—you have a filthy temper—but no one could mistake you for a mastermind. I expect acting through proxies would but little satisfy your lust for violence. Indeed, I don't suppose it would ever occur to you. Yours is a simple mind, I collect."

"Your compliments put me to the blush, madam," he said, grimacing.

"Well," she said, shrugging her shoulders, "you need not come to dinner, you know. You are not really wanted, and we have nothing in the house but mutton."

"But your cousin has been gracious enough to invite me, and seized by temporary madness, I have accepted," he said. "What a splendid relative you have in the Reverend Dr. Cary! First, he accuses me of sabotage; then he tries to toadeat me!"

"Toadeat!" Her eyes blazed. "Why, you *are* a Barbary ape! No, I tell a lie—"

"What? Another lie?" he taunted her.

"A Barbary ape would have more brains," she told him. "Dr. Cary did not ask you to dinner out of any deference to your rank, you know."

"What was it then? My polished manners? My stern good looks?"

"You were stupid enough to tell Mrs. Cary you had something particular you wished to say to me," she very kindly explained. "They think you have come here to press your suit."

"My valet does that," he said scornfully.

"Not very well by the looks of you," she retorted. "In any case, you see how you will not be wanted for dinner. They will think I have refused you, that's all."

"Ha!" he said, reddening. "You would like that,

wouldn't you? You would like it spread about that
you declined an offer of marriage from the Marquess
of Swale!"

"You must take your lumps, Ginger," she told him
heartlessly. "If you are fool enough to come running
after a girl because you have something *particular* you
wish to say to her, well, hard cheese on you if people
are misled! As it is, I'd say you were getting away with
hardly any damage. Just imagine the spot you'd be in
if I told the Reverend Dr. Cary that, whilst we were admiring his rhododendrons, I entertained . . . and
accepted . . . Lord Swale's offer of marriage!"

He stared at her, openmouthed. "Of all the mean
tricks—!"

"I daresay," she went on amiably, "if you were at all
good-looking or gentleman-like, I might be tempted
to use you so shamefully, for what girl would not like
to be a Marchioness? But you, my dear Ginger, are a
pill that cannot be gilded. If you were to get down on
your knees and beg me to be your wife, I would not
scruple to laugh in your face!"

"Let us be clear about one thing, madam! I did not
come here to ask you to marry me."

"No," she said, smiling triumphantly. "You came
here to ask me *not* to marry your father! Well, I *will*
marry old Auckland if I wish to, and that is all I have
to say about it." She turned abruptly on her heel and
walked away, saying, "I will make your excuses to
Cousin Wilfred. Good-bye, Ginger! Go back to
London. There are many, many lovely things you can
break in the British Museum, you know."

Seething with unrequited rage, he walked rapidly
back to the Tudor Rose. Not even Mrs. Sprigge's
rabbit pies could soothe him. "Dust off the old dinner

jacket, and look sharp about it!" he told Bowditch. "I am invited to dine at the Vicarage tonight."

Bowditch beamed at his master. "I take it the conquest has been made, my lord?"

"What conquest?"

"I take it your lordship has succeeded in winning Miss Wayborn's affection?"

"Oh, that conquest."

"It must be going well if Miss Wayborn has invited your lordship to dine at the Vicarage," Bowditch pointed out, unable to fathom his master's black mood.

"The bloody harpy cornered me in the shrubbery!" Swale swore violently as he ruined the neckcloth he was attempting to tie. "The shrubbery, Bowditch. You may imagine what I felt. Then she threatened to tell her cousin that I had asked her to marry me. She had the temerity to suggest it was my own fault for saying I had something particular I wished to say to her."

Bowditch recoiled. "My lord! Do you mean to say you are engaged to Miss Wayborn?"

"Don't be an ass, Bowditch!"

"No, my lord."

"I, engaged to the female plague? No, she declined to spring her trap on me."

"That is very fortunate, my lord."

"We are to understand," said Swale angrily, "that my person does not attract her sufficiently. My person, you understand, is repugnant to Miss Wayborn."

"I see, sir."

"Not even my rank is sufficient to tempt her, you collect. I am a pill that cannot be gilded. I am an orangutan. Incidently, you do not press my suits to Miss Wayborn's satisfaction. You must do better, Bowditch."

Bowditch, who had never pressed his lordship's suits to anyone's satisfaction, started in surprise. "My lord?"

"I won't have her sniping at me," said Swale. "I can't help my face, which she does not like, but I won't have her sniping at my clothes. They are expensive clothes, are they not? With a little care, Bowditch, I am convinced they might be made to *look* expensive."

"Does your lordship mean to dine with Miss Wayborn after all?"

"The Vicar invited me, and I accepted," Swale said piously. "It would be churlish of me to break the engagement."

"I expect she has refused him," said Dr. Cary with a sigh. "If his lordship does not mean to dine with us, I expect she has refused him. Do you suppose we might ask her, my dear?"

His wife, who was busily sorting shards of porcelain at his desk, was giving him but half her attention. "Ask who what, my dear?" she said absently.

"Ask Juliet if she has refused the Marquess," said the Reverend.

Mrs. Cary gasped. "You can't ask a young woman whether or not she has refused an offer of marriage, Dr. Cary. That is rather a personal matter."

"I don't *wish* to ask her," he replied. "But if she has refused him—if there is no possibility of the marriage—I should like to be compensated for the damages. Or we might throw Cynthia in his way. She's very pretty. She might tempt him. His Grace of Auckland has many livings in his gift, you know. There might be a bishopric for me yet, Mrs. Cary! I wish I *were* her father—I would make her marry him."

This caught Mrs. Cary's attention. "But you *are* Cynthia's father, my dear."

"Hm-m? Yes, I know I am Cynthia's father," he snapped. "I wish I were *Juliet's*. Then I could make her marry Lord Swale. What does she mean refusing an offer that she is a good fifty thousand pounds shy of deserving?"

"Well, if she does not wish to marry him, my dear, it is only right that she should refuse him," Mrs. Cary said sensibly. "Even the most bashful girl must see it is her duty to be disobliging on such an occasion. I daresay it can be mended," she added hopefully.

"Mended!" cried Dr. Cary, forgetting in his upheaval the fractured shepherdess his wife was sweeping into a box. "But *what* it would have meant to our Cynthia! That is what occupies my mind. Why, if her cousin were Marchioness of Swale, that would throw open the doors of the very best society there is."

"And some of the very worst," she told him wisely. "Pray, do not trouble yourself about it, my dear. Put it out of your mind."

"I fear that one day, Juliet will come to regret her stupidity," Dr. Cary said forebodingly. "One does not lightly spurn a nobleman of his lordship's rank and fortune. And such a disagreeable man he is, too. Full of bile, I think. He will make her miserable for refusing him. She would have done better to accept him, no matter how much she dislikes him."

"Better he make her miserable for refusing him than for accepting him," said Mrs. Cary. "It is possible for even the most agreeable suitor to prove himself a disagreeable husband, but if a man does not trouble to make himself agreeable *before* the marriage, he can scarcely be expected to make himself agreeable *after.*"

Dr. Cary was forced to admit the wisdom of this assessment, though it pained him to relinquish the Marquess from his imagination. "Why could he not be well-favored and agreeable as a Marquess *ought* to be?" he moaned.

Down in the garden, Juliet and Cynthia were discussing this very thing.

"Well, Cynthia!" said Juliet. "I did not exaggerate when I described Lord Swale as a stableboy with nettlerash."

"His hair really is quite horribly red," Cynthia murmured. "I thought he was going to *hit* Papa."

"Why do gentlemen persist in marrying attractive red-haired ladies?" Juliet wondered. "Do they think they will bear only attractive red-haired daughters? Don't they know they are just as likely to give birth to ugly red-haired sons?"

"I would not call him ugly exactly," said Cynthia. "He is too terrible to be merely ugly."

"You would not call him ugly—not to his face, perhaps," said Juliet, laughing. "For he has the most vile, loathsome temper of anyone I have ever met!"

"But . . ." Cynthia bit her lip. "You do not think he is behind the attack on Cousin Cary?"

Juliet sighed. "No, I expect I must give all that up. He is incapable of guile. His face bursts into flame at the slightest provocation. I am inclined to think him a mean-spirited bully, but quite innocent of hurting my brother. He actually thought those paltry grays had a chance against Cary's chestnuts! But then, he hasn't very much sense."

"Oh, Juliet!" Cynthia admonished her. "Do you not see you have falsely accused an innocent man? Small wonder he is angry."

Cynthia was right. Juliet's cheeks burned, but she

said crossly, "Rely on it—he has done *something* for which he deserves a cruel setdown."

"Well, perhaps," Cynthia said unhappily.

"I expect I should not have said 'if,'" Juliet admitted more gracefully. "'If I have wronged you, I am sorry.' I should not have said that. That is what made him throw the basket. Now *there,*" she said suddenly in quite a different tone. "There is a man who looks—and behaves—like a marquess."

Cynthia looked up and saw her eldest brother walking toward them from the house. "Horatio?" she said in some surprise.

Juliet pinched her arm. "Yes, you goose! Don't you know your brother is the most handsome man in London?"

Cynthia laughed. "To me, he is simply Horatio. Do you not think his mustache rather too absurd? Whoever heard of a seafaring man with a mustache and whiskers?"

"I think they become him very well," said Juliet, smiling at the Captain. "Now, a mustache on Ginger—that would be too absurd!"

"You must not call his lordship Ginger!" cried Cynthia.

"Indeed, you must not, Juliet," Horatio, who had heard this remark, said sternly. "It implies an intimacy that, I trust, does not exist!"

Juliet blushed. "No, indeed, Cousin," she murmured. "I assure you it implies only my contempt for the man."

"When I heard he had taken rooms at the Tudor Rose, I was appalled," said Horatio. "Now I discover he has been here, imposing himself on my pretty cousin."

Juliet, accustomed to his gallantry, did not blush at

the compliment but laughed. "Rather his lordship has imposed upon your father's shepherdesses!"

"Was that not your doing, Juliet?" inquired Horatio with a frown, for he had heard from his father the tale of the playful basket tossing.

Juliet hurriedly explained. "I could not allow your father to form any ill ideas about his Grace of Auckland, who really is an honorable old gentleman."

"Then . . . Lord Swale has not proposed to you?" Horatio seemed relieved.

"Heavens, no!" said Juliet, laughing.

"I expect the offer of a coronet would be difficult for any young lady to refuse," Horatio said thoughtfully.

"Despite my youth," Juliet replied teasingly, "I believe I could withstand the temptation. He really is the most disagreeable man. He shouted at me until my ears rang; he flattered me with the sobriquet of 'harpy'; he told me how delighted he would be to break my neck and how he wished I were a man; then he topped it off by snatching my basket from my hands and pitching it across the room! I wish he *had* proposed to me. Then you would see how quickly I could send him away with a flea in his ear! Not," she could not help adding, "that he didn't *arrive* with a flea in his ear."

"What has he come for?" Horatio wondered. "That he would dare show his face—"

"Juliet is convinced he did no harm to Cousin Cary," Cynthia broke in. "You must not think him such a villain as that, though he does have a frightful temper."

Horatio smiled grimly. "And he came here to swear his innocence, did he? I say, that's a bit oily, isn't it?"

"His lordship has many faults," said Juliet, "but being oily isn't one of them. He resolutely refused to swear to me he was innocent, which I thought rather well of him."

"Indeed?" said Horatio. "Then he has convinced you he is innocent."

"He did convince me," Juliet admitted. "What's more, he thinks he knows who *did* do it."

"Who?" Horatio demanded. "Do you mean to say he actually accused someone?"

"Yes," said Juliet, recalling just in time that Lord Redfylde was Horatio's patron. To spare him pain, she said quickly, "You will forgive me if I do not repeat his accusation. There really is no proof, you see."

"Then it does you credit not to repeat it, Cousin," said Horatio warmly. "What sort of fellow is this Swale to accuse someone without proof?"

"He is the very worst sort," Juliet told him confidently. "If you will excuse me, Cousin, I should write to my brother Sir Benedict. I should ask him what he knows about this strange matter. If I hurry, I can send it by the afternoon post."

Horatio caught her arm. "If the Marquess of Swale has not come to make love to you, Cousin Juliet, and he has not come to swear his innocence, why is he come to Hertfordshire?"

Juliet flushed. Under no circumstances could she tell her cousin that Swale had come to satisfy himself that she had no designs upon his aged father. "You had better ask Ginger that," she said. "Lord Swale, I mean."

Horatio was given an early opportunity for doing so when the Marquess, in defiance of Miss Wayborn, arrived at the Vicarage promptly at six o'clock, looking like he meant to eat. Juliet was astonished when he walked into the drawing room where she and Cynthia were sorting fragments of china plates and figurines into their respective piles. The parlormaid,

Mary, sketched a curtsey and announced belatedly, "My lord, the Marquess of Swale!"

"Very good, Mary," Swale congratulated her, smiling so amiably that Mary blushed and Juliet scoffed indignantly.

"What are you doing here?" she demanded, getting to her feet.

"Miss Cary," he said warmly, bending over Cynthia's hand. "My dear child, you look perfectly charming this evening."

"How very good of you to come after all, my lord," Cynthia whispered, trembling. "If you will—Oh!" She broke off in confusion as he pressed his lips to the back of her hand. "If your lordship will please excuse me," she hurried on, "I do not suppose my mother knows you are coming."

"But why should she not, my dear child?" Swale inquired pleasantly, still holding her hand. "Your father graciously has asked me to dine, and I graciously have condescended to be fed."

"Let her alone, you monster," Juliet said coldly. He turned to her, and Cynthia vanished from the room in a flurry of pink muslin. "I told you you're not welcome here."

He looked at her. She had changed into a fitted gown of Tuscan red cambric for dinner. The short, tight sleeves and the deep décolleté were trimmed with rows of silky golden fringe that shimmered provocatively with her slightest movement. The cut and color suited her dark hair and brought out the dusky gypsy tint of her skin, which he had not noticed before. A heavy gold Etruscan-style bracelet worn above the elbow of her right arm was her only ornament. While not as pretty as her elfin cousin, she was definitely a handsome girl. He wondered, with a flash of annoyance, if she had chosen that dress especially to please her cousin Captain Cary.

Carefully averting his eyes from the smooth round tops of her breasts, he paused at the mantelpiece and stooped down to pat the spaniel curled up in its basket. "If one only went where one was welcome, Miss Wayborn, one would never go out," he told her gravely.

"Well, you had jolly well better behave yourself," she said. "Don't you *dare* play the overweening aristocrat here. You will eat everything put in front of you, and you will like it, sir. And you will tell Mrs. Cary it is the best roast mutton you ever had in your whole life, or I shall *kick* you under the table."

"As long as it is not dressed as lamb," he returned coldly, "I like mutton above all things. Except possibly cheese. Also rabbit pie."

"Cheese! Rabbit pie!" Her lip curled in distaste.

"Don't you like rabbit pie?" he inquired innocently.

"I have certainly never eaten it!" she snapped.

"To say the truth, it is only good with a tankard of ale," he admitted with a sigh.

"Well, there's no ale or rabbit pie here," she said impatiently. "So you had better go back to your room at the Rose. *And* you had better not walk out on the Sprigges without paying your bill."

He squatted down to scratch the dog behind the ears. Her skirts, he noticed, were fashionably short, and they were trimmed with more of that seductively swaying silky fringe. Her slim ankles were clad in ruinously expensive white silk stockings, and on her feet were high-heeled slippers, the velvet tongues of which were threaded into little heart-shaped diamond buckles. Rather overdressed, he decided, for dinner at a small country vicarage.

The dog he was petting suddenly whimpered,

startling him. As he bent down to look at the spaniel's paw, the animal cringed.

"Get away from him," Juliet said angrily, prodding him with the pointed toe of her slipper. "Can't you see you're frightening him?"

"Can't you see he's got something stuck in his paw?" he retorted.

"Oh!" she said, kneeling down to look.

Swale spoke gently to the dog, and gradually, the animal allowed him to touch his front paw. "What's his name?"

"Sailor," she answered. "It looks like a sliver of china," she added, bending her head over the dog. One long, dark curl fell across her shoulder, following the curve of her breast and disappearing like a snake into her cleavage. "He must have gotten into the room before the pieces were all swept up, poor thing."

"It is my fault then, Sailor," he said softly. "Go and fetch me tongs or something, can't you?" he told the girl curtly. "And something to wash the wound. And a bit of bandage."

They were joined at this moment by Captain Cary. Juliet performed the introductions hurriedly. "Horatio, Sailor is hurt!" she cried, rushing from the room.

Swale looked the other man over with a critical eye as he continued to stroke the spaniel's head. The Captain was not so very handsome, he told himself. And the fungus on the upper lip—that was hardly the height of fashion. Quite unlike his own magnificent sideburns, which plunged in fiery splendor down the length of his jaw. Had the Wayborn truly decked herself in golden fringe and diamond buckles for this pretty coxcomb?

"How do you do, my lord?" said Horatio, bowing

correctly. "What brings your lordship to our little village? Besides the practice of veterinary medicine?"

Swale could scarcely admit that he had come there to break the heart of Miss Juliet Wayborn. He fell back on the excuse he had used at the Tudor Rose. "I am looking for a small country place convenient to London," he said as Juliet returned with the necessary items tucked into a small enamel basin. "I understand that Mr. Cary Wayborn owns Tanglewood Manor. It sounds just the thing."

Juliet blinked at him in surprise.

"Tanglewood is not for sale, my lord," Captain Cary said.

"Indeed, it is not," said Juliet, finding her tongue. "It was my mother's girlhood home. I should die before I see it leave the family. My brother will never sell you Tanglewood." She knelt down beside him at the hearth and gave him the tweezers.

"Oh?" said Swale. Carefully, he removed the shard from the soft pad of the dog's paw while Juliet held the poor animal still. "I heard at the inn that Mr. Wayborn does not concern himself much with the place. Neglects it, one might say."

Juliet flushed hotly. "How dare you!" she said, keeping her voice hushed for Sailor's sake. "When my brother marries, I expect he will settle there. In any case, what business is it of yours?"

"Why, none," he said mildly. "If it is not for sale, even my enterprising mind cannot tell how I may buy it, so there I must leave the matter. There are other places. I am not one of these overweening aristocrats, my dear Miss Wayborn."

He finished cleaning the spaniel's paw and watched as Juliet wrapped it in a bandage. "Your finger, my lord," she said, and he thought he detected a softening in her wide gray eyes. Or was she playing the demure little angel to catch Captain Cary's heart?

"What about my finger?"

"If you could just put it there for the knot? It needs to be good and tight." He obliged, and she pulled the ends of the knot tight over his fingertip. "You can pull it out now," she said gently, almost shyly, but in the next moment, she turned to the dog. "There now, Sailor. Next time, tell us when you are hurt." And she left the room to put away her basin.

Dinner was not the simple mutton affair that Juliet had led Swale to anticipate. The Vicar prided himself on a good table, and Mrs. Cary, without any pretensions to elegance, provided it. Dr. Cary was quite shocked when Swale said carelessly, "Oh, do not throw away your claret on me, sir. I don't object to Madeira."

Mrs. Cary, thinking that Madeira must be the height of sophistication if Lord Swale preferred it, silently berated herself for all the Anjou, Beaujolais, and Amontillado upon which she had squandered her husband's money.

"Let me assure your lordship," Horatio said dryly, "that *we* do." He watched with his lip curled as Swale swilled the fine wine and smacked his lips.

For his part, Swale watched with a sneer as Captain Cary mixed the ladies' wine with water. Juliet, who knew that his scorn was directed chiefly at her, glared at him.

As she had ordered him, he ate everything put in front of him—loudly. He slurped his soup, then picked up his bowl in his hands to drink the dregs. He wolfed down the next two courses greedily, either swallowing his food whole or chomping it lustily, all the while moaning and rolling his eyes in exaggerated delight. Anything that fell from his plate was fed to the dog under the table. He twice spilled his wine, apologized profusely, and begged for more. His snowy neckcloth and waistcoat were soon speckled with crumbs and gravy, and he licked his greasy fingers with unprecedented enthusiasm.

Cynthia and her parents watched him almost in disbelief, neglecting their own plates. Horatio turned away in disgust. Juliet, well aware that he was attempting to provoke her, pretended not to notice, but when he actually asked Mrs. Cary for a little *honey* to make his peas *stick* to his *knife,* she could take no more.

"Carrots!" she said sharply.

He frowned at her. "What did you call me?"

"Why nothing, my lord." She smiled innocently as she held up a pretty celadon bowl full of julienned carrots. "May I offer you some carrots? A little specialty of mine. I glazed them myself with *ginger* and . . . oh, all sorts of good things. May I serve you, my lord?" She was already on her feet. "It would be such an honor if you would tell me what you think. You are obviously an authority on food."

He leaned back from the table and patted his belly lovingly. "Serve away, Miss Wayborn, and I'll give you my honest opinion," he said magnanimously.

She came around the table and set the bowl on the sideboard behind his back. "I think you'll find it's rather a special dish, my lord," she said cheerfully, adding liberal amounts of black pepper and brandy to the innocent carrots. In the drawer she found the old brass candlelighter.

Smiling sweetly, she set the dish before him, then set it ablaze just as he leaned forward to begin shoveling it down.

As the brandy ignited, a tall flame leaped from the bowl, causing Mrs. Cary to shriek in dismay. The

Marquess of Swale nearly fell over backward in his chair, the tips of his precious sideburns sizzling. In the pretty celadon bowl, the flame petered out, leaving behind a glistening burnt orange mass.

"I find that a little brandy makes a marvelous foil for the ginger," Juliet said serenely, returning to her seat. "Unless my lord objects, I shall call it *carottes flambeaux a la Swale.*"

"Juliet!" Horatio rebuked her as Cynthia tried desperately not to giggle. "How could you? You might have injured his lordship!"

Swale spared him a look of scorn. "Nonsense," he said, forcing himself to smile at the gray-eyed pyromaniac who was now seated across from him with a look of triumph pasted on her patrician face. He picked up his fork. "Yum, yum. Looks absolutely delicious!" he commented while stretching out his foot to grind those pretty heart-shaped diamond buckles into her foot with his heavy shoe. As he cautiously felt around under the table, he forced a blob of her cooking down his throat, smiling grotesquely. In the next instant, he was reaching for his water glass, draining it in one gulp, and holding it out for more and choking.

"Not too much pepper, I hope?" the cook inquired with pretended anxiety.

"No, indeed," he assured her, despite the fact that his tongue felt as though a hive of bees had stung it and he knew he would *never* get the filthy taste out of his mouth. "Perfectly perfect! Just what I like." As he spoke, he extended his leg under the table until he felt a foot on the other side, then bore down on it with a vengeance.

Horatio started up in his chair and frowned at him.

Juliet, of course, *would* keep her pretty velvet slippers tucked underneath her chair, well beyond the reach of even long-legged Viking giants. Realizing his error, Swale hastily withdrew his foot, saying, "I thought it was no longer the fashion for nice young ladies to meddle in the kitchen. Not ladylike."

"Not ladylike to cook?" Dr. Cary shook his head, and Swale could tell this was going into the old boy's next sermon. "Too many ladies live lives of vanity and indolence. Not ladylike to cook indeed! My dear Mrs. Cary, did you not make the trifle?"

"You're not eating, my lord," Juliet said with apparent distress. "You don't like my cooking after all. I am excessively sorry I have failed to please you."

"That's quite enough, Juliet," said Horatio. "The joke has gone too far, my lord. Mary, take that foul concoction away."

"I see no joke," said Swale coldly, shooing Mary away. He really didn't like the high-handed manner in which this pretty fellow corrected the evil, yet unquestionably magnificent, Juliet, almost as though he owned her. "I will eat every bite of this decidedly non-foul concoction, thank you."

He grimaced at Juliet as he forced the last of the gruesome stuff down his throat. She watched him in wide-eyed disbelief. "My compliments on your excellent cookery, Miss Wayborn. I have never tasted anything quite like it. Perhaps, one day you will allow me to return the favor and serve you a dish named in *your* honor? A dish served cold, I think." He snapped his fingers. "I have it! *Oysters.* Raw oysters served on a block of ice and garnished with lemon. Oysters to match your eyes, Miss Wayborn. Ice to represent the ice in your soul, and lemon reminiscent of your tart personality. I give you . . . Oysters a la Juliete."

The blaze of scorn in her eyes made him smile, but the others at the table were alarmed.

"What a splendid compliment!" cried Mrs. Cary, who did not wish to see anything else set afire in her dining room. "His lordship means to pay a compliment. Your—your eyes *are* gray, my dear."

"Indeed they are," agreed Dr. Cary nervously, for he wanted nothing else broken.

"And you know you like oysters, Juliet," Cynthia pointed out. "I could never bear the horrid, slimy, squishy things myself—" She broke off as she realized that her remarks were unlikely to promote peace. "But *you* have always liked them."

Juliet thoughtfully took a bite of cold asparagus. She had underestimated Swale, she realized. First, his hands, and now, his tongue. She had not supposed him capable of matching wits with her, any more than she would have guessed him capable of easing a sliver of glass from a wounded animal's paw. Several witty rejoinders suggested themselves to her, each icier and more tart than the last, which meant, of course, that she could not use them, not *now*.

"I do like oysters," she conceded, inclining her head graciously to her opponent. "I like them smoked and stewed. But I would not be adverse to trying them served cold with lemon."

Horatio had listened to Juliet and Swale cross swords with growing displeasure. He was not accustomed to sharing his cousin's attention with other gentlemen, and it troubled him deeply that Juliet had allowed herself to be goaded into exchanging rather vulgar insults with the man. It showed a want of propriety that, he feared, might reflect badly on himself and his family. He took control of the conversation as the sweet was brought in and steered it toward Walter Scott's poetry, a subject that he knew always interested Juliet.

Swale, who had no stomach for poetry, maintained a sullen silence as the cherry sorbet did its best to eliminate the taste of burnt carrots from his mouth. In due course, the ladies withdrew. Dr. Cary unburdened himself of his political views for three quarters of an hour, and then the gentlemen rejoined the ladies in the little drawing room. All signs of the afternoon's disaster had been removed, but a large pale square on the wallpaper showed where the broken cabinet had once stood.

Dr. Cary being set against cards and all forms of gambling, Mrs. Cary proposed alternative entertainment. At her insistence, each of them was required to perform a speech from Shakespeare.

Juliet, rather than choosing anything from her namesake, did Portia's "The quality of mercy is not strained" from the courtroom scene of *The Merchant of Venice*. The Vicar regaled them with Marc Antony's "Friends! Romans! Countrymen! Lend me your ears!" Cynthia, after much indecision, rather surprisingly settled on Cleopatra's lament. "No more but e'en a woman, and commanded/ By such poor passion as the maid that milks/ And does the meanest chares." It went on and on. Swale could make neither head nor tails of it, but he noticed Juliet wiping a tear from her eye as Cynthia's soft voice faded into the air.

Horatio stood up and smiled fondly at Juliet. "What shall I do, my dear cousin? Macbeth? Hamlet? Othello?"

"Hamlet," she said promptly, clapping her hands together like an ecstatic child. Swale did not much like the way her gray eyes glowed as she looked at her handsome cousin. She seemed to have forgotten entirely how the rude fellow had insulted her cooking!

Horatio honored her choice with "O, that this too

too solid flesh would melt/ Thaw, and resolve itself into a dew."

Swale was sitting on the sofa next to Cynthia with Sailor in his lap. "No such bloody luck," he muttered under his breath, but he added his applause when the long soliloquy at last was laid to rest. "You might have had a career treading the boards, Captain," he said, stifling a yawn.

"Thank you, my lord," Horatio said coldly.

"So that's *Hamlet,* is it? The man's mother marries his father's brother—have I got it right?" asked Swale. "Fairly beastly, what? I must say, I can't approve. English people ought to behave better, set an example for the world, even in our plays."

The Family Cary did not know what to say.

"Ancient Rome, yes, obviously. And the Greek chap who married his own Mamma—Octopus or Edifice or what is it?"

"Oedipus," Horatio said contemptuously.

"Well, foreigners, after all. But one expects better from the English race, by God."

"They're not English, you ridiculous man," said Juliet severely. "They're Danes."

"They're what?"

"Danes. The play is set in Denmark." Juliet shook her head, almost unable to credit the extent of his ignorance. "For heaven's sake, it's *called* Hamlet, Prince of Denmark."

"Which explains his rather poor grasp of the English language," said Swale. "Such an obvious Dane, Hamlet. That part about the old shoes following the dead fellow's body around the place, all teary-eyed—"

Juliet angrily picked up the book. "A little month or ere those shoes were old," she read, "With which she followed my poor father's body/ Like Niobe, all tears—"

"Is that good English?" Swale wanted to know. "I ask you, even in Denmark, are those lines to be considered the King's English? Hm-m-m, Miss Wayborn? I think not."

Juliet slammed the book shut. "And what will you do for us, my lord?" she inquired, tilting her head to one side. "Sir John Falstaff, perhaps?"

Swale regarded her blankly. "Sorry?" he said. "Thought it was Shakespeare night."

"Don't you know any Shakespeare at all?" cried Juliet, appalled.

"Shakespeare, my dear infant," he informed her while scratching Sailor's tummy, "is the name of the horse that won the Lincolnshire in '03."

Chapter 8

His lordship returned to his room at the Tudor Rose in high dudgeon. "If *that* is the sort of man she likes!" he fumed as he tore off his neckcloth. "Poetry, Bowditch, and a lip covered in fungus! He is a great eater of *poulet roti au cresson* and salmon *en croute* and God knows what! No rabbit pie for *him*, Bowditch! Not the great Captain Cary."

Bowditch was already in bed, reading by the light of his candle, and where another valet might have felt the need to get up and attend his master, Bowditch merely turned the page.

"They call him Phoebus in town, you know. One of those ruddy Parthenon gods, I expect."

"The god of the sun, my lord," Bowditch informed him. "Sometimes known as Apollo."

Swale sat on the edge of his bed and availed himself of the bootjack. "I expect they call the Wayborn after one of those bally Parthenon goddesses too."

Bowditch closed his book with a firm clap and looked sharply at his master. "Miss Wayborn, my lord? Did your lordship find her to be goddess-like?"

Swale crossed the room and set his boots outside

the door to be polished. "Oh, not one of the really juicy goddesses, not Venus or anything like that. Take your mind out of the stews, Bowditch. One of those queenly, stiff-necked, fully clothed goddesses, if you see what I mean. Prone to flinging lightning bolts at the heads of defenseless mortals. You know the type. Supply the name."

"I believe that Juno was the queen of the gods, my lord. Something of a jealous shrew, or so I understand. Always trying to kill Hercules."

"No, no," Swale said impatiently. "Nothing Junoesque about the Wayborn. Quite a slim girl, Bowditch—I daresay I could span her waist with my two hands. I can't think how she managed those chestnuts. What's the name of the one that jumped out of Jove's head with her spear at the ready?"

"Minerva, my lord."

"That's the one. Goddess of war? Chaos? Doom?"

"Wisdom, my lord, though Minerva did side with the Greeks in the Trojan War. She was the patroness of Ulysses."

"The Trojans won that one, didn't they?"

"No, my lord. Troy fell."

"Did he? Stubbed his toe? Serves him right." Swale yawned. "I'm going to bed now, Bowditch, where I shall sleep like an infant. Why? Because I deserve a rest after the evening I have had. Tomorrow, we return to London."

"London, my lord?"

"Yes, Bowditch, London. Hertfordshire is a foul wasteland. Nothing but trees, sunshine, and grass. There's nothing to amuse us here."

"But surely, my lord, your revenge upon Miss Wayborn is incomplete—"

Swale sniffed. "I have decided it is not the behavior

of a gentleman to trifle with a lady's affections. She don't deserve to have tender, womanly feelings awakened in her by me. I'm for London, Bowditch. I'd like an early start, so mind you don't drag your feet!"

"No, my lord," said Bowditch, blowing out his candle.

Some time later, while it was still dark, Swale awoke with a start from a dream he was having in which a long, slender snake had gotten inside the shimmering red dress of a tall, dark-haired lady, causing her great distress, and in which he was pleasantly engaged in helping her to locate it. The search had reached a most interesting point when suddenly, his eyes popped open. It took him a moment to realize what was amiss. The loud, regular snoring of his valet had ceased, desisted, and stopped altogether.

"Bowditch?" he croaked softly. There was no answer. It briefly occurred to Swale that he ought to investigate. Then he rolled over and went back to sleep.

The next thing he knew, his excellent landlord was standing over him. The room was filled with light. The air smelled beautifully of bacon, sausages, and steak and kidney pie.

"My lord?"

Swale eyed the man blearily. "What is the time, landlord?" he asked gruffly.

"Half-past ten," came the incredible answer.

"Damnation!" cried Swale, throwing back the covers. "I wanted an early start, landlord. Did my man not tell you?"

"No, my lord. I haven't seen Mr. Bowditch this morning."

"Tea, landlord," Swale said decisively. "And something to revitalize the tissues," he added, patting his growling belly. "Another rabbit pie, perhaps?"

"Yes, my lord," said Mr. Sprigge.

Swale rubbed his face vigorously, and his whiskers rasped against his knuckles. "And I don't suppose you could shave me, landlord?"

"Certainly, my lord," Mr. Sprigge said readily enough, but Swale could not help noticing he seemed rooted to the spot.

"What is it, man? Bowditch didn't run off with the pewter, did he?"

"No, my lord. There is . . . a lady . . . waiting to see your lordship."

"A lady?" Swale chuckled. "Well, perhaps when I am stronger, Mr. Sprigge. Right now, all I want is my breakfast. And lots of it."

"It is Miss Wayborn, my lord," said Mr. Sprigge a little coldly. "She's been waiting for your lordship for three quarters of an hour already. She asked me to wake you, my lord. She says it is important that she speak to your lordship."

"Miss Wayborn?" He was so startled he stopped midway through a yawn. Certain images from the previous night's dream entered his head, causing him some embarrassment, which he covered with a show of annoyance. "What the devil does she want?"

"The young lady did not confide in me, my lord."

"I wish she'd told you to wake me up two hours ago," he grumbled, beginning to shove on a few clothes that happened to be lying around. "I might be in London by this time. Where is she?"

"The parlor, my lord."

Swale nodded. "Very well, Sprigge. I will join her anon, as Shakespeare said. For the nonce, whatever you do, don't let her near my breakfast. She has rather a nasty habit of setting a man's food on fire."

He found his boots outside the door, put them on, and made his way to the private parlor. Miss Wayborn

was standing at the window looking down onto the
High Street. She was very neatly dressed in a dark
blue redingote that reminded him, as it was meant to,
of a Naval officer's coat. In her gloved hands, she held
a riding crop.

"Well, harpy?" he greeted her with his usual lack of
courtesy. "What do you want?"

She turned, frowning, but for a moment, she was
struck speechless by his appearance. His shirt was
badly wrinkled, and it lay open at the neck. His coat
was unbuttoned. He wore breeches and boots. He was
unshaven, and his red hair was standing on end.

"Good God, man!" she said, appalled. "Your face
looks like an anthill. Did you sleep in your clothes?"

"No, my dear young lady, I slept in my bed. What
did *you* sleep in?"

"That, Ginger," she spat, her hands tightening on
the crop, "is none of your business."

"Quite!"

Juliet resumed an air of queenly dignity. "I have come
to speak to you on a matter of some importance."

"It may very well be important to the harpy population," he said, "but what chiefly matters to me is
breakfast. Ah! Here is Mistress Sprigge."

The landlord's wife bumped into the room carrying a jug. She was closely followed by a sturdy young
man carrying a heavy tray.

Swale sat down at the table and rubbed his hands together as various dishes were set before him. As he
began to eat, Mrs. Sprigge looked askance at the young
lady.

"Thank you, Mrs. Sprigge."

"Oh, now, Miss Julie—"

"That will be all," Juliet said firmly, and Mrs. Sprigge
reluctantly withdrew.

Swale, his mouth full of heavenly bacon, chuckled. "You've shocked her," he observed. "You should be more careful, you wicked doxy. What if I were to tell the Sprigges I had offered you *carte blanche* and you had accepted? Who would be in a spot then, eh, my girl?"

He expected a pale face and a gasp of horror, but she baffled him with a puzzled look. "What is *carte blanche?*" she asked. "White card, I know, but what does that signify?"

He felt his own cheeks grow hot.

"Never mind!" she said hastily. "Whatever it is, the Sprigges have known me since I was a baby. They would take my part against *you,* Ginger, rest assured."

He grunted and reached for the jug Mrs. Sprigge had left. It turned out to be buttermilk. Not as refreshing as ale, of course, but it helped the sausages go down. "A gentleman offers a courtesan *carte blanche* when he wishes to become her only client," he told her.

"Oh!"

He leaned back and looked at her. Righteous indignation, affronted prudery . . . these would have amused him. But in her expression, he saw only disgust. "If you don't want to be offered *carte blanche,* my dear," he told her roughly, "you might refrain from requesting private meetings with strange gentlemen at your local inn. Appearances and all that."

"Do you keep a manservant called Bowditch?" she asked abruptly.

He polished off a few slices of toast while considering the matter. "Is there some reason I shouldn't keep a manservant called Bowditch?"

"Well, if you *have* a man called Bowditch, which I think you do, I have two very good reasons why you should turn him off immediately. First of all, you look like you just woke up."

"I did just wake up," he informed her.

"You *always* look like you just woke up!" she retorted.

"And the second reason?" he said. "The first carries no weight with me, you understand."

"Your Bowditch has been imposing on my Fifi!"

He nearly choked on his buttermilk. "Your Fifi?"

"My maid," she explained with dignity. "Josephine."

He looked her up and down. She did not appear in the least to have just woken up. Parthenon goddesses never do. "The maid that curls your hair over your ears?" he inquired. "Why do you let her do that? I don't think your hair *wants* to be curled over your ears."

"Hairdressing advice from the Viking berserker," she scoffed. "Never mind my hair, you insufferable oaf! What are you going to do about this Bowditch? You may as well know that Fi—that Josephine is an orphan. Her parents were émigrés who fled the Terror in France and arrived here with nothing. I am responsible for her."

"A touching story," he said, trying unsuccessfully to disguise a belch as a hiccough.

"Last night, I found her in tears!"

"Your Fifi?"

"You may be accustomed," she said icily, "to laughing at the tears of a friendless young girl, but I am not!"

"I beg your pardon," he said, ringing the bell, "but surely you do not expect me to console your Fifi?"

"I wish you would tell your Bowditch to stay away from my Fifi!" she snapped. "For how can I doubt his character when he is the servant of *such* a master!"

He stood up and threw down his napkin. "What did you say?"

She did not scruple to repeat the insulting words. "Perhaps you do not care that your servant is imposing upon a defenseless female," she went on. "Perhaps you are so licentious yourself that your servants see no need to curtail their own behavior!"

His green eyes narrowed. "Licentious! So I'm licentious now, am I? No serving wench is safe from me?"

Too proud to withdraw, she stoutly declared, "If I were a servant girl, I wouldn't trust you as far as I could throw you."

He crossed the room to her in two long strides. "By God, if you were a man—!"

If she had been a man, he would have punched her in the nose. But she was not a man, so he grabbed her by the elbows, lifted her bodily from the floor, and kissed her, causing her to drop her riding crop. When he was finished, he let her go so quickly, she nearly fell as well.

"Call me licentious," he said, a little short of breath. "I'll teach you licentious!"

For a moment, she was too surprised to say anything. The sound of the boots clearing his throat in the doorway brought her to her senses.

"What is it, Jackey?" she said crisply, then wiped her mouth hard with the back of her hand.

The boy's eyes were open to their fullest extent, and judging from his cheeky grin, he had witnessed the entire disgraceful incident. "Begging milord's pardon, Miss, but milord's man asked me to give this note to his lordship when his lordship woke up."

He held up a bit of folded paper and added apologetically, "I was in the cellar filling the lamps, milord, or I'd have brought it sooner."

"Never mind, Jackey," said Swale, giving the lad a breezy smile as he unfolded the letter. "I was quite agreeably occupied, as you saw. Clear the table, will you; there's a good lad. And bring Miss Wayborn some hot tea. She has had a bit of a shock. I daresay she has never been kissed before, which explains both the ineptitude of her response and her present confusion."

Juliet was not to be goaded so easily. "What does Bowditch have to say for himself?"

"Ha!" said Swale, waving the page under her nose. "I knew it! It is not my Bowditch that has imposed upon your Fifi. Rather, it is your Fifi that has imposed upon my Bowditch. The frisky minx has prevailed upon him to take her away from this provincial backwater. It would appear that your Fifi regards you as a sort of a jailer, Miss Wayborn."

"What nonsense," Juliet scoffed. "He has abducted her. I tell you, I found her *crying*!"

"Quite," he told her happily. "It says here she meant to employ some ruse to get you out of the way. In sending you here to confront me about Bowditch's supposed crimes against her, I'd say she has succeeded. You've been outmaneuvered by your own Fifi, Miss Wayborn."

"My maid would never run away from me," said Juliet. "Not willingly! Your vile Bowditch must have exercised some terrible influence over her, some coercion . . . "

"Begging your pardon, Miss Julie," said the ever present Jackey. "But I happened to see his lordship's man yesterday—"

"Not now, Jackey!"

"But he had a piece of paper, Miss Julie! When he spied me looking at it, he folded it up real quick-like and stuck it in his pocket."

Juliet sighed. "What of it, boy?"

"I asked him what that paper was, Miss Julie," Jackey went on enthusiastically. "And he told me it were a special license!"

"Special license!" Swale was thunderstruck.

Jackey grinned. "Aye, milord! Only I thought it was milord's!"

"Oh?" said Swale. "I look like the sort of fellow who goes scampering about the country with a special license in his pocket, do I?"

"Aye, milord!" said Jackey, unabashed.

"Oh, dear God," cried Juliet, sinking into a chair. "He means to force her to marry him."

Swale glared at her. "Why do you persist in this delusion that your Fifi was unwilling? She seems to me about the fastest bit of goods since—since that filly that won the Newmarket!"

She flushed angrily. "That is a thoroughly commonplace thing to say. For your enlightenment, allow me to tell you that Mademoiselle Huppert has an understanding with Bernard, with Mr. Bernard Corcoran, my brother's groom. The attachment is deep and of long duration."

"What?"

"They are engaged, Ginger," she snapped. "So you see it's quite impossible that she would elope with your Bowditch."

"I see nothing of the kind," he returned. "Why, that worthless jade! My poor Bowditch has been deceived very thoroughly by your diabolical Fifi."

"Nonsense! He has abducted her! Don't let's argue, Ginger," she added quickly. "We agree on one thing, I hope—they must be stopped! I suggest we go after them at once."

"Yes," he said grimly. "Then we'll see who's right. Jackey, go and ready my curricle."

"If your Bowditch has a special license, he could marry her anywhere," Juliet pointed out. "He would hardly dare ask my cousin to perform the sacrament.

The nearest village is Little Straythorne. If you've brought your grays, we may be able to catch them in time. My Fi—Josephine was yet at the Vicarage when I left it at half-past nine."

"We've already established who it was that gave you those ridiculous curls."

"You ought to let me drive," she said, following him from the room. "I know the country better than you."

The resourceful Jackey had brought the curricle into the yard. "Shut up," Swale replied to Juliet's suggestion, "or I shan't take you with me at all." He watched her climb up into the seat beside him but did not offer to help her. "You drive my precious grays?" he scoffed. "I had rather see them fed to my hounds."

"In case you've forgotten, I drove my brother's chestnuts," she snapped.

"Ha!" he replied. "And a fine mess you made of it too, you miserable brat. Stopping in the middle of the road like Balaam's ass! I nearly broke my neck getting 'round you. Which way do I go?" he asked abruptly, for the grays had reached the end of the yard.

"South, down the High Street, over the bridge, then take the eastern fork. It's four miles to Little Straythorne."

As he took up the reins, she looked at his hands critically. In his haste, Swale had forgotten his gloves, if he had any. His hands were large, with red knuckles and thick, coarse fingers. They were not the hands of a gentleman. They did not appear capable of delicacy, but she had seen them very gently doctoring the paw of a hurt dog, and the horses seemed to respond to him gladly. He did not use the whip. "It may be of interest to you," she said slowly, "that I had no choice but to stop in the middle of the road."

"Is that so?"

"Indeed," she answered, "because, you see, I did not know where we were racing to."

"*What?*"

"I thought Southend," she went on blithely. "But then I thought, perhaps Colchester after all. What else could I do? I was obliged to stop at the crossroads and let you go first so that I could follow you."

"Let me go first—!" he choked, then swore violently under his breath.

"But then I saw you veer to the right, and I knew you were trying to get inside me—inside the right hand turn, I mean," she amended hastily. "So I—so then I knew it was Southend after all. It was just bad luck that you collided with me."

"Damned bad luck," he agreed. "Damned, wretched bad luck. I should never have met you, let alone collided with you!"

"What I mean to say is, if you were a *very* bad driver, you *would* have overturned. But you didn't," she added unnecessarily.

"I expect you were sorry I didn't overturn and break my neck!"

"Well, yes," she admitted. "At the time, I would not have been sorry to see you overturn. But that is when I thought . . ." She completed her sentence with a faint sniff.

"First, a compliment, and now, an apology," he said mockingly. "It would appear, Miss Wayborn, that I have gentled you with a kiss."

"I was gently born, Ginger," she informed him. "That is why I haven't slapped your horrifically ugly face. You only did it to embarrass me."

"Succeeded too," he laughed. "You blushed to the roots of your hair."

"I did not indeed," she said. "If I blushed, it was only

for your stupidity. But tell me, why Southend? Cary always races to Brighton."

"The turnpikes," he told her.

"Of course," Juliet murmured. "There are none between London and Southend. Otherwise, I should have had Bernard with me, and he would have told me the way."

"I would have gladly hazarded my grays against Mr. Wayborn's chestnuts," Swale said, "but I hadn't a decent groom to manage the turnpikes. Your brother was very fair to me when he hit on the Southend scheme. I'm as good a driver as he is," he added forcefully, anticipating argument.

"Perhaps you are," she said thoughtfully and colored up as he flashed her a look of surprise. "You could never have beaten him though," she went on quickly. "You are a much bigger man. Heavier, I mean. You simply couldn't ask it of the horses."

"You had a decided advantage there," he said irritably. "You weigh next to nothing."

"Good morning, Mrs. Croft!" Juliet called out suddenly, waving to a grim-looking matron coming down the street with her two unmarried daughters. "I expect little Jackey Lime will be only too pleased to tell the world what he saw today at the Tudor Rose. And now Mrs. Croft."

"What of it?" Swale said as the curricle went over the bridge.

"Honestly, Ginger," she said severely. "Are you a simpleton?"

"I am not a simpleton," he said. "I suppose you think me a simpleton because my blowhole don't spout poetry like your precious Captain Phoebus."

"Horatio has had fewer advantages than you and has accomplished considerably more," she said vehemently.

"But even if you had all the Bard's plays and sonnets learned by heart, I would still think you a fool. Let's review the facts, shall we? Yesterday, you came to the Vicarage looking like some wild Old Testament prophet and told poor Mrs. Cary you had something *particular* you wished to say to me. Today, you are clever enough to be caught by Jackey Lime kissing me in the private parlor of the Tudor Rose. Now you are driving me at what can only be described as a spanking pace through the village in full view of one of the busiest bodies in all Tanglewood Green. If I didn't know better, I would think you were trying to force *me* to marry *you!*"

"You may wish."

Her curiosity was aroused. "Were you never in your life warned against designing females? I have two brothers. Benedict, of course, never gets into scrapes, but Cary—well, even he knows better than to go about the place kissing people unless he very much wishes to marry them."

"Well, I don't wish to marry you, madam," he snapped. "Depend on it!"

"Indeed, I hope I may," she shot back.

"As a matter of fact, I have already chosen my match."

"Indeed? Where does one find a female grotesque?"

"Female grotesque?" He laughed. "I wouldn't call Lady Serena Calverstock a grotesque, would you?"

Juliet's mouth fell open, but she closed it with a determined snap.

"She's quite twenty times as pretty as you are, Miss Wayborn," Swale continued to goad her. "What is the matter? Why do you not wish me happy? Dear me, can it be that you actually entertained hopes of becoming Marchioness of Swale?"

"Not so much a hope as a nightmare!" she retorted.

"That's it," he responded cheerfully. "Save yourself

for my aging father. He has two sets of teeth, you know. One ivory and one wood. At night, he soaks them in vinegar in a glass on his bedside table. Which do you want him to wear when he kisses you?"

After that, they did not speak for a long time. As they came upon the third mile, Juliet suddenly gave a cry of surprise. Another curricle was in the road, coming toward them from the opposite direction.

"Look, Ginger! Isn't that—aren't those—?"

"I see them," he said, shaking off her hand. "I don't need you to tell me—"

"But aren't those *Cary's chestnuts?*" she cried.

Swale's head jerked around as the other curricle passed them. It was unfortunate that at just that moment, one of his grays would trod upon a stone and stumble. In the next moment, the curricle sprang several feet in the air, then came down with a crash on its side. The grays inexplicably turned off the road and fled a good twenty feet across the muddy meadow before Swale was able to get them under control.

Juliet, who had been flung clear of the car, was already getting to her feet. Her face and clothes were splashed with mud. "This would not have happened if you had let me drive!" she shouted angrily as she fought to keep her balance in the slick grass.

Swale's heart began to beat again. When he had looked over and seen his passenger gone from the seat, he had feared the worst. Nonetheless, he bristled at the criticism. "Is that so?" he shouted. "If you had not pulled my arm like the damn fool you are—!" He climbed over the side of the curricle and jumped down, sinking several inches in the squelching grass.

Juliet, reminded of why she had pulled his arm, turned to look down the road. The driver of the other curricle had turned and was coming back up the road toward them.

"Those *are* Cary's chestnuts!" she cried triumphantly. "It's Bernard!" Jumping up and down, she began waving her arms. Then, with a sharp cry of pain, she fell again. This time, she did not get up.

Swale, who had begun looking over the grays for signs of injury, heard her cry out and ran to her. Bernard heard her too and brought the chestnuts to a stop. "I'm coming to you, Miss Julie!" he shouted, but it was Swale's red hair that swam before Juliet's eyes first.

She said through gritted teeth, "My leg."

Swale's face, usually so ruddy, was almost white. "Your head is bleeding, you damn fool!" he muttered. "Will you be still?"

"I tell you, it's my leg," she argued weakly. "I can't stand up."

"You mustn't try," he said decisively. In the next moment, he had flung her over his shoulder like a sack of grain. "Go to the village at once and fetch the doctor," he told Cary Wayborn's groom. "Miss Wayborn is hurt."

Bernard stood his ground. "Miss Julie?"

"What are you doing here, Bernard?" she asked, her head somewhere beneath Swale's shoulder blades.

"Why, I came to see the wee Mademoiselle," he said, surprised. "Did she not tell you, Miss Julie? I knew she wouldn't like being stranded out here in the country. But never mind all that. Himself is after sending me for the doctor!"

"I am taking Miss Wayborn *there*," said Swale, pointing across the meadow.

Bernard squinted and saw in the distance a snug little farmhouse with a thatched roof and a reassuring curl of smoke coming from its chimney.

"Yes, Bernard," Juliet said, biting her lip. "I think you had better get the doctor."

Swale picked his way across the meadow. It was slow going. The ground was slick and treacherous, and he did not want to risk a fall.

"I beg your pardon," Juliet gasped, acutely aware that her bottom was bobbing up and down on Swale's shoulder, "but all the blood seems to be rushing to my head . . ."

With a groan of impatience, he shifted her from his shoulder into his arms. "You are not the slender wisp you appear," he said presently, grunting under her weight. He was obliged to ask that she put her arms around his neck as he foundered in the mud. She did so, but only with her eyes closed.

"Try to stay awake. Force your eyes open," he advised.

But Juliet preferred to screw her eyes shut and grit her teeth. The pain in her leg made her want to scream, and her head had begun to ache as well, but she would be damned before she broke down in front of Swale. It seemed an eternity before he got her to the farmhouse. He burst through the door unceremoniously, calling for the woman of the house.

Despite the fire and other signs of recent occupation, no one came forward to meet them. Swale found a chair near the fire and placed Juliet in it. Her face was ashen, and she was nearly unconscious. Her forehead was damp with perspiration, as though *she* had just carried *him* across the field. Her eyelids fluttered.

"You're looking green, Miss Wayborn," he said. "No, don't fall asleep on me!" He slapped her cheeks rapidly, and her eyes snapped open. "Where does it hurt?"

"Your grays . . . " she murmured, and he had to lean close to catch the feeble words. "Your lovely grays . . ."

"Never mind the bloody cattle."

"Please," she moaned, "my leg. I can't bear it."

He was more worried about the cut on the side of her head, just above the ear. Still calling for the woman of the house, he searched for something to stanch the flow of blood.

"Please!" Juliet was gritting her teeth. "Please help me!"

Swallowing a curse, he got down on his knees at her feet. "Is your left ankle usually so fat?" he inquired presently. "Have you a clubfoot?"

To his horror, she did not snap at him but silently gave way to tears, her face white and drawn.

He found a knife to cut the buttons from her walking boot. When he pulled it off, Juliet cried out in pain. He tore her stocking almost to the knee, noticing as he did so that she wore long, filmy lawn drawers trimmed with lace. From ankle to knee her leg was puffed and bright red, rapidly turning purple.

"I think it may be broken, Miss Wayborn," he said grimly. "Try and sit still. The doctor will be here soon. Why are there never any peasants at hand when one actually needs them?"

Suddenly, he thought of his flask. Quickly, he took it out of his pocket and handed it to her. She turned her face away, moaning.

"Drink it," he commanded.

"What is it?"

"Whisky," he told her, pressing it to her pale lips. "It will make you feel better."

She drank it, spluttering. For a second, she felt as if she had inhaled fire, then a pleasant, warm, tingling sensation invaded her limbs. She took another drink, then another. "I feel much better now," she said, smiling dreamily. "I feel like dancing."

"That's wonderful," he said. "No, sit still. No dancing for you, my dear."

"But, Ginger, I want to," she said stubbornly.

"Your head is bleeding," he told her sharply, "and your leg very likely is broken. Be a good girl, and sit still while I find something to bind your head."

"May I have more whisky, please?" she asked hopefully.

"No!"

"But I want—" she began, trying to climb to her feet.

"Dammit!" he said. "Will you do as you are told!" Putting his arms around her, he dragged her back down into the chair and held her there. She struggled weakly, then relaxed, going quite limp beneath him. He feared for a moment that she had slipped into unconsciousness, but he soon saw that her eyes were fixed on something over his shoulder.

"Hullo, Horatio," she said very gravely.

Then she began to giggle.

Swale hurriedly disentangled himself from her and turned to face the captain. Horatio Cary was staring at him with cold blue eyes. In his mind, he was back on the deck of his frigate about to order a round of flogging for the crew.

"I have sent the groom for the doctor," said Swale. "She is . . . Miss Wayborn is hurt, as you see. *Where* is the damned woman who lives here?"

Horatio continued to stare at him coldly.

"I daresay this appears worse than it is," said Swale.

"How so?" Horatio inquired.

"Well, you see, Cary, my Bowditch and her Fifi—"

"*What?*"

"My valet and Miss Wayborn's maid," he explained, "have eloped. We were just attempting to retrieve them when we met with an accident."

Horatio's eyes swept over him once more, then moved to Juliet. "Is this true, Juliet?"

With effort, Juliet's eyes focused on her handsome cousin. "He kissed me, Horatio," she blurted out, her gray eyes wide and serious. "But he did not offer me *carte blanche*."

Chapter 9

Sir Benedict disliked anything that took him away from his beloved Wayborn Hall, so to be called to Hertfordshire because of his sister's wild behavior was a severe trial for him. His resentment was tempered only slightly by the fact that she was bedridden with a badly bruised leg.

Upon arriving at the Vicarage, he spent half an hour closeted with Dr. Cary and Horatio in the Vicar's study. Both gentlemen assured the baronet that his sister had been compromised very thoroughly by Lord Swale.

"He came here determined to marry Cousin Juliet," Dr. Cary said flatly, "and he did not mean to go away without achieving his objective. A more determined man I never saw! His lordship arrived on Thursday and interviewed her alone in the drawing room and then again in the shrubbery after a . . . slight accident involving my china shepherdesses. Dear Juliet, with the usual feminine delicacy, swore she would not have him. Why, Mrs. Cary swore the same to me, but I didn't carry her off the next day! Anyone knows that a gently bred girl will always profess to be amazed and confused at the gentleman's first proposal. How would the world be if we men went about the thing with special licenses in our pockets, and at the lady's first refusal—"

"Had he a special license in his pocket?" Benedict exclaimed.

"He did indeed!" said Dr. Cary. "The boy at the Tudor Rose saw his lordship's valet unpacking the damned thing. I don't much care for the special license, Sir Benedict. A Christian man ought to marry in the parish of his baptism or in the parish of his betrothed's baptism. None of this gadding about the country or making a spectacle of one's self in St. George's! Vanitas, that is what I call these damned society weddings at St. George's."

Horatio intervened before his father's diatribe against the special license began in earnest. "When I confronted his lordship at Brisby's Farm, Sir Benedict, his lordship claimed the special license was for his manservant." Horatio's lips curled under his well-groomed mustache. "We are to believe that his lordship's valet and my cousin's maid were eloping. His lordship has even gone so far as to have his man carry off Juliet's maid. No one has seen either of them for nearly two days."

"I confess I am amazed," Benedict said slowly. "To learn that Lord Swale has come into Hertfordshire is puzzling enough, but that he should be so fixed upon my poor sister—! I should tell you, Dr. Cary, that not five days ago, I received from his Grace of Auckland a communication proposing marriage between Juliet and his son Geoffrey."

The Vicar regarded his guest with astonishment. "That is fortunate indeed, Sir Benedict," he said after a long moment, "for it is now imperative that the two young people marry. They were alone in Brisby's house for quite some time before my son arrived, you know. I don't doubt his lordship behaved as a gentleman," he added quickly. "Still, it is the appearance of the thing."

Horatio frowned. "But if his father is in favor of the match, why should Lord Swale come into Hertfordshire with a special license? He is bizarre, I think."

"I refused to give my consent to the match," said Benedict, frowning, "and Juliet is yet a minor."

Dr. Cary goggled at him. "You did what? Good God, man, are you mad? It is the match of the century. Our little Juliet, Duchess of Auckland! She could do no better."

"I do not like the man," said Benedict coldly. "I am convinced he would make my sister unhappy. He cannot control his temper, and his temper is *very* bad."

"My dear Sir Benedict," said Dr. Cary, scandalized. "One does not refuse a marquess merely because one does not like him. The Aucklands are very rich, you know, and Lord Swale is the heir. His father's influence is felt in the very highest circles. His Grace of Auckland has raised mere younger sons to the Cabinet, mere country curates to bishoprics—"

"Nonetheless, I have refused him," Benedict replied, unmoved. "Until Juliet comes into her majority, it is my duty to prevent her from making a foolish match."

"Foolish!" Dr. Cary was incredulous. "Foolish, the man calls it."

"We cannot agree, Dr. Cary," said Benedict with a small smile. "I would not see my sister wed to a violent, abusive man for twice the sum you have named. Lord Swale would be certain to make Juliet miserable. Naturally, if she wishes to sell herself to the Aucklands when she has reached the age of twenty-one, she will be within her rights to do so. But for now, I am her guardian, and I shan't sell her to anyone."

Dr. Cary grew red in the face. "That is not at all what I meant, sir!" he said huffily. "It is not a question of selling—!"

Horatio interrupted smoothly. "If it were Cynthia whom we were discussing, Sir Benedict, I'm sure my father would not be so ready to hand her over to this brute Swale!"

"Cynthia? Marry Lord Swale!" Dr. Cary laughed bitterly. "His Grace of Auckland would not be so quick to favor the match. We are not as illustrious as the Wayborns, you understand."

"Only consider what Lord Swale has done, Father," said Horatio quickly. "Juliet's guardian refused his consent, and what does the fellow do but run her to earth and press his suit anyway! Then, when Juliet refuses him, he has her maid carried off, knowing that Juliet will feel obligated to go after the silly thing and bring her back. I begin to suspect that his Grace of Auckland has threatened to cut off his lordship's allowance if he does not make the match."

"Or, perhaps I offended his lordship's pride," Benedict said thoughtfully. "I did not hesitate to give my reasons for refusing my consent. Perhaps it was wrong of me to excoriate him so, but I had just seen him break the nose of Mr. Eustace Calverstock in St. James's Street, and my feelings were offended in every way."

"Whatever the reason, his lordship obviously came into Hertfordshire to force Juliet to marry him," said Horatio angrily.

"And he has succeeded very handsomely," said Dr. Cary with as much disapproval as pleasure. "They *must* marry now. There is nothing else for it. Dear Juliet will be ruined if they do not marry."

Benedict smiled coldly. "And who knows what the Aucklands' influence may do for us in exchange?

Perhaps I shall be raised to the Cabinet. Perhaps *you* will be raised to a bishopric."

Dr. Cary nodded. "Exactly so, Sir Benedict. Exactly so. If I am to officiate at the wedding of the Duke of Auckland's heir, a bishopric would not be such a far-fetched thing."

Benedict got to his feet. "I would like to see my sister now, if I may."

Juliet was in bed, her injured leg propped up with feather pillows. "It isn't broken," she said quickly, setting aside her book as Benedict entered the room. "The splint is to keep me from bruising it again, that is all. Actually, the swelling has gone down a great deal, don't you agree, Cynthia?"

Benedict had not seen Cynthia upon entering the room. "Miss Cary," he said now, bending over her hand. "I hope my sister has not distressed you too much."

"No, indeed, sir," said Cynthia quickly. "Though I was very worried that her leg *was* broken. And her head was bleeding when they brought her home to us. Mr. Elliott put four stitches in her scalp, you know." She glanced at her cousin. "She's very worried, Sir Benedict, that you will make her marry Lord Swale. I—I wish you wouldn't! I daresay you think me impertinent, but I wish you wouldn't! His lordship has the most dreadful temper. In a fit of anger, he broke one of my father's cabinets."

"Was that not an accident?" Benedict asked.

Cynthia shook her head. "Indeed, it was not, sir! Though Juliet told my father it was—" She broke off unhappily. "I do not mean to say that she *lied*—"

Benedict smiled at her. "I am glad you still regard my sister well enough to defend her, Miss Cary. Would you be good enough to grant me a private interview with her?"

"Is she not the loveliest, sweetest, most divine creature you ever saw?" Juliet inquired brightly when Cynthia had left them alone. "She's an absolute angel. When are you going to declare yourself?"

Benedict frowned at her. "Do not think to distract me, Juliet. This is the second time in a week you have escaped your guardians to go driving in the country with Lord Swale."

Juliet was astonished. "How can you compare one thing with the other?" she cried angrily. "The race was completely different! I see now it was wrong of me to dress up like Cary and humiliate Ginger in that shabby manner. But you can not fault me for *this!* I thought my Fifi to be in the gravest danger. My intentions were good, Benedict, and really, it would have been all right if we hadn't overturned."

"You're right, Juliet. By comparison to the present situation, the race was completely innocent! On that occasion, you stayed in your brother's curricle, and Lord Swale stayed in his. There was no contact between you. Have you no sense?"

"I expect you think I don't," she answered sullenly. "I expect you have come to lecture me on the error of my ways. Well, I don't see what I have done that is so wrong. I was only trying to save my Fifi, and I won't apologize for that."

Benedict sighed and sat down in a chair near the window. "My dear Juliet," he said, "if your maid has been carried off by a villain, there are things that can and should be done. You ought to have reported the incident to the authorities and left them to it."

"I did not know she had been carried off when I went to see Ginger—Lord Swale," she corrected herself hastily. "Fifi told me that his lordship's man had been imposing on her. I went to make Swale put a stop to it, that's all. But when I was there, the boots brought his lordship a note from his Bowditch saying that he and my Fifi were eloping. We had to go after them, Benedict! I couldn't let my Fifi be carried off by his Bowditch." She sighed. "I am bound to say that I was never more deceived in my life! If Bowditch has married her, he is to be pitied."

"You wanted a French maid," he reminded her. "Against my advice, you hired Mademoiselle. At Wayborn Hall, you will have a dependable English girl—"

"Wayborn Hall!"

"Yes, my girl," he told her curtly. "You didn't think I would continue to inflict your society upon the good people of Hertfordshire after this, your latest adventure?"

"You can't take me away *now*," she pointed out. "I can't even walk."

"As soon as you are well enough to travel," he assured her, "I am taking you home myself. You are grown quite wild, Juliet! I don't know what I am to do with you. You have always been willful, but I never thought of you as bold and unmanageable. Your character, which I was always used to admire, is in need of a severe correction."

"My God, Benedict," she cried weakly. "I had rather you *beat* me than say such terrible things! Indeed, I do not deserve it!"

"Never mind," he said in a gentler tone. "I will say no more about it. You will want to know how Cary is recovering."

"Oh, yes," she breathed, grateful for the change in subject. "How is he?"

"Much vexed to be kept in bed while his bones knit," said Benedict. "Not best pleased that Lord Swale has broke young Calverstock's nose."

"What?" cried Juliet, her eyes lighting with excitement. "Ginger broke Stacy's nose? I expect it was at the boxing saloon?"

"No, indeed," said Benedict. "It happened on the street in front of White's. And a more disgusting display of temper I have never seen. Anyone else would have been expelled permanently from the club, but he is a duke's son. They will allow him to return next year. Disgusting."

"Was he provoked?"

"I daresay he was," Benedict responded dryly. "I imagine that having one's nose broken can be quite provoking."

"Not Stacy!" Juliet said scornfully. "Ginger. Stacy must have jolly well provoked him to get his nose broken. Was there a duel?"

"Certainly not," said Benedict, appalled by her bloodthirstiness. "Mr. Calverstock quite rationally declined to issue a challenge."

"Rather poor-spirited of him to be rational at such a time," Juliet observed scornfully. "But I expect Swale is the one they will condemn. It's so unfair! He says he did not hire anyone to break Cary's arm, and I believe him. He told me you believed him too. He says it was Lord Redfylde."

"He actually named Lord Redfylde as the guilty party?" Benedict shook his head. "That is very wrong of him when he has no proof. At best, he is a suspect."

"No proof? Redfylde placed a wager of ten thousand pounds—on Ginger, if you please!"

"That is singular," said Benedict, "but it is not proof he is behind the attack on our brother."

"I think," she said stubbornly, "it was very clever of Ginger to put it all together."

Sir Benedict's mouth twitched. "Yes, indeed. Very clever. His lordship is to be congratulated on his mental dexterity."

"Then you don't believe my Lord Swale is guilty?" she asked eagerly, a great deal too eagerly for her brother's comfort.

"I never thought he had anything to do with the attack on our brother," Benedict replied. "It is not in his lordship's character to hire mercenaries. He would enjoy the experience of breaking a man's arm, I think. Possibly even a woman's."

Juliet laughed. "Come now, Benedict! That is absurd. I'm sure I have said things far more provoking than Stacy Calverstock, and *my* nose is intact. The worst he could do to a woman is grab her knitting basket and fling it across the room." She thought suddenly of his lordship's kiss, and her cheeks turned pink. Fortunately, her brother did not notice.

A smile touched his lips. "That is how Dr. Cary's cabinet was broken, I collect."

"And several of those wretched shepherdesses of which he is so proud," said Juliet. "You are *quite* wrong about Ginger if you think he would ever harm a woman. I admit his temper is very ill-governed, but I think it must be very hard to be accused falsely of a crime. Even *you* might lose your temper, Benedict, under such trying circumstances. To be called a coward and a cheat and a liar and then to be humiliated by a— a girl—! Yes, I think it must be very hard for a proud man like Ginger."

Benedict looked at her intently. "Then you're not afraid of him?"

Juliet laughed. "Afraid of Ginger? Really, he's all thunder and no lightning. Practically an infant when it comes to women. In fact, I'm amazed some enterprising female didn't scoop him up long ago. Just look at the scrape he got into with me."

"Yes, my dear. Let us look at it very carefully."

Juliet gave him a hard look. "If I were an ambitious,

designing female—if my excellent brother were greedy and unscrupulous, which of course, he isn't—Ginger would have to marry me, I suppose. Fortunately for him, I am *not* ambitious, and you're not greedy. We mayn't like him very well, but he doesn't deserve to be tricked into a marriage he doesn't want."

Benedict appeared relieved. "Then you don't wish to marry him."

"What a piece of nonsense anyway," Juliet said irritably. "Just because he kissed me!"

Benedict turned pale. "Did he kiss you?"

"It was not at all romantic!" she said hastily.

"No?"

"Not in the least," she assured him. "It was quite horrid—he'd been eating sausages. He only kissed me because I was saying something he didn't like. I expect if I had been Stacy Calverstock he might have broken my nose."

"I expect he would have," said Benedict grimly. "God help me, for a moment when I was speaking to Dr. Cary, I wavered. I thought I might actually have no choice but to welcome him into the family. But it is impossible. I would not see you married to a man we can't respect, and a man who won't govern his passions can never be respected. I'm glad you dislike him, my dear."

"Well, I don't dislike him," she said haltingly, "and I wish you would not hate him, Benedict. Not everyone has your marvelous self-control. I don't, anyway, and neither does Cary. Really, no one has it, but you! As for Ginger, do you know he carried me all the way to that farmhouse?"

Benedict shrugged. "He could do no less—he was responsible for your injuries. That he would come here against my expressed wishes and make love to you is intolerable."

"Make love to me!" Juliet cried. "I think perhaps my ears deceive me. Did you say that Ginger came here to make love to me?"

Benedict frowned. "Did he not ask you to marry him?"

"Certainly not! You have been listening too much to Horatio and Cousin Wilfred."

"Do you know he came here with a special license?"

"That wasn't his," she told him. "It really was Bowditch with designs upon Fifi. Lord Swale only came into Herts looking for a small, comfortable place within easy distance of London. I expect his inquiries about Tanglewood led him to the Vicarage, and to me."

"He told you he was looking for a house in the country?"

"Yes."

"Then he is a liar!" said Benedict grimly. "I knew he was an ill-tempered brute when he broke Mr. Calverstock's nose—that is why I refused to consent to the marriage—but I didn't think him a liar."

Juliet was bewildered. "Stacy asked for your consent, and you refused him because his nose was broken? This is intolerable. How dare he go behind my back and ask you when I refused him!"

"Not Mr. Calverstock," Benedict told her. "Swale. More accurately, Swale's father."

Juliet gasped. "The Duke of Auckland wants to marry me? Oh no!"

Benedict chuckled softly. "His Grace was convinced that a marriage between our two families would quiet any scandal arising from Cary's injury and the curricle race, but he did not mean to sacrifice himself, my dear. The match his Grace proposed was between his son and my sister."

"Ginger and me?" Juliet turned pale. "But that is

impossible. He's fixed on Serena Calverstock. He told me so himself."

Benedict frowned slightly. "I've seen no notice in the papers. I expect that is wishful thinking on his part. Undoubtedly, if you married the scapegrace, Society would conclude his innocence. That is the chief appeal of the marriage. I daresay his Grace made certain concessions that would make it still more attractive to his son."

"Then you truly believe he came here to ask me to marry him? He *did* tell Mrs. Cary he had something particular he wished to say to me," Juliet said thoughtfully. "But I never dreamed . . . Oh, Benedict, I made fun of him."

"He came here *after* I told him I'd never consent to the marriage," said Benedict. "I call that underhanded and ungentlemanlike, thoroughly in keeping with what I know of Swale."

"Oh, poor Ginger," she murmured. "I was really horrid to him. I wouldn't even milord him. What he must think of me."

"What must he think of *you!* Juliet, you astonish me."

"But he came all this way to ask me to marry him," she protested, "and I laughed in his face. I threw yarn at him, and I set his dinner on fire too, poor man. If I'd known his father had sent him here to solicit my hand, I should never have been so cruel. Especially when he didn't really *want* to ask me to marry him and was probably frightened to death I'd accept!"

"Good God," Benedict murmured. "Would you have accepted him?"

"Of course not," said Juliet. "No. But I ought to have listened to him politely, thanked him for the honor, and refused him with civility at least. Especially him. I've wronged him so much. If he is in disgrace, it's my fault. I publicly accused him. If I hadn't done that—"

"If you hadn't, Mr. Calverstock undoubtedly would have."

"Yes, but *I* did do it. It's no use dodging blame. You were absolutely right," she continued in bitter self-deprecation. "It was stupid and rash. I can never show my face in Society again, and I've damaged the reputation of a man who did not deserve it. I'm so sorry, Benedict."

Benedict climbed to his feet. "Don't dwell on it, my dear. Swale's reputation was pretty corroded at the start. I expect I must go down to the Tudor Rose and tell his lordship you do not wish to force him to marry you, after all."

Juliet was startled. "Has he not gone back to London?" Her eyes widened in alarm. "His grays— were his horses very badly injured? Oh, God! How selfish of me not to inquire before!"

"I'll ask him when I see him, if you like. Did you truly not know he was here?" Benedict frowned. "Dr. Cary tells me he called only this morning, anxious to be of assistance to you."

"Did he? No one told me."

"Do you wish to see him?"

"Oh no," his sister replied, looking rather flustered. "If he did call, it was only from a sense of obligation, I'm sure. I daresay he has no wish ever to see me again. It would be terribly awkward if we were to see each other again. But do please inquire after his horses, Benedict. Cattle, he calls them."

Juliet looked down at her hands in embarrassment. "And will you please tell him that I'm excessively sorry? I may have said some very foolish things when we were in the cottage . . . I never meant to cause him so much trouble. It must have been the whisky."

Benedict sighed and, with an air of weary detachment, resumed his seat. "Whisky?"

"Does this mean our Miss Julie is going to be a Duchess?" Jackey Lime inquired excitedly as he polished Lord Swale's boots in the private parlor of the Tudor Rose.

"She will be a Marchioness," Swale told the boy. "She won't be a Duchess until my father shuffles off the mortal coil, and between us, the old fool plans to live forever."

"A Marchioness." Jackey appeared doubtful. "Is that good, milord?"

Swale smiled at the boy. It was remarkable, really, how calm he was in the face of impending doom. "It's very, very good, Jackey," he assured the boy.

"Will she have jewels and carriages?" Jackey demanded.

"She will have all the jewels and carriages she can eat," Swale promised.

Mrs. Sprigge came in and glared at Swale. "Sir Benedict Wayborn is here to see your lordship," she said. "He don't look happy," she added with a malicious gleam in her eye.

The man himself appeared in the doorway, pallid with anger.

"This is a respectable establishment," Mrs. Sprigge said, lingering. "That Miss Julie should be insulted in my parlor is intolerable, sir! You mustn't blame Mr. Sprigge, Sir Benedict. How was he to know the lordship would be so naughty? You're a wicked, wicked lordship," she scolded Swale, "and I don't mind telling you there's no place at the Tudor Rose for a rake's progress!"

This was not the first time it had been suggested to

Swale that he leave the inn, but he did not take it seriously since no shortage of rabbit pie had developed. He ignored Mrs. Sprigge and addressed himself to Juliet's brother. "Is she well, sir? Is Miss Wayborn quite well? Those damned Carys won't let me near her! They won't tell me a thing. Should I send to London for my family's surgeon? Mr. Norton would come at a moment's notice."

"Will you leave us, please, Mrs. Sprigge?" said Benedict. For a moment after she had left, taking Jackey Lime with her, he seemed busy fiddling with his stick, polishing its silver head obsessively with his thumb. In reality, he did not trust himself to speak. He seated himself and said quietly, "There are surgeons enough in Hertfordshire, my lord."

"Dammit, man!" Swale exploded. "Is she all right?"

"My sister need not concern you, my lord," Benedict informed him coldly.

"Not concern me? Sir Benedict, I was driving. I accept full responsibility for the accident. Naturally, Miss Wayborn's injuries concern me. They concern me very much."

"First, my brother's arm, and now, my sister's leg," Benedict remarked in exasperation. "Are we never to be rid of you, sir? You destroy all in your path. You cling like ivy. You persist like the plague. I heartily wish you to the devil."

"If we're to be brothers, you mustn't wish me to the devil, Sir Benedict."

Benedict lifted a brow. "Brothers, my lord? Why should we be brothers?"

"Come now," said Swale, shrugging his shoulders like a pugilist preparing to enter the ring, "I know perfectly well I'm caught like a rat in a trap. If I'm to marry your sister—"

"You must allow me to tell you that you will never marry my sister," said Benedict.

Swale was taken aback by this calm statement. "But haven't I ruined her or something?" he demanded. "Your sister, of course, is quite innocent, but the Carys seem to think I've compromised her. Dammit, man! Is her leg broke? Is she crippled?"

"My sister will make a full recovery, as I hope, my brother will." Benedict looked at him coldly. "I am Juliet's guardian. I value her happiness above the opinion of the world. I won't be bullied by this shabby trick into giving my sister to you, my lord, particularly since the marriage is disagreeable to her."

"What shabby trick?" Swale's face was red, and his green eyes narrowed dangerously. "I used no trick. All of my dealings with your sister have been honest, which is a sight more than she can say about her dealings with me! Did she say the marriage was disagreeable to her? Not half as disagreeable as it is to me, let me tell you!"

"Do you deny that you came to Hertfordshire to make my sister marry you?"

"I do deny it," said Swale hotly. "I never had the least intention of marrying your sister."

"No, indeed," Benedict murmured. "Milord is here looking for a house within easy distance to London!"

Confronted with the lie, Swale blushed a dark red. "As a matter of fact," he said with dignity, "I *do* want a house within easy distance of London. Doesn't everyone?"

"It seems to be quite the thing indeed," said Sir Benedict with a very grave expression. "My Lord Redfylde is also seeking a house within a few miles of London."

"Redfylde!" Swale's eyes narrowed to slits.

"Yes, my lord," said Benedict. "Redfylde."

"Is he in Hertfordshire?" Swale demanded. "Lead

me to him. I have a crow to pluck with my Lord Redfylde!"

"And yet," Benedict observed, "rather than stay in London and pluck it, you chose to pursue my sister into Hertfordshire. Is that not a trifle curious?"

"I told you," Swale said coldly, "I was interested in purchasing a country estate within easy—"

"Easy distance of London," Benedict finished. "Very well, my lord. My sister's being in this very place, in her cousins' house, must have been a very shocking coincidence for you."

"Well," said Swale, wilting beneath Benedict's fierce gaze, "I had an idea she was here. I had an idea of seeing her. I had an idea that things must have been very rough on her after the race."

"And you came here to smooth out the rough?" Benedict snorted unpleasantly. "Well done, my lord. She is now *much* better off."

"I didn't mean to make things worse, you know," Swale said. "I've . . . I've no animosity toward her. She owned her mistake, and she has apologized to me. Well, perhaps I exaggerate when I say she apologized. But, at any rate, if she wants me to marry her, I will. Reluctantly."

"That is handsome of you, my lord," said Benedict, "but, alas, you must seek some other young woman upon whom to practice your amazing condescension. My sister seems to prefer the ignominy of being known forever as the Young Lady Who."

"Your sister, if you don't mind my saying so, is an ass," said Swale. "And if you were any sort of guardian, you would make her marry me. She has been alone with me here in this very room. That infernal boy saw us together. You know we were seen driving through the village together. We were quite alone at that bloody farm, and when that ass Captain Cary walked in, she was in my arms. Well, dammit! Who's going to marry her now?"

"Since it is definitely not to be Lord Swale," Benedict replied, "the question does not overly concern me. But, in case it concerns *you*, my lord, you should know that Captain Cary has asked my permission to marry Miss Wayborn. So you needn't worry she will die an old maid."

"She's going to marry *him*?" Swale scowled. "The man is a pompous ass and a dead bore."

"That will be my sister's decision," Benedict replied.

"That *is* a great relief to me," Swale said after a moment. "Yes, she *should* marry him, and quickly too, before he changes his mind. He'll make her a famous husband. They will suit very well indeed—they have matching coats with shiny brass buttons already."

"I'm excessively glad your lordship approves."

"Let me be the first to toast the happy couple. I suppose he is with her now, holding her little hand and reciting Shakespeare's poetry in the original Danish. I daresay *he* wouldn't know what to do if a snake got inside her clothes!"

"I have nothing more to say to you, my lord." Benedict seemed about to leave, but he hesitated. "My sister, however, asked if I would inquire after your horses."

"My grays?" Swale appeared distracted. "She asked after them, did she? You may tell her that Jupiter has quite a nasty scratch, and Mercury has a big knee."

"Will they recover? It would grieve my sister if they had to be put down."

"Put down? Oh, no. The curricle was smashed, of course—"

"Miss Wayborn did not inquire after your curricle, my lord," Sir Benedict informed him curtly, then coldly took his leave.

Chapter 10

In the elegant reception room of her London town house, Lady Maria Fitzwilliam extended her hand to Mr. Alexander Devize.

"Good evening, my lady. My mother and my sister have asked me to convey their regrets."

Lady Maria inclined her head. She was a snub-nosed, red-haired young woman of twenty-eight. If she was considered attractive, it was chiefly due to a pair of mischievous, laughing dark eyes, but when she was angry, the nostrils of her snub nose tended to flare and her expressive eyes grew very cold. The nostrils flared now as Alex bent over her hand.

"Indeed?" she said in a rather hard voice. "What excuse did they give? Headache? A sick relative? Believe me, I have heard every possible excuse in existence tonight!" With an angry snap, she opened her painted ivory fan. "Though I did expect more from my Lady Devize and my Lady Cheviot!"

Alex's face reddened with embarrassment as he looked around the elegant ball room. By ordinary standards, the ball was well-attended, but the very best Ton were conspicuous by their absence. This was the

Fitzwilliams' first ball as a married couple, and the Duke's daughter was livid. It ought to have been a runaway success. But the only ladies in attendance were the wives of the officers of her husband's former regiment, many of whom she had invited merely as a courtesy to her husband. And she very much suspected that many of these ladies had attended only as a courtesy to *their* husbands and that they would have preferred to stay away.

Having never supposed that the spurious accusations leveled against her brother by people she had never heard of would ever affect her own family's consequence, Maria was seriously vexed. Who were the Wayborns? Old County, she was told, which she took to mean little country nobodies. Her husband could never explain to her how a mere baronetcy—and a Surrey baronetcy, at that!—could trump all the wealth and influence of the Duchy of Auckland.

"Well?" she demanded of Mr. Devize. "They asked you to make their excuses. Make them!"

"It's little Harry Cheviot, I'm afraid," the baron's son was obliged to say. "My nephew is quite ill, and his Mamma and Grandmamma have stayed at home to nurse him."

"Are you quite certain he did not fall out of a tree?" Maria inquired coldly. "Quite a few children appear to have fallen out of trees today."

The lady's husband, Colonel Fitzwilliam, coughed lightly. "My dear, it's not Mr. Devize's fault."

"My brother," Maria said in a low, stifled voice, "does not cheat! It is my opinion that Mr. Wayborn was set upon by footpads and only concocted this bizarre story because he knew he would lose the race by default!"

"Mr. Wayborn *did* lose by default," Alex reminded her. "Miss Wayborn conceded."

"Oh, the despicable sister." Perhaps it was unreasonable, but Lady Maria held Miss Wayborn entirely responsible for her brother's disgrace and the poor turnout at her ball. "Miss Whip, they call her! I do not know the young woman, Mr. Devize. I was away on my honeymoon when she came out, though I understand this is her *second* season. No surprise she was unable to find a husband in her *first* season," Maria added spitefully, quite forgetting that she herself had enjoyed nearly ten Seasons as a spinster before finally leading Colonel Henry Fitzwilliam to the altar. "Are you at all acquainted with Miss Wayborn, Mr. Devize?"

"I know her a little," he admitted.

"I hear such things as make me shudder," said Maria. "She crops her head like a boy, smokes cigars, wears trousers, and takes snuff!"

"I have never observed the lady engaged in any of those activities," said Alex, and Maria heard the slight stress he placed on the word 'lady.'

"And the *lady's* family?"

"The Surrey branch of the Wayborn clan. That is all I can tell your ladyship."

"There is an Earl Wayborn," said Colonel Fitzwilliam. "His lordship's seat is at Westlands, not far from my own boyhood home of Matlock."

"I expect his Surrey relations trade freely upon Earl Wayborn's good name," Maria said scornfully. "Let us hope Miss Wayborn does not drag them all under. Miss Wayborn herself is quite sunk. All good society must be closed to her now."

"She is to be pitied," the Colonel murmured.

"Pitied?" Maria frowned. "Rather, she is to be ostracized. She is to be punished for her impropriety, her insolence, her impudence . . . her willful disregard of civility and the deference due my brother's rank!"

Alex was taken aback. "You are aware, are you not,

that your father has been at some pains to arrange a marriage between your brother and Miss Wayborn?"

Maria was appalled. "My brother marry Miss Wayborn?" she cried. "I *don't* think!"

"You needn't worry anything will come of his Grace's efforts," Alex assured her. "Sir Benedict Wayborn, the lady's brother, strangled the idea at birth. Apparently, he does not desire my Lord Swale as a brother. He would not confide his sister's happiness into your brother's keeping."

Maria's cheeks reddened with the Ambler nettlerash. "How dare he say such a thing!" she cried, trembling with rage. "My father honors him too much, and this is his answer? Insupportable! Insufferable conceit!"

Alex chuckled. "Swale was also enraged. You will laugh, my lady, when I tell you the revenge your brother is plotting against that family."

"Well?" said Maria, her nostrils flaring.

"Geoffrey means to find Miss Wayborn wherever her family has hidden her and make her fall in love with him. Then he'll spurn her, breaking her heart." Alex's eyes danced at the absurdity of his red-haired friend in the role of Casanova, but Maria recoiled in alarm.

Colonel Fitzwilliam frowned. "That is very bad of Geoffrey. Miss Wayborn must be wretched enough without he makes her a figure of fun."

"But—where *is* my brother?" Maria demanded. "I haven't seen Geoffrey since the damnable race. I expected him to attend my ball, you know. He does not even send his regrets."

"Perhaps," Alex said, "he has fallen from a tree."

"I had rather he were dead at the bottom of the Thames than anywhere near Miss Wayborn," Maria declared stoutly.

"My dear, you do not mean it," Fitzwilliam murmured.

Maria seemed about to defy her husband and say that, Yes, she did mean it, but she was forestalled by the unexpected arrival of Lord Redfylde and his sister-in-law, Lady Serena Calverstock. There was a stir among the little gathering of ladies and gentlemen as the raven-haired beauty with shining violet eyes entered the room escorted by the tall, fair-haired Marquess.

Lord Redfylde bowed over his hostess's hand and apologized for the absence of his wife, who was awaiting the birth of their third child. Lady Maria civilly offered her wishes that the child would be a boy this time. Redfylde needed an heir, and his wife seemed to breed only daughters, and these with the greatest of difficulty. Redfylde then presented his sister-in-law.

Lady Serena greeted Maria with a degree of familiarity that the Duke's daughter might have found objectionable at another time, but on this occasion, she was so pleased Lord Redfylde had not snubbed her that she accepted Serena's effusive compliments on her ballroom decorations almost with pleasure.

The two ladies knew one another slightly, and they had shared a number of London Seasons but had never been friends. Maria had been clever enough to realize that all her own vivacity and wit would be as nothing compared to Serena's exquisite beauty and taste, so she had always avoided the lady celebrated with the sobriquet of La Serenissima.

Serena was dressed very simply in a white pleated dress with a spray of spotted orchids on one shoulder and diamond pins sprinkled in her jet black hair. Maria felt overdressed and stuffy in her own gown of garnet velvet, as dumpy and out of date as any poor lieutenant's wife. Whatever they felt, the two ladies studied each other's gowns, correctly identified the modistes who had made them, and with brilliant smiles, pronounced their creations universally charming. Maria then politely inquired after the health of Serena's sister, Lady Redfylde.

"Dear Constance," murmured Serena. "She is not at all well. Mr. Norton has advised a remove from London—and in the midst of the Season. So inconvenient! My Lord Redfylde has been very busy this week seeking a comfortable house within easy distance of London."

"It is most inconvenient at the top of the Season," Redfylde added, "but it cannot be helped."

Serena spoke in a lowered tone to Maria. "Please do not be offended if we don't stay long, my lady. Indeed, I was determined to stay at home with my sister all evening, but Redfylde insisted we come. My lord feels very keenly any slight upon the honor of a fellow nobleman, and he hopes that these dreadful rumors about your brother may be crushed at once. If it were not for her condition, do please know that Lady Redfylde would be here herself."

"Thank you, my dear," said Maria with real gratitude. "We are discovering now who our real friends are."

"Did you not attend the race, my lord?" Alex asked, turning to the Marquess of Redfylde. He cast into his memory, but he could not recall seeing Lord Redfylde's proudly sculpted face and ash-blond hair either at the Black Lantern Inn or at the finish line in Southend. Surely, that was a curious lapse in a man who had hazarded ten thousand pounds on the outcome!

Incredibly, Lord Redfylde begged to know which race, as Ascot had not yet taken place. When told Mr. Devize was referring to the infamous curricle race from London to Southend, he coolly replied, "I haven't time for such nonsense, Mr. Devize. I have been looking for a country house. Redfylde, for all its beauties, is too far from London to be of any use to us on this occasion."

"My Lord Redfylde has just taken Silvercombe in Surrey," Serena told the company. "I wish he had not! We will be rubbing shoulders with the Wayborns, for Sir Benedict of Wayborn Hall is to be our nearest neighbor."

"Your ladyship was not always so adverse to rubbing shoulders with the Wayborns," said Alex a little sharply. "Mr. Cary Wayborn's attentions had grown very marked in these last few weeks, and I had often seen you riding with Miss Wayborn in the Park."

"My dear Mr. Devize," murmured the lady, her dark lashes sweeping her cheek. "I did not see you there. Yes, I am a little acquainted with the Wayborns, but, you know, that was *before* . . ." Her beautiful violet eyes glinted. "But where is your dear Mamma, Mr. Devize? Where is Lady Cheviot? I long to see your charming sister."

"They did not trouble to come," said Maria, linking her arm with Serena's. "Most of the ladies and half the gentlemen have stayed away tonight. I consider it very insolent, their taking the Wayborns' part against the Aucklands'!"

"Oh, my dear Lady Maria," cried Serena. "I could not—I would not—abandon you in your darkest hour. It is most unfair! What your poor brother must be feeling!"

"Most unfair," Lord Redfylde echoed.

"I am sure it is all a dreadful mistake," Serena went on blithely. "There is no possible way that Lord Swale would employ such hole-and-corner tactics."

"You're very kind," murmured Lady Maria.

Alex's eyes narrowed. Like many gentlemen of rank and fortune, he had enjoyed a brief flirtation with Lady Serena, and he had never quite forgiven her for ending the affair before he was ready. "Was it not your cousin Stacy Calverstock who accused Lord Swale?"

Lord Redfylde made a choking sound. "Calverstock is an ass!"

Serena lightly touched his arm. "My poor cousin!" she murmured. "He is bewitched by Miss Wayborn, I think. He'll do anything to please her. He says even now that he will not give her up. I fear he will do something quite foolish."

Lord Redfylde patted her hand reassuringly. "He will give her up indeed, my dear. I will see to that. There is no possible way I will allow him to connect my family to such an immodest young lady."

Alex was shocked. "Lady Serena does not mean to suggest that Mr. Calverstock accused Lord Swale merely to please Miss Wayborn?"

"No, indeed," Serena replied. "Eustace and Mr. Cary Wayborn have been friends since boyhood. He feels it is his duty to support his friend and his friend's sister."

"If the gentlemen both say Mr. Wayborn's attackers mentioned Lord Swale by name," said Alex, "I think we must take them at their word."

"Why," demanded Maria, "when it is so obviously a lie?"

"Let us say they *did* mention his name," said Lord Redfylde irritably. "What does it signify? They are villains. They will say anything. Lord Swale is a Peer of the Realm, like myself. Surely, that places him above reproach."

"Precisely," said Maria. "It is absurd that my brother should be condemned by a few words from the uncivilized curs who attacked Mr. Wayborn. If indeed he was attacked."

Serena scanned the ballroom restlessly. "Indeed," she said. "Anyone who knows my Lord Swale would never credit it for a moment. Why should he wish Mr. Wayborn any harm?"

"I believe the inference is that Lord Swale wanted to win his race by default," said Redfylde.

"Where is the sport in that?" scoffed Maria. "There is no possible way my brother would deny himself the pleasure of defeating Mr. Wayborn's chestnuts."

"A great deal of money is hazarded on these events," Alex said, watching Lord Redfylde closely. "Someone else may have wanted to deny your brother that pleasure, Lady Maria."

Redfylde stiffened perceptibly. "What do you mean by that remark, sir?"

"I believe it is more than a coincidence that Mr. Wayborn was attacked on the eve of the race," Alex replied. "I believe the attack was carefully planned to prevent him from ever reaching the Black Lantern on the morning of the race."

Redfylde's lip curled in disdain. "Are you Mr. Wayborn's champion, sir?"

Alex bowed to him. "When Mr. Wayborn's attackers implicated my friend in their crime, they made an implacable enemy of me. My friend's name is blackened, and while Mr. Wayborn is going to recover, it was a very near thing. Whoever is responsible for this outrage, my lord, will be found out. I am determined he will be found out."

Lord Redfylde smirked. "I wish you luck in your endeavors, Mr. Devize. Will you take up the cudgels for poor Miss Wayborn as well? Do you mean to assist her back into Society?" He laughed briefly.

"I don't doubt she has gone back to Surrey," said Maria, shrugging her shoulders, "and has no idea of ever moving in society again."

"I pray not," said Lord Redfylde with a shudder. "If she has, I wish Sir Benedict would not call on me at

Silvercombe. I certainly do not wish for my Lady Redfylde to be nuisanced by Miss Wayborn."

Alex regarded him with loathing. If, as he suspected, Lord Redfylde was behind the attack on Cary Wayborn, his lordship's disdain for the family seemed singularly ill-bred.

"Don't worry on that score, my lord," Lady Serena assured her brother-in-law. "Poor Captain Cary was taxed with the duty of escorting his cousin into Hertfordshire, not Surrey. It seems unfair to burden the lady's cousins, but we cannot blame Sir Benedict for not wanting her in Surrey. I pity Captain Cary."

"Captain Cary!" exclaimed Maria. "That handsome young man is Miss Wayborn's cousin?"

"I only hope," said Lord Redfylde, "that her unladylike escapade will not cost him his chances for a knighthood. It was due to my influence, you know, that he received his commission in the Navy."

"I had no idea she was such a hoyden," said Serena with unwholesome relish. "I am sure no one was as shocked as the poor Captain to discover her true character, but he feels an obligation to her that she is certain to exploit to her own advantage."

"It would seem Miss Wayborn has bewitched the Captain, as well as poor Mr. Calverstock," said Maria. She drew Serena away and whispered to her as they took a turn together around the room. "I am loath to concede anything to Miss Wayborn, but if Captain Cary marries her, at least my brother and your cousin will be safe."

"Your brother!" Lady Serena was clearly startled. "What do you mean, Lady Maria? Do you mean to say that Miss Wayborn has pretensions of becoming . . . becoming *your sister?*" She clucked her tongue. "She must be a clever puss indeed to have *three* gentlemen languishing in her toils."

"I don't care who the poisonous wretch marries as long as it is not my brother!" Maria's dark eyes flashed dangerously. "I married for love, and I am determined my brother will also."

Serena sighed wistfully. "Are you very much in love, ma'am? Your husband, I collect, was a military gentleman. I hope you were not too long parted by the war."

"Four years," Maria said rather proudly. "Four long years I waited for my Henry to come back to me. I would have married him before he went away, but neither he nor my father would consent to it. I should be free, they both said. What nonsense!"

"How dreadful it must have been for you, my dear Maria."

"But how happy I was to hear of his advancement," the Duke's daughter replied, gazing fondly across the room to where her husband stood. He was a quiet man of thirty-five with a plain, grave face, but she clearly adored him. "And how happy I was when he returned to me. He is truly the best of husbands."

"You are very fortunate indeed," said Lady Serena. "This dreadful war has separated some lovers for eternity."

Lady Maria was startled. "You, Serena?"

Serena smiled sadly but apparently could not express herself on such a painful subject.

Maria bit back the hundred questions that leaped into her mind. *Her lover must have died,* she thought, giving the other woman's arm a sympathetic squeeze. "I'm so sorry, my dear," she said softly. Then she thought suddenly, *Why should not my brother be the one to console her?* "We must distract you from your sorrows, if we can. We shall take a small, intimate party to Vauxhall Gardens next week, and you shall be part of it."

Serena demurred. She would be far too busy preparing for her sister's removal to Surrey to even think of her own amusement. And after that, she would be in Surrey with her sister. She had no more thought of returning to London until Constance was safely delivered of the child.

Upon Maria's expressing every regret at losing her dear friend to that unworthy county, Serena promptly invited her ladyship to visit her at Silvercombe, and this offer was promptly accepted.

The next morning, Lady Maria rose late and breakfasted with her husband. With a feeling of dread, she picked up the society page of the morning paper. Due to the scandal, her ball had not been a success, a fact that she imagined the loathsome members of the press would lose no time in broadcasting.

She nibbled halfheartedly on a muffin as she scanned the vitriolic columns, and her husband was thrown into panic when she suddenly began to choke. Leaping to his feet, he pounded her on the back until she begged for mercy. A cup of tea seemed to restore her, but her face was redder than he liked.

"Read this!" she cried, pushing the paper into his hands.

Colonel Fitzwilliam did not ordinarily read the society columns. As a man of sense, they embarrassed him. But dutifully, he read the offensive paragraph.

"*Apparently eager for a Rematch with the notorious Miss Whip, Lord S—recently pursued that lady into the country, and it must be reported that she was quite Overtaken by his lordship's Swift Maneuvers! These two fierce competitors were seen racing North in but a Single Curricle drawn by his lordship's famous grays. Is it to be supposed that Miss Whip has relinquished the reins of her chariot to Lord S—? Or can*

*it be that his lordship is content to be Miss Whip's
GROOM? Only Time will tell."*

Colonel Fitzwilliam was pale with disgust. "Good
God!"

"It is my brother they mean," cried Maria, tears of
vexation welling up in her eyes. "My brother and that
Wayborn chit! They mean to say they have eloped!"

"That cannot be true," Fitzwilliam assured her.
"Geoffrey would never be so undutiful as that."

"To be sure, my brother would not. But I don't
trust the notorious Miss Whip a jot! I will not rest," said
Maria, "until I have removed her talons from his flesh.
She is staying with her cousins in Hertfordshire. I believe I will pay the insolent strumpet a visit."

"Absolutely not," cried her husband. "I am persuaded there is not a shred of truth in this vile pub-
lication, but your going into Hertfordshire to quiz
Miss Wayborn will be seen as proof of it."

Maria did not like it, but she was forced to forego
the pleasure of telling Miss Wayborn to her face what
she thought of her. The rest of the week was a trial for
her, and by the end of it, she believed that Lady
Serena Calverstock was her only true friend. Serena
alone refrained from teasing her about the latest
gossip. Serena alone entered into her fears for her
brother's happiness. More than ever, Maria was convinced that Serena was the only woman in the world
who she could bear to see joined to her brother, and,
in due course, take her mother's place as Duchess of
Auckland.

The following week, Swale returned to London. As
he was now banned from the clubs in St. James's
street, he took up residence in Auckland House. The

Duke was not best pleased with him. The initial interview took place in his son's bedroom several hours before Swale had any idea of getting up.

"I told you to make her an offer, not elope with her!" his parent began, flinging newsprint at the figure in the bed. "You have bungled the matter hopelessly, my boy. If anything, the scandal is worse. But never mind all that. Where is your bride? In a few years, no one will remember that you eloped."

Great was the father's disappointment when Swale could produce no bride.

"What do you mean she wouldn't have you?" he demanded. "She is quite lost now to all good society unless she makes a good marriage. We must appeal to her guardian. Sir Benedict is a reasonable man—"

His son snorted. "He is not at all reasonable when it comes to his sister, let me tell you! She hurt her leg, Father, and I was not even permitted to see her. All my letters and gifts were turned away. She wants nothing to do with me."

"Then I shall go to Earl Wayborn himself," declared the Duke of Auckland.

"Earl who?"

"His lordship may only be a distant relation, but he must take an interest in the fortunes of his young relatives," his father informed him. "He is the head of the family. He will *make* Miss Wayborn marry you."

"Force her, you mean?" Swale thought of Juliet being dragged to the altar of St. George's, pale-faced and tear-stained, and then submitting joylessly to him in the marriage bed. He flung back the covers and jumped out of bed. "I wish you wouldn't, sir," he said violently. "Do you want it said that the only way your son could ever get a wife is by brute force?"

"If Miss Wayborn does not know what is in her best interest, then so be it," snapped the Duke, but Swale knew him well enough to know he was deeply distressed. "What sort of marriage does she expect to make now? Oh, she's quite celebrated at the moment among the young rattles and rakes about town. But what happens to her next year when her notoriety wears thin?"

"What rattles?" Swale demanded. "What rakes?"

His father waved a dismissive hand. "Does it matter? No respectable woman will receive her. The Patronesses of Almack's are all set against her, I can tell you. Indeed, they are so suspicious of the poor girl that my perfectly innocent attempts to defend her have only served to increase their suspicion. Sally Jersey had the temerity to imply that Miss Wayborn is—is my mistress!"

Swale turned white. He looked positively ill.

"Geoffrey, are you hung over?" the Duke demanded angrily.

"Everything we do seems to make things worse for her," Swale muttered. "And really, she is . . . she's not a bad girl. Oh, damn it! She's a magnificent little creature! I admit it."

"Well, if she won't marry you, there's nothing we can do," his father cried in exasperation. "The ungrateful little wasp. My influence is not unlimited, you know. I cannot merely wave my hand and make her respectable. If your mother were here—" He snapped his fingers. "Maria! Of course! Why did I not think of her before? Maria will take her up, and all will be well. You'll show her your hidden depths, Geoffrey, and *then*, she will marry you."

"I'll show her my what?"

"Your depths. You've got them, haven't you?"

"With knobs on," he said, rubbing his head. "But—"

The Duke put one hand on his son's shoulder.

"Good," he said. "I'm counting on you, Geoffrey. I want that nose. You've seen the nose?"

"I have," Swale admitted, "and it is something to behold."

"I told you," said the Duke, looking very pleased. "Not too short, not too long, not too thin, not too fat. Perfectly straight."

"It looks pretty nice when she wrinkles it up at me too," Swale said, "and the gray eyes."

"They will not clash with your red hair," said the Duke smugly.

"On the contrary, Father, those particular eyes clash with everything."

"Well, then, what are you waiting for?"

Swale did not have the heart to tell his father that he hadn't a duckling's chance in a maelstrom of marrying Miss Wayborn. She was slated to marry a man with no hidden depths at all, and a dead bore besides. When his father had gone, Swale picked up the pages of the *Morning Post,* but he could find no announcement of a forthcoming marriage between Miss Juliet Wayborn and Captain Horatio Cary.

One would think the Wayborns would have put the notice in as soon as possible. Curious, he thought. Frowning, he tossed the paper aside.

Alexander Devize ran him to earth the next day at Auckland House and got the whole story from him. "Do you mean to say the Wayborn had you in her clutches and then she . . . *let you go?*" Alex was half-amused, half-incredulous. "Full reprieve in fact?"

"Threw me back as if I were a bloody minnow!" Swale flung himself into his favorite chair and reached for the Madeira. In a reflective mood, the reprieved man was glad of his friend's company. "When the effects of the whisky wore off, she had no wish to marry me, thank God."

"Yes," said Devize agreeably. "It is always pleasant to hear that a handsome, spirited girl does not wish to become one's wife. At least, when the effects of the whisky have worn off."

Swale's face turned red. "You know what I mean, dammit! She could have had me with a word. The bloody Vicar sent us out into the shrubbery right off, then the bloody boots walked in on us at the inn when I was kissing her, and Bowditch—!" He paused to pour a river of Madeira down his throat. "Bowditch was waving the special license about the place like a bloody flag."

"I see," Alex said gravely.

"Even Sir Benedict, when he was apprised of all facts, thought it might be his duty to bring about the marriage, and that man certainly despises me."

"Indeed," said Alex. "You were seen mauling his sister in the local tavern. What did you expect?"

"I can see his side of things," said Swale. "We were alone in that beastly cottage for ages. The whisky on her breath could not be denied. But, really, she was in such pain! I would have done as much for a dog with a hurt leg. I meant well."

Alex frowned. "If she were my sister, the announcement would be in the *Post* already, I promise you."

"It was all perfectly innocent."

"All the more reason the girl deserves the protection of your name," Alex said inexorably. "If she were guilty, no one would blame you for deserting her. But an innocent girl—!"

"Well, I didn't kick," said Swale grumpily. "The minute I saw Captain Cary's face, I knew I was caught. It's not as though I could rely on my father to extricate me. *He's* potty about this girl's nose. He'd have taken her part against me and made her family a generous settlement, I don't doubt."

"And it would serve you right, old man. One simply doesn't go about the place kissing girls like Juliet Wayborn!" Alex scolded him. "We live in liberal times, but the Wayborns are Old County, I'm afraid, like the Devizes. We don't put up with you lecherous Hanoverian aristocrats trifling with our women. You should be more careful, Geoffrey. You're fortunate that Sir Benedict let the foolish girl have her own way. I wouldn't have done it myself, had I been in his place."

"Oh, Sir Benedict despises me," said Swale. "He was pleased to let her have her way. He don't want to be connected to me in any way, shape, or form."

"Whatever possessed you to kiss her—and at the local inn, of all places?"

"I had to kiss her," Swale explained. "The sound of her voice was annoying me. I couldn't very well punch her in the nose, could I? Especially not that nose— it's bloody perfect. Anyway, it was only a kiss."

"That kiss nearly cost you your life. Your freedom, Geoffrey!"

Swale frowned. "As I have said, I know I was well caught."

"I expect Miss Wayborn was sorely tempted," Alex said thoughtfully. "Twenty thousand a year and a coronet? I believe *I* would marry you for twenty thousand a year!"

"I don't think she was tempted for a moment," Swale admitted ruefully.

A smile touched Alex's lips. "But, my dear Swale, did you not go there to make her fall in love with you? As I recall—"

"Never mind what you recall!" Swale said quickly.

"Can it be you failed to make yourself agreeable to

her?" said Alex, laughing. "Did she not think you a matrimonial prize? Indeed, I am all astonishment!"

"It was all I could do to convince her I didn't break her brother's arm," said Swale sullenly. "But I think I've managed that at least."

"The first step is now gained," said Alex, enjoying his friend's discomfiture. "The way is open. Don't say you mean to give up the game entirely?"

Swale summoned his dignity. "I decided it would be cruel for me to sport with the feelings of such a noble girl."

Alex arched a brow. "Then am I to infer that you remained in Hertfordshire for a week to allow the noble girl to trifle with *yours?*"

"You are talking stupid," Swale informed him loftily. "After the business with the curricle and the farmhouse and the whisky, do you imagine that I was permitted to see the noble girl? I presented myself at the Vicarage every morning for a week in case there should be some task I might perform for her, but there was nothing Miss Wayborn required of me. Sir Benedict never allowed me to see her."

Alex was astonished. "You mean you placed yourself at her disposal?"

"Certainly," said Swale. "I was responsible for her injuries, and it seemed reasonable that since I could walk and she could not, I should help her if I could."

"And she asked nothing of you?" Alex seemed skeptical.

"She had Captain Cary at her disposal as well, you understand," Swale said, his resentment apparent. "She is engaged to Captain Cary, or so her brother informs me. I have not seen it announced anywhere. H-have you?"

"I don't read the obituaries," Alex said blithely. "How grateful you must be to Captain Cary! Here I was thinking the lady unaccountably noble, but as she is already engaged, there could be no question of her marrying you."

"She has this coat," Swale said bitterly, "a dark blue coat with wide lapels and gilt buttons. You see what that means, don't you? Picture it with gold braid and epaulets, aboard the deck of a ship. I believe she had that coat made especially to please *him!*"

"That is a grave accusation indeed!" said Alex, trying not to laugh.

Swale was scowling ferociously. "The thing is, Alex . . . the thing is, I didn't mind being caught. I mean, I'm going to be caught one day. Why not by her?"

"My dear Geoffrey," Alex murmured, chuckling.

"What I minded was being turned loose as if I were too small a fish to be bothered with. I'm a big fish! A bloody big fish!"

"A whale," said his loyal friend.

"That she would spurn me in favor of a Captain Cary—! That is chiefly what I minded."

Alex's response was forestalled by a sound from the hall.

"What the devil!" Swale murmured. It sounded like the door opening and closing. In the next moment, Bowditch shuffled into the room, dragging a worn valise.

The sight gave Swale no pleasure. "Well, Bowditch, if you have come for your wages, you should know I have spent them on Madeira. It is cheap, but I find I require large quantities."

"No, my lord," said Bowditch. "I have come to resume my duties. I have decided that I am not the marrying kind."

"Not the marrying kind!" cried Swale. "After all you put me through? Not the marrying kind, eh? Well, you might have made the discovery sooner—*before* you eloped with the ghastly Fifi. Good God, man!" A sudden thought required him to sit up and set down his glass. "Don't tell me you've abandoned Miss Wayborn's Fifi somewhere along the road?"

Bowditch assumed an injured expression. "No, my lord. Mademoiselle Huppert left me for a man she met on the stage."

"The stagecoach, you mean?"

"No, sir, the stage. Mr. David Rourke may currently be seen in Drury Lane in the part of Tony Lumpkin in Mr. Sheridan's excellent production of *She Stoops to Conquer.*"

"What about Cary Wayborn's groom?" Swale demanded. "There was an understanding there, I believe, an attachment of long duration."

Bowditch shook his head. "Mr. Corcoran has vowed never to marry until all three of his late master's children are married themselves. Mademoiselle Huppert became impatient. Not even Mr. Corcoran's fortune of ten thousand pounds could induce her to wait."

Swale started in surprise. "What's a bloody groom doing with ten thousand pounds?"

Bowditch cast his master a look of reproach. "His late master, Sir Anthony Wayborn, left him a handsome bequest in his will, my lord. Some masters do value their loyal servants, you know."

"Do they?" Swale retorted. "You may as well know, Bowditch, that I intend to outlive you."

"Yes, my lord," said Bowditch, withdrawing.

"You don't mean you're letting him stay?" Alex cried in amazement.

Swale looked at him in equal surprise. "This is his home, isn't it?"

"It seems to me that half the business is his fault," said Alex. "If he hadn't run off with the damned Frenchy, you wouldn't have gotten yourself into this scrape."

"I'm not in a scrape," Swale pointed out.

"Only because Miss Wayborn is already engaged," Alex said. "You may wish to stay away from Hertfordshire—Miss Wayborn may decide she would rather be the wife of a Marquess than of a mere swaggering Naval officer!"

"I have no intention whatsoever of returning to Hertfordshire," said Swale. "At the earliest opportunity, I intend to call on my Lord Redfylde."

"That may be impossible," said Alex.

"Why do you say so? His lordship evidently holds me in such high esteem that he would hazard ten thousand pounds on my skill. Surely, he will consent to meet me."

"But his lordship is not in London," Alex told him. "Due to Lady Redfylde's frail health, he has taken a house in the country."

"Then I shall meet him there," said Swale.

"But my dear Geoffrey," Alex protested, "you can't shoot him merely for placing a wager on a race. In any case, you can't shoot him at all. Lady Redfylde is breeding, you know, and her health is poor."

"Hang Lady Redfylde," said Swale.

Alex sighed. "And you were so chivalrous with Miss Wayborn—it gave me hope. You *cannot* challenge Lord Redfylde. I would not second you if you did."

"I would like to beat him until he admits what he did," said Swale.

"You can't do that either."

"What *can* I do?" Swale wanted to know.

Chapter 11

It was well for Juliet that she liked her apartment at Wayborn Hall, for it was only by going into it and closing the door that she could escape the society of her aunt Lady Elkins. How that lady had learned of her niece's tête-à-tête with Lord Swale at Brisby's Farm was never clear to Juliet, for Juliet was certain that Benedict had never spoken of it, but know of it she did, and in the two weeks that followed Juliet's arrival at her childhood home, the widow never ceased scolding her niece. Not even the presence of Miss Cynthia Cary, who had accompanied her cousin into Surrey, could stop her ladyship's tongue. On this subject, her energy was boundless and her voice so strident that it made Juliet long for the days when her aunt was too weak to lift her head from the pillow.

Aunt Elinor's favorite venue was the small parlor where the ladies gathered for tea every afternoon.

"I wish I were your guardian, Juliet. I would have *made* you marry Lord Swale!" A dreamy smile would smooth her aging face. "Lord and Lady Swale! Marchioness of Swale! You are a wicked girl indeed to be depriving me of the pleasure of being the aunt of a marchioness."

Juliet always endured her aunt's displeasure in silence, but Cynthia usually felt obliged to defend her cousin. "But, my lady," she protested, "if you knew Lord Swale, you would not for a moment consider such a thing. If you had seen him drink his soup from the bowl like a savage . . ." Cynthia shuddered delicately. "He has a cruel, black temper, you know, ma'am, and besides, he insulted poor Juliet in so monstrous a fashion—"

"Would you say it was an insult?" Lady Elkins retorted. "Twenty thousand a year for a mere baronet's daughter and a marquisate besides? Make sure of it, Juliet; if his lordship kissed you, it is because he secretly wished to marry you but was too shy to ask!"

Juliet laughed heartily at this. The notion of Swale being shy was too absurd. As for his secretly wishing to marry her . . . no, indeed. Swale's idea of a partner in life was Lady Serena.

"Depend upon it, my dear," said Lady Elkins. "He must be wild in love with you."

"Indeed, it would be a miracle if he did not hate me," said Juliet. "I blamed him for the attack on Cary, and I was wrong. I blamed his Bowditch, when all along it was my Fifi—wrong again! Then, was I to force him to marry me against his own expressed wishes?"

"He is so awful in appearance," Cynthia said with a shudder. "Truly, Lady Elkins! A horrible giant with long red hair like a Viking marauder."

Lady Elkins rounded on her angrily. "What do his looks signify, Miss Cary? He has *twenty thousand* a year! That is my idea of handsome!"

"Oh, my dear aunt," Juliet murmured, chuckling.

"Do you suppose that your uncle, Sir Thomas, was handsome? He was a respectable gentleman of large fortune. I considered myself very lucky to get him. He was forty-three years my senior and in very frail health, but he made me comfortable in life before he died. So comfortable, indeed, that I never considered marrying again. That is *my* idea of a good husband."

Cynthia's eyes stood out like cornflower blossoms on stems. "But, Lady Elkins," she could not help exclaiming, "you would not want your niece to marry an . . . an old man!"

"That is my point exactly, miss," Lady Elkins snapped. "Lord Swale is not old. I consider your reasons for rejecting him very trivial, Miss Juliet!"

"I did not reject him," said Juliet. "The marriage was proposed by other people, not ourselves. I would never use my honor as an excuse to make a man marry me. I am sure my uncle, Sir Thomas, was not forced to marry Miss Elinor Wayborn."

"No, indeed," Lady Elkins sniffed. "He had a falling out with his nephew and decided to disoblige him by marrying me. He hoped to have a son and so dash the impertinent young man's hope of succeeding to his title, but that, of course, proved impossible, and the ungrateful nephew triumphed after all."

Lady Elkins spoke matter-of-factly, as though there was nothing unseemly about a marriage entered into out of spite on the gentleman's side and greed on the lady's, but Cynthia was appalled. Juliet, who knew her aunt's history, still could not hear the facts without wincing.

"The man I marry will have a better reason for marrying me," she said firmly. "And I shall have a better reason for marrying him. Swale never dishonored me. Why then, should he be forced to marry me? And if he *had* dishonored me, do you suppose there would be any force on earth that could compel me to accept him as my husband?"

"Force!" cried Lady Elkins. "What do you mean? His lordship is not a child. He must know there are consequences to such reckless behavior as kissing Miss Wayborn in a public house. And you say he did not dishonor you! He would not *dare* resent you for insisting on a marriage."

"You do not know him, Lady Elkins!" protested Cynthia. "I should be *afraid* for Juliet if she married him. He is so evil-tempered. If he felt himself ill-used, he would certainly take his revenge on my cousin. And the Aucklands are so rich and high, what could we do to stop him?"

"I am not afraid of Swale," scoffed Juliet. "His temper is not at issue. Rather, I should never marry a man who does not at least *wish* to marry *me!* It is a little requirement of mine that must be satisfied before I will even consider whether or not *I* wish to marry *him.* Swale doesn't love me, Aunt Elinor. He told me himself he is fixed on quite another lady."

"For myself," Lady Elkins declared, "I consider myself *married* to any man seen kissing me in a public house! Let him try to escape!"

In vain, Cynthia tried to stop her giggles by biting her knuckles. It was no use. The image of Lady Elkins being kissed by the pot-boy at a village inn was too much for her.

Juliet began to laugh too. "Take care, my dear aunt! If this fact is made known to the general population, you will find yourself in constant danger of being kissed. Wealthy widows are always attractive to young men who have only their handsome faces to recommend them. How would you like a vigorous young man for a husband?"

Lady Elkins gathered her dignity and threatened to quit the room.

"I mean no disrespect, Aunt Elinor," Juliet said contritely, "but my views on marriage are nothing like yours. Let us avoid the subject. Tell me, what changes do you suppose Lord Redfylde will make to Silvercombe?"

This was the one subject that could divert Lady Elkins from scolding her niece. Lord and Lady Redfylde had hired Silvercombe, the nearby country estate of Lord Skeldings, who had taken up permanent residence in Bath. My lord and lady were to remain in the neighborhood for the period of her ladyship's confinement. Lord Redfylde was not often under the roof, however, and it was well-known that, due to her condition, Lady Redfylde was not receiving visitors, so Lady Elkins was obliged to rely upon servants' gossip for all the Silvercombe news.

Juliet had already quizzed Sir Benedict about Lord Redfylde's sudden appearance in the neighborhood, running to his study the moment she had heard that Redfylde had hired the house, demanding, "And what are you going to do about it?"

Benedict had given her a measured look and dismissed his estate agent from the room. "What am I going to do about what?"

"*It,*" she clarified. "Lord Redfylde. Are you going to call on him? Have you—have you already called on him?"

"Certainly I have," Sir Benedict replied. "Some time ago, I recommended Lord Redfylde to Lord Skeldings. On my recommendation, he has taken the house."

"Some time ago? Before the race, you mean? I did not know you were so well acquainted with Lord Redfylde."

"I am not," he told her. "But when I heard his lordship was seeking a place near London where his wife might be comfortable without being deprived too much of her husband's company, I spoke to him on Lord Skeldings's behalf. You know Bertram needs the money, and it is better for the neighborhood if Silvercombe does not stand empty all the time."

"Redfylde! Better for the neighborhood?" Juliet scoffed.

"Yes, Juliet. And better for our friend Lord Skeldings. At the time, I had no reason to question his lordship's character."

"But you must have some plan to expose Lord Redfylde now that he is here," she said impatiently. "Have you questioned him yet? How does his lordship explain betting monstrous sums on Lord Swale?"

Benedict held up his hand as he completed figuring a column of sums. "I am no magistrate, you know, to be questioning my neighbors."

Disgusted by his unruffled calm, Juliet kicked the carpet with her toe. "I might have known you wouldn't think it proper! If I were a man, I'd walk right up to him and demand answers."

"That would be the height of impropriety. It won't do, Juliet, to accuse a Peer of the Realm." He gave in to her curiosity reluctantly. "I called on him, and I can tell you, if Lord Redfylde was involved in the attack on our brother, he feels absolutely no remorse. He is quite the most disdainful man I ever met. He did not so much as inquire after Cary's health."

"But what are you going to *do?*" she cried, stamping her foot in frustration.

"The Bow Street Runners are at their inquiries in London," he told her. "Cary and Mr. Calverstock were able to give a good description of the attackers. If the miscreants are found, they can be made to give evidence. If they were hired and if they can identify Lord Redfylde as their employer, then his lordship may be questioned by the proper authorities. Does that satisfy you?"

"No!" she responded. "Let his lordship prove his innocence if he can."

"My dear Juliet, he is innocent until proven otherwise."

His sister did not appear to agree with this cornerstone of English jurisprudence. "I would like to hang him up by his thumbs until he talks!"

"Have you learned nothing?" he rebuked her. "It was not so very long ago you accused Lord Swale—falsely as it turns out. Now you propose I cast suspicion over Lord Redfylde."

"All the more reason to question him," she said. "We must at least *try* to shift the blame to where it belongs. What if the Runners cannot find Cary's attackers? Cary will recover, I daresay, but Swale will always be under a cloud." She twisted her hands together in embarrassment. "You must do something, Benedict, because, you know, it was my fault. If I had not raced with him to Southend and accused him so publicly . . . if I had gone to you instead . . . you would have handled it quietly."

"My dear," he said gently, "the Runners will find them. Do not concern yourself about Swale so much—unfortunately, there will always be a place in Society for the Duke of Auckland's heir."

She went away far from comforted. More than ever, she felt herself to be in Swale's debt. During her recovery in Hertfordshire, he had come to the Vicarage every day to inquire after her progress. Despite Benedict's constant rebuffs, Swale came anyway every morning and every evening without fail. Certainly, he had no real wish to see her, and it must have been humiliating for him to be turned away day after day, but still he came. She would not have blamed him if he had left Herts and returned to London and Serena Calverstock. But he had remained until the very morning of her own departure.

He would have married her, she knew, out of a sense of obligation because despite all his bluster and soup slurping, he really was an honorable man. As Lady Swale, she would have passed instantly from disgrace to the very highest circles of the Ton. But what a depressing way to catch a husband! And a husband who loved Serena Calverstock would be a poor prize indeed, whatever Lady Elkins said about it.

And what her aunt chiefly had to say was this: "Depend upon it. He will marry as soon as he can and will forget all about you. Men never like to have their generosity thrown in their faces. And when he is married and his wife is decked in diamonds from head to toe, don't think you can cry on my shoulder! When you are an old spinster, you will weep tears of bitter regret, for who will marry you now?"

For weeks, Juliet was forced to listen as her aunt condemned her to a life of no children, no home of her own, and no place in Society. Much to Lady Elkins's surprise, her threats and sermons only served to make Juliet's views on the subject grow stronger. That she should marry as the means of conceiving a child, or for architecture, or for the right to be gossiped about by people she neither liked nor respected—all were equally unthinkable. "I should only want to bear children if I loved the man," she declared. "And I should only wish to share my home if I loved the man. And I should consider my place in Society a sham if I did not *love* the man. I would not deserve the honor of his name if I didn't love him."

"I confess I feel the same," said Cynthia.

Lady Elkins eyed them with contempt. "You modern girls!" she said scathingly. "You want too much. The moon and the stars are nothing to you. Not only must your husbands love you, which was considered *more* than sufficient in my day, but you must love your husbands too! If that is your course, you will see many inferior girls find husbands and happiness while you advance into spinsterhood. I am speaking mainly to you, Miss Cary, for it goes without saying that Juliet will never again receive an offer of marriage."

"If only that were true, Aunt," Juliet said wryly.

"What?" cried the lady, clutching her heart. "Juliet, you sly thing! Have you received an offer of marriage?"

"No, indeed," Juliet laughed. "How could it be so when your ladyship has declared it impossible! I only wish, as you claim, that it went without saying."

"Cruel, wicked, abominable girl!" replied her aunt, falling back into her chair. "To raise my hopes and then dash them so cruelly. I have a mind to leave all my money to my nephew instead of to you, ungrateful, selfish Juliet. I'm glad you'll never be a marchioness—I am sure you don't deserve it!"

In the first week of April, Lady Serena Calverstock accompanied her sister to Silvercombe. It was she, and not Lady Redfylde, who took over the duties of mistress of Silvercombe. The neighborhood buzzed with excitement, for she had brought with her a small party of fashionable London friends, including a Colonel Fitzwilliam and his wife.

Sir Benedict Wayborn called upon Colonel Fitzwilliam as courtesy demanded and reported him to be an amiable gentleman. "And do you know who his wife is?" he asked his sister upon returning to the Hall. "She is the Duke of Auckland's daughter, and a very proud, disagreeable woman besides."

"Swale's sister?" Juliet guessed that an association with Swale's sister would bring Serena that much closer to the splendid marriage she had been waiting for. "Is . . . is his lordship a member of the party?" she asked, forcing her voice to remain neutral.

"Lord Redfylde was not at home when I called," her brother replied.

"Not Redfylde—Swale! Has he come with his sister?"

"No, thank heavens. We saw quite enough of Lord Swale in Herts, I think. I daresay we will not be obliged to see very much of the Silvercombe set either. The ladies are occupied in amusing Lady Redfylde, and the gentlemen mean to have some sport. I have given them leave to fish in my lake, so do not be alarmed if you see strangers there."

Juliet scarcely heard him, for her mind was so busily considering what it meant that Serena was a particular friend of Lady Maria Fitzwilliam, Swale's sister. Her ladyship was certain to promote the match between her friend and her brother. Or, was the match already made? Every day, she searched the newspapers for any information, but there was no sign of an engagement notice in the papers.

Aloud, she expressed only some mild curiosity to know Lady Maria. Lady Elkins, on the other hand, could scarcely be restrained from calling upon the Silvercombe ladies until the respectable hour of eleven was reached the next morning. In her view, it was imperative that the ladies of Wayborn Hall be the first to call upon the newcomers, even before the Parson's wife and daughters.

Cynthia was nervous. At home in Hertfordshire, there was no one more awesome for her to call upon than Squire Mickleby's wife, and that lady was as big and comfortable and well-meaning as her own mother. Juliet's description of Lady Serena scarcely comforted her nerves. "She is extremely haughty, but so rich and so beautiful, with black hair and the most exquisite violet eyes, that everyone is obliged to pretend to like her."

"Only consider what it means, my dear," Lady Elkins interrupted, "that Lady Maria has come into Surrey with Serena Calverstock."

"Pray, what does it mean?" Juliet asked with an arch smile for Cynthia.

"Lady Maria must be making a match between her brother and Lady Serena," Lady Elkins declared, startling her niece with her perspicacity. "Why else would she so distinguish an unmarried lady? The marquisate is lost to you forever, you stupid girl, and the duchy too. If Serena has not already made him very much in love with her, she is certain to do so. Oh, was there ever anything more vexing! When I think that you had him in your grasp and let him go—!"

Juliet merely laughed. "Serena and Lord Swale! Beauty and the Beast! I wish them happy, I am sure. He will acquire her beauty, and she will acquire his wealth and position. Don't tell me you don't approve, Aunt Elinor. It is precisely that mercenary kind of marriage that you always recommend so kindly to me."

Her feelings on the subject, however, were very

different. She could not help but doubt the lady who had until quite recently given the world every reason to believe her in love with Cary Wayborn, and Juliet's own dislike of Serena made it impossible for her to believe that Swale truly loved her. He would not be the first man blinded by Serena's beauty, but what was she to do? It would be the very height of presumption for her to interfere in the lives of two relative strangers, however strongly she felt that their marriage was wrong.

Silvercombe was obtained after a drive through a long avenue of lime trees. Lady Elkins was perplexed when Driscoll, the butler at Silvercombe, walked out to the barouche and informed her ladyship that the Silvercombe ladies were not at home. The slight infuriated Juliet, for a slight it undoubtedly was; she had known Driscoll all her life, since he had always been Lord Skeldings's butler, and his apologetic air spoke volumes. Lady Serena and her dear friend Lady Maria were certainly at home, but they were not *at home* to Miss Juliet Wayborn. Her disgrace had followed her into Surrey.

Lady Elkins passed from bewilderment to indignation to dizziness, and the coachman was obliged to turn the barouche around and carry them all home again. Though wounded, Lady Elkins left cards at Silvercombe, so they waited at home every morning for three days afterward for the Silvercombe ladies to return the call, but they did not so much as send cards. Lady Elkins was mortified. Never in her life had she been treated so shabbily, and for days, she spoke of nothing else.

Cynthia was relieved. "It is well you did not agree to marry Lord Swale," she whispered to her cousin, "if his sister is so haughty. She would have crushed us with her contempt."

Juliet, who had rather the opposite thought, did not reply.

If the Silvercombe ladies had considered themselves above all company in the neighborhood, Lady Elkins might not have felt the slight so keenly. But Lady Maria and Lady Serena were not shy in receiving other visitors. They even made several well-publicized trips into the village to the delight of the local ladies.

And everywhere their ladyships went, wherever possible, they cut Miss Wayborn and made glad the ears of the neighborhood gossips with tales of her exploits in London and Hertfordshire. To Mrs. Wyndham, they expressed astonishment that Sir Benedict permitted his sad romp of a sister to move at all in Society, and Sir George Brabant was warned against letting his daughters visit the notorious Miss Whip, lest their own reputations be tarred. In church, their ladyships occupied the Skeldings's pew, which stood opposite the Wayborns', but they never looked in that direction. With the utmost civility, Colonel Fitzwilliam would speak to Sir Benedict after the services, and Lord Redfylde, when he was in the neighborhood on a Sunday, which was not often, would gravely nod his fair head, but the ladies refused to acknowledge the very existence of their female neighbors.

It was not long before the women in the neighborhood, overawed by the fine London ladies at Silvercombe, began to follow their lead. Juliet accepted her own disgrace with little more than prickly irritation, but the slights dealt to her aunt and her cousin were insupportable. She was indeed the notorious Miss Whip and was perhaps deserving of contempt, but Lady Elkins and Cynthia had done nothing to deserve such cruelty.

"I daresay they think you should lock me up in the attics and not even permit me to attend religious services!" she remarked to her brother as they left the village church. Cynthia and Lady Elkins had taken Sir Benedict's barouche back to Wayborn Hall, but Juliet and her brother always walked home in fine weather, cutting through the meadow to take the path along the lake. "I might think they had come to Surrey with no other object than to ruin me in my own county!" she added bitterly. It filled her with indignation to see people who had known her all her life and who liked her, now pretending not to see her, huddling their children away from her, and whispering about her behind their hands.

Benedict was plainly so aggrieved that she felt obliged to make a light remark. "At least my disgrace keeps you safe from Lady Serena," she teased him. "I had feared she might wish to be mistress of Wayborn Hall. I daresay it would amuse her to flirt with you after breaking poor Cary's heart." *At least,* she thought viciously, *until she receives a firm offer from Swale.*

"I doubt Wayborn Hall is enough to tempt Lady Serena," Benedict said dryly. "And I am not at all the sort of friend she would like. I think I am safe from her indeed, my dear."

"She liked Mr. Devize very well until she saw Castle Devize in Suffolk, not at all a modern place, I think. She dropped poor Mr. Devize like a hot potato, I can tell you, and began to pursue our brother. As for her brief interest in Cary, I can only believe that someone exaggerated the importance of the Tanglewood estate."

"Hot potato?" Benedict sighed. "Did you learn that vulgar expression from Bernard?"

"No—Cary," she replied. "But very likely, he learned it from Bernard. It answers the situation very nicely, I think, though I have never actually handled a hot potato. After my disgrace, her ladyship wanted no more to do with Cary or me. I hope—I hope he doesn't blame me. Her affection could not have been sincere in any case. And now, if the rumors are true, Lord Swale is pursuing her. Won't they make a charming couple? Her beauty and his money?"

Benedict shuddered. "She is to be pitied, I think. Lord Redfylde is unlikely to advise against the match, and without his lordship's consequence behind her, she may well capitulate."

"I think Swale is more to be pitied," said Juliet. "She has a pretty face but a cold heart. How you can take her part when she has snubbed your aunt and worked so much mischief against your only sister, I shall never understand. I knew I should have difficulty in London, but in my own county, with my own people—! Mrs. Oliphant has invited my aunt and my cousin to a card party on Wednesday, but Miss Juliet, you know, need not trouble to come!"

Benedict sighed.

"And poor Cynthia! There is nothing for it, Benedict. As sorry as I am to see her go, Cynthia can no longer stay here. Every day, she joins in my disgrace. She says it does not matter; she will not play cards at Mrs. Oliphant's, but it can't be pleasant for her. She must go home unless . . . unless you wish to make her a tenant for life and mistress of Wayborn Hall?"

She gave his arm an encouraging squeeze, but Benedict agreed, with less reluctance than Juliet liked, to write to Dr. Cary at once. "Oh, Benedict!" she rebuked him. "She'll be going to London next Season, and very likely, she will marry someone else if you do not ask for her soon."

"I am thirty-six years of age," he told her irritably. "Miss Cary is a child of seventeen. It would be ridiculous, not to say repugnant, for me to form any serious design on a mere child."

"Gammon! What does age matter if you love her?"

"I have the greatest respect for Miss Cary," said her brother with maddening sangfroid. "She seems a very good little person. She is very pretty. She does not distress her family by racing across the country with strange gentlemen. I don't underrate her value, I assure you. But if I love her, Juliet, it is only in the fertile territory of your imagination." And he laughed at her expression of bitter disappointment. "I am equally certain that Miss Cary's affection for me is made of much the same stuff. Do not matchmake for me, sister. You would not like me to choose your husband for you."

"No," she admitted. "You would choose someone very dull indeed."

The following week, in response to Benedict's letter, Horatio arrived at Wayborn Hall driving a very smart new barouche pulled by a beautiful pair of bays. Lady Elkins was overjoyed to receive him and was excessively sorry that he did not mean to stay. There was nothing she would have liked better than to be driven about town by the handsome Captain in his new barouche. Juliet, of course, would sit beside Horatio on the barouche box, and Mrs. Oliphant and the Brabant girls would gnash their teeth with envy.

Alas, it was not to be. He meant to leave that very

afternoon for he had pressing business in London. However, since Horatio's rapid advancement in the Royal Navy had been largely due to Lord Redfylde's influence, he naturally felt it was his first duty to call at Silvercombe. "Though for your sake, Juliet, I take no pleasure in it," he told his cousin apologetically.

Juliet tried not to show her disappointment, but she felt that again the Silvercombe ladies had triumphed over her. She had hoped that since Lord Redfylde himself was not at home, Horatio might escape the obligation, but it was impossible. Not even the reports of Lady Serena's coldness to his sister could deter him. "I do not say it is a pleasant duty, Cousin Juliet, but it is nonetheless a duty. I daresay her ladyship will receive Miss Cary with every indication of pleasure when I present her."

"Oh no!" Cynthia cried in dismay. "I could not go to Silvercombe, Horatio. Lady Serena and Lady Maria have been monstrous cruel to Juliet and to Lady Elkins too! I will not set foot in any house where my cousin isn't welcome."

Horatio insisted. "You must consider your brother, Cynthia, and you must consider yourself. Juliet will not feel you have betrayed her simply by paying a morning call to your neighbors. Your first loyalty must be to your brother. And I need hardly add, you will not do yourself any good by making enemies of their ladyships."

But it was only after Juliet urged her to go that Cynthia consented.

The duty visit was accomplished before luncheon, and Juliet received a full report from her pretty cousin during the meal that was to be Cynthia's last at Wayborn Hall. Not only had Lady Serena received Miss Cary with every appearance of delight, but Lady Maria Fitzwilliam had also been everything kind.

"She asked me to take a turn in the garden with her, and we walked arm in arm while Horatio waited on Lady Serena. Her ladyship is not at all haughty, Juliet. She said I was a dear, sweet girl and that if I should go to London, I should be a great success and she would help me."

"And how did you like Lady Serena?" Juliet asked slowly.

"If anything, she was even more kind to me than Lady Maria. She privately told me she hoped to be married soon and to have the nicest sister in the whole world. She must really mean to marry Lord Swale and be Lady Maria's sister! Oh, Juliet!" she fretted. "Do you think I ought to have warned her ladyship about Lord Swale? I am convinced no one could be happy married to him."

"I don't think happiness will be Serena's chief reason for marrying Swale," Juliet said dryly. "And so," she went on, "you are persuaded that all good society will be opened to you if you will only deny your scandalous cousin Miss Wayborn."

"Oh no," Cynthia cried in dismay, but there was a guilty shyness in her eyes.

"I daresay Lady Maria has promised to obtain vouchers to Almack's for you when you go to London next year, and Lady Serena to take you for drives in her pony phaeton."

Cynthia's lower lip began to tremble so violently that Juliet relented and hugged the girl. "Never mind! I am not in the least angry. The truth is they will be of greater assistance to you in Society than ever I could be. And as I shall not be in London next year, you need never have to choose between them and me."

"Horatio is convinced your disgrace will be forgotten by next year," said Cynthia, her smile charged with meaning. "I think you *will* be in London next year if my brother has anything to say about it, my dear Juliet. And next year, I hope, you will be more to me than a cousin, and much closer too!"

Upon taking the hint, Juliet was seized with blind panic and a sneaking guilt. She could not deny that she had given Horatio a great deal of encouragement since his return to England. In those first weeks, she had liked him very well indeed and had even cherished a hope of marrying him one day. When had her feelings begun to change? It was not difficult for her to know exactly—it was the moment he had rebuked her for setting Swale's carrots on fire. A quiet word at a later time would not have been amiss, she felt, but he had publicly taken the enemy's part over hers. Even after the enemy had ceased to be an enemy, she had nursed a secret resentment against her handsome cousin, and in the week following the injury to her leg, when Horatio had been at his most attentive, she had formed the opinion that they would not suit after all. Her cousin had a tendency to correct her that she had not noticed before and that reminded her unpleasantly of Benedict. She certainly did not require a husband who criticized her as freely and severely as her own elder brother!

But had she given him as much *discouragement* since the change in her feelings as she had given him encouragement before? She *had* tried by spurning his efforts to induce her to read this book over that to show him that he was no more her idol, but she feared he had merely thought her irritable because of her injury. A proposal now would force her to be more plain and lay her open to a rebuke that, she felt, she must justly deserve for awakening his hopes.

When Horatio asked to take his leave of Juliet in

private, there could be no mistaking his intentions, but despite her niece's frantic and surreptitious signals, Lady Elkins cheerfully agreed. A very faint and unhappy Aunt Elinor had been carried out onto the terrace to recover from her disappointment at not being taken for a ride in Captain Cary's barouche, but she happily returned to the house quite under her own power, leaving Juliet no choice but to hear Horatio's proposal.

"My dear Juliet," he began, "I have been separated from you too much, and here I am taking leave of you again. I wish—"

"Indeed, it must be *Fate* keeping us apart," Juliet said quickly and emphatically.

Horatio did not take the hint. "I do not believe in fate," he replied, seizing her hands. "I believe it is up to us to order and arrange our lives in such a way as to secure our future happiness. To secure my future happiness, I would make a life with *you*. In this new life, I would never again take leave of you. I know my happiness would be safe with you, and I believe, dearest, loveliest Juliet, that I could make you happy too. Will you consent to be my wife?"

Juliet bit her lip. Anything she said would be certain to cause him pain. He clearly had no inkling she meant to refuse him, and that too was her fault.

"Do not answer me now," he quickly begged. "Do me the honor of considering my proposal with the same sober thoroughness with which I decided to make it. I am leaving now to bring Cynthia back to my mother, but I will return in three days. Dear Juliet, may I have your answer then?"

"I don't know what to say," she stammered, feeling very much a coward. How many women, she wondered, had begun from a desire not to injure the gentleman's feelings, only to find themselves married to men whom they did not properly esteem?

"You need not say anything now," he assured her. "May I have your answer in three days?"

"I would not dream of keeping you waiting so long," she protested.

"Please do give my proposal the attention it deserves," he urged her. "It is a very important decision, after all. You must consider the matter very carefully. Do me the honor of thinking about it while I am gone. If you decide to have me, I should like to know your decision was entirely rational and in no way hurried by the violence of my own feelings or the suddenness of my declaration."

It would give her time, she reflected, to find the least hurtful way of refusing him. In the course of three days, she might compose a long, thoughtful letter in which she somehow excused her own shameful behavior and lessened his pain.

"Of course," she said faintly. "I will consider it very carefully, and you must know I am sensible—and grateful—for the honor. But you have caught me in surprise!"

"You have also caught me in surprise," he said softly, making her blush. "My dear cousin, it was the happiest surprise of my life when I realized my love for you. I will leave you now to your thoughts. I shall count the minutes until I am with you again."

With a bow, he left her.

Chapter 12

The smart new barouche took her cousins away, but the afternoon post brought a letter from London, so the day was not entirely lost. Juliet did not recognize the handwriting when Benedict handed it to her at luncheon. Opening it, she saw that it was from Cary. It was not in Cary's hand or style, both of which were usually careless. Juliet at first supposed that a secretary had written it out for him, but the first few lines informed her that he had taught himself to write with his left hand since his right arm still pained him.

"Why, he is coming home at last," she cried when she had read it half through. It had been two months since she had seen her brother. He had never been a diligent correspondent, and despite his promise to write every day, this was his first letter to her since she had left London, though she had written him at least twice a week during that time. "He will be here tomorrow. He means to bring someone with him, but he don't say who."

"Doesn't say who," Benedict corrected her wearily. He disliked the affectation of poor grammar that seemed so prevalent among the youth of the day, so he corrected Juliet as solemnly as if she were truly ignorant of proper speech.

"I daresay it's only Stacy Calverstock. I wish Cary wouldn't bring him here."

"That is uncivil," remarked Lady Elkins, who was pettishly toying with her cutlets. "Mayn't your brother bring anyone he chooses to his own home?"

"Indeed he may," said Benedict, frowning.

"And, you know, my love," Lady Elkins added, "he may be coming to ask you to marry him."

"Ugh!" said Juliet.

"I had thought you liked Mr. Calverstock, Juliet," said Benedict.

"Oh, I like him well enough," she said crossly. "But you know he'll be obliged to call on his cousins and their fine friends at Silvercombe. You know, the beautiful people who can't be persuaded that I exist? Really, why doesn't he stay there with them?" she wondered aloud. "It is excessively annoying, you know, to have one's guests always visiting at Silvercombe."

"It is quite your own fault if you are not welcome there," Lady Elkins told her in a voice filled with injury. Thanks to the neighborhood gossips, she was now in possession of all the facts, as well as a great many of the embellishments, concerning Juliet's exploits in London and Hertfordshire, and she had vowed never to forgive her niece. "Haring all over the country in your brother's clothes! Shame on you! Shame on you!"

"Yes, yes, shame on me," Juliet muttered. "You and Stacy Calverstock will have a grand old time lecturing me, Aunt. And I shall have a grand old time putting newts in his bed."

Benedict set down his fork with a clatter. He knew his sister well enough to know this was not an idle threat. "No newts, Juliet! While Mr. Calverstock is our guest, you will make him welcome here. That means no newts and no sulking—it doesn't become you."

"Very well," Juliet said, rising from the table and declaiming from Shakespeare: "'To beguile the time, look like the time; bear welcome in your eye, your hand, your tongue; look like the innocent flower, but be the serpent under it!' Rest assured, I shall!"

Benedict did not particularly enjoy his sister in the role of Lady Macbeth. "Really, Juliet," he said in a despairing voice.

"The raven himself is hoarse that croaks the fatal entrance of *Stacy* under my battlements!" replied his theatrical sister as she left the breakfast room.

"No newts," she murmured thoughtfully as she roamed the halls. Going into battle without newts was a serious handicap, but it was not insurmountable. There were things worse than newts, even in Surrey, and she knew where they were to be found.

First, she hurried to the housekeeper's room with the news that Master Cary was coming home. "And make up the Hastings Room for Mr. Calverstock," she added carelessly.

Mrs. Spinner frowned. "Hastings, Miss Julie?" she said doubtfully. "Mr. Calverstock always stays in Quebec."

"Quebec is excessively comfortable," Juliet informed her. "One night in Hastings, and poor Mr. Calverstock will run to Silvercombe where he belongs. And you needn't bother making up a fire—you know how that chimney smokes."

Outside the stables, she bargained successfully for a dead rat. Carrying the box in gloved hands, she mounted the stairs to the Hastings Room, which was situated most inconveniently underneath the servants' attics. There, she lifted the pillow on the narrow bed and deposited the rat under it, her face turned resolutely away, then tossed the empty box into the cold, black hearth. For good measure, she disconnected the servant's bell. Not as ideal as a bed full of cold, wet newts, of course, but a good start.

Having prepared for the early departure of her guest, she went to her own room, which afforded an excellent view of the avenue. At last, her vigilance was rewarded by the sight of a small cloud of dust moving very quickly toward the house. She ran downstairs, flying past the drawing room where her aunt was sitting, and nearly collided with Benedict's page, a boy of ten. "He's come, Miss Julie!" cried the boy. "Master Cary's come!"

Juliet grabbed his hand, and together they ran outside. Two curricles were in the avenue, one drawn by two perfectly matched chestnuts, and the other by two perfectly matched grays. Juliet clutched the boy's hand, her heart in her throat. She would know those grays anywhere, and the bright red hair of the driver could only belong to Swale.

Billy beamed with pride. "I'd know them anywhere, Miss Julie. Beautiful steppers they are." He wrinkled his nose. "But who's the other fellow? That's never Mr. Calverstock!"

"No," Juliet said faintly. "No, it isn't."

"Funny-looking sort of cove," said Billy critically, his lip curling as Swale brought his curricle up to the steps. "Red hair like Judas Iscariot. What is he atall, Miss Julie? A prizefighter?"

"That cove is the Marquess of Swale, Billy," she told the page severely.

"That burly, red-haired cove is a lordship?" cried Billy in unalloyed amazement. "They'll let anyone in the House of Lords these days, won't they? There was a time we had standards."

"That's quite enough, Billy," said Juliet crisply.

"Even if his lordship were not a Peer, he's still my brother's guest, and you will treat him with respect."

"Yes, Miss Julie," the boy said doubtfully.

"Now, go and tell Sir Benedict that Master Cary has lost his reason and brought that burly, red-haired cove to Wayborn!"

Billy flashed her a grin. "Yes, Miss Julie."

"Well, Juliet?" called a familiar voice, and she realized with a start that she had been staring at Swale and completely ignoring her brother.

Bernard Corcoran, who was driving Cary's chestnuts, tipped his hat to her. "Good day to you, Miss Julie, and is not himself looking better today than he was when you did see him last?"

She looked at Cary now and released a hoot of laughter. Cary was wearing a mustache and a neatly trimmed goatee. With his dark good looks, it made him appear faintly satanic, and he evidently felt its cultivation had been a valuable use of his time. Juliet supposed that many ladies must find his new look very attractive, but she did not agree. It reminded her of a rat.

A dead rat.

A dead rat under a pillow.

Cary's vanity would not be denied. "Well, Julie?" he prodded her. "What do you think? Am I not handsome?"

"At last! Some clever person has found a use for small, furry dead animals," she said, acutely aware that as she chattered brightly, Swale was looking at her with steady green eyes. "I have often been grieved by the appalling waste of merely shoveling them off to the dustman!"

Cary's color was good; his eyes were bright; and with his arm in a sling, he looked like some dashing war hero returned victorious from battle. Cary frowned at her, looking very much the dark angel. "Now is that a proper greeting? For your information, Miss Wayborn, it is the fashion. Horatio wears small whiskers," he reminded her. "You don't seem to mind it."

"No, because he's fair-haired," she replied as Bernard opened the curricle and Cary stepped out, disdaining the helping hand his groom offered. Her natural exuberance checked somewhat by Swale's presence, she went down the steps and hugged her brother. "Careful, child!" he protested. "My arm is far from mended."

She sprang back, apologizing profusely, then demanded, "Where is your tricorn? Where is your purple coat?"

"I have given all that up," he said airily. "A tiresome affectation—makes it too easy for naughty young ladies to assume my identity! May I present Lord Swale to you?"

She turned and faced Swale for the first time, her cheeks burning. She was not sure why she was blushing, she only knew she wished she had checked her appearance in the mirror before dashing outside with Billy. She managed to sketch a curtsey and said faintly, "You are most welcome, sir."

"Miss Wayborn," he said, and she realized that he must be as embarrassed as she was. "You're not limping. May I assume you're quite recovered from the accident?"

"I am quite well, I thank you. And you are driving your grays," she said with a forced smile. "I take it they are fully recovered as well? Mercury and Jupiter?"

"Oh yes," he answered, shuffling his feet to rid his boots of excess dust. "They're ready for the race. When your brother's arm is completely healed—"

"The race!" she exclaimed. "You don't actually intend to go through with that, do you?"

"Certainly," said Cary curtly. "The club has voted to

honor all bets placed on the previous race, which as I recall, you won, Juliet. Swale and I are to be constant companions until I'm well enough to drive. That way, if I am attacked, he will be with me and can defend me." Cary's voice was laced with sarcasm. "The members have voted to place his lordship on probation."

"I see," said Juliet, wondering if Lord Redfylde had participated in this vote.

"My bones are knitted," Cary told her. "I have only to recover my strength. I drove part of the way here. I had meant to go the distance . . . but it was useless. Bloody useless. I haven't the strength of a baby." Before his sister could reply, he turned away to speak to his groom.

Alone with Swale, Juliet felt unaccountably shy.

"How keenly you must be feeling the loss of your Fifi," he said, smiling at her.

"What?" she said sharply, her color rising.

"Poor Miss Wayborn. You have no one to curl your hair over your ears."

Self-consciously, Juliet touched her hair. Her new maid was a local girl, who was so inexperienced she could manage little more than a simple twist. Today, her hair was pulled back in a long queue and tied with a smart blue ribbon. She would never dream of wearing her hair loose in town, but it was not inappropriate for the country, she thought. "My new maid wants more practice before I let her near my hair with hot tongs," she said a little tartly as she started back up the steps.

"I like it," he said, following quickly. "I had a setter with hair just like yours."

She looked at him incredulously, and he became a little flustered.

"Well, I was damned fond of that little bitch," he muttered. "Sweetest little bitch I ever had."

Juliet tried not to laugh and very nearly succeeded. "I think perhaps you are ill, my lord," she said. "You have not shouted at me yet or thrown anything at my head, except this truly amazing flattery."

"But I never threw anything at your head," he protested. "And, what's more, I never would. I—I like your head."

She laughed. "You had a setter with a head like mine, I daresay."

"What's all this?" Cary demanded suddenly, and Juliet, remembering that he was hampered by his injury, hurried down the steps to help him.

"I was just telling your sister I brought her some new books from London," Swale lied.

"Did you?" asked Cary with a slight frown.

"What books, my lord?" asked Juliet curiously.

Swale snapped his fingers, and a servant brought the package from his curricle.

"It was very good of you to think of me, my lord," Juliet said doubtfully as she helped Cary up the steps, "but you need not have troubled yourself. We do have books in Surrey, you know."

"The clerk at Hatchard's said they were very new and smart," Swale said, shrugging. "You would not let me do anything for you after the accident, but I did want to do something. I'm sorry to say Mr. Shakespeare's output is not what it ought to be. Nothing at all new from him this year or last year either. Probably, he will never recover from the whole *Hamlet* fiasco."

Recognizing that he was making a joke, and a joke at his own expense, Juliet stared at him openmouthed.

"What room have you made up for Swale, Julie?" Cary interrupted. "His lordship will want to make himself presentable before he meets my aunt."

Juliet's eyes were big and round. "I have made up

Hastings, but—oh, Cary! You don't mean—He's not staying *here?*"

"He has to stay here," Cary told her grimly. "God help us."

She gulped as she thought of the disabled bell; the hideous furniture; the cold hearth; the general disorder; and, above all, the R-A-T. "Perhaps another room—"

Cary's lip curled beneath his mustache. "Hastings will do nicely, Julie. Billy will see to you, Swale," he added, looking around. "Where is that infernal boy?"

Juliet felt her cheeks reddening. Cary knew as well as anyone that Hastings was the worst room in the house, even without the charming modifications she had made to it. It had the most hideous, stiff Restoration furniture. Prisons boasted more comfortable beds. Swale would think the Wayborns were poverty-stricken! "I could have Quebec made up," she whispered to her brother.

"No, indeed," Cary snorted. "Hastings will be quite good enough for *him*. We ain't friends, Julie. We're tied together until this bloody race is over."

"Just put me anywhere, Miss Wayborn," Swale said cheerfully. "I'm not particular. And do please take the books. I always fork over a little present when I make an extended visit. And if you find I've caused any damage, do please present me with a bill."

Cary looked at him with contempt and strode into the house, leaving them to follow—or not.

"I will give them to my aunt, sir," Juliet said, accepting the little package. "And thank you. My lord," she remembered to add.

Inside the house, four curved walls formed a grand circular entrance hall. A star-shaped pattern was laid out on the floor in black and white marble. The walls were painted pale blue, and they looked even paler in the brilliant sunlight spilling from the glass dome far overhead. Matching staircases flanked the hall, one curving east, the other curving west.

A footman appeared in the hall to help Cary up the eastern stairs. Swale started up the staircase after him, but Cary said rudely, "You're on the other side of the house, Swale. I'm going to my room, Julie. Send some tea up to me right away, will you? And make sure you cut the crusts off the sandwiches; otherwise, I won't eat them."

Swale frowned up at him. "Does he always order you about like a servant?" he asked Juliet.

"Certainly he does," she replied, covering her nervousness as best she could, "but I never attend him. Billy went to tell Sir Benedict you have arrived, my lord. He'll be back directly to show you your room. Please excuse me," she added, desperate to get away and speak to the housekeeper.

"No, don't," he said immediately. "Don't go!"

She turned to look at him, wide-eyed.

"You don't dare leave me alone in this place," he pointed out. "I'm sure to break something." With a sweep of his arm, he indicated the tall Wedgwood vases in various niches along the curved, pale blue walls.

"Oh, break anything you like," she cried, darting toward the hall. "They're quite fake, you know."

He stepped in front of her. "Fake vases? Can't put flowers in them or anything?" He stood with his arms behind his back, his face open and friendly, but he seemed determined not to let her leave. "How curious."

"No, of course they're real vases," said Juliet impatiently. "I meant they're not real *Greek* vases. They're just plain, ordinary Wedgwood. If you break one, I'm sure the factory still has the mold. We could always replace it. They're reproductions, I meant. Not fakes."

"Ah."

He looked at her so sharply that her resentment was aroused. "I expect there are no reproductions at Auckland Palace," she said. "I expect that Wayborn is quite a cottage compared to Auckland Palace. Is there really a drawing room with walls paneled in amber?"

"I daresay there is," he said, wrinkling his brow. "I know there is one in turquoise and one in malachite. Or is it lapis lazuli?"

She laughed. "Don't you know?"

"Auckland is so far north I go there but once or twice a year. You are fortunate, Miss Wayborn, to have two such charming places so near to London."

"Yes, I have Tanglewood and Wayborn," she replied, giving up all hope of escaping. "You are interested in purchasing a small estate near London, as I recall."

"Am I? Oh yes," he stammered, turning red.

"Need it be small?" she asked curiously. "That is, Lord Skeldings might be persuaded to part with Silvercombe. It is very bad for the neighborhood that he lives now almost entirely in Bath. The house is so big it is rarely let for more than a month or two out of the year, and really, it is not modern. The plumbing is quite dreadful. But it is the only place in the neighborhood that might be available. Lord Redfylde has taken it through the end of the year, but I daresay he will give it up after Lady Redfylde is safely delivered."

"I came to Surrey—" he began, then corrected himself. "One of the reasons I came to Surrey was to have speech of Lord Redfylde. Try as I may, I could not find him in London."

"Unfortunately, his lordship is not at Silvercombe now," she told him. "He spends but little time there, though his wife is ill and she carries his child. I do not know when he means to return. It is said that business takes him to London, but you say he is not in London. I wonder where he could be."

"Never mind—he will return eventually," said Swale quickly, guessing that the man had a mistress somewhere.

"You mean to ask him about his wager," she guessed.

"Certainly."

She looked at him with approval. "I told Benedict to ask him, but he refused. He said it wouldn't be proper."

Swale smiled. "There is some difference, I think, in my case. I may safely ask his lordship why he would hazard ten thousand pounds on me. Sir Benedict would look a damn fool asking Redfylde why he had wagered against his brother."

"I suppose you are right," she said reluctantly.

"Of course I am right," he told her as Billy appeared at last.

"Your room is not quite ready," Juliet said quickly. "Billy will show you to Sir Benedict's dressing room. I will—shall I send his man to attend you?" she asked doubtfully, eyeing his disheveled clothes and wild hair.

"Thank you, no," he answered. "Bowditch will have arrived by now."

Juliet was startled. "Bowditch! Have you taken him back? But what about Fifi?"

He was obliged to tell her of Fifi's perfidy. "She has betrayed my poor Bowditch just as she betrayed Mr. Wayborn's groom. So you see, my dear Miss Wayborn, she really was a shocking strumpet." He chuckled. "It must be rather tiresome to always be wrong. First, you misjudge me, then poor Bowditch."

"If you think," Juliet said, her eyes flashing, "that your Bowditch will ever set foot in this house, you very much mistake the matter! I will send Pickering to you."

His eyes flashed like emeralds. "Do it," he

answered, considerably annoyed, "and I'll bloody well throw him at your head!"

"'Ere now!" Billy objected instantly. "There's no call for your lordship to be using such language in front of Miss Julie! We don't go in for that sort of thing at the Hall."

Juliet braced for an explosion of resentment from Swale, but he merely smiled. "You're quite right, Master Billy. My apologies, Miss Wayborn. Unforgivably rude." He gave Juliet a short bow and the impertinent Billy a pat on the head. "Send me all the Pickerings you like, my dear Miss Wayborn. Bowditch can sleep in the stable."

"Well!" Juliet said to herself when he had disappeared with Billy. She did not know what to make of Swale's sudden reappearance in her life. She had assumed when she had first seen him, that he must be staying with his sister at Silvercombe and that he had only come to pay his respects. He would certainly have an added reason for wanting to stay at Silvercombe, since it was Serena's residence. But he was to stay at Wayborn Hall. She couldn't think of the events in Hertfordshire without profound embarrassment, and she supposed he must feel the same. After all, they might be engaged now or even married. And yet he had not seemed embarrassed. He seemed to be trying to make himself agreeable. He seemed . . . happy.

"Julie!" Cary shouted from somewhere above her. "Where is my tea?"

Something must be done about the rat in Hastings immediately, she decided, hurrying off to find Sir Benedict's personal manservant. "I've two rather desperate cases for you, Pick," she apologized. "Lord Swale don't care how he looks, and Master Cary has grown a rat—I mean, a beard!" she corrected herself hastily before rushing off to find Mrs. Spinner.

* * *

Sir Benedict's dressing room was a large compartment that smelled handsomely of cedar. Billy filled the basin with water, and Swale stripped to the waist to wash. Billy picked Swale's coat and shirt up from the floor, then obligingly poured icy cold water over his head with a suddenness that quite took Swale's breath away.

"I am gratified, Master Billy. You have reminded me of my school days."

Billy began vigorously toweling the lord's shoulders, but Swale preferred to do this himself. "Don't worry," he told the disappointed boy. "There's a big tip in it for you if you don't mind earning it."

Billy's eyes narrowed suspiciously. "How's that?"

Swale finished drying off and hung the towel around his neck. "All I want is a little information."

"Like what?" Billy wanted to know.

Swale shrugged. "Like . . . for example . . . who's going to marry the daughter of the house?"

Billy's eyes started from his head. "What, milord?"

"Come now!" Swale said amiably. "The servants at Auckland Palace had a pool going on my sister. Robert, the second footman, made out with a hundred pounds, I understand, when his candidate won the fair Lady Maria Ambler."

"A hundred pounds, milord!" Billy cried, adding an appreciative whistle.

"The man she married was a bit of a dark horse," Swale explained. "So tell me, who's your money on, Master Billy?"

Young Billy stuck his finger in his ear and performed a thorough and pleasurable search of its contours before answering. "Well, there's no pool or nothing, milord—Mrs. Spinner don't hold with servants gambling and all. But there's no law against speculating, now is there? Mrs. Spinner speculates herself."

Swale, while having no idea who Mrs. Spinner was, asked solicitously, "And who does the good Mrs. Spinner favor?"

"Mr. Calverstock," said Billy with a shrug. He leaned against Sir Benedict's dressing table and folded his arms, beginning to enjoy the man-to-man chat. "But he's only a younger son, and anyway, Miss Julie couldn't like his wet mouth. He's always licking his lips. See?"

Billy was a gifted mimic. Swale made a note to himself never to lick his lips in Miss Wayborn's presence. "Mrs. Spinner is bound to be disappointed," he said. "Who do you favor, Billy?"

"Captain Cary's coming on nicely," said young Billy, after a moment spent exploring his other ear. "He made his fortune in the war, and he's dead handsome into the bargain."

"And what about me?" Swale demanded.

"Cor!" said Billy, looking at the Marquess in cool surprise. "You, milord?"

Swale tapped the side of his nose. "Remember the dark horse, Billy."

Billy shook his head sadly. "I wouldn't give you false hope, milord. If Miss Julie put you in Hastings, she must have had her reasons."

"Oh? Has—has she put me in Hastings?"

"Aye, milord. So, you see, it seems hopeless."

"Thank you, Billy," said Swale, producing a handful of small gold coins. Selecting one, he gave it to the boy. "You've been very helpful."

The boy's eyes widened with new respect. "Are you rich, milord?"

"I have twenty thousand a year," Swale told him.

"Cor!" said Billy, shaking his head. "And not a far-thing of it spent on clothes."

"Moreover, in case you don't know this, Master Billy, I have expectations."

"I thought you was a Marquess," said Billy suspiciously.

"I am," said Swale. "But my father is a Duke and unlike the unfortunate Mr. Calverstock, I am not a younger son."

"A Juke is it?" said Billy with a sniff. "When her mother, Lady Wayborn, was on her deathbed, she made Miss Julie promise her she'd marry for love, so a Juke is nothing to her."

"Indeed," Swale said. "Then it would appear to be a hopeless case, Master Billy."

Billy nodded sympathetically. "Not but that we wouldn't like to see our Miss Julie marry a Juke or even a Marquess," he said kindly. "And I don't much like Mr. Calverstock. As for the Captain—"

"Oh? Don't you like the great Captain Cary?" Swale asked, grinning. "Hero of Trafalgar?"

"I don't, milord, and that's a fact," said Billy. "I don't hold with a man getting above himself, if you like, and this Captain is only the son of a clergyman, Trafalgar or no Trafalgar. Why should Miss Julie throw herself away on a sailor?" He looked at the Marquess frankly. "I'd say it's a bloody shame, milord, that you wasn't born with the Captain's looks."

"I am glad you don't hold with a man getting above himself," Swale observed dryly.

"No, milord," said Billy. "That I do not. No good ever comes of it." He looked at Swale shrewdly. "If Miss Julie was to marry you, milord, would the ladies at Silvercombe be at home to her?"

Swale frowned. "What do you mean? What ladies?"

"Lady Serena Calverstock and Lady Maria

Fitzwilliam," Billy answered in a hard voice. "Very fancy ladies they are, from London. Damn them to hell."

Swale was taken aback. "Maria is at Silvercombe? Maria *Fitzwilliam?*"

"Aye, milord. And a very proud, disagreeable, nasty bit of goods she is too!" sniffed Billy. "Flouncing around the village with her nose in the air, speaking nothing but ill of poor Miss Julie, who never did a wrong deed in all her life."

"Red hair, Billy? Pug nose and a rather tall, solemn-looking husband?"

Billy nodded. "The Colonel. Do you know the lady, milord?"

"My sister, Master Billy."

"Gorblimey!" said Billy. "Is it any wonder Miss Julie put you in Hastings?"

A tall figure dressed very correctly in black entered the room and cleared its throat.

"You're Pickering?"

"Indeed, my lord," Sir Benedict's valet answered, surveying with a cold eye the water dripping over the carpet of his master's closet. "Miss Wayborn asked me to offer my services in the absence of your man." His exacting blue eyes raked over Lord Swale's person. "I am a little acquainted with Mr. Bowditch, my lord."

"Are you indeed?"

"There was a time when Mademoiselle Huppert, Miss Wayborn's *femme de toilette*, regarded Mr. Bowditch as almost a gentleman. I was obliged to disillusion her."

"Ah! The fatal Fifi strikes again," said Swale, pulling his shirt on over his head and raising his braces over his shoulders.

"Indeed, sir. Mr. Bowditch will be quite comfortable with the coachman in the coach house," said Pickering, picking up Swale's coat and tossing it to Billy.

"Take it away, William, and give it a good brushing," he instructed.

"I could do with a good brushing as well," said Swale ruefully, "if I am to be presentable to the ladies. And I won't say no to a shave."

"And a trim, my lord?" Pickering produced a pair of shears from his pocket.

"I shouldn't think so," said Swale, gingerly touching the shaggy red hair covering his ears. "My crowning glory and all that sort of thing."

"What do you think, Mr. Pickering," exclaimed the exuberant Billy. "His lordship wants to marry Miss Julie. He's a Marquess, but there's an expectation of a Jukedom, and he's got *twenty thousand* pounds a year."

"Indeed, my lord?" Pickering smiled. "Miss Wayborn confided in me that she finds a cropped head enormously attractive."

Swale recoiled. "What? A crop? What, bald?"

"Yes, my lord."

"I'll look a fool," Swale protested, eyeing his image in the mirror over the dressing table.

"Yes, my lord."

"I daresay a trim wouldn't hurt," he said, reluctantly taking the chair Pickering offered. "A little off here and there."

"Yes, my lord," agreed Pickering, tying a cloth around his lordship's neck and going to work with the scissors.

Chapter 13

Benedict stood at the window in his half-brother's bedroom. For several moments, he stood there, but he was not admiring the view of the lake. Cary had removed his sling, and he was now sprawled across the bed, flexing his weak arm. "You must be mad to bring him here," Benedict said at last. "He is most unwelcome, Cary. If you don't care what he's done to your friend Mr. Calverstock, at least think of your sister."

Cary scowled. It always chafed his pride to be scolded by his older brother. "Stacy Calverstock! I confess I am heartily disgusted with Stacy. He wouldn't even challenge Swale to a duel—after having his nose broke, if you please! I was never more sick in my life. Old Auckland sent him a fat cheque for his nose, and the nincompoop took it. Can you believe? I know he's desperate for money, but a gentleman does not accept a cheque for a broken nose." His scowl deepened. "But what has Swale done to Julie?"

Benedict gave his brother a brief history of Lord Swale's activities in Hertfordshire. "Now you can see it's impossible for him to stay here. Juliet will be embarrassed—horribly embarrassed!"

Cary was on his feet, striding from one end of the room to the other, his face dark with fury. "So Horatio thought they ought to marry, did he? Swale! Marry my sister? Not bloody likely! What does he mean, pretending he wants to buy Tanglewood—as though I should ever sell to the likes of him!"

"Are you thinking of selling Tanglewood?" Benedict asked sharply. "Are you in debt?"

"No, my dear brother, I am not in debt," said Cary bitterly. "That is, no more so than any other gentleman of my acquaintance. I wouldn't take a cheque from Auckland if Lord Swine broke my nose, I can tell you, however straitened I might be."

"If you have bills—" Benedict began.

"Naturally, I have bills," Cary haughtily interrupted. "But if I were to sell Tanglewood, the last thing I should do with the money is squander it by paying tradesmen's bills. I honor them with my custom. Is that not enough? If anyone asks for my tailor's name, I give it freely."

"Then you *are* considering selling Tanglewood," exclaimed Benedict. "I can't believe it."

"Why shouldn't I sell it if I wish to?" Cary demanded. "My grandmother left it to me. I own it outright. The house stands empty, and I have no wife and brats to put in it. All I want from it is the income."

"Your mother was born at Tanglewood," Benedict chided him. "Your sister has some love for the place, if you do not. How will Juliet like it if you sell?"

"She may like it very well," returned Cary, "if I sell it to Horatio. As a matter of fact, I told him I *would* sell it to him if he marries Julie. She'd be mistress of the manor."

Benedict shook his head. "And how do you suppose

your sister will feel when she discovers that Captain Cary wishes to marry her merely as the means of obtaining Tanglewood?"

Cary was genuinely surprised. "What should it matter why he marries her if she loves him? The estate will be hers too, and as you pointed out, she loves Tanglewood."

"It will be worse for her if she *does* love Horatio," said Benedict, raising his voice. "It will be agony for her when she discovers that *he* does not love *her*."

Cary scoffed. "You seem to think it impossible that anyone could love our sister. I tell you, she had half a dozen young pups falling at her feet in London, and since the race, it has only gotten better. Bosher has composed a sonnet in her honor called 'The Chariotrix,' I'm sorry to say, and Lord Meadowsweet sent one of his American Indians to the house in Park Lane to be her servant. Don't fret—I sent him away," he added quickly.

"Mr. Bosher and Lord Meadowsweet are of no consequence," said Benedict. "But Juliet may actually care for her cousin Horatio. Did you actually tell Captain Cary you'd sell him the estate if he marries Juliet?"

"I don't see the harm," Cary said sullenly, breaking off abruptly as Juliet backed into the room with the tea tray. Juliet stood looking nervously from one brother to the other. Being so different in character, they were often at loggerheads, and she was a poor peacekeeper.

"What harm?" she inquired, setting down the tray.

"Prepare yourself, my dear," Benedict said gravely. "Your brother's guest is not Mr. Calverstock after all, but Lord Swale."

"Yes, I know," said Juliet. "I've seen him. Swale has

to stay with Cary until the race takes place. He's on probation with his club. But, Cary, does he have to stay in the same house with you? Couldn't he stay at Silvercombe? What am I supposed to *do* with him?"

"What race?" Benedict demanded. "Good God, Cary! Haven't you had enough racing?"

"I could never make you understand," Cary said airily. "But as soon as my arm is healed, the race will take place as originally conceived. Too right it will. My chestnuts against his lordship's grays from London to Southend. Until that time, Swale and I are chained together. Whither I goest, he goest too. And yes, Julie, he has to stay in this house with me."

"Why on earth did you bring him *here?*" Benedict said sharply. "You couldn't stay in London?"

"I don't care to practice my driving before a London audience," Cary replied. "My bloody arm shakes! Do you think I want all of London gawping at me when I drop my own bleeding ribbons?"

"Mind your language," Benedict snapped. "Why didn't you take Swale to Tanglewood?"

"Tanglewood!" Cary scoffed. "The house is in disrepair. I wouldn't trust the roof as far as I can throw it."

"Whose fault is that?" said Juliet angrily. "I wish Grandmamma had left it to *me*—I'd make something of it!"

"And there's no housekeeper," Cary continued breezily. "Swale might enjoy camping out in a ruin, but I'm a civilized fellow. I like my meals on time. In any case, he'll have a devil of a time hiring ruffians to disable me in my own neighborhood."

Juliet bit her lip. "But, Cary," she said, "Swale didn't do that. We think it was Lord Redfylde, and he *is* at Silvercombe. All the bets are to be honored in the new race," she told Benedict. "Lord Redfylde still stands to lose ten thousand pounds if Cary beats Swale. Which he is certain to do," she added for her brother's encouragement, "as soon as his arm is completely healed."

Cary sniffed. "I've heard this crackbrained theory that Lord Redfylde is behind the attack on me. It's rubbish."

"What?" cried Juliet. "Indeed, it is not rubbish. Lord Redfylde bet ten thousand pounds on Swale to win. He must have known something was going to happen to you, Cary. How else do you explain it?"

"Simple, my dear infant," her brother replied. "I had the whole story from Stacy. Lord Dulwich goaded Redfylde into taking that absurd bet, saying he was too chickenhearted or too straitened to hazard a mere ten thousand on the outcome. Redfylde was provoked into taking it, and of course, ten thousand is nothing to him."

A plausible enough explanation, she supposed, given male vanity, and yet every feeling rebelled against it. Swale *must* be innocent. "Benedict," she pleaded, "tell him he's wrong."

Cary's lip curled. "So Swale has deceived you as well. Poor Julie! Just you look at this note he sent me— along with Bernard's money—then tell me I'm wrong." Reaching into his wallet, he almost flung the scrap of paper at her.

It was a pompous and condescending communication; she could scarcely believe that *Ginger* had written it.

His lordship, the Marquess of Swale, sent his compliments to Mr. Cary Wayborn and trusted that the latter's touch of influenza made him not too uncomfortable.

It is to be regretted that such a trifling illness must prevent you from keeping our appointment, sir, and even more regrettable that you must choose to take the ungentlemanlike step of sending an imposter in your place. I daresay you instructed Miss Wayborn to cheat as well, and the abominable transvestite was more than happy to comply, but I must remind you that our wager was upon a race between myself and yourself, and while I congratulate you on having a mustachio'd amazon for a sister, I cannot, in good conscience, keep your five hundred pounds. Therefore, I am returning your money until such a time as you are recovered from your sickness and may meet me in person at the Black Lantern Inn. I urge you to leave your unnatural sister at home where she belongs.

Cordially,

Geoffrey Ambler, Lord Swale

Juliet's face was scarlet by the time she finished reading this.

"He has me struck down like a dog in the street," Cary said through clenched teeth, "then he taunts me with this! And he dares to insult Julie—abominable transvestite! Mustachio'd amazon!"

Juliet tore the note into tiny pieces and flung it into the fireplace. "That is an unforgivable letter, and I will make him pay for it, but it don't signify his lordship's guilt. He was angry when he wrote those words, and you know, we *did* put it out for Aunt Elinor's sake that you had influenza."

"Listen to the poor lamb defending the wolf!" said Cary. "If you like him so well, why did you not marry him when you had the chance?"

"I never said I liked him," she protested. "He is coarse and rude, and—and let me tell you, his face belongs in a grotto! Indeed, I do *not* like him."

"Let us be thankful for that!" said Cary. "If you

ever start to feel you might like him, just remember that note, my dear, sweet mustachio'd amazon. He accuses you of cheating too, my dear, sweet, unnatural sister. My abominable transvestite!"

"Oh!" cried Juliet furiously.

"His lordship is here now, Juliet," said Benedict, giving her shoulder a sympathetic pat. "Whatever we feel, we must afford him the dignity and respect due to a guest."

"Does that include you, Sir Benedict?" she responded.

The baronet raised his brows. "What have I done?"

"It's what you *will* do that worries me," she retorted. "And that is provoke Lord Swale with your cold disdain! I expect you to be an amiable host. And though it costs me, I shall be an amiable hostess. I've decided to put him in—in Quebec."

"I put my *friends* in Quebec," Cary objected. "Put him in Hastings."

"I can't put him in Hastings," Juliet cried.

Benedict shuddered. "Certainly not! I had understood Hastings to be unsuitable for all human habitation. The servants use it as a sort of a storage cupboard, I think."

"I might put him in Agincourt," she said slowly.

"Certainly not!" both her brothers cried at once.

"I'm sure we have no reason to show off for Lord Swale," said Benedict. "Runnymede will be more than sufficient for his lordship's needs, and it has the advantage of being on the other side of the house from the family's rooms. Put him in Runnymede."

Juliet looked mutinous but said nothing.

"Go on, Juliet," said Benedict. "See to your guest."

"And send up more tea," Cary added imperiously. "This has grown cold, my girl. Did you even boil the water?"

In the hall, Juliet nearly collided with Pickering, who was leaving Sir Benedict's dressing room. "Ah, Pickering," she said, giving him the tea tray. "Have you finished his lordship?"

"Yes, Miss Julie," he replied. "I sent him down to Lady Elkins on the terrace."

"And?"

"I think you'll be pleased, Miss Julie."

"Master Cary wants more tea," she told him. "And see if you can't get him to shave that fungus. If he refuses, we can always do it while he's sleeping."

"Yes, Miss Julie."

"Thank you, Pickering," she said, running down the hall to the stairs. "Pickering?"

"Yes, Miss Julie?"

She chewed on her bottom lip for a moment, then said decisively, "I'm moving his lordship to Agincourt. Will you please inform Mrs. Spinner?"

Pickering was startled. "Agincourt, Miss?"

"Yes, Pickering," she said testily. "Why shouldn't I put him in Agincourt if I wish? I'm the mistress of this house until my brother marries, and I shall put him anywhere I please. I defy anyone to question my right to do so!"

"Yes, Miss Julie."

"Inform Mrs. Spinner there's to be a fire and fresh flowers and every good thing. Except—and I am firm on this, Pickering—under no circumstances is his lordship's man Bowditch to be admitted into the house."

"Yes, Miss Julie," said Pickering with unusual fervor.

Feeling rather flustered, she paused at the mirror in the hall to smooth her hair before descending the stairs to the drawing room. It was a mild spring afternoon, and the French windows all stood open, and she could see the terrace beyond. Lady Elkins was seated outside with a shawl wrapped around her shoulders, her face set in an expression of peevish disgust.

"More tea, my lord?"

Juliet was startled by the coldness in her aunt's voice. What on earth had Swale done to Aunt Elinor? It was not in Lady Elkins's nature to be anything but amiable to a young bachelor of great fortune and rank.

But perhaps, Juliet thought with a smile, Lady Elkins had accepted that Lord Swale was beyond her niece's grasp, so she very sensibly had decided to hate the very man she would have delighted in calling nephew.

"I wouldn't say no, Lady Elkins," Swale replied cheerfully. At first, Juliet could not see him, but then he crossed the terrace to hand his cup to his hostess, stopping in front of the open window.

"Oh, my dear, sweet Lord!" Juliet murmured, shocked into blasphemy.

His head was bare, almost completely bare. Less than a quarter inch of red hair covered his skull in the severest crop she had ever seen. She could only stare, stupefied, as he turned, and catching sight of her standing within the house, he smiled.

"Here she is, Lady Elkins. Miss Wayborn, will you not join us?"

Juliet stepped onto the terrace, moving automatically, her eyes trained on Swale's shorn head.

He ran his hand across the stubble self-consciously. "She's speechless, Lady Elkins. That's a good sign, isn't it?"

Once the shock had faded, she discovered that the cut actually suited him. It made him look more gentlemanlike, and his skull had a good shape. His ears were rather long, but they did not stick out too much. All the same, much to her own surprise, she missed the rumpled red mop. She did not, however, miss the rumpled clothes. Thanks to Pickering, his lordship was neat without being fastidious in a dark blue coat and buckskin breeches.

"He scalped me, Miss Wayborn," said Swale, rubbing his shorn head. "Not so much as an inch of stubble did he leave me. But I was told that a *certain lady* preferred a cropped head, and . . . one must make sacrifices when one is"—he cleared his throat in embarrassment—"in love."

Juliet's mouth was suddenly as dry as a desert.

"Lord Swale," Lady Elkins said icily, "has come to Surrey to make himself agreeable to a *certain lady*. I think we can guess who that lady is."

"You see the lengths to which I am willing to go to please her," said Swale.

Juliet's breath caught in her throat. She now understood her aunt's coldness, but strangely, she was not amused. So Swale really had come to fix things between himself and Serena Calverstock! Perhaps they were already engaged. If Juliet knew anything about Serena, she would certainly seize the chance to become Lady Swale. Maria Fitzwilliam would be pleased in her new sister, and she supposed his Grace of Auckland could have no real objection to the lady, who was beautiful and well-bred and rich.

But Swale! Could he be taken in by a phony like Serena? Did he truly believe that the lady, after loving Alex Devize, then Cary Wayborn, two very handsome and dashing young bucks, could suddenly transfer her affections to Swale, who was neither handsome nor charming?

And how dare Swale come to Wayborn Hall and use

her home as a base of operations for his pursuit of another woman, and a woman she detested too!

She had no claim on him of course, but she considered it inexpressibly rude of him to court another woman under her very nose—and to brag about it to her face. Had he so little regard for her dignity as that? The knowledge that Serena could not possibly return his affection and that she would certainly make him miserable did not console her in the least.

"The Beast has come to claim his Beauty, in fact," she said lightly.

"Precisely!" he said, holding out his cup to Lady Elkins and beaming proudly.

"I seem to be out of tea, my lord," snapped Lady Elkins bitterly.

Juliet folded her hands and said with tolerable nonchalance, "I had understood, my lord, that you had quite a different reason for coming into Surrey. I had understood that you are on probation with your club and that one of the terms of your probation is that you stay near my brother and make sure no harm comes to him until the race."

"Well, yes," he admitted. "But the neighborhood has another attraction for me. I think you know me well enough, Miss Wayborn, to know that I'd tell every man jack of my club to go hang himself. But for my own reasons, I want to be here. This lady . . . well, London is pretty flat without her, let me tell you! Life, Miss Wayborn, is pretty flat without her, to say the truth."

"Excuse me," Juliet said in a strangled voice. "I've only just remembered—I must speak to Cook about the savory."

He bowed to her. "I'll eat anything you put in front of me, Miss Wayborn. Even if you set it on fire!"

"I remember," she said coldly.

He called after her as she made her escape. "I'll even eat cheese with pleasure."

"Odious, odious toad!" she muttered, mounting the stairs that led to the splendid guest suite that bore the name Agincourt. She could scarcely believe that for one half moment, she had actually thought she was glad to see him! That, as Cary had accused, she liked him!

"Toad!" she cried aloud.

"Miss Julie?"

The two footmen carrying Swale's trunk into Agincourt's dressing room looked at her curiously. "Are you all right, Miss Julie?" asked Albert. "You look a mite feverish."

"Take that back to Hastings at once!" she snapped. "Agincourt would be quite wasted on a philistine like Lord Swale! I will teach him to make love to another woman right under my nose! I will teach that bald man to tell me life is pretty flat without Serena Calverstock!"

The footmen exchanged bewildered glances. "Yes, Miss Julie."

"And if a dead rat was good enough for Stacy, it's more than good enough for *him!*"

Returning to the terrace, she found Swale alone and the servants clearing the tea away. "Where is my aunt?" she asked him in an accusatory tone.

"I didn't break her, if that's what you mean," Swale answered, laughing.

"Lady Elkins has the headache, Miss Julie," one of the servants told Juliet. "Miss Huddle is with her now."

"Thank you, Jem." She waited until the servants were gone before she said, "Cary is resting, and Sir Benedict is with his estate agent, my lord."

"And Lady Elkins has the migraine. If you wanted

to be alone with me, Miss Wayborn, you only had to say so!" He smiled, but inwardly, he was rather nervous.

He had arrived uncertain of his reception and anxious to please. The sight of her waiting on the steps—fleetingly he had fantasized that she waited for him—had firmed his resolve. Really, until that moment, he had almost convinced himself that his sudden desire to marry her was a fancy that would soon pass. But it was all he could do not to rush up the steps and carry her off in his arms. Life *was* pretty flat without her.

She had received him civilly at first, but in the entrance hall, he could not help but notice her evident desire to get away from him. Indeed, he had been on the verge of offering to go if his presence was so unpleasant to her. But that would never do—if she accepted his offer, then he would have to leave Wayborn Hall, and that would be the end of a very good thing.

He had succeeded at least in making her laugh, and that was his only encouragement.

Her aunt he had found rather cold to him, even after he had confided to her that his purpose in coming to Surrey was marriage. But that coldness, he supposed, was to be expected after his conduct in Hertfordshire. Lady Elkins was a good aunt, not one of these ambitious, matchmaking females who look only at a fellow's fortune in judging his worth. He would have to work hard to gain her good opinion. He congratulated himself on his suavity in that initial interview.

And he must have made some inroads into the old lady's heart, for had she not excused herself, giving him the chance to be alone with Juliet?

Dear Juliet! The poor girl was trying very hard to maintain her composure, he could tell, but clearly, she was deeply affected by his declarations of love. Cutting off his hair merely to satisfy her whim—that was pure genius. The poor girl was trembling, but she clung to her pride and tried to appear aloof.

"Being alone with you is precisely what I don't want," she retorted, tossing her head. "But since no one else can stomach you, Ginger, I suppose it is my duty to entertain you. Or, perhaps you would prefer to go now to pay your respects at Silvercombe? Our stable is far from complete here, but I'm sure we could manage to find something for you to ride."

"Silvercombe?" he repeated innocently. Thanks to Billy, he was ready for this test of his mettle. "But you said Lord Redfylde is not at home. Why should I go to Silvercombe?"

Juliet frowned at him. "Redfylde isn't there, but Lady Serena is and your sister, of course, and her husband, Colonel Fitzwilliam. Indeed, I wonder if you would not be more comfortable *staying* at Silvercombe."

"I have not been invited to stay at Silvercombe," he pointed out. "I have been invited to stay here, and I have accepted your brother's kind invitation. Besides, you have already spoken to the cook about the savory. It would be churlish of me to leave you now."

"No one could ever say Lord Swale was churlish," she remarked dryly. "It is three hours until dinner . . ."

"I am at your disposal, Miss Wayborn," he said quickly.

Was he practicing lines on her that he meant to use later on his ladylove? she wondered in a fit of ill temper. "Would you care to see the house and grounds, my lord?" she asked stiffly.

He accepted the grudging offer with enthusiasm. "I've already seen the terrace. Most impressive. Another few days and the rhododendrons will give a lovely display. Remember the rhododendrons at Tangle-wood Vicarage? Where you explained to me the folly of having something particular to say? I think of those rhododendrons fondly."

"Actually, we have two terraces," she told him briskly. "But this one has a view of the lake."

"Man-made?" he inquired politely, following her back into the house.

"I have no idea," she sniffed. "It is simply the lake. It's always been there. This is the drawing room," she continued, moving quickly through the room. "These are the tables. Those are the chairs. Paintings, as you see, on the walls. That one is Benedict's prize— a Constable. Rugs on the floor."

"A Constable, Miss Wayborn?" he said, squinting at Sir Benedict's prize painting. "I think not. It appears to be a landscape with some sheep."

"Constable is the name of the painter," she told him acidly. "Don't you know anything about the arts?"

"I'm fond of music," he answered, "but I daresay I couldn't tell you a thing about art."

She rushed out of the room before he could betray any more of his appalling ignorance. In similar style, she showed him the morning room, the breakfast room, the dining room, the main library, and then she brought him upstairs to show him the smaller in-formal library.

"And I brought books to this place," he said ruefully. "Like coals to Newcastle, I see."

"Our serious books are in the library downstairs," she told him. "This book room is devoted to plays, novels, poetry." She ran her fingers over the volumes on a shelf. "Some old journals. My aunt is inordinately fond of horrid mysteries. You're welcome to read anything you like. We generally get the London papers by noon each day."

"Excellent," he said cheerfully. "That is what I call an easy distance."

Lady Elkins's bedroom was next to the upstairs library, then Juliet's own room, then Cary's. She passed all three of these rooms, then opened the door to the fourth. "This is Quebec."

Quebec was a large, octagonal room with windows overlooking the lake. The walls were paneled in dark green watered silk, and a huge black bearskin lay on the parquet floor before the white marble hearth. Huntsmen's trophies lined the walls. The only other ornament was a large painting of a military gentleman that hung over the mantle. "Sir Roger Wayborn, the first baronet," Juliet explained. "The fifth son of the third Earl Wayborn. He went to Canada with Baron Dorchester in 1759. They fought together in the Battle of Quebec, hence the name of the room."

Swale was looking at the large head of the animal mounted opposite Sir Roger's portrait. It had the largest, strangest antlers he had ever seen. "That is called a caribou, I believe," he said. "And the smaller head next to it is a beaver's."

"I think you are right," she said, surprised.

He stood under the head of a large, snarling cat. "This, of course is a mountain lion. I have been to Canada. Oh, not in a military capacity," he said quickly when he saw her eyes light up. "One of my disreputable cousins has an estate on the St. Lawrence River. I spent an enjoyable six months there when I was seventeen, paddling around in a canoe with an Indian guide. Do I get points off in your accounts, Miss Wayborn?"

She laughed. "For paddling in a canoe?"

"For being sent down from Oxford. That's why I was sent to Canada in the first place."

"Yes, indeed," she said. "But points back on for the canoe-paddling scheme."

He grinned at her. The bed in Quebec, he could not help but notice, was a huge carved box of walnut topped with a thick feather mattress and hung all around with heavy curtains of green and gold brocade. "Sir Benedict's chamber, I daresay," he remarked. "Very handsome."

"Quebec," she told him, "is one of our guest rooms. You're wondering why I didn't put *you* in Quebec," she guessed, toying with the polished brass door handle.

"It does seem a comfortable chamber."

"Yes, but unfortunately, it's haunted," Miss Wayborn apologized.

"By the first baronet, Sir Roger?"

"Certainly not," she said. "There are no ghosts in my family, thank you. It's the caribou. The last person to sleep here was butted out of the window by the caribou."

"The ghost of the caribou."

"M-m-m," she smugly agreed. "So you see, I could not in good conscience put your lordship in Quebec. If the caribou were to take you in dislike . . ."

"Now, Miss Wayborn," he chuckled. "Do you really expect me to believe you don't wish me to be butted out of the window by the ghost of your caribou?"

"There is a tree outside the window," she explained, moving smoothly out into the hall, "so it is not as though you'd break your neck."

The next bedroom she showed him was Agincourt. Her pride was evident, and he could easily see why. The carpet was dark blue with the gold fleur-de-lis of France, while the bed hangings were the red and gold of the English king. The scarlet walls were hung with tapestries depicting the famous victory of Henry V over the French at Agincourt in 1415.

"Splendid, isn't it?" she said. "I did think of putting you here, but as a matter of fact, this chamber is reserved for my cousin, Captain Cary."

"And a fire has been lit," Swale observed. "Do you expect him momentarily?"

"Oh," Juliet said airily, "there is always a fire in Agincourt in honor of our ancestors who fought there."

Runnymede was on the opposite side of the house, up the western staircase, just three doors from Hastings. While not as splendid as Agincourt, it was a handsome, comfortable chamber with dark blue hangings around the bed and a view of the rolling green farmland of Surrey from the tall windows.

"One of your illustrious ancestors was at the signing of the Magna Carta, I collect?"

"Baron Wayborn," she affirmed. "There is a lovely effigy of his lordship and his wife atop their tomb in the family crypt, if you're interested in effigies."

"Not as a general rule."

"Baron Wayborn's great-grandson became the first Earl Wayborn in the reign of James I. The Earl was granted his father-in-law's estate in the Midlands, but his younger brother remained here in Surrey without a title until Sir Roger was made a baronet in 1760. There have always been Wayborns in Surrey." She cleared her throat. "I would have put your lordship in Runnymede, but then Sir Benedict would not have a place to put a friend if a friend were to visit him unexpectedly. You understand."

"Certainly. Don't give it another thought."

"And this," she said, throwing open the door to the last chamber on the hall, "is Hastings."

The room was cold and dark and cramped. There was a faint smell of mold clinging to the bed hangings. Swale entered cautiously, the floorboards creaking under him, and upset a collection of old cricket bats set on one side of the door. "I take it one of your ancestors was also at the Battle of Hastings in 1066?" he inquired with forced cheer.

"Yes," she replied, remaining at the door. "But we lost that one."

Swale looked around slowly, taking in the narrow, lumpy bed that sagged in the middle, the hideous, unupholstered black chairs and benches that were the only furnishings. In one corner was a stack of boxes. "The room is not yet ready," he guessed.

"What do you mean?" she asked innocently. "Here's your trunk now," she added as two footmen carried Swale's trunk into the room. "Open the window, John," she instructed one of the footmen airily. John obeyed, opening a tiny window choked with ivy. "This is a most convenient chamber to put guests in, my lord," she told Swale. "The footmen are in the room directly above you."

Swale suddenly chuckled. "This is where I lose my temper and start throwing things, is that it, Miss Wayborn? You're testing me."

Juliet inclined her head. "Why should I test you, my lord?"

He tapped his nose. Naturally, his Juliet would not be inclined to discuss personal matters in front of the servants. He had always been raised to ignore servants, but Juliet evidently worried about wagging tongues. "Right," he said. "Mum's the word. Test away."

"Would you like to see the grounds now?" she inquired coldly.

"Passionately," he said, lavishly tipping the footmen.

"May I suggest we ride?" said Juliet. "You do ride, don't you?"

"The question is not do I ride," he informed her, "but can you keep up with me?"

Twenty minutes later, he met her downstairs in the circular entrance hall; she was dressed in a dark green riding habit and no hat, he in buckskins and a simple black coat. The horses were brought to the front steps, and he balked when he saw the nondescript brown mare she expected him to ride.

"I'm not riding that," he said stoutly. "I see you have something nice for yourself," he added resentfully, nodding toward the dancing black mare the groom was walking up and down.

"Dolly is mine," she told him irritably. "The black mare is Cary's. As you are his guest, you may ride his horse. She's very fresh. You'll probably break your neck."

They agreed to race for a half mile to the crest overlooking Silvercombe. To her chagrin and despite his weighing sixteen stone compared to her eight, he reached it first. "You ride well," she said grudgingly as she overtook him.

"I had the better mount," he said truthfully. "I wonder your brother hasn't found you a better horse. That brown mare is no longer young."

"I know," she said, leaning forward to pat Dolly's neck. "Cary bought me the prettiest saddle horse for my nineteenth birthday, but Benedict made him send her back. He was certain I'd break my neck on her—as though I should!" She sighed as she thought of the beautiful, swift black mare that had been hers so fleetingly. "Benedict doesn't ride, so he's not the best judge when it comes to horses."

He nodded absently as he looked out over the valley,

observing a vast white house with spires and battlements that reminded him of a wedding cake. "Silvercombe appears to be a large, handsome house with a very fine prospect," he remarked. "Is it really for sale?"

"I expect you would like to buy it for a *certain lady*," she said sourly, "as a wedding present."

He stared at her, amazed by this unexpected boldness, his heart pounding. Before this moment, he had been uncertain as to the feelings of his Juliet, but this must remove all doubt. When a lady asks a gentleman to buy her a country house for a wedding present, then the gentleman is on solid ground indeed! His battered heart filled with gratitude; while he had been dreading all those humiliating declarations that must accompany the courtship of any well-bred young lady, Juliet had apparently judged it best to dispense with all that and move straight to the wedding gifts. For sparing him the indignities of going down on bended knee and pleading in the wettest terms his violent love, he considered a country estate of some six thousand acres not too extravagant a tribute.

"I daresay I will," he said, smiling brilliantly. "If a certain lady desires me to purchase Silvercombe, I will of course be commanded by her."

Juliet was trembling with rage. The thought of Lady Serena—*Lady Swale*—as mistress of Silvercombe made her positively ill. "You would do that to me," she said bitterly. "You'd buy a house not a mile from my brother's door, and—and *live* there!"

"Possibly not," he said, now thoroughly confused. "I am fond of Sir Benedict, but I suppose it is possible to be settled too near him."

"Quite!"

"Then I shall look for something farther afield, shall I?" he asked cautiously.

"Indeed!" she snapped, turning her mild brown mare back toward Wayborn Hall. "I must return to the house now, but you mustn't let me keep you from paying your respects. Just keep to the path; Silvercombe is less than a mile. You must be most anxious to see your sister and your—your *friends*."

"Why don't you come with me?" he suggested.

Juliet snorted. Lady Maria Fitzwilliam would certainly be confounded if the notorious Miss Whip arrived at Silvercombe in the company of Lord Swale—she could hardly claim not to be at home to her own brother! And her ladyship's displeasure at being forced to receive Miss Wayborn would be richly worth savoring.

Reluctantly, she shook her head. However rude and insolent the Silvercombe ladies had been, she would not retaliate with behavior that would make Sir Benedict cringe. "I can't leave my brother's property without telling anyone where I have gone," she said. "Besides, it's nearly six o'clock now, and we dine at six-thirty."

"Country hours," he remarked. "It *is* rather late for a visit, I suppose. If I were to call now, Serena might feel obliged to invite me to dinner."

"She might," Juliet agreed. "Would that not be desirable? Do not imagine we'd be offended at Wayborn Hall if you were to find the company at Silvercombe more to your liking."

"Pretty shabby I would look, riding over at this hour in all my dirt and hanging out for an invitation to dine," he said, rubbing his head. His head felt vulnerable and itchy now that it bore nothing but stubble, and he found himself rubbing it almost continuously. "I may be an ill-mannered brute, but I think I am better than that."

"As you please," she said coldly. His anxiety to please Serena Calverstock annoyed her like nothing else, even though apparently, his love for the lady was encouraging him to look and behave more and more like the gentleman. The Swale she knew had never given a second thought to being an ill-mannered brute. Rather, he reveled in it. She was not entirely sure she liked the new Swale. His pleasantries grated on her ears all the way back to the house.

She would have gone straight up to her room to change, but he stopped her in the hall. "Before we part, Miss Wayborn, would you be kind enough to provide me with some paper? I would like to send my sister a note since I won't be visiting her until tomorrow."

Certain that he really meant to write to Lady Serena, Juliet was too irritated to be gracious, though of course, such a civil request could not be denied. She brought him to the morning room where her aunt kept an escritoire well stocked with writing supplies. He watched, amused, as his hostess, with every appearance of ill humor, sat down in her green habit and began to rule lines onto a sheet of hot-pressed paper with a little silver pencil.

"My dear Miss Wayborn," he murmured, chuckling, "I am well able to line my own paper. I have been doing it since I was a boy. It is excessively kind of you; I thank you for it with all my heart, but I wish you would not go to such trouble for my sake."

Cheeks flaming, Juliet immediately sprang up from her seat. It must look as though she were eager to perform any little service for him, however menial, and this was decidedly not the case! "It is only force of habit," she explained quickly, anxious to remove the impression of obsequiousness that she had unwittingly created. "I always line my brothers' paper for them. They never do it for themselves. Benedict can't and Cary won't."

"I see," he said, his green eyes twinkling. "My own sister claims to love me, but she has never given me such a practical proof of it as this."

"I will leave you to write your letters, sir," she said coolly. "But don't forget that dinner is at half-past six. If you're not punctual, don't think I'll keep the others waiting! There's nothing worse than cold soup."

With a haughty toss of her head, she swept from the room.

Chapter 14

The family customarily gathered before dinner in a small lounge across from the dining room. Juliet was the first to come down, and she immediately set about tidying up the little room. Her brothers and her aunt were constantly taking books from the library, leaving them scattered around the lounge, and never putting them back. And as it seemed unfair to tax the servants with replacing books that they probably could not read to their proper places, the task almost always fell to her. When Swale joined her a few minutes later, looking surprisingly elegant in his formal evening dress, she was carrying a stack of books over to a side table. He stopped in the doorway and looked in, rubbing his head self-consciously, and to her annoyance, he did not offer his assistance. She did not want his help, of course, but she would have enjoyed telling him so.

He said merely, "More books, I see."

She plunked them down on the table, snatched the top one, and sat down with it.

"Your brothers will very likely be late," he said.

"We are all three of us sharing the same valet, and I got him first."

He was looking as well as she supposed it was possible for him to look. His neckcloth was spotless, and his coat had been thoroughly ironed. She doubted he would ever be polished enough for Lady Serena, but she was obliged to admit he was quite elegant enough for herself. His figure was not fashionably slender, but he was very tall, and Nature had given him a deep chest, broad shoulders, and good legs. While his physique was nowhere near as pleasing as that of her cousin Horatio, or indeed, her brother Cary, there was a vigor about Swale, an appetite and a restless energy, that she liked. But for some reason, he was repressing it and acting like a milksop. Such unexceptional behavior might win him the fair Serena, but why was he acting the courtly tulip with her? They were not even friends.

"My aunt will be late as well," she told him. "She's having her hair crimped over her ears. Could take hours."

He merely looked at her for a moment, and she wondered if he were evaluating her appearance as she had already evaluated his. It was a disconcerting thought, and she braced herself for the comment she expected him to make. Compliment or insult, it was likely to be embarrassing. She was the first to admit that her appearance had suffered greatly from the departure of Mademoiselle Huppert.

She was wearing one of her new London gowns, a white silk with a pale green gauze. About as daring as she dared, it left her neck and arms bare, while clinging provocatively to her tall, proud figure. She had declined Huddle's expertise in crimping and had dressed her hair herself, pulling it back from her face in a simple twist, with one long curl draped across her breast. She was wearing her mother's pearl-drop earrings and no other ornament.

"You seem to have a goodish number of china bits in there," he observed, turning his attention from her to the room. "Shall we risk it? Or, do I remain in the hall where I can't hurt anything?"

She shrugged, unaccountably annoyed not to be likened again to his favorite dog. "I only wish we had better things for your lordship to knock about—perhaps our ornaments are not up to your standard?" She pointed out two tall Sevres vases that graced the mantelpiece. "You would not be ashamed to break those, I think," she said civilly.

"No, indeed," he said, grinning at her. It really was a charming, boyish grin, she noted, and quite wasted on her. Boyish charm could not affect her. "Eminently breakable. Expensive?"

"Ten thousand pounds for the pair, but I daresay you have Sevres bowling pins at Auckland."

"At a mere ten thousand pounds a pair, why not?"

She frowned at him, tired of the jest though she herself had initiated it. "Ten thousand pounds is all I have in the world, you know!" she said sharply.

"Is it?" he said, blinking at her in surprise. "Well, I daresay when you marry, Sir Benedict will make you a handsome settlement. My father gave my sister fifty or sixty thousand."

Juliet's anger deepened. "That is well for your sister, my lord. But when I say all I have in the world is ten thousand pounds, I mean it. That is my dowry, and I wouldn't take a penny more from my brother."

"That is a pity," he said, rubbing his head. "I think women need more inducement to marry than a mere ten thousand pounds—we men are such beasts. If I were a woman, I wouldn't marry for a penny less than fifty thousand guineas."

She regarded him in astonishment. "If you were a woman!"

"Marriage is all well and good for a man," he went on, "but what's in it for her? I don't see."

"Companionship," she answered slowly. "A partner in life, and a home of one's own. And . . . and children, of course." Unbidden, her imagination painted a picture of about half a dozen ugly, red-haired children sporting on a green lawn with a number of long-haired setters. Instantly repressed, of course, but impossible to forget.

"I don't blame you for refusing to marry me in Hertfordshire," he said presently. "If I were you, I wouldn't take me for a hundred thousand pounds."

"You make it sound as though you asked for my hand and I refused," she protested.

His brows were drawn together in a straight line as he looked at her. "If I had asked you, would you have refused me then?"

She stared back at him, almost appalled by the turn the conversation had taken. He was certainly not speaking to her like a man whose heart was engaged elsewhere. "Certainly, I would have refused you," she said. "Why should I have to marry you simply because I hurt my leg? Fortunately, my guardian cares more for my happiness than my reputation."

He grimaced. "Perhaps Sir Benedict was thinking more of himself than of you."

"What do you mean?" she said, offended by any criticism of her brother.

"It's no secret he doesn't want me for a brother," Swale replied. "But he don't consider how difficult it will be for you to marry anyone else. Perhaps he's content to keep you here forever to rule his paper for him."

"If he doesn't want you for a brother," she snapped back, "I'm sure I don't blame him!"

"Fair enough," he said with a faint smile. After that, he prowled around the small room, looking at things, and they were unable to make conversation, though he kept a half-mocking, half-respectful distance from the Sevres vases. Finally, he stopped at a small picture hung on the wall. It showed an Elizabethan house of red brick with dozens of gables and mullioned windows. "I like this picture," he said. "I like all the colors and the way things in the background are fuzzy."

Juliet could not resist leaving her chair to stand next to him. "My mother always said that was the worst picture in the house," she informed him. "She painted it when she was a girl."

"Well, I like it," he said stubbornly. "It's Tanglewood, isn't it?"

"Yes," she said, surprised that he should recognize it.

"I thought so. I'm sorry I didn't have the chance to see the house, except in passing."

"You'll like Silvercombe better," said Juliet. "Tanglewood is really a glorified farmhouse, you know. In fact, the main hall was once a cow byre, or so the story goes. You wouldn't find anything worth breaking there."

"Do you know," he said suddenly, "it seems to me that your ten thousand pounds, taken in proportion to Sir Benedict's estate, is quite as handsome as my sister's dowry, in proportion to the Duchy of Auckland."

"I've always thought it handsome," Juliet agreed. "If

I had fifty or sixty thousand pounds like your sister, I should be a mark for fortune hunters. I don't mean to imply that your brother-in-law is a fortune hunter," she added quickly.

"Oh, he's not," said Swale good-naturedly. "Maria was the despair of all fortune hunters. Very early, she fixed upon a Major of Brigade in the Derbyshire, a younger son, if you please, and to everyone's amazement, my father declined to put a stop to it."

"Astonishing," Juliet murmured.

"Well, the war was on then, and women are bound to find soldiers dashing in times of war," said Swale with a shrug. "Soldiers and sailors. I expect your cousin Captain Cary has quite a following amongst the debutantes in London."

"Any admiration that comes his way is entirely justified," said Juliet. "He is every inch the gentleman, and a hero besides."

"And he spouts poetry from his blowhole like a giant whale," said Swale grumpily. "He is indeed a paragon. Rich too, if you like new minted money."

"What he was born without, he managed to acquire by virtue of his talents," Juliet said coldly. "I am excessively proud of my cousin Horatio."

"He seems to return your admiration," said Swale. "I half expected to find him here, lodged in your bosom. Tell me, what sinister forces have conspired to take him away from you? Has the war started up again?"

"He has gone to Hertfordshire for a few days."

"But you expect him to return soon?"

"Yes," she answered, puzzled by his overweening interest in Horatio.

"He's very jealous of your honor," Swale observed.

"You remember he threatened to shoot me—and all I was guilty of was touching your foot!"

Juliet was silent for a moment as she wondered whether she ought to remind his lordship that he was guilty of worse than touching her foot. Could he really have forgotten kissing her in the private parlor of the Tudor Rose? While perhaps not pleasant, it was surely unforgettable! In the end, she decided against mentioning that disgraceful incident. Let him think that she too had forgotten it.

"Yes, if Horatio has a fault," she said pertly, "it must be a quick, fiery temper!"

Swale laughed out loud. "Why, that's what I like best about the fellow! I've a bit of a temper myself, you see."

"It seems to have disappeared, along with your fiery hair, like the strength of Samson," she observed wryly. "Pickering is to be congratulated. He has turned you into a gentleman."

"I can make myself agreeable when I want."

"You are able to laugh at yourself, at least," she said grudgingly. "You're not pompous."

"No, indeed," he laughed. "Of pomposity, I am never accused. I'll never be perfect like your seafaring cousin, but I ain't pompous."

"I sometimes think that if Horatio had been born into wealth and privilege as you were, he might be a very bad man," Juliet confessed. For want of anything else to do, she replaced her book on the table and pretended to select another from the stack. "Perhaps I wrong him, but I think if he were a marquess, he might be very pompous indeed."

"I think he is very pompous indeed already," said Swale, also pretending to select a book. "Why should I not drink Madeira if I like it?"

"Or Malta? Or Mallorca?" said Juliet, laughing. "Who is he to tell your lordship not to drink this island or that?"

"Precisely," said Swale. "I don't tell him to raise the mainsail or weigh anchor, do I?"

"Yes, I think you're right about poor Horatio," Juliet said with a laugh. "He *is* pompous. And there's some talk of elevating him to the knighthood. Only think how pompous he'll be when we have to call him *Sir* Horatio!"

"You would not wish to marry a pompous man," he said. "You would find it tedious."

She sobered, suddenly ashamed of herself for making fun of her cousin. "There are worse qualities," she said rather primly. "For example, I know a man who throws knitting baskets."

He grinned. "On the occasion to which you refer, Miss Wayborn, I was sorely provoked, and by the most impudent young miss I ever met in my whole life! Under the circs, I'd say I was restrained."

"Our notions of restraint clearly differ," she said. "But on that occasion, we were neither of us restrained, I think," she conceded.

"*You* certainly weren't," he said. "You accused me of every crime in the calendar and threw yarn at me, too. That is not the treatment, you know, which my situation in life has accustomed me to receive from single young ladies. Just between us, Miss Juliet, there *is* something worse than cold soup, and that is a woman pretending to like you when in fact, she does no such thing."

She felt her color rising. Had he discovered Serena's sham? "So I would imagine," she murmured.

"If a woman is inclined to fling her knitting at my head, I should a thousand times prefer her to do that rather than grit her teeth, smile at me sickly, and milord me."

"But then you would be covered in knitting," she pointed out. "No, you must allow us to practice our forbearance and civility on you, as you practice yours upon us. You must allow us to grit our teeth, smile at you sickly, and milord you. In this way, a great deal of unpleasantness is avoided, and much knitting saved."

"Practice away, dear lady," he said cheerfully. "And I too shall practice restraint."

"No, you must be as provoking as possible," she told him with mock seriousness. "The greater the provocation, the greater the triumph of overcoming the urge to assault you."

"I wouldn't know where to begin provoking you," he protested, laughing.

"Wouldn't you?" she retorted, sitting down with her book, which turned out, horribly enough, to be Adam Smith's *The Wealth of Nations*. "It is scarcely gratifying to be told one is reminiscent of a favorite dog," she informed him. "I can assure you I have practiced a great deal of restraint on you already!"

He frowned. "Dammit, *you* don't remind me of a dog—just your hair. It's long and silky and sort of brown just like Daphne's. But that is where the resemblance ends, sadly. Your eyes are gray, not brown; you have only two legs; your ears are far too small. . . ."

In spite of herself, Juliet began to laugh.

"She used to knock me down and lick my face," said Swale, becoming wistful. "How I miss Daphne. Did you never have a dog, Miss Wayborn?"

She shook her head. "My aunt doesn't like dogs in the house. The barking gives her migraines. And since Benedict was hurt by a dog, there's never been one in this house."

"I'd forgotten that," Swale said. "But surely, you're not afraid of dogs?"

"Oh no," she replied. "I daresay I know every farm dog in the parish, and my Tanglewood cousins keep dogs at the Vicarage. You must remember Sailor?"

"The little spaniel? His paw is better, I hope."

"Yes, thank you," she said. Nothing made her feel more guilty about putting him in Hastings than remembering how kind he had been to the Vicarage dog. "Some days, I wish I had a dog to take with me on my walks here. They are pleasant companions. One doesn't always like to ride, you know, and a dog is just the thing. I'd often take Sailor on walks when I was with my cousins."

"And when you are established in your own home, you will have dogs?"

"I should like to," she said slowly. "But what if my husband does not like dogs?"

"He will," Swale told her, but before she could question his assurance, Sir Benedict joined them. Billy had delivered Swale's note to Silvercombe and had returned with a reply, which Benedict now handed to his guest.

Juliet concentrated very hard on her book while Swale went to one corner of the room and broke the seal of his letter. Several minutes passed awkwardly before Cary arrived, escorting Lady Elkins, and they were able to go across the hall to the dining room.

The meal was accompanied by very little conversation. Benedict had nothing to say to his guest; Cary did little but complain to his sister about the various dishes set before him; and Lady Elkins, still miffed that Lord Swale had spurned her niece in favor of the rich and beautiful Lady Serena, preserved an icy silence, though his lordship inquired solicitously about her headache.

Swale sat alone in the middle of the long table opposite Juliet and Cary, who sat together, Juliet at Benedict's right and Cary at Lady Elkins's left. Juliet, who had begun the meal as determined as her aunt to punish Lord Swale's presumption with silence, soon felt the pangs of a guilty conscience. Whatever Swale was guilty of, he was behaving just now as a gentleman ought, while the proud Wayborn family was behaving with the utmost incivility to a guest.

Benedict seemed to feel it too as Swale cordially complimented his host on the house and grounds that Juliet had shown him that afternoon. "I trust," said the baronet, "that your lordship is very comfortably settled in Runnymede?"

"Runnymede!" Swale exclaimed, flashing a look at Juliet. The color rose in her cheeks, but she glared back at him defiantly.

"My mother had a fanciful streak," Benedict said with some slight embarrassment. "She named all our guest rooms after famous battles. When she came here as a young bride, she was quite impressed with the long history of the Wayborns."

"Runnymede," Swale said gravely, casting Juliet a look of strong reproach, "is an excessively comfortable chamber, thank you, Sir Benedict."

"You have an excellent view of the village and the church from the windows," said Sir Benedict complacently. "And if you should require anything else, don't hesitate to tell the servants."

Juliet cringed as she thought of the ivy-encrusted window in Hastings.

"The view from my window is indeed extraordinary," said Swale. As he spoke, the servants removed the second course, and a covered dish was placed before him. The footman lifted the silver lid to reveal a proud little wheel of white cheese and nothing else.

"Ah," said Swale. At least it was not on fire.

Sir Benedict hastily set down his knife and fork. "Good God!" he softly exclaimed. "What is that appalling object?"

Juliet smiled with feigned innocence. "It's a cheese. His lordship is very fond of cheese."

"Indeed I am," Swale said with forced cheer. "But you need not have done anything special for me, Miss Wayborn."

She blinked at him. "Did you not command me to serve you cheese, my lord?"

"I? Command you?"

"Aunt Elinor, you are my witness. Did his lordship not say to me 'I would eat cheese'?"

"I can't think what he said," Lady Elkins replied crossly. "My head was throbbing so!"

"I said I would *even* eat cheese, Miss Wayborn," Swale corrected her gently. "I meant you were to order your table as usual without any thought to me."

"Dear me," Juliet murmured. "I understood you to mean that you would eat nothing *but* cheese. I went to a great deal of trouble to secure a suitable quantity for a man of your appetite. This cheese is from the Home Farm. Mr. Quince tells me it is a very brisk seller on Fair days. Apparently, the people eat it with hunks of bread and wash it down with ale or stout."

"Thank you, Miss Wayborn. I daresay cheese is not a fashionable dish. I daresay my tastes are boorish and unrefined, but I do like it."

Lady Elkins turned away in disgust, but Juliet and her brothers watched, fascinated, as the marquess cut a wedge of cheese and consumed it with every appearance of enjoyment. "Delightful!" he pronounced. "Miss Wayborn, you may tell Farmer Quince he has produced the finest cheese in all England. Such a delicate, smoky flavor! I approve. I should like to roast it on a stick."

"Roast it on a stick?" Juliet echoed, her eyes round. "Whatever do you mean?"

"One cuts it into wedges, puts it on a stick, and roasts it over a fire," he clarified. "It sounds quite savage, I know, but it is one of the truly delicious things in life. Why should it be that only peasants enjoy cheese? Or potatoes, for that matter?"

"Do potatoes truly enjoy cheese?" Juliet wondered. "I had no idea."

Benedict recoiled. "Potatoes! Juliet, pray do not tell me you mean to put *potatoes* on my table? I put my foot down at potatoes."

"Certainly not," she said faintly. "But you have not finished your cheese, my lord. Shall I send it back to the kitchen and have it roasted on a stick for you?"

"I should like that very much indeed, Miss Wayborn," he replied. "However, I am learning to practice restraint, no matter how great the provocation."

"Provocation, my lord?" Juliet inquired. "Has the cheese provoked you in some way?"

He grinned at her. "What sort of man do you think me, Miss Wayborn, to be provoked by a cheese? No matter the *temptation*, I should have said. Though I am sorely tempted to have my cheese roasted on a stick, I shall restrain myself. It will be good practice for me."

"Do you require a great deal of practice in self-restraint, sir?"

Sir Benedict clearly was not enjoying his sister's conversation with Lord Swale. "I believe," he interrupted, looking at Juliet so gravely that she blushed, "that we all require some practice in self-restraint."

"For example, some young ladies talk too much," Cary added rudely, "and wear too little."

"And some young men grow mold on their faces!" Juliet responded in kind.

"Magpie," he muttered under his breath, stroking his little beard protectively.

"Mossy!" she hissed back.

Benedict appealed to Lady Elkins to withdraw, which she could scarcely do quickly enough. As Juliet rose to follow her aunt to the drawing room, Cary caught her hand and whispered to her fiercely, "For God's sake, put a shawl on or something! The insolent wretch has been staring at your shoulders all evening."

Startled, Juliet looked at Swale for some confirmation of his interest but found none. His lordship was wholly occupied in brushing crumbs from his waistcoat.

The gentlemen were not long parted from the ladies, and Cary scowled at Juliet when he entered the drawing room and saw she had disdained his advice to cover herself up. "I am not in the least cold, thank you," she told him sharply when he offered to fetch her shawl.

Since there was no hope for civil conversation, the four young people agreed to play at whist, while Lady Elkins, pleading headache, went up to her room supported by her maid.

Juliet accepted Swale as a partner, and it proved an unhappy, if not disastrous, alliance. He was consistently bold but only occasionally brilliant. His attention would wander if he sensed the rubber was lost, and when this was the case, their losses were greater than necessary due to his carelessness. *Her* caution irritated him; he liked to play large so that his winnings might offset his losses. This style of play was entirely foreign to her, and she found herself making blunders, which increased his irritation.

Yet Cary and Sir Benedict were even more ill-matched, for where Swale was merely bold, Cary was reckless; and between Cary's wildness and Swale's unpredictability, Benedict's well-ordered mind was confounded again and again. In the end, Juliet and Swale won, though not by as much as his lordship would have liked. "If you had only trusted me a little," he complained, and she retorted that she had trusted him more than he deserved.

At nine o'clock, Juliet went upstairs, and not long after that, Cary and Benedict withdrew, the former pleading exhaustion and the latter pleading business accounts requiring his attention. Swale took his candle and mounted the lonely western stairs to Hastings. The chamber was dark and frigid, and he shivered as he undressed and pulled his nightshirt over his head. The coal scuttle was empty of coal, but he did find a few pieces of what appeared to be a broken spindle.

The bell rope, when he found it, came away in his hand.

"Restraint," he told himself firmly. He was Geoffrey Ambler, Marquess of Swale. He would not be defeated by Hastings. He was not helpless. He had ingenuity and intelligence. An investigation of the fireplace unearthed an ancient bedwarmer, which consisted of a large covered pan of copper mounted on a pole. The pan was discovered to contain nearly two dozen old coals that were, of course, ice cold now. He emptied them into the grate and lit them with his own matches, hoping to add the broken spindle to the flames.

Alas, it was not to be. There were no flames. The white rind covering the coals burned reluctantly at first and then not at all, filling the room with thick, acrid smoke. Coughing, he opened the window and stuck his head out into the sweet-smelling ivy.

Covering his nose and mouth with his arm, he plunged back through the smoke to the door. For a few minutes, he stood in the hall, fanning the door back and forth and dispersing most of the smoke.

With longing, he thought of Runnymede just three doors down. True, there was unlikely to be a fire lit, but the bed was large and comfortable, and the servants' bell might actually be connected. Sir Benedict's casual inquiry at dinner had more or less granted him the right to that chamber, but he could not escape the fact that his hostess had, for whatever reason, placed him in Hastings. In Hastings, he would have to stay.

He found his dressing gown, wrapped himself in it, and laid down on the bed only to discover that it was fully as uncomfortable as it appeared. More of an iron maiden than a bed, really. The pillow had a hard lump in it, and the sheets were so cold that he thought at first they were wet.

He pulled the thin covers up over his head but felt no warmer, and a strange smell seemed to be emanating from the pillow. "What in hell's name . . ." he muttered, sitting up to investigate.

The next moment, he jumped out of bed, accompanied by an earsplitting shriek. Almost immediately, as he used the bedwarmer to make sure the rat was quite dead, there began a persistent rhythmic banging from the direction of the ceiling. Recalling that Juliet had told him that the chamber immediately above Hastings was occupied by servants, Swale guessed they were footmen who had achieved their present positions in the household by virtue of their ability to stomp their feet with undreamt of ferocity. He grasped the ancient bedwarmer in his hand and, leaping atop the bed, began striking at the ceiling with it with all his might, shouting, "Quiet, you buggers!"

The stomping ceased as suddenly as it had begun; the copper pan of the bedwarmer parted from its pole; and the door to Hastings swung open almost simultaneously. A branch of candles was thrust into the room, and the copper pan rolled across the floor and spun at Juliet's feet before falling with a clatter to the parquet floor.

Behind her appeared the worried face of Fenwick the butler. Behind Fenwick, young Billy jumped up and down, trying to see into the room.

"Julie!" Swale cried, jumping down from the bed and still holding the pole, which he used to surreptitiously flip his pillow back over the dead rat. "The noise!"

"Yes, Ginger, the noise," she replied, coming into the room. Her hair was loose, and she was wearing a rich purple dressing gown that made her look even more Minerva-like than usual. "I have come to ask you to stop it. The servants are trying to sleep."

"Oh-ho! The servants are trying to sleep, are they?"

"Please, my lord," the butler interjected nervously, "if your lordship would not mind putting down the stick . . . ?"

Swale ignored him and addressed Juliet. "For your information, madam, your servants have been dancing a bloody jig on my head for the past twenty minutes! Or perhaps . . . perhaps, it was the ghost of the caribou?"

"You have broken my bedwarmer," she accused him.

"Believe me, dear madam, it had ceased to function as a bedwarmer long before I came upon the scene," he told her angrily.

"What is that smell?" she then demanded. "Have you been smoking in this room?"

"I was cold," he informed her haughtily. "I made a small fire." He was finding it difficult to maintain his hauteur, however, as he was in his nightshirt with his dressing-gown flapping around his bare legs. "I usually have my hair to keep me warm, but as I have been scalped . . ."

Juliet coolly noted the miserable little coals in the grate. "*Where* did you get the coals?"

"I am not without resources," he told her. "I found them in the bedwarmer."

"That bedwarmer should have been emptied long ago," she muttered. "But then, I daresay you would have broken up the furniture for fuel! I had no idea you were one of those thin-skinned aristocrats who must be bundled up like an old woman to guard against trifling little drafts! Poor Ginger! Would you like Fenwick to fetch you a shawl?"

He glared at her. "Julie, I daresay when I am an old married man surrounded by my affectionate children, it will amuse me to relate all I suffered the time I went to Surrey to win the hand of their beautiful mamma, but at the moment, for me, the joke has worn pretty thin!"

In her view, this was really too much. For him to boast of his conquest in her very presence—and in front of Fenwick too—!

"Kindly do not stick your chin out at me, sir," she said with gritted teeth. "Since you have made Hastings quite uninhabitable, I suppose I am forced to move you to Runnymede. I suppose you think you're very clever. But if you think setting fire to Runnymede will gain you Agincourt, you quite mistake the matter!"

"Thank you, Miss Wayborn. I should be delighted to move to Runnymede."

"Good night, Ginger," she said with queenly hauteur.

Fenwick was swept away in her wake, but Swale enticed Billy to remain by showing him a gold coin. "I'm going to need newts, Billy," he said solemnly. "And lots of them!"

Chapter 15

Never before had the written word affected Lady Maria Fitzwilliam so violently as when she broke the seal of her brother's note and read the fatal words: "If you want to see your only brother alive, I am currently lodged at Wayborn Hall. Your affectionate Geoffrey." She could not have been more shocked if she had received a ransom note demanding huge sums of money for her brother's return. She cried out in distress and sank into a chair in her dressing room.

"She has him!" she cried in a choked voice when her husband came to inquire what was wrong.

"Who has him, my love?"

"Miss Wayborn! She has taken him prisoner."

"Of whom are you speaking?" he asked patiently. "Who has been taken prisoner by Miss Wayborn?"

"Geoffrey! My brother! She has him at Wayborn Hall!" Maria cried theatrically. "I must go, Henry, and rescue him from her clutches."

"Nonsense," he replied. "Remember what Mr. Devize told us. Your brother is intent on making Miss Wayborn fall in love with him. He means to break her heart. Rather wrong of him, of course, but I don't see any danger of a marriage. I daresay your brother has a greater disgust for the young woman than even you do."

"Depend on it," his lady said fiercely, "she will make him fall in love with her if she can. The scheming little minx! She will use all her arts and allurements to inveigle him. Wouldn't she fancy herself as Marchioness of Swale! Henry, you must order the carriage at once."

Colonel Fitzwilliam, however, was not as biddable as the average Henry. "My dear, it is dinnertime. We can hardly call on Sir Benedict now, particularly when you have been so rude to his family these past weeks. It will have to wait until the morrow."

Lady Maria acceded to her husband's good sense, but she ate very little dinner, slept very ill, and could scarcely be prevailed upon to eat two bites of a gooseberry tart at breakfast before she was on her way to Wayborn Hall. Lady Serena was enlisted to accompany her friend, who felt in need of an ally on this trying occasion, and Colonel Fitzwilliam said he would call on Sir Benedict.

Lady Elkins was alone at breakfast when the Silvercombe ladies arrived. Never an early riser, her mornings of late had been devoted to long bouts of self-pity and headache. She stayed very long in the breakfast room and while eating very little, reflected very long on how badly her friends were treating her over this nonsense about Juliet. The arrival of visitors, and such unexpected and desirable visitors, struck her with the force of a lightning bolt. Forgetting entirely the weakness in the legs that had plagued her all week, she scrambled for the better of the two drawing rooms and received the two ladies with something like composure.

Lady Serena, looking very dashing in a new hat decorated with ostrich plumes, apologized effusively for neglecting poor Lady Elkins, and Lady Elkins effusively forgave her. Serena then made the baronet's widow known to her friend Lady Maria Fitzwilliam, and the duke's daughter inquired immediately into the whereabouts of Lord Swale.

"Oh!" Lady Elkins was confused and flustered by the cold abruptness of Lady Maria. She began to make her excuses rather incoherently. She had been ill—she was always the last of the household to rise—she was utterly alone. Sir Benedict would be in his estate office, if he had not gone to inspect the new cottages. Mr. Cary Wayborn had gone to a neighboring village to view a horse. Perhaps Lord Swale went with him?

"I expect," said Lady Maria dryly, "that Miss Wayborn went along to view this horse? What an exceptional animal it must be."

"I do not know, my lady," stuttered Lady Elkins, feeling all at once that it was wrong of her not to know where her niece was, though it had never entered her head before. "All these comings and goings! I am too old and infirm to keep up with these energetic young people."

Lady Serena seemed almost ready to give up and go away again, but Lady Maria was prepared to endure more. "Which farm?" she wanted to know. "When did they go?"

Lady Elkins grew more confused. "Perhaps it was yesterday they went to view the horse," she murmured. The arrival of a servant with refreshments spared her any further embarrassment. "Peter, where did the young people go? Did they go to view the horse, or was that yesterday?"

The servant, whose name was Robert, answered

cheerfully, "Mr. Cary has gone to Wexton to see Mr. Martin's mare, your ladyship. Miss Julie is just back now from her ride."

"Ah," said Lady Elkins, as pleased as though she had remembered this herself.

"Is my Lord Swale with her?" Lady Maria demanded.

Juliet herself answered this by entering the drawing room with absolutely nothing Swale-shaped at her elbow. Her tousled brown hair was pulled back by a wide ribbon of black silk, indifferently tied in a bow, and her scarlet, military-style habit was stained with grass. The fierce light in her eye matched the style of her habit. She had found out the identity of the morning callers and had come directly from the stables to defend her aunt.

Lady Maria experienced something of a shock. She had previously viewed Miss Wayborn from a distance at church and had found her tall and slim, though unremarkably pretty and too sun-browned to be fashionable. But she could see now how an impressionable, foolish young man like Geoffrey might be intrigued by her flashing gray eyes and queenly bearing. *Artful, presumptuous strumpet,* she thought.

"I beg your pardon," said Juliet coldly. "My aunt has not been well. Perhaps your ladyships would be good enough to visit us another time?"

"Nonsense, my dear," cried Lady Elkins. "I am so much better today, I would delight in company. Indeed, I am quite recovered. It is so excessively good of Lady Serena and Lady Maria to return our call."

"My dear Miss Wayborn," Serena called to Juliet, "may I present you to my friend, Lady Maria Fitzwilliam? Her brother, Lord Swale, is your guest, I believe."

"Ma'am." Juliet made only the barest sketch of a curtsey.

Lady Maria, exerting the privilege of her rank to the utmost, remained seated and inclined her head in slight acknowledgment of the tall, athletic young lady standing before her in a scarlet habit. Her dark eyes, however, betrayed a vociferous contempt. This treatment was usually enough to send impudent girls crying to their matchmaking mammas, but evidently, Miss Wayborn was made of sterner stuff. She merely looked back at Lady Maria like an equal.

"I am a little acquainted with Earl Wayborn," Maria said in her coldest, haughtiest voice, which really did not go with her pert, pug nose. "His lordship is a relative, I collect?"

"I am also a little acquainted with the Earl," Juliet replied carelessly, pulling off her gloves. "The day I was presented to Her Majesty at court, he gave me two fingers to shake and made me free to use my own surname, which I thought pretty well of him since I already had my father's permission. But you won't meet his lordship here. He never comes here, and we never go there, to Westlands."

"I have been to Westlands," said Lady Maria smugly. "Rarely have I ever seen a house so happily situated. Why, it is twice as large as Wayborn Hall!"

"No doubt you wish you were there now," said Miss Wayborn. "How pleasant it would be, indeed, if your ladyship were there now."

Lady Elkins interceded as Maria's nostrils began to flair. "But there is nothing at Westlands older than the year 1700, my lady. The first Earl left everything in Surrey to his younger brother, including all the pictures of our ancestors, when he took possession of

Westlands. Juliet, you must take her ladyship to the gallery and show her the pictures."

"Oh, no one cares to see pictures of other people's relatives," said Juliet. "Lady Maria can have no more interest in our pictures than we have in hers."

"Indeed," Lady Maria returned smartly. "There is no comparing ancestors with me, as I am sure you must know, Miss Wayborn."

"I have had occasion to look up the Aucklands quite recently," Juliet admitted. "The Amblers came over with the Hanoverian Elector," she whispered to her aunt before returning to Lady Maria with a bright smile. "To which of the many *tribes* of Germany did the Amblers belong, Lady Maria? That information seems to have been left out of the latest edition."

Lady Maria choked on her fury, her little heart-shaped face turning red.

"I must apologize," Lady Serena said quickly, her violet eyes wide and scandalized, "for not returning your call sooner, Miss Wayborn. As I was telling your aunt, with so many calls to return, somehow, I must have overlooked your little cards. Do forgive me."

"Juliet could never take offense at any trifling thing," Lady Elkins said before her impetuous niece could turn her wrath on Serena. "Indeed, she is the dearest, sweetest girl who ever lived."

"Indeed, I must be," Juliet agreed carelessly. "For, not only do I forgive them for not coming sooner, I truly believe I could forgive them for not coming at all! Now, please do excuse me, your ladyships. I must go and change my dirty clothes."

"You have been riding, Miss Wayborn," Lady Maria called after her, eager to exert her authority and force the insolent Miss Wayborn to remain standing before her when she clearly wanted to leave. "Was my brother not with you?"

"Your brother? With me?" Juliet smiled. "Certainly not, ma'am. I haven't seen Ginger since very late last night when he broke the bedwarmer!"

Lady Elkins slumped as though she had fainted, but unfortunately for her delicate sensibilities, it was only a pose. When one most craved oblivion, one remained stubbornly conscious.

"Ginger!" exclaimed Lady Maria, unable to conceal her astonishment. "Why, you impudent—"

"But, now you mention it," Juliet continued sweetly, "as I was passing the breakfast room just now, I heard some rather disgusting wet noises coming from within. I daresay it was your brother. He makes those noises when he eats, I have noticed."

She saw with great satisfaction that Lady Maria was seriously discomposed. Her ladyship appeared on the verge of inflicting violence upon Miss Wayborn.

"Excuse me," Juliet said sweetly, offering a graceful curtsey before sauntering from the room in the most nonchalant manner. This time, Lady Maria did not seek to detain her.

Lord Swale was not with Mr. Cary Wayborn, as Lady Elkins had supposed. Nor was he in the breakfast room, as Juliet had suggested. In fact, he was standing in the hall outside Juliet's room with a bucket of newts, and that is where the daughter of the house found him. He frowned at her. "You went out riding and didn't tell me," he complained. "I'd have gone with you."

"Bernard was with me, thank you," she answered.

"You prefer his company to mine, do you?"

"You appear to have been rather too busy to take me riding," she pointed out, bending to look in the bucket. Two or three brightly colored newts paddled around in the water. "Newts, Ginger?" She shook her head in disapproval. "Not very original."

"But damned effective! I'm a traditionalist, Miss Wayborn. I don't apologize for that."

"I'll take those," she said hastily as a door opened further down the hall. "Your sister's come to take you away from this terrible place. You'll find her in the drawing room with a . . . a *certain lady.*"

"Many thanks, Julie," he whispered. "It wouldn't do for me to be caught this close to Agincourt, eh? See you downstairs in two shakes." He trotted away, leaving her to face Benedict with the bucket in her hands.

"Juliet, I understand we have guests," he began rather crankily, then broke off as he saw the pail she could have no hope of concealing. "*What* is that?"

"It's a bucket."

He looked inside and recoiled. "What did I tell you about newts?"

"You said, 'No newts.' I remember it distinctly."

His lips thinned. "Juliet, I realize you must be even more eager to banish Lord Swale than you were Mr. Calverstock, but you can't go about the place scattering newts. Give me the newts."

"Don't hurt them," she said quickly. "It isn't their fault, you know."

"I'm not going to hurt them," he told her coldly. "I'm going to have Billy take them back to the lake where they belong. If I can ever find Billy . . ." he added under his breath.

Juliet suddenly grasped his arm. "Do you hear that?" she demanded. "Someone is playing my pianoforte!"

Benedict listened for a moment to a rather frank and yet sensitive interpretation of Beethoven's Moonlight Sonata. "Playing it rather well, too. You could play like that, Juliet, if you would take the time to practice."

"Serena!" Juliet seethed. "How dare she come into my house and exhibit on my instrument!" In a flash of scarlet, she rushed down the stairs.

"Juliet, slow down! You'll break your neck." He did not expect her to heed him, and she did not. With a sigh, he trudged down the stairs after her, carrying the bucket. He was astonished to find his sister listening at the doors of the drawing room, her face a mask of misery.

"Are you sulking because Lady Serena has more talent at the pianoforte?" he teased her. "I doubt she sings as well as you do."

"That is not Serena," she answered. "It's *him*. How I detest him!"

"Who?"

"Ginger!"

Benedict was astounded. "Swale? Swale is playing the instrument?"

"He plays like an angel," she said bitterly, clenching and unclenching her fists. "Couldn't you just strangle him? He said he was rather fond of music! Fond!"

"Now, Juliet," he admonished her. "I know how you feel about him, but—"

"I hate him!"

"Quite," said Benedict. "But you can't stand out here in the hall. You must go in. It is not right that our aunt is left to entertain so many visitors."

"I have to change my clothes," she said, running past him and up the stairs to the safety of her room and slamming the door. The sight of a smiling Swale bent over the instrument, with a smiling Lady Serena bent over *him*, had been more than she could endure when she had looked into the room.

"How dare he play my piano?" she panted furiously as she tore off her scarlet jacket. "How dare he!"

She wiped tears from her eyes and told herself firmly that they were tears of anger. If Ginger was content to be Serena's fool, it was nothing to her. If Serena wanted to be his wife, it was only his rank and fortune that attracted her, of course, but again, that was nothing to *her.* If they would only get out of her brother's house and not force her to watch the sickening progress of their romance, she would be quite content.

That there might be a deeper reason for the turmoil of her emotions did occur to her, but it was ruthlessly suppressed as she recalled with loathing Serena's simpering expression as she was turning the pages of Swale's music. Her ladyship's ostrich plumes and rich attire Juliet thought rather ridiculous for the country. For herself, she chose a light green sprigged muslin and soft kid boots. She gave her hair a good brushing and tied it back with a green ribbon, then went down half hoping that the proud Silvercombe ladies had made the most of her absence and taken Ginger away.

Her disappointment at finding him in the drawing room was not very pronounced, however. He smiled at her, and she smiled back with a queer little fluttering, melting sensation in her chest.

"Here is Miss Wayborn," he said almost as if he had discovered her on the other side of the world and brought her back as his trophy. "May I present my brother to you? Colonel Fitzwilliam, this is Miss Wayborn."

A gentleman she had not noticed before came forward. She wondered if he had been in the room earlier when she had met Lady Maria and decided that he could not have been. He seemed a mild gentleman of nondescript appearance, but there was something in his countenance that convinced her he would not stand by and allow his wife to be abused as she had abused Maria.

"I have heard a great deal about you, Miss Wayborn," said the Colonel, bending over her hand. She detected a note of reproach in his grave, gentle voice and blushed.

"And this is my sister Maria," Swale continued. "Serena you know, of course." He rushed over to the pianoforte where Serena was seated. "This is your instrument, I collect, Miss Wayborn?"

She nodded, forcing herself to speak. "I did not know you played, sir. You put me to shame."

"I learned chiefly to annoy Maria," he said. "How she struggled, poor girl, and how easily it came to me! It just sort of flows off my fingertips."

Colonel Fitzwilliam interrupted as he saw his wife's temper rise. "I was hoping you could give me a game of billiards, Geoffrey," he said. "With Redfylde away, Silvercombe is a bit of a henhouse, I'm afraid."

"Yes, Geoffrey, do come to Silvercombe for dinner, and give poor Henry a game afterward," cried Maria.

"But Miss Wayborn plays billiards," said Serena with an impish smile on her lovely face. "Don't you, Miss Wayborn? Miss Wayborn could give you a game of billiards, Colonel Fitzwilliam."

Juliet stiffened. "My brother Cary taught me," she said coldly, "but I only play against him."

"Indeed," Lady Elkins cried. "It was very bad of Cary

to have taught her, but as she only plays with him, I don't see the harm."

"Why shouldn't he teach me?" Juliet said irritably. "Benedict can't play, and there are times when Cary would have no opponent if I hadn't learned."

"You should teach Maria to play," Swale suggested to his brother. "Then you would never lack for a partner, Fitz. You'll give me a game after dinner, won't you, Miss Wayborn?"

"You have been invited to dine at Silvercombe, my lord, and I only play with my brother," replied Miss Wayborn severely.

"Oh, Maria can't invite me to Silvercombe," said Swale. "It ain't her house. I couldn't possibly accept an invitation from anyone other than Lord Redfylde."

"Oh, but do come *here* for dinner, Colonel Fitzwilliam," cried Lady Elkins, recognizing her cue. "You and your lady wife and dear Serena. Dine here with us, and his lordship will give you a famous game of billiards."

"You forget, Aunt," Juliet said gently. "Tonight is Mrs. Oliphant's card party. Their ladyships are engaged for the evening."

"But that's not for hours yet," said Swale, running his fingers over the keys. "We can invite them, can't we, Miss Wayborn, to come along with us on our excursion?"

Juliet frowned at him. "What excursion?"

"You did promise to take me to the church and show me the effigies of Baron Wayborn and his lady. You haven't forgotten?"

"I seem to have forgotten the part where you expressed an interest in the scheme," she said. "I had the impression you were rather disdainful of our effigies."

"A night in Runnymede has changed me forever," he said. "I feel very close to Baron Wayborn. I am agog with curiosity to see his effigy. This is the real twelfth century stuff, I trust?"

"Certainly."

"You won't find any twelfth century effigies at West-lands," Lady Elkins smugly announced. "But we have some quite good effigies in the private chapel, and such beautiful stained glass windows too. There is scarcely a stone in the village church that doesn't have the name Wayborn carved into it."

"I daresay the ladies are not at all interested in ef-figies," said Juliet doubtfully.

"We were going to have a picnic in the meadow," said Lady Maria.

"We were?" Lady Serena appeared startled.

"Yes, we were," said Maria firmly. "Doesn't that sound nicer than exploring some moldy old church, Geoffrey? You won't mind relinquishing him, will you, Miss Wayborn? I haven't seen my brother in some weeks—I want his company."

Juliet realized with a sick thudding feeling in her belly that she did mind. She minded very much. "No, indeed, Lady Maria," she said faintly, meeting Serena's mocking smile with difficulty. "Take him away and feed him. He eats all our muffins here. It's very tiresome."

"I could eat," Swale admitted. "But I'd like to see the chapel too."

"Why can we not do both, my lord?" Lady Elkins brightly suggested that the young people walk down to the church to see the effigies. "I'll follow in the barouche with the picnic lunch. Juliet knows a short-cut through the meadow—it's scarcely above half a mile. Quite a pleasant, shady walk."

Swale was all enthusiasm, Maria less so, and Lady Serena not at all, but the scheme was universally adopted when Colonel Fitzwilliam was promised a game of billiards afterward. "I'll get the key," Juliet said wearily, returning a few minutes later wearing the key to the Wayborns' private chapel on a ribbon around her neck and carrying a battered, broad-brimmed straw hat and a stout, straight limb of ashwood.

Clapping her hat down over her head, she led them by way of the terrace down to the lake. Swale followed with Serena on his arm. She needed his arm, for the high-heeled slippers she was wearing did not agree with the trek through the woodland. Behind them, Colonel Fitzwilliam gravely escorted his wife.

Juliet had the pleasure of overhearing Serena's conversation with Swale. The lady was chiefly concerned with complimenting his lordship on his new head. "I have always preferred a cropped head, my lord, and yours is such a handsome shape."

Juliet savagely stabbed the earth with her walking stick and was horrified when she couldn't pull it out again. A glance behind told her that Swale was much too occupied with Serena to notice her struggles, but Lady Maria was watching with amusement.

"It feels like I've been scalped," Swale complained, running a hand over the short red stubble on his head. "But . . . anything to please the ladies." He laughed pleasantly.

The stick pulled free suddenly, almost sending Juliet sprawling. Grabbing it, she stomped off in the direction of the village.

"Slow down, Miss Wayborn," Swale called to her presently. "Serena's thrown a shoe."

Juliet waited, tapping her foot impatiently, as Swale knelt and restored Serena's pretty shoe to her pretty foot. "Thank you, my lord," said Serena softly, coloring up. "I didn't know I would be tramping through the fields when I left home this morning." She laughed prettily.

Juliet, for no apparent reason, laughed too.

"On a glorious day like this, with such pretty country all around you, the only place to be is outside," Swale told Serena. "Exercise and fresh air, that's what you need."

"Yes, my lord," she agreed meekly, her lashes sweeping her cheeks.

"Look at Miss Wayborn—she's brown as a berry," Swale added. "I'd be willing to bet Miss Wayborn could walk as far as Richmond without missing a breath. Show me a milkmaid who can do that!"

Serena tittered. "I confess I am no milkmaid, my lord."

"Perhaps my lady needs to sit down and rest now," Juliet said waspishly. "There's a bench just ahead if you are feeling faint."

Serena, leaning heavily on Swale's arm, said she would adore a bench above all things.

The bench, however, was occupied by a rather grubby young man with a bucket. He grinned at Swale. "Will you be needing any more newts, milord?"

"No, Master Billy, thank you," said Swale, and Lady Serena hastily declared that she did not need to rest after all. She had found a hidden reserve of strength. The march continued, and several times, they were passed by villagers. Lady Maria withdrew from a particularly bucolic farmer driving a wagon. He respectfully took off his hat and greeted Miss Wayborn, guiding his mule off the track to allow them to pass.

"Good heavens!" Maria cried loudly. "Does your brother know all these people are using his property,

Miss Wayborn? I shouldn't allow it. That man looks like a gypsy!"

"This is a common path, my lady," Juliet told her. "It has been used by the local people for centuries. Wexton is six miles out of the way by the King's road, less than two by this route. And that good man is no gypsy. That is Mr. Quince from our Home Farm."

"That excellent fellow is responsible for the little white cheese?" exclaimed Swale. "I must speak to him." Matching deeds to words, he abandoned Serena and rushed over to the wagon, returning with a wheel of cheese wrapped in brown paper.

"We'll add it to our picnic," he told Juliet as he tucked it into his waistcoat. "It is the nicest cheese I ever ate," he told the rest of them. "I'm sending them to everyone I know for Christmas, and Farmer Quince has promised to show me how they are made. He likes his toasted on a slice of crusty brown bread."

Serena was clearly repulsed. "It has rather a strong smell, does it not, my lord?"

"Wait until you taste it, my dear. It is exquisite."

Serena's smile was forced, and she could not suppress a shudder. Despite her earlier lack of enthusiasm, she was now only too pleased to reach the church, having grown very hot on the walk. The sanctuary was dark and cool. Juliet led them to the small private annex where the Wayborns had honored their dead for centuries, propped her stick in the corner, and unlocked the door of carved oak. The miniature chapel was bathed in the light filtering through the brilliant stained glass windows showing the Wayborn coat of arms. The effect was dazzling, sheer drops of color dancing in the air like butterflies.

Serena balked at the entrance. "Are there . . .

bodies in there?" she whispered in horror, clutching Swale's arm.

"The crypt is underground," Juliet told her curtly. "This is our private chapel. These are merely statues, monuments. There's nothing to be afraid of."

"Extraordinary," murmured Colonel Fitzwilliam, following Juliet into the chapel. "I have never seen anything like it. So well-preserved! The colors in the windows are so rich. The blue is the true cobalt. It is quite as lovely, in its way, as Chartres."

"Thank you, sir," Juliet said, rather surprised by his interest. She had never been very interested in it herself. She led him up to the altar where life-sized marble statues of Baron and Baroness Wayborn lay stretched at full length on a marble dais. Their hands were clasped in prayer, and from above, the rose window tossed dozens of brightly colored gems over their peaceful faces.

"I detect a marked resemblance to the lady," Colonel Fitzwilliam said, looking from Juliet to the marble sculpture. "It must be a wonderful thing to have one's ancestors so close at hand. I have no record of my own ancestors until the early part of the last century," he admitted ruefully, "though my mother is very keen on inventing stuff for Mr. DeBrett and Mr. Burke! Don't believe half of what you read about the Matlock Fitzwilliams in the Peerage," he told her, chuckling. "We are mere overnight mushrooms compared to the Wayborns."

Behind them, Lady Serena sneezed, and Lady Maria called, "You have the bar sinister in your coat of arms, Miss Wayborn! Pray, why is that? Were not all of your ancestors above reproach?"

"Evidently not," said Juliet dryly. "The name Wayborn is as much a clue to our history as the bar sinister, Lady Maria. The first Wayborn must have been just that, born by the way on the side of the road. But it was an English road and by the Grace of God, a Surrey road. For that, I'm thankful."

"Bravo, Miss Wayborn," said Fitzwilliam, which did not endear him to his lady.

Serena sneezed again. "The smell of . . . of *death* is everywhere," she complained.

"Have you seen enough?" Juliet asked Swale. He was contemplating the crude medieval knights carved into the pillars of the altar. "We've got rubbings from those at the house, if you would care to study them."

"They look very stern, don't they?"

"Yes, and very short in stature, have you noticed? One wonders where they found the strength to walk around in all that chain mail."

"From what I hear," said Swale, "Fitz would have been glad of a little chain mail at Waterloo."

Juliet's eyes widened. "Were you at Waterloo, Colonel Fitzwilliam?" she exclaimed.

He bashfully averred that he had been, just as his wife cried out in vexation, "I think we had better go, Henry! The air here is very cold and damp. Poor Serena is sneezing." It did not suit Lady Maria at all to see Miss Wayborn monopolizing both gentlemen in the party, and she demanded her due. "Geoffrey, help poor Serena."

Swale caught Serena in his arms as the lady crumpled in a rather picturesque faint. "Julie!" he cried in astonishment. "Julie, she's fainted."

Miss Wayborn was unimpressed. "So I see," she said coldly.

Swale lowered Serena, still holding her in his arms. "Give me your hat, Julie," he said, reaching out a hand without looking away from his charge. "I'd better fan her face."

"You'll get more wind from her ladyship's hat than mine," Juliet objected sourly.

"Fork it over, miss! And look sharp doing it!"

Miss Wayborn angrily snatched at the green ribbons of her old straw hat and flung it at him. After being struck several times in the face during his lordship's zealous fanning, the lady was revived and helped to her feet.

The chapel was cleared, and by the time Juliet had locked it up again and put the key back around her neck, the rest of her party had walked outside into the sunshine. Swale was speaking to Serena with real concern. "You should not have gone from such a warm place to such a cold place all at once, Serena," he scolded her. "You'll jeopardize your health."

"Oh, I can't bear places like that," she said. "It's so dark . . . so ghoulish! I can hardly breathe. Look! I am trembling."

It took all of Juliet's restraint not to swat the silly peahen. "We'd better dispense with the picnic then," she said, "if you're *trembling,* my lady, though I daresay you'll be excessively disappointed not to sample the cheese! Here is my aunt now. I'm sure she'll be pleased to convey you all back to Silvercombe in the barouche."

"Yes, I think you're right, Miss Wayborn," Serena said faintly. "I hate to spoil the afternoon, but my head does ache so."

Lady Elkins's driver brought the barouche up to the wall of the churchyard, and Juliet went to explain to her aunt that Lady Serena was too ill to consider pic-nicking in the nearby meadow. Lady Elkins, who had been looking forward to driving through the village in her barouche with Lady Serena and Lady Maria in full view of all her friends, like a Roman general at his triumph, gave up her carriage with very bad grace.

"Help Serena into the carriage, Geoffrey," Lady Maria commanded, as if Lady Elkins's barouche were not equipped with a driver and two footmen.

"Oh, you mustn't all forego the picnic just because of me," cried Serena. "Go and enjoy yourselves."

"Geoffrey will see you home," said Maria. "Poor Serena! Make her lie down, Geoffrey, when she gets home, and bathe her temples in violet water. And send the carriage back to fetch us." Her instructions continued at length as Lady Elkins was handed down from her vehicle. The footmen unburdened the barouche of two large picnic baskets, and Swale and Serena set off for Silvercombe. "I do love a picnic," said Lady Maria, smiling meanly at Juliet. "What a treat!"

The picnic was set out in the nearby meadow, and Juliet was obliged to help her aunt assume an undignified pose on the cloth spread on the ground. The pain had returned to Lady Elkins's legs with the relentless cruelty of a nemesis, and there was now absolutely no reason for Aunt Elinor to mention that her niece had made the salmon mayonnaise herself.

Chapter 16

Lady Maria's landau arrived before Swale returned with Lady Elkins's barouche, and Juliet was forced to endure another of that lady's triumphant smiles. "I daresay my brother is reluctant to leave dear Serena in such a fragile state. He's very protective of her, you know. When a certain happy event takes place, I daresay he will never leave her side."

She was pleased to see Miss Wayborn flinch. Sweetly, she offered to convey Juliet and her aunt back to Wayborn Hall. Lady Elkins, complaining of an evil pulse in her head, heart flutters, and shooting pains in her legs, readily accepted, but Juliet, with a toss of her head, declared her intention of walking home.

Lady Elkins halfheartedly tried to persuade her niece that it was not at all the thing to be seen walking through the village without a hat, but her own suffering soon overcame any thought of Juliet, and she sank back onto the bleached leather cushions of the landau. Colonel Fitzwilliam made a more sustained effort, but Juliet, clutching her walking stick, started down the High Street in the opposite direction taken by Maria's carriage, all but daring anyone to say a word to her.

Someone took the dare as she was passing the White Hart. The upper window was suddenly flung open, and a young man with a cropped, dark head stuck the upper half of his body out so far he was in danger of falling into the street. He was in his shirt, which was open at the throat. "Miss Wayborn, we have just been talking about you!"

Juliet was startled, to say the least, never having been shouted at by a young man hanging out of the upper window of a country inn. With a great deal of embarrassment, she recognized Budgie St. John–Jones, a London acquaintance and a nincompoop if ever there was one. She walked on.

"Oh, I say!" he cried, slamming his head against the casement in his eagerness to withdraw. To Juliet's amazement, a few minutes later, he was on the street, pursuing her and struggling to put his coat on over his shirt. Another gentleman followed at a more sedate pace.

Not wanting to quicken her pace to escape a mere flea like Budgie, Juliet walked steadfastly on, her eyes fixed ahead, preserving the icy, depressing silence of a lady as Budgie overtook her. She knew him from the drawing rooms of London, and she very quickly had determined he was too stupid even to be trusted to fetch lemonade at Almack's.

"I say, don't rush off," said Budgie, but he then was overcome with giggling.

"I understand you have an interest in racing, Miss Wayborn," said the other gentleman, drawing alongside Juliet. Without seeming to hurry half so much as Budgie, he had easily reached her side. He was unknown to her, but he bore the unmistakable London

mark in his clothes and address, and his cool blue eyes
moved up and down Juliet's figure in a speculative
manner that made her dislike him instinctively. "I
wanted to see for myself how fast you are, Miss Wayborn," he said warmly. He lifted his hat from his well-
coifed head, imbuing the respectful gesture with the
most unflattering irony. "I am disappointed to find
you so easily caught. Dare I hope you wanted to be
caught? But perhaps I flatter myself?"

Juliet gripped her stick tightly but made no reply.
She was not going to be provoked into an argument
with gentlemen who were determined to insult her,
and she certainly would not run away from them in
tears like—like some wretched, ignorant milkmaid.
She was a gentlewoman, a fact that was well-known to
Budgie. Her brother was a baronet and an MP; she
was not in any real danger; and only a perfect wet
goose would allow herself to be bullied.

As they neared the little bridge arching over the
brook, they were overtaken by a wagon. With relief,
Juliet recognized Mr. Quince.

"Drive on, man," said Budgie's friend with the impatient authority of a child used to getting his own
way. "This is a private conversation."

Farmer Quince seemed not to hear the fine gentleman from London. He halted his mule and raised
his hat respectfully. "Good afternoon, Miss Julie," he
said in his slow, stolid way.

"Good afternoon, Mr. Quince," she replied in what
she hoped was her normal, steady voice.

"I have it in my power to take you as far as your back
gate, if you please, Miss."

Juliet climbed up next to him gratefully, and Mr.
Quince drove on, forcing Budgie and his friend to
step aside. Mr. Quince drove over the bridge, then

turned off the road onto the well-worn track leading through the woods. As they drew away from the village, Juliet glanced back. A third man had joined Budgie and his rude friend in the street. She had almost convinced herself that she could not possibly recognize him from such a distance when he suddenly reached up and, in Lord Swale's characteristic way, rubbed a hand across his head. His other hand, she could not help but notice, was holding a battered straw hat with green ribbons. She saw Budgie throw back his head and laugh, and she knew her face was burning.

"How is your wife, Mr. Quince?" she inquired brightly. "And the new baby?"

She scarcely heard that good man's answers. What she chiefly wanted was to sneak off somewhere and have a good, purifying cry. Mr. Quince talked on in a steady, even voice, almost a drone, as if he were soothing a disturbed animal. Juliet heard only snatches here and there until a name suddenly drew her complete attention. "Swale! What about him, Mr. Quince?"

If Farmer Quince was surprised by the young lady's vehemence, he did not show it. "His lordship has asked me for two hundred cheeses, Miss. What could his nibs want with so much cheese? I didn't think the gentry ate a deal of cheese. I'd have to take on a few extra lads to fill the order, and even then . . . where am I to get my hands on so much milk? He's the sort of man I'd never dare refuse anything, Miss Julie, but I honestly don't know how it's to be done."

"You had better speak to Sir Benedict," Juliet advised him. "Two hundred cheeses! I daresay it is his lordship's idea of a joke. You know how these high-strung Hanoverian aristocrats can be."

"Oh now, Miss Julie," he said mildly. "I'd say his lordship is a man who means what he says. But I'll speak to Sir Benedict, I will, about taking on the extra lads and maybe buying a few more milch cows."

As he spoke, Juliet became aware that someone was running down the shady lane behind them and calling her name.

"Well, I'm blowed," said Mr. Quince, whistling for his mule to stop. "'Tis the man himself."

Juliet sat up very straight and looked ahead resolutely. "Your hat, Miss Wayborn," said a breathless Swale as he climbed up beside her. Juliet was obliged to squash up next to Farmer Quince to make room for him.

"You weren't very gracious to Serena," he admonished her as he arranged the straw hat on her head. "I really expected better from you, my girl. Serena's not like you, Julie. She's delicate. She needs someone to look after her."

"Oh!" said Juliet bitterly. "Oh, it only needed that! Why don't you go back to your friends, my lord? You seemed to be having such a merry time."

"What? Oh, Budgie and Dulwich, you mean? Guess my surprise when I met them in the street. What do you suppose could have induced them to leave London?"

"There was a bit of unpleasantness, milord," Mr. Quince said quietly.

"What kind of unpleasantness?" Swale wanted to know.

"Nothing to interest you, Ginger," Juliet snapped, tying the green ribbons together under her chin with trembling fingers. "And where, pray, is my aunt's barouche?"

"Her footmen have taken it home," he answered.

"I went to the church to fetch you, and they told me you were on foot with no hat."

"What does it matter? I'm brown as a berry!"

Swale frowned. "Did I say that? I meant nut. You're brown as a nut, Julie. A little color is good, but I think perhaps you overdo it. Serena's skin is like alabaster or mother of pearl."

Juliet simmered in silence.

Farmer Quince cleared his throat. "I was telling Miss Julie, please your lordship, that I'd have to take on extra labor to fill the order for the cheese."

"Then do it," Swale replied carelessly.

"You can't actually *want* two hundred cheeses," Juliet protested.

"Oh, don't I?" he retorted, pulling something wrapped in brown paper from his waistcoat. "Taste this, Miss Wayborn, and tell me I don't want two hundred wheels of it!" He unwrapped the cheese and cut off a hunk with his pocketknife.

"Thank you," Juliet said coldly, "but I do not eat cheese."

Farmer Quince confounded her by laughing. "There was a time when you liked it well enough, Miss Julie! When my mother was alive, milord, and this young lady was only a bit lass with pigtails braided down her back, she'd come clamoring at the back door of our cottage, and my mother would give her cheese until she was fit to pop!"

"Now I'm a grown-up lady, Mr. Quince," Juliet said primly. "And ladies don't eat cheese."

"Julie!" said Swale in a voice filled with reproach. "Have you had it toasted on brown bread?"

"Oh, she has, milord," said Mr. Quince. "And she's had it baked into an onion tart as well, and she used to especially enjoy it with fried slivered apples."

"Now then, Mr. Quince," said Swale, laughing. "You mustn't tell all a lady's secrets."

Eventually, the back gate was reached, and Mr. Quince drove on without them. Juliet had no key for the stout, iron-bound gate, so she was obliged to seek Swale's assistance in climbing over the wall into the orchard. "I can't think why Benedict keeps this locked," she exclaimed in disgust as he knelt down and allowed her to step up on his knee, then his shoulder, to reach the top of the wall. "No one wants to steal his nasty little apples."

Swale was obliged to give her rump a helpful push, and she was over, falling unceremoniously into the shrubbery on the other side of the wall. Almost before she knew what was happening, her brother Cary was hauling her to her feet. "Julie, where the devil did you come from?" he demanded. Naked to the waist except for a pair of leather gloves, he was sweating profusely.

She gaped at him, her straw hat now hanging under her chin by its ribbons. "What are you doing here?" she cried, pulling at the ribbons that were threatening to strangle her. "I thought you'd gone to look at a horse."

"I did," he replied. "I've got a sweet little four-year-old half bought for you—I thought I would train her myself. When I got back, everyone was gone, so I thought I'd come out here and do some strengthening exercises." He picked an old sword up from the grass where he had dropped it and gave it a half-hearted swing with his right arm before dropping it in disgust.

"Uncle George's rapier!" she exclaimed, picking it up. "So heavy!"

"I haven't the strength of a baby," Cary said disgustedly, flexing his arm.

"You mustn't try to do too much," Juliet urged, resting the flat of the blade against her shoulder. "I'll carry it back for you. Good heavens, you're sweating like a racehorse. Where is your shirt?"

They were interrupted by a small cheese flying over the wall.

"Excuse me," cried Swale from the other side. Jumping up, he caught the top of the wall and began struggling to throw his leg over.

"What the bloody hell are you doing here, Swale?" Cary demanded as the Marquess was forced to relinquish his hold on the wall without making it over. "Mind your language in front of my sister!" he added as they heard Swale's muffled curses.

In the next moment, Swale was again hanging from the wall, his chin planted on the top as he tried in vain to haul his leg over.

"Cary, have you got a key to the gate?" Juliet asked, just as the brick wall rather dramatically gave way under Swale's weight. "Or . . . he *could* just knock the wall down and walk through it, I suppose!"

"Julie, I've cut my chin," Swale complained, holding a handkerchief to his jaw.

"You've broken the wall, sir," said Cary. "And my sister's name, you ignominious oaf, is Miss Wayborn."

"Oh, don't be such an ass, Cary! Ginger, my foolish brother has been exercising too much. You see how pale he is. Do you think you can carry him back to the house?"

"I am perfectly capable of walking!" Cary protested, shaking violently.

"Cary, do you feel light in the head?" Juliet inquired anxiously. "Oh, Ginger, I think he has a fever!"

"I do *not* have a fever."

"The silly ass has given himself a fever," said Juliet in fierce disgust, appealing to Swale. "You'll have to carry him. You will, won't you?"

Cary snatched his shirt from the branches of a nearby tree. "Don't you dare!"

"Go on up to the house, Julie," said Swale. "I'll get him home. Go on, girl! No red-blooded Englishman is going to allow his sister to watch him being carried home like a baby."

Juliet bit her lip. "Very well," she said reluctantly. "But I hold you responsible, my lord. If anything happens to him—"

"Run along, Julie!" said Cary, harshly.

"All right, I'm going," she snapped back, marching off into the trees with the rapier over her shoulder.

"Don't you dare," Cary said warningly.

"I wouldn't dream of it, old chap," Swale coolly replied.

Cary pulled his shirt over his head and reached for his coat. "As soon as my strength comes back to me, I am going to shoot you, Swale. You have but to name your second. And none of this Hyde Park nonsense. I will shoot you right here, dig a hole, and bury you."

"Julie won't be very pleased if you shoot her husband-to-be," Swale replied. "And between you and me, the girl has a ruthless element to her personality that is more often found in people named Genghis, Attila, and Tamerlane."

A vein pulsed in Cary's forehead. "You, Swale? You expect me to believe that you're engaged to my sister?" he sneered.

"I have an understanding with your sister, yes."

"Understanding? What the devil does that mean?"

Cary scowled suspiciously. "What sort of understanding?"

"*Julie* has given me leave to buy her a house in the country as a wedding gift," said Swale.

"*Miss Wayborn* would never do that!"

"I was rather surprised myself," Swale admitted, "but she did it all the same. I'm perfectly happy to buy her a house, you know. I have pots of money, and I simply adore the little monkey."

"You're a damned liar, sir," said Cary. "My sister is engaged to Captain Horatio Cary. Captain Cary is going to buy Miss Wayborn a house in the country, namely Tanglewood, which is the one place in the world upon which you, for all your beastly money, will never get your scabby paws!"

"I haven't seen an engagement notice in the papers," said Swale belligerently, "and believe me, I have been looking for it! Your sister is going to marry me, Wayborn. Accustom yourself to the idea. I may never get my scabby paws on Tanglewood Manor, but your sister—Julie is her name, by the way—that's quite a different matter!"

Cary swung a fist unwisely, missed his mark, and nearly fell.

"Don't try to hit me again," Swale advised him. "I'm pretty handy with my fives."

"So am I," said Cary. "And I warn you, I don't take cheques! You'll pay for that disgusting remark in blood."

"I withdraw the remark," said Swale. "It was unworthy of Miss Wayborn's betrothed. I shall have to endeavor to be a better man from now on, for Julie's sake. I can see I'm going to have to put up with a great deal of nonsense from my brothers-in-law."

"You'll marry Julie over my dead body," said Cary.

"No, I won't," said Swale, turning toward the house. "I was thinking I'd marry her in the quaint little church in the village, and we'd release a few doves afterward as a symbol of our . . . what in hell's name are doves a symbol of, anyway?"

"You bastard!" Cary leaped onto the bigger man's back and tried to dig into his eyes with his fingers.

"Oh, did you want me to carry you up to the house on my back, after all, Mr. Wayborn?" Swale inquired solicitously.

Some time later, his lordship entered the house by the French windows on the terrace. Inside, the housekeeper was changing the flowers. "Miss Wayborn?" he inquired politely. "There is something particular I wish to ask her."

At these magic words, Mrs. Spinner instantly directed him to a small room at the back of the house. There he found Juliet struggling to hang Uncle George's rapier back in place on the wall. It was but the work of a moment for him to do this for her.

"Thank you," she said coolly, her patrician face red with exertion. She tried to step around him neatly, but Swale blocked her. "Your left eye is swollen," she remarked.

"Your brother did a few strengthening exercises on my face."

"You brute!" she exclaimed. "Did you hit him? I swear, if you hit Cary—! Is he all right?"

"Is *he* all right?" Swale huffed. "What about me? And no, I didn't hit him. Turns out he didn't want me to carry him up to the house after all."

"You left him out there in the wilderness!"

"I tried to," he admitted, "but the cheeky fellow chased me all the way to the house. I have only just given him the slip."

She shook her head in disgust. "You ran away."

"He kept hitting me," Swale explained. "I have a great deal of restraint, as you know, but it *is* a finite amount. Sooner or later, I would have hit him back, sore arm or no sore arm."

"Excuse me," she said coldly, "I must go to my brother."

"Not so fast," he said, catching her by the arm. "I have a straight question for you, Miss Juliet. And I should like you to give me a straight answer."

"Oh yes?" she asked politely, letting her arm go slack rather than struggle against his superior strength.

"Julie," he said, letting her go. "You know my feelings. You know the real reason I came to Surrey. Do I have your permission to place an engagement notice in the newspaper?"

If she had not been brown as a nut, Juliet's face would have been quite white. "W-what?" she stammered. "Why ask me?"

"After everything that's happened between us, I should look a bloody fool if I put *my* notice in twenty minutes after Captain Horatio Cary puts *his* in, don't you think, Julie?" He looked at her intently. "Or, is that what you wanted all along, to make a bloody great fool of me?"

Juliet took a deep, shuddering breath. "Is it so very important to you that your notice is put in before his?" she asked quietly.

"You know that it is!" he answered furiously. "It means everything to me. It makes all the difference in the world!"

"Then, by all means, make your preference for a certain lady known to all the world just as soon as you can, Ginger," she said with what she hoped was the coolest, barest, most indifferent shrug in the world.

"Put in as many notices as you like, my lord. Put a hundred in the *Morning Post*—no, a thousand. Have monograms printed up on cream-colored, hot-pressed paper embossed with your coat of arms. While you are about it, commission a few dozen commemorative plates from Mr. Spode. Hire men to walk around Hyde Park from dawn 'til dusk wearing giant sandwich boards. Never let it be said that my Lord Swale does things by halves."

By the end of this remarkable speech, her beautifully sculpted nose was red as fire, and her gray eyes were bright with unshed tears. She gave him a fierce shove and ran out of the room, slamming the door behind her.

"Impetuous little madcap," he murmured fondly.

He particularly liked the idea about the sandwich boards.

Chapter 17

Swale was not present at tea, and when the ladies went upstairs to dress for dinner, he still had not put in an appearance. Juliet dressed automatically in the last of her London gowns. It had been made for a ball that she had never attended, having been forced out of London before the end of the season. Beginning with almost a white décolleté, the fine silk gradually, almost imperceptibly proceeded through a half dozen deepening shades of blue until finally the hem reached a rich ultramarine. She was brushing out her glossy, walnut-brown hair when Mrs. Spinner tapped at the door.

"Dear me! Don't you look fine, Miss Julie!"

Juliet was too depressed to entertain compliments. "What is it, Mrs. Spinner?"

"No one seems to know whether or not his lordship means to return for dinner," replied the housekeeper. "Mr. Corcoran says he ordered his grays put into the traces of his wee car—"

"His curricle?" Juliet guessed with a faint smile.

"Aye, and no one's seen him since. Master Cary said he didn't know and didn't care where his nibs had gone . . . and I do hate to bother Sir Benedict. I have to tell the cook something—it's *boeuf en croute* and sherry trifle for the sweet. Do you know if his lordship means to return, Miss?"

"I believe he had urgent business in London," said Juliet slowly, attempting a look of cool indifference. "But I had not thought—I did not think he meant to go immediately."

"He ought to have taken his leave of Sir Benedict and Lady Elkins like a gentleman," said Mrs. Spinner indignantly. "What am I to tell the poor cook?"

"That man," Juliet said crossly, setting down her hairbrush, "has no conduct! He is the rudest man in England! Go and see if he's left his things in Runnymede, Mrs. Spinner. Then we'll know absolutely if he means to return for dinner."

Mrs. Spinner, who was all of fifty-two, with a lace cap and a huge gold cross hanging from the edge of her massive bosom, blushed like a girl. "Oh, I couldn't, Miss Julie!"

Juliet sighed as she rose from her dressing table. "I'll go."

"Oh! Do you think you should, Miss Julie?" cried Mrs. Spinner.

"He can't eat me if he's not there," Juliet pointed out dryly.

The first thing she saw when she entered Runnymede was a handsome pair of silver-backed brushes on top of the chest of drawers. Red hair in the bristles left no doubt about their ownership. The sight of them made her ache. She slipped her hand through the strap of one of the brushes and picked it up.

How absurd that she had not recognized her feelings before! She should be engaged to Ginger, not Serena, and she might have been so. The knowledge that she had behaved honorably in Hertfordshire when she had declined to force him to marry her hardly consoled her. Honor, she decided, was ridiculously overrated. Honor was going to trap Ginger in a loveless, miserable marriage and herself in loathsome spinsterhood.

She slipped the second brush over her other hand and clapped the two together violently, as though she could crush honor between them.

"Hullo, Julie," said a friendly, familiar voice from behind her.

She nearly jumped out of her skin and frantically tried to shake his hairbrushes from her hands. One fell to the floor, but the other clung stubbornly to her hand.

Swale slipped it off easily and returned it with its mate to the top of the bureau. If he was surprised to find his hostess in his room handling his toiletries, he didn't show it. He did, however, show a dark, puffy ring around one eye where Cary had planted his fist earlier. The black eye had not dampened his spirits, however. "Don't have much use for those currycombs anymore, thanks to Pickering," he said cheerfully. "Nothing on my head left to curry."

"I'm so sorry," she stammered. "I never meant for him to scalp you."

Now he was surprised. "Don't you like the crop?"

"I miss it," she admitted.

"So do I," he said. "Oh well. It'll grow back, I daresay. Did you wish to speak to me?"

He looked at her very directly with his clear green eyes.

Cleopatra, she knew, had been given a moment like this—or rather, she had taken it for herself when she had rolled herself up in a carpet and had herself delivered to Caesar's chamber. Just a few minutes alone with him, and the great Julius Caesar had abandoned his wife, his country, and his honor and had made Cleopatra Queen of Egypt. History did not say what exactly the Egyptian beauty had done to poor Caesar to make him so compliant, but Juliet guessed it was probably fairly naughty.

She was not Cleopatra, of course, but then, he was not Caesar, and the fact that she had not spent the last few hours rolled up in a carpet must be seen as an advantage.

"Julie?"

"I beg your pardon, sir," she answered with a violent shake of her head. "I thought you'd gone, or I should never have presumed—"

"I'm just back now," he replied easily, taking off his coat and flinging it onto the bed. "I have been in the village, enriching the special messenger service."

"Oh," said Juliet. "I thought you might have gone to London. I didn't know what to tell the cook. It's *boeuf en croute*," she added lamely, "so the cook absolutely has to know how many she's feeding."

"Definitely put me down for the *boeuf en croute*," he said, patting his belly.

"Right," she said, knowing she ought to go at once. She could not even begin to tally how many standards of propriety she was violating merely by being alone with a man in his bedroom, but her feet refused to move. "You went for a drive?" she asked.

"Just to the village. I sent my instructions to my father's man of business—urgent post. The announcement will appear in all the morning editions with any luck."

Juliet stared at him, a huge hollow feeling opening in her chest.

"Congratulations," she said, forcing a smile. "I'm sorry if I was rude to you earlier . . ."

He seemed surprised. "You, Julie? Why, you were bursting with great ideas. Minerva never had a better idea in her whole life than those sandwich boards. That'll make 'em sit up and take notice. That ought to convince certain people the marriage should take place sooner rather than later."

Juliet's mouth fell open. "S-sandwich boards?"

"Yes—announcing our engagement. I don't think it's ever been done before." The idea of being the first man in history to announce his engagement via sandwich board held great appeal for him, she could tell. The priceless ass!

She very much doubted that his betrothed would share his enthusiasm. Serena would almost certainly die of mortification. She might even reconsider her decision to become Lady Swale. After all, any woman would balk at having her name printed up on a sandwich board to be displayed in Hyde Park, and what woman in her right mind would marry a man capable of such an absurdity, such an unforgivable lapse in propriety? Perhaps not even a greedy, grasping, long-in-the-tooth, ambitious schemer like Serena Calverstock.

Juliet felt a ray of hope. If only . . .

Of course, no honorable gentleman would ever break an engagement to a lady, but there was nothing to prevent Serena from changing her mind. Her rival was not unintelligent; she would be certain to realize how insupportable it would be to marry an uncivilized brute like Swale. And if Serena jilted Ginger . . . then Miss Wayborn could certainly console him!

"Indeed, my lord," Juliet said, now able to smile with

genuine delight. "I hope this marriage brings you great happiness."

"I believe it will make us both happy," he replied. "When two people are such good friends and so well-matched in spirit, the marriage is bound to be happy."

"I'm sure you're right," she agreed quickly. "I'd better go finish dressing. I'll send Pickering to you—with a poultice for your eye."

"You look dressed to me," he said, holding the door for her. "I'm a fair judge of when a lady is dressed or not dressed. And you, Julie, are dressed. Very clever the way it shifts color, that dress."

He was not looking at her dress at all, she could not help but notice. He was looking deep into her eyes. With his swollen eye, he looked more than ever like a fantastic creature from a grotto. Why then did she feel the strongest urge to take his face in her hands and kiss him?

"It's called ombre," she told him in a faint voice.

"Ombre," he murmured. "That's French, isn't it? Clever little buggers, the French. Always coming up with natty new words and phrases. Bouillon—that's gold, but also soup."

"*Carte blanche,*" she suggested archly.

She saw him swallow hard. "*Bon appetit,*" he said huskily. "*Cherchez la femme.*"

"*Le coeur a ses raisons que la raison ne connait point.*"

"Good Lord," he breathed. "What in God's name does that mean?"

"The heart," she translated, looking up at him through her lashes, "has reasons of which Reason knows nothing."

The effect on him was everything she could have wished for. Abruptly, he closed the door, forced her up against it, and kissed her, his hands buried in her thick hair. It was a fiery, undisciplined kiss, his tongue leaping wildly as he discovered her openness. Juliet welcomed it, her heart beating wildly as again and again his mouth closed over hers. When he was finished, he reluctantly released her, but leaned his hands against the door on either side of her head. He was panting as he touched her forehead with his own.

He must realize now, she thought joyfully, that he could never marry Serena Calverstock.

"Now I expect I've earned this black eye," he said ruefully. "It is impossible to practice restraint when you look at me like that, and you say those things, and you smell so good, and your skin is so soft, and your eyes . . . Julie . . ."

She reached up very deliberately and kissed his mouth. Unlike his kiss, hers was gentle, savoring, sweet. She touched his lips with the tip of her tongue, tasting nectar. "There is not the least need for restraint with me, Ginger," she whispered. "I'm yours if you want me."

He laughed shakily. "Careful, Julie. I'm not made of stone, you know."

The weakness she saw in his eyes made her feel all-powerful, irresistible. Slowly, she pulled the laces of her ombre dress and shrugged out of it. As he watched, stunned, the silk crumpled at her feet, and she stood before him wearing only her white silk drawers, stockings, and satin slippers. Her hair covered her breasts, but almost defiantly, she pushed the long, dark curls aside.

"*Mirabile visu,*" he murmured, and all restraint left the room.

The snowy white sheets felt cool against her burning skin as he crouched over her. "That's Latin," he murmured, his head moving between her breasts. His tongue trailed down her breastbone, and she felt the tips of her breasts swell almost to bursting. "It means 'wondrous to behold.' You, my darling, are bloody wondrous to behold."

She cried out in pleasure as his mouth covered her upstanding nipple. She had never thought of her body as sensual before. She had compared its physical lines to Greek and Roman engravings and to garden statues of nymphs, to which, she thought, it compared rather favorably. But never this. Every inch of her skin was wild with feeling where he had touched her and where she longed to be touched.

He suckled at her breast tenderly until the wildness calmed into a dreamy pleasure.

"I know quite a bit of Latin," he went on, lifting his head. "I read Latin at university."

"I thought you were sent down from Oxford," she murmured, staring at his wide, red mouth. She had not noticed before, but his lips had a sensual pout to them. Kissing was what they did best. How many women, she wondered, had he driven mad like this? Actresses and opera dancers. He was certainly rich enough to keep a string of high-priced mistresses. Jealousy and insecurity bit her suddenly. How paltry her offering of love must seem to him after the practiced ministrations of skilled courtesans! Her breasts were too small, her body too thin and awkward . . .

"I learned a thing or two before I left," he whispered in her ear, his tongue flicking against the sensitive lobe. "Cunnilingus. Do you know what that is, my sweet?"

She propped herself up on her elbows and looked at him, irritated because he had stopped fondling her breasts. Were they really too small to please him? What if the nipples were too hard? She could not understand it—usually, they were soft. And there was a strange wet feeling between her legs that was not at all normal. She felt all at once that her body had betrayed her. Decidedly, she was not in the mood for a Latin lesson.

"Is it important?" she asked impatiently.

He chuckled, his hand slowly exploring the soft hummock of her belly. She gasped as, dipping lower, he pulled the string of her drawers. She was horrified that he would discover the mysterious and embarrassing moisture.

"Please, Julie . . ." he begged, his voice dark with desire, and she melted. As long as she was certain of his desire for her, she could not be reluctant. She closed her eyes tightly, and the sensation of her drawers being pulled off both excited and terrified her. He kissed her down the length of her body, driving her almost to sobs, but her body jumped involuntarily as he pressed his hand between her thighs. He sucked in a ragged breath and slowly opened the petals of her sex. She willed herself to be still; the sensation was unlike anything she had ever experienced in her life, and she meant to feel it to the utmost. "You have such clever, sensitive fingers," she murmured happily as he continued to explore the exquisitely sensitive flesh. More and more honey flowed from her body, but she was no longer embarrassed. All she could feel was him, his hands, his lips, his desire for her. His head moved lower, his lips trailing sweet fire over her skin.

"If you enjoy my fingers, you will like my tongue even better," he murmured.

Juliet's eyes popped open. With a shock, she realized that he intended to kiss her *there*. "You can't—!" she protested weakly.

"You are about to experience all the benefits of a classical education, my love, without any of its inconveniences," he announced firmly, taking her powerless legs over his shoulders.

In the next moment, his mouth was on her, and she forgot all the half-hearted protests that had formed in the back of her mind. In her innocence, she had thought his mouth on her breast the pinnacle of pleasure, but she soon realized her mistake. The first crisis shuddered through her body almost before she knew what was happening. The blood rushed into her ears, and she bit her lip hard to keep from shrieking like a newborn babe. The most exquisite, wringing pleasure overtook her entire body in a seemingly never ending spiral of torrential emotion. She had not thought herself capable of such strong feeling; the closest she had ever come to this had been—she nearly laughed as the thought entered her reeling brain—the closest she had ever come to this feeling in her life was when she had heard this man play Beethoven. Now he was playing her, though not with those remarkable hands, which looked so clumsy but were so sensitive. He was playing her with his tongue, and the music was divine.

When at last he lifted his face, she was a changed woman, and her lover's face, with its black, swollen eye; short nose; and wide mouth, was exquisitely beautiful. "The Romans were a curiously oversexed bunch," he told her. "I expect it's why Italy is such a popular destination for travelers."

She blinked at him in confusion, her ability to think and speak returning slowly. "What are you talking about?" She wanted to ask why he was talking at all. Tears streaked her cheeks. She was now his forever. Surely words were unnecessary?

"Cunnilingus. *That* was cunnilingus. From the Latin *lingere,* meaning 'to lick,' and *cunnus* . . . well, I will leave you to guess what *cunnus* is Latin for."

"Oh." She sat up and, for some absurd reason, pulled the blue velvet coverlet up over her naked breasts. *A bit late for that, miss!* her conscience mocked her. The second before she had offered herself to him, she had felt proud and powerful; now, she was horribly weak and shy. "It was not what I expected," she said slowly. "I had thought the gentleman would have to undress in order to perform the act of love."

He had not even removed his boots!

"Good God, no," he said, sitting on the edge of the bed. "If I were to unleash my poor, tortured pego, your virginity wouldn't be worth the paper it's printed on, my dear."

"What? You mean there's more?" It was an exhausting thought. An exhilarating thought. Moments before, she had thought herself entirely depleted, but the desire returned now at double strength. If the mere preliminaries had transported her into bliss, what would the act itself do to her fantastically responsive body? And what would it do to him? She was dying to find out.

"Of course there's more," he said brusquely, averting his eyes from her. The velvet coverlet had slipped from her breasts. They were bigger than he had anticipated, with a soft round weight to them and proud nipples, still red from his wild mouth. The sight made him short of breath. If she gave him the barest provocation, the barest sign, he knew he would lose all control.

"You don't think I'm going to take your virginity, do you?" he asked.

"I thought you had," she whispered. "You mean you didn't? Don't you want to?"

He groaned.

"I'm not a complete cad, you know," he said, acute sexual frustration making him more curt than he meant to be. "I don't go about the place violating well-bred young ladies, you know. I'm a guest here. Your brothers would hardly thank me—"

"My brothers aren't here," Juliet said quickly. "I'm here. I'm here, Ginger." She pulled his hand to her and placed it on her breast. "I want to belong to you . . . forever. You must know that. More than anything in this world, I want to be your wife."

Her skin was warm and throbbing with life. In vain, he had tried to kill his desire for her. "You win," he muttered as he swiftly unbuttoned his trousers. This time her legs fell open to him easily, without any nervousness. The neat little sex he had kissed and sucked so shamelessly looked like a full-blown rose now, a rose drenched in dew. She instantly closed her legs around his waist, clasped her arms tightly around his neck, and arched her back to receive him. She made only the barest complaint as he broke through her maidenhead, and then they moved, fiercely in tune, Nature teaching her to match her rhythm to his, until he was fairly exhausted. With a last, violent thrust that almost frightened her with its intensity, he emptied himself into her.

Then he rested, his body heaving as he tried to draw breath. After a moment, he came to his senses and raised himself on his elbows so that her body, which was drenched in his sweat, was not crushed under him.

"I know I should regret this, but I don't," he said, smiling at her.

"No, indeed," she murmured, feeling shy now, acutely aware that he was still inside her.

"Oh?" he chuckled, bending his head to tease her nipple. "Then milady is pleased with her victory? *My* honor is in shambles. My conscience in shreds. But I am dead to shame. I don't care, if it gives you even a little pleasure."

"Considerably more than that, my lord," she admitted, her face hot.

"Will we go again?" he asked seriously.

She felt him inside her, nudging, lengthening, and despite a great deal of soreness between her legs, the thrill was undeniable. "Yes, please," she moaned, but she could not help wincing as he thrust into her again.

"Oh, it's too much for you," he murmured, rolling away from her.

"No," she protested, clinging to him.

"My dear girl," he said firmly. "You've had quite enough. Don't stick your chin out at me—you oughtn't to have had any. I've indulged you too much as it is. You do realize, don't you, that Pickering walked in on us just now?"

Juliet sighed. "I thought I felt a draft. How awkward for him, poor man! But I do think we were past the most embarrassing part, don't you?"

He shrugged into his shirt, pulled up his breeches— he still had not removed his boots!—and picked her shades of blue dress up off the floor. Reluctantly, she pulled it over her head, and he did his best to tie the laces at the back. "I'm not usually this clumsy," he apologized.

"I know it," she answered, laughing. "My piano will never let me touch it again, now that it has been played by the master." She became serious. "Will you play the Moonlight Sonata after dinner just for me?"

"Of course," he promised, desperately trying to smooth her tangled hair. "Off you go, Mademoiselle Ombre," he said, giving her rump a playful swat. "Try not to look so bloody gorgeous at dinner— I might just leap across the table and ravish you on the spot."

She found the little blue beaded slipper that had rolled under the bed and sat down on the bed to slip it onto her foot.

"Julie."

She looked up at him, startled by his serious tone.

"I wish—" he broke off, unable to find the words. She guessed that he was thinking of Serena, and a stab of guilt pierced her happiness. Not for Serena's sake, but because she had made him do such a dishonorable thing as making love to one woman when he was promised to another. But it could not be helped. She loved him; Serena didn't. Where was the honor in letting him marry a woman who didn't love him?

But Swale was thinking no such thing. "I was your first," he said, falling on his knees before her and seizing her hands. "I wish to God you had been mine!"

Juliet listened in astonishment.

"I have never been with a woman who wasn't paid for her services. I'm sorry to pain you, Julie, but I couldn't go on without telling you the shameful truth about me. You had every right to expect me to be as chaste as you are, but I can't deceive you."

"I was not deceived," she assured him gently. "Young men are expected to have . . . experiences. It is the way of the world. And perhaps, it was your experience that made it so . . . so pleasant for me." Silently, she cursed the inadequacy of the word. Pleasant! Rather, she had been shaken to her very soul.

"Don't ever think that," he said with shocking bitterness. "The only pleasure *they* ever felt was when they counted my money. Believe me, there's no comparison between what we have and that . . . that cold commerce."

She kissed him very gently on the lips. "Well, of course there's no comparison, Ginger, you priceless ass," she said softly. "*I* love you."

"What are we going to do, Julie?" he whispered. "Sir Benedict has already told me he'll never consent to our marriage while you're still a minor. He isn't likely to change his mind. I thought I could do the time standing on my head, but you . . . *this* . . . Dammit, I want you again right now."

"Leave all that to me," she said, suppressing the unladylike desire to whoop with joy. Her gamble had paid off. To hell with honor, she thought recklessly. "One thing at a time, my darling. First, let the announcement appear in the papers. That will do much of the work for us. Did you really hire men with sandwich boards?"

"I did exactly what you said, Julie," he said earnestly.

"Good," she assured him, stroking his face. "Good, my darling. These things have a way of working themselves out. You'll see."

"I should speak to Sir Benedict, all the same. I should like to speak to him. I should like to convince him I shall be a worthy husband for his sister."

"And you will," she said quickly. "You will. But not just yet. I'll tell you when the time is right to speak to Sir Benedict. I know my brother. I know best how to handle him."

"I feel like that Macbeth chap plotting to murder

his king," Swale complained. "Wheels within wheels. Secrets and lies. I want everything out in the open, Julie. Well, perhaps not everything," he amended hastily. "You know what I mean. I want to deal frankly and plainly with Sir Benedict."

"I know, my darling," she answered, biting her lip. "I know any form of subterfuge and deceit is abhorrent to you. It is abhorrent to me! But it's the only way we can be happy. You could not marry anyone but me, and I can't wait two years to be your wife."

"Marry anyone but you, Julie?" he cried passionately. "No, indeed. I'm ashamed that I ever thought of marrying the Calverstock . . . or poor little Coralie Price, for that matter. The soul recoils in horror. But this, Julie . . . skulking around like a pair of thieves . . . I think it would be better if I spoke to Sir Benedict now, *before* the notice appears in the London papers. How am I ever to face him after *that?* He will think me the most dishonorable wretch that ever drew breath, if he doesn't already."

"No!" she cried in panic. She could just imagine Benedict's reaction if Swale spoke to him tonight about marrying Miss Wayborn, just a few hours before the notice of his engagement to Serena was printed in the papers. "Ginger, you must *not* speak to Benedict before that happens! That would be a catastrophe. Not only would he refuse to give his consent, but he would also never speak to me again." She leaned down to kiss him, her voice growing soft and, she hoped, seductive. "I understand how you feel about skulking, but it's not all unpleasant, is it? It has a few consolations, does it not?"

"As a temptress, you are nothing short of diabolical," he moaned. "No! No more kissing," he protested weakly as she pressed her lips against his. "If you go down to dinner with swollen lips, your brothers will put their heads together and then their arms together, and before you know it, Uncle George's rapier will be snicking off my head."

"As though I should ever let anyone snick your head off," she crooned soothingly. "Will you trust me to know what I'm doing? I have a plan."

"You're worse than Lady Macbeth, you know that?"

Juliet laughed. "Nonsense. If I had been Macbeth's lady, he would have gotten away with it."

"I don't know," he muttered. "It seems wrong somehow. Devious."

"'Art thou afeard to be the same in thine own act and valor as thou art in desire?'" she countered. "'Wouldst thou have that which thou esteem'st the ornament of life, and live a coward in thine own esteem'—"

"Oh, shut up," he interrupted crossly. "I can see it now. Amateur theatricals at Auckland Palace. Stupid, burbling actors soliloquizing on my blessed lawn. I daresay you'll want a bloody outdoor amphitheater too? God help us."

She observed him rather frostily. "Did you just tell me to shut up?"

"Less persiflage rather," he amended hastily.

"We're not married yet, Ginger," she informed him from the doorway. "I can still change my mind. If I were you, I'd keep the rudeness to an absolute minimum. Points off for rudeness, in fact. Macbeth never told his lady to shut up, did he, Pickering?"

"No, Miss Julie," replied the servant who was waiting politely in the hall.

Swale admitted the valet into the room.

"I have taken the liberty of preparing a poultice for your lordship's eye," said Pickering. "It is composed chiefly of chamomile and witch hazel. I have used it in the past to reduce the appearance of swellings and bruises, particularly in the eye region, with some noticeable success. If my lord would sit down . . . ?"

Swale submitted to the poulticing. Appearing at dinner with a shiner would scarcely endear him to Sir Benedict. And since that gentleman was Juliet's legal guardian and he was more than capable of withholding his consent for his sister's marriage until Juliet reached the ripe old age of twenty-one, it was best not to antagonize him. Juliet was definitely worth a poulticing. Definitely worth a black eye, if it came to that. Which it had, of course.

"What did he say, Pickering?" he asked, resting comfortably in the chair with something wet and sticky plastered to his eye.

Pickering looked at him in some surprise. "Who, my lord?"

"That Macbeth chap. He must have said something to that scaly wife of his. Holdeth thy tongueth, O lady?"

Pickering thought a moment. "'Prithee peace,' my lord. Act One, Scene Seven."

"Prithee peace . . . meaning, of course, shut up?"

"Indeed, my lord."

"Or, if one prefers the Latin, *Quieta non movere.*"

"Indeed, my lord."

"Prithee peace. Pretty well for a Scotsman," he observed.

"Indeed, my lord," said Pickering.

"A man can safely say 'Prithee peace' to his lady love without suffering the slings and arrows, I trust?"

"Indeed, my lord."

"Good man, Macbeth. Excellent fellow. Whatever happened to him?"

* * *

Swale was sixteen minutes late for dinner, but the swelling in his left eye was barely noticeable, and his shirt and waistcoat were snowy white. He took his place across from Cary, making his apologies to Juliet, who was seated at the foot of the table in her aunt's customary place. Juliet accepted his excuses very demurely and explained that her aunt had grown over-tired during the picnic and was taking supper in her room.

"We thought you'd gone, Swale," Cary said rudely. "We were looking forward to a quiet evening. I have lost my appetite." Angrily, he slung down his napkin and left the table, despite Benedict's order for him to remain where he was and not be a fool.

"I seem to be decimating your household, Sir Benedict," Swale said ruefully. "First, Lady Elkins, then your brother. Take care. Miss Wayborn may be next."

"I apologize for my brother, sir," Benedict said coldly, his embarrassment magnified by having to apologize to a man he disliked. The report that Cary had given him before dinner of Swale's actually being engaged to Juliet, he had already dismissed. He could not conceive of any lady regarding Swale with anything but revulsion, and Juliet was not likely to be seduced by the promise of riches and a title.

The cold soup was taken away, and the main course was brought in.

"Do you know," Swale said suddenly, "what happened to Macbeth? The fellow in the play, I mean. His head was cut off and put on a pole underwrit with the words, 'Here may you see the tyrant.'"

Benedict stared at him in appalled fascination. "You have just discovered this, my lord?"

"Just now," Swale confirmed. "Pickering told me.

Guess my shock! Things were going so well. And his poor wife, Chuck."

Benedict could not contain himself. "Chuck?"

"Yes, her Christian name was Chuck."

"Was it?"

"Of course," Swale said irritably. "Act Three, Scene Two, if you don't believe me. 'Be innocent of the knowledge, *dearest Chuck*, till thou applaud the deed.' One of your less popular Scotch names. Understandably so."

With the greatest effort, Benedict kept his countenance, but Juliet could not.

Swale gave her a hard look as she collapsed into giggles. "Do you know what happened to Chuck, Miss Wayborn? It is popularly believed that Chuck—Queen Chuck she would have been—threw herself from the battlements, which I gather are pretty high things to be throwing oneself from! *That* is what comes of plotting and scheming, Miss Wayborn. I think Shakespeare is trying to tell us something, huh? We could learn much from the lessons we draw from the fate of Chuck and her Macbeth."

"The tragedy of Macbeth surely is more complicated than a mere morality play," said Benedict. "In his grasping ambition to enlarge himself in the temporal world, Macbeth throws away his immortal soul, the only thing that truly makes man greater than the sum of his parts."

"Very well put, Benedict," Juliet congratulated him.

"And poor Chuck, after all her scheming, is driven to suicide by her guilt," said Swale.

Juliet looked at him sharply. "That never rang true to me, my lord. Mrs. Siddons was very moving in the sleepwalking scene, of course, but *I* never thought Lady Macbeth had a conscience. Macbeth had a conscience, but he suppressed it like she told him to." She leaned forward and spoke deliberately. "'Screw your courage to the sticking place, and we'll not fail.'"

"Easy for you to say," Swale grumbled, tucking into his *boeuf en croute*.

"Actually," said Benedict, "I think—"

"They're calling this dish Beef Wellington now," Juliet brightly informed them.

"What's next?" Swale asked resentfully. "The Wellington hybrid tea rose? Wellington suspender buttons? Wellington toothpick holders?"

Juliet frowned. "His Grace is so modest he has insisted the new bridge be called Waterloo Bridge and not Wellington Bridge, as originally proposed. It's not his fault everyone wishes to honor him. He has saved all Europe from the Bonapartists. What have *you* done?" She looked down the table at her brother. "Benedict, I think we should call our little cheeses after the Duke of Wellington, don't you?"

Benedict shuddered. "That could scarcely be considered a compliment to the man," he said repressively. To his dismay, his sister and Lord Swale spent the rest of dinner suggesting various names for the Home Farm cheese, none of which could be considered for a moment. A more inane conversation he could not have imagined, but the young people pursued it vigorously, the lady suggesting absurd French phrases, the gentleman responding in Latin. Resolutely, Sir Benedict looked up at the ceiling and concentrated on chewing his food thirty times per bite.

He actually started in surprise when Juliet rose from the table.

"Don't forget—you promised me the Moonlight Sonata," she was saying to Lord Swale. Her eyes were sparkling, and her color was high. She also seemed rather grotesquely overdressed for a quiet meal at home in the country. The shimmering blue dress was daringly low cut, showing a high rounded bosom; white shoulders; and a long, slender neck. Not at all the sort of dress an elder brother wishes to see his sister wearing. Dresses like that, in fact, were one of the many reasons he avoided London altogether.

Without actually touching Juliet, Swale was glued to her side. He reminded Benedict, odiously, of a fawning puppy. Was Cary right? He suddenly wondered. *Was* Juliet engaged to the odious Swale?

She had not been tempted to have him in Hertfordshire, but, he reflected, life had become very trying for his sister since the arrival of Lady Maria Fitzwilliam in Surrey. Miss Wayborn had gone from being of first importance in the neighborhood to anathema, and she might be tempted to accept the first offer of marriage that came her way. After the scandalous race to Southend, she could not expect to receive many. And becoming Marchioness of Swale offered the unique opportunity of being revenged upon Lady Maria, her chief tormentor.

It broke his heart to think of his sister marrying for such unworthy reasons.

"My lord," he said sharply before the other man was out the door. "May I offer you some port?"

Chapter 18

"Yes, do," said Juliet quickly. "I must go up to my aunt in case she may need anything."

She pulled the doors closed behind her, and though Benedict observed her very closely, he could detect no special regard in the last glance she gave Swale. His lordship, however, was horribly transparent. The uncivilized brute actually had designs on Juliet!

Albert brought out the port, but Benedict made no move to pour. Instead, he fixed a flaying eye on Swale and said, "Farmer Quince tells me you have taken a fancy to our cheese, my lord."

Swale first appeared confused, then relieved. Clearly, he had been expecting quite a different question. "Oh yes, Sir Benedict. The cheese."

"You have asked him to sell you two hundred cheeses, I believe? Two hundred, is that the correct figure?"

"I think so."

"You think so?"

"Yes. Yes, two hundred is the exact number."

"At forty pence a cheese?"

"Oh, round figures, if you please," said Swale easily. "A guinea a cheese."

"Naturally, we will draw up a contract," said Benedict. "In that way, both parties are protected."

"Farmer Quince requires no protection from me."

Benedict smiled coldly. "A contract makes explicit the obligations of both parties."

"For heaven's sake," Swale said impatiently, "I give him two hundred guineas, and he gives me two hundred cheeses."

"It does seem simple," Benedict agreed. "But what size cheese? And when are they to be delivered? If they cannot be delivered by such and such a date, is the contract void? If, for example, Mr. Quince is unable to provide more than, say, one hundred and seventeen cheeses by the date specific, is the contract void, or should your lordship be obligated to purchase the one hundred and seventeen cheeses? If so, should the price of one guinea per cheese be reduced to, say, one pound?"

Swale made a gesture of impatience. "Details, details."

"A contract spells out the details of any agreement for easy reference, my lord." Benedict lifted the decanter and poured a glass of port. "Take marriage, for example."

Swale's eyes widened as he attempted to appear innocent. "Were we . . . were we talking of marriage, Sir Benedict?"

"*I* am talking of marriage, my lord. Deceptively simple, marriage, like the buying of cheese. A man and a woman discover a deep admiration and regard for one another. They pledge their feelings publicly; then before God and man, they are joined in holy matrimony. What could be simpler? And yet, the devil is in the details. Marriage is a legal contract between two parties. I would be a poor landlord if I allowed Mr. Quince to enter into a burdensome contract with you, my lord. After all, if he were to go to the trouble and expense of making two hundred cheeses and get nothing for it in the end, the poor man would be ruined."

The baronet poured a second glass of port, and Swale accepted it gratefully. All this talk of marriage had made him thirsty. "All this talk of cheese is making me thirsty," he said with a shaky laugh.

"In the same way," Benedict continued smoothly, "I would be a poor guardian of my sister's happiness if I allowed her to enter into a burdensome contract."

Swale frowned in concentration. "But . . . I don't wish to buy any cheese from your sister. My bargain is with Mr. Quince."

"No, sir. Your bargain is with me," Benedict informed him. "But you have not touched your port, my lord. Can it be that the stories are true?"

Swale started. "Stories?"

"Would you prefer Madeira?"

The time had come to seek wiser counsel. "No, thank you, Sir Benedict," he said, almost jumping to his feet. "In point of fact, what I need is the closet."

Ignominiously, the Marquess of Swale quit the field.

Juliet was waiting for him in the dark hallway outside her aunt's room. "Good God!" she whispered fiercely. "You nearly frightened the life out of me."

"He suspects," said Swale, trying to gather up her hand.

Impatiently, she snatched her hand away. "He certainly *will* suspect if he finds you here," she snapped. "You must go back down and drink port with my brother."

"No, I think I'd much better hide," he retorted. "I can't drink the man's port and not tell him I'm in love with his bally sister. I won't do it."

"Ginger—"

"I'm not bloody Macchiavelli, you know!"

"Steady on, my darling," she said quickly, soothingly, realizing that her coconspirator had been pushed to his limit.

"*This,* Julie, is worse than cold soup. A secret engagement! I never in my life heard of anything so shabby. It would be better to elope. A good, honest elopement is just what we need."

"Scotland? I *don't* think," said Juliet hotly. She could just imagine the contempt that would follow her all her days if she eloped with Serena Calverstock's betrothed within days of the announcement in the *Post.* Not to mention the sandwich boards in Hyde Park! "I've had enough scandal, thank you. We must think of our families. Benedict would never forgive me."

"My father would never forgive me either," he agreed woefully. "He believes in the nobility setting an example for the commoners, you know."

"And my poor aunt," Juliet added with a faint smile. "Only imagine the pains in her legs if we eloped." She touched the side of his face. "You must be strong, my darling."

"Couldn't we tell Aunt Elinor, at least?" he begged without much hope. "I shouldn't feel as much the snake in the grass—the *anguis in herba*—if someone in the household knew our secret."

"Are you mad?" Juliet scoffed, but in the next instant, she felt a flash of inspiration. "Aunt Elinor has always been in favor of our marrying," she said thoughtfully. "She is our only possible ally since both my brothers detest you, and it will make her happier than words can express. Yes, I think we should tell Aunt Elinor."

Swale followed her a little doubtfully into the room, remembering how that lady always seemed to develop headache in his presence. Lady Elkins was abed with a cold compress over her eyes, her back supported by a mountain of pillows. A lace cap covered her hair, and a heavy shawl was wrapped around her shoulders. She wore a voluminous robe of copper-colored silk, and on her feet were thick, black stockings. Only two or three candles lit the large room.

"Aunt Elinor?" Juliet called softly.

"Wicked, ungrateful girl," whined Lady Elkins pathetically. "I have been lying here in the most excruciating pain for a full twenty minutes, not that *you* care two straws for that. Bring my vinaigrette. No— the hartshorn."

Juliet sat on the edge of the bed and took her aunt's hand gently in her own.

"You handle me so roughly," complained Lady Elkins. "I am too weak even to lift my head."

"I have brought you something better than hartshorn, my dear aunt," Juliet whispered.

"Pray, do not scream at me, miss. Is that a young lady's voice or a trumpet blast? Oh, how my head aches! I expect Mrs. Oliphant's card party would have been too much for me. Indeed, I should not have gone, Juliet, even if you *had* been invited. When I think I might have been the aunt of a marchioness—! You are far too particular, my dear. What does it signify if the man has a face out of a grotto? What does it matter that he is a red-haired ape of a man? He has *twenty thousand* a year!"

Swale could not hear this with universal pleasure.

"My dear aunt," Juliet said quickly, "would you be *very* pleased to call him your nephew?"

"Certainly not," she bitterly replied. "The stupid man has made himself so disagreeable to everyone that I cannot blame you for refusing him. I wish he would go away and leave us all in peace."

"I'm very sorry to hear you say that, Aunt, because I am secretly engaged to him."

"Oh, don't tease me," moaned the widow. "You wicked, wicked girl. My heart cannot bear the strain."

Juliet peeled the compress from her aunt's eyes. "But it is quite true, Aunt Elinor. His lordship is here with me now. His lordship very much wishes to be your nephew."

Lady Elkins regarded Swale almost with horror, as though fearing he might be a ghost.

"Hullo, Aunt Elinor," he greeted her. "Direct from the grotto, as you see."

Lady Elkins spoke cautiously. "You're really going to marry Juliet? You're not toying with me?"

"Our engagement is secret at the moment," said Juliet, "for obvious reasons. But his lordship said we must tell Lady Elkins. Lady Elkins will be our ally. We must have Lady Elkins's approval and advice. Lady Elkins is the only person in the world who can help us."

"Oh!" Lady Elkins cried, her bosom beginning to heave. She was deeply flattered to be drawn into such an important secret. "My approval? Of course you have it, my dear children! Oh, you dear, sweet boy!" she cried, throwing her arms wide to Swale. "I am speechless with delight! Words cannot express my happiness! I do not know what to say! Twenty thousand a year!"

"Do you feel well enough to come down, Aunt

Elinor?" Juliet gently suggested. "It's so difficult with Benedict glaring at us the whole time."

"I'll carry you downstairs if you like," Swale offered.

Lady Elkins was indignant. "Young man, I am perfectly capable of walking downstairs! Certainly, I will come down. Juliet, fetch me my good shawl—no, no, the cashmere from India. And my silk slippers. Juliet embroidered these for me, my lord. Is that not exquisite workmanship? An E on each toe for Elinor Elkins. Isn't that clever?"

"Very," Swale affirmed, not in the least distressed that his future wife possessed one very silly aunt. It was pleasant to meet someone in this house who did not regard him with the flaying eye. He offered her his arm.

Juliet ran down before them and was engaged in opening the piano and setting out the music when Sir Benedict found her. "Is Swale in here?"

Juliet cheekily stooped to check underneath the piano before answering, "I don't see him."

"Where's he gotten to?" Benedict looked at his sister suspiciously. "Are you wearing rouge?"

"Certainly not. Only old ladies and opera dancers wear rouge."

While not entirely convinced, Benedict did not pursue the matter. "Look here, Juliet. I must speak to you. I can remain silent no longer. Cary tells me you have received an offer of marriage? Is this true?"

Juliet was startled. Cary could not possibly be aware of her arrangement with Swale since it had only been decided just before dinner. Benedict must be referring to Horatio's offer. "I have received an offer of marriage," she told Benedict. "But I have decided I cannot accept."

"Thank God," said Benedict. "I could not stand by and let you marry a man you do not love."

"I have no intention of marrying a man I do not love," Juliet replied rather crossly.

"I was afraid that your recent trials might have made you vulnerable," said Benedict. "It is hard, I know, to be snubbed by your friends, but that hardship would seem as nothing to the abject misery of a loveless marriage. Have you told your suitor you will not have him?"

Juliet sighed. "He begged me to take some time to consider his offer, or I should have given him my answer immediately. I daresay he is assured of a very different answer than he will receive, but I cannot help that."

"You have greatly relieved my mind."

"If I ever do come to you and tell you that I am engaged to be married," Juliet said slowly, "you will know it is because I am in love and for no other reason."

"Yes, yes, of course," said Benedict, smiling at her. "You have no idea of the weight that has been lifted from my heart. Yes, I daresay his arrogance has led him to believe you will have him, Juliet. When do you give him your answer?"

"Tomorrow."

"Good," said Benedict. "There is nothing to be gained from drawing this thing out." He went on almost sheepishly, "I don't suppose I could persuade you to retire very early this evening? With Cary gone and my aunt indisposed, I can scarcely leave you alone with Swale, and you know how insupportable I find his society. I had much rather be going over my accounts in my study."

Juliet was spared the embarrassment of answering

by the arrival of her aunt. Bundled in a shawl, Lady Elkins arrived, clinging to the arm of Lord Swale like a burr.

"Look who I found," Swale said proudly.

"My dear aunt, you should be in bed," said Benedict. "You are unwell."

"Nonsense," she replied. "All I needed was a little rest. I'm fit as a fiddle now. His lordship has promised me an evening of music. Music is just what I need to carry away all the pains in my limbs. An evening of cards would be insupportable, of course, but music is always delightful."

"There, Benedict," Juliet whispered to her brother as Swale settled Lady Elkins into a comfortable chair with a footrest. "Now you may go to your accounts any time you like." She looked back at him innocently as he studied her with narrowed eyes.

"Are you quite sure you're not wearing rouge?"

"Quite sure."

Lady Elkins took her knitting onto her lap, while Juliet slipped a shawl over her own bare shoulders and stood next to the piano, turning the pages for Swale as he began to play. His lordship concentrated on the piece, and Benedict was forced to admit the man was a gifted musician. The baronet quietly withdrew before the second movement, wishing them all a pleasant evening.

Juliet collapsed on the piano seat next to Swale, who blew out his breath as if he had been holding it for an hour. "He doesn't suspect anything," she assured him quickly. "He was afraid I was going to marry Horatio. He was very relieved when I told him I wasn't."

"That *would* be a burdensome contract," said Swale, considerably cheered. "He don't like Horatio either? That shows some good sense."

"Of course it does. And I swore to him if I ever did marry, it would be for love." She leaned across him and smoothed the pages of the score. "Better go on playing now, Ginger. If he doesn't hear music, he may think your hands are straying."

He grinned at her, his hands moving lightly over the keys. "Tonight, my love . . ."

"Oh, yes?"

His voice dipped lower and lower. "'Ere the sooty winged bat hath flown night's yawn, there shall be done a deed of dreadful note.' Points on for Shakepeare?"

Juliet grimaced at the mangled quotation. "One point for trying, but two points off for mucking it up, I'm afraid. But what are you planning to do?"

"Be-eth thou innocent of the knowledge, dearest Chuck, till thou applaudeth the deed," he told her solemnly, making her convulse with laughter.

"What is so funny?" Cary Wayborn suddenly demanded from the doorway.

His surly disapproval had nothing like the effect of Benedict's cold contempt. Juliet stood up and faced him defiantly. "You're drunk," she said coldly. "You've been carousing in the village tavern, I suppose?"

"And the society there was infinitely better than the society here," he replied rudely.

"Thank you, sir," his sister responded tartly. "You had better go to bed before Benedict sees you."

"Indeed, my love," said Lady Elkins in a more gentle tone. "You do look peaked."

"I will go to bed," Cary declared, sweeping his arm up in a grand gesture worthy of Napoleon himself. "I will conserve my strength. I will sleep the sleep of the innocent, while *he* sleeps the sleep of the guilty." He pointed at Swale, who stared doggedly at his music.

"Good night, my lord," he added, executing a bow with difficulty.

"Go to bed, Cary," Juliet snapped. "Go to bed before you fall over."

"You defend him!" Cary cried, beginning to slur his words. "That'sh rich. He'sh made you the talk of London, my dear shister. They are placing bets on whether or not Swale will swucceed in marrying you."

"What?" Juliet and Swale cried at once.

"Look at the innocence on his face," Cary sneered. "One would almost believe he knew nothing whatever about it. It was hish friend Devize that started the pool."

"What are the odds?" Swale asked curiously, but Juliet quelled him with a glance.

"You see, Julie! The fiend don't deny it!"

"I can't help what they are betting on in London—I have been here," Swale pointed out. "*I* haven't bet on anything."

"As though my sister would ever make such a degrading marriage merely for worldly advantage!" said Cary. "That is what I told Budgie and Lord Dulwich when I saw them in the thillage. I will swoot Shale before I let him marry my sister."

"I'm sure he doesn't mean it, my lord," said Lady Elkins.

Juliet suddenly felt quite depressed. Tomorrow, the announcement of Swale's engagement to Serena would appear in the London papers. That obstacle would have to be removed before she could even think of how she would make her brothers accept her own engagement to Swale, but right now, it all seemed impossible.

"Go to bed, Cary, please," she said wearily.

Satisfied that he had broken up their gaiety, Cary went away.

"I swear, Julie, if he weren't your brother—" Swale muttered.

"I know," she sighed. "Suddenly, I'm very tired. Would you mind awfully if I went to bed now? Tomorrow is going to be rather a big day for us."

"Not yet," he said, seizing her hands. "In just a few moments, you will hear your obnoxious brother give an impression of a rooster laying an egg."

Cary's piercing scream brought Benedict from his study. Aunt Elinor complained violently that her heart had just burst, and Juliet let her head fall into her hands in despair.

"Not so much a rooster laying an egg," Swale said critically, "as a pig trying on a hat."

"What did you do?" Juliet asked sternly.

Cary himself answered, bursting through the doors of the drawing room like an avenging angel, with Benedict not far behind him. Cary was wild-eyed, he was dressed in his nightshirt, and his hair was standing on end. "Newts!" he roared. "That blackguard has put newts in my bed. Dozens of slimy, wriggling, nasty newts! I will teach you, sir, to put newts in my bed."

"Juliet!" cried Benedict at once. "How could you do such a thing to your brother?"

Cary blinked in surprise.

"Me?" Juliet was indignant.

"Don't deny it, Miss," said her eldest brother, glaring at her. "I caught you red-handed in the hall with the bucket in your hand! At the time, I assumed I'd caught you *before* you had committed your crime. But now I realize the truth—you were just finishing up."

"Oh," said Juliet. "It was only a harmless little

prank. W-welcome home, Cary!" She laughed gaily. "Nothing says welcome home like a merry prank."

Cary gritted his teeth. "I beg your pardon, Swale," he said curtly. "As for you—!" He shook his fist at his sister. "I'll take your room since you have made mine uninhabitable. How is that for a merry prank?"

He turned on his heel and strode off.

"I suggest we all go to bed," said Benedict. "You may board with your aunt tonight, Miss Juliet, after you have rid my house of newts. Shame on you!"

"Just a moment, Sir Benedict," Swale interrupted. "Whatever happened to one's being innocent until proven guilty? Miss Wayborn is entirely innocent. *I* put the newts in Cary's bed."

"You cannot protect her by lying, my lord," said Benedict. "I saw her with my own eyes."

"Cary put a dead rat under my pillow," said Swale. "Naturally, I retaliated."

"No, he didn't," said Juliet, wincing. "*I* did that."

"What?"

"I put the rat under your pillow," said Juliet miserably, unable to meet Swale's blazing green eyes. "You said no newts, Benedict, but you never said a word about rats."

"An unforgivable lapse, as it turns out," Benedict murmured.

"I didn't know it was *your* pillow," Juliet went on, turning to Swale. "Cary's letter said he was bringing someone home. I thought he meant Stacy Calverstock. I thought if I put him in Hastings and put a rat under his pillow, he'd go away again the next morning."

"You have been very busy, I see," said Benedict severely.

"I thought it was Cary that put the rat under my pillow," said Swale, frowning.

"I'm sure it was all a merry prank, my lord," said Lady Elkins desperately. "Juliet has a very lively sense of humor. Not everyone appreciates it, of course, but here we laugh all day long."

"I am not laughing," said Benedict, rather unnecessarily Juliet thought. Rather obvious that he was not laughing. "Juliet, you will rid my house of all newts and all rats without any help from the servants. Then you will go to bed. You will not ride your horse for two weeks. Is that clear?"

"She'll grow horribly fat," said Juliet, but weakly.

"Billy will exercise her."

"Look here," said Swale. "I am responsible for the newts. I saw that filthy rat, and all I could think of was newts."

"I thought you were on your way to put them in *my* room," said Juliet. "I never dreamed you had already put them in Cary's room."

"I suppose you had Billy put the rat under my pillow," said Swale.

"Certainly not," said Juliet, deeply offended. "I did it myself! I don't send servants to do my skullduggery for me. I did *buy* the rat," she added a little sheepishly.

"Oh, I paid Billy for the newts," Swale admitted freely. "Couldn't risk being seen down by the lake. But I put them in your brother's bed myself. You see, Sir Benedict, I'm not the kind of man who pays people to do shady things on my behalf—and neither is Julie."

"Congratulations to you both," Benedict said dryly. "Only consider my point of view. I don't actually consider my residence a suitable habitat for newts. Since you and I do not agree on this, my lord, I must respectfully ask you to leave."

"But he only did the newts because of the rat," Juliet wailed. "You can't punish him for something *I* did! Besides, he has to stay. He has to remain with Cary until the race."

"He can stay at the village inn," said Benedict inexorably.

"They will say he left because of *me*," Juliet objected. "You may as well turn Wayborn Hall into a leper colony."

Lady Elkins added her lament. "I will never be invited to another card party as long as I live!"

Swale drew himself up to his full height. "If I give you my word as a gentleman, Sir Benedict—no more newts or rats—and if I remove all the offensive little creatures from the house, will you allow me to stay?"

Benedict looked in exasperation at his female relations and silently threw up his hands.

"I'll help you with the newts, my lord," said Juliet, following Swale from the room. "It is only fair, Benedict. He disposed of my rat."

"My dear aunt," said Benedict. "May I escort you to your apartment?"

In Cary's room, Juliet poured a little water into a basin with steep sides, and she and Swale began collecting the various members of the *Triturus* family that had taken up residence in the vicinity of the bed.

"It's not going well, is it?" Juliet said worriedly.

"Temporary setback," he assured her.

Grimacing, she held up a wriggling aquatic salamander by its hind leg and threw it in the basin. "But what if it doesn't work?" she persisted. "What if my famous plan fails to free us of our present entanglement? Did you mean what you said about eloping with me?"

"Of course," he said instantly. "I've a hunting box in Scotland, so establishing residency is no difficulty."

"We wouldn't be able to come back to England until

I'm twenty-one," she warned. "Benedict is perfectly capable of having the marriage annulled."

"Has the man ever smiled?"

"I don't really think Cary would shoot you, but . . ."

"Then you don't know him as well as I do," said Swale. "Don't worry about that though. I'll let him go first. With his shaky hand, he'll miss me, and I shall fire into the air."

"You're rather a big target, my love," said Juliet. "Would you take me to Canada? Your cousin still has a house on the St. Lawrence River, doesn't he?"

Swale nodded. "Whatever you want, Julie," he said cheerfully. "We'll paddle around in a canoe for a while until the dust settles, and then we'll come back to England."

Juliet rubbed her temples. "It would be better for your father's sake if we were closer. Could Ireland possibly be as bad as they say?" She sighed. "I'm so tired I can't think."

"Go on to your aunt then. I'll manage these little buggers."

"No, don't," she murmured distractedly when he reached for her. "I'm all newty."

"Don't care."

"In my day," Lady Elkins greeted her niece as the latter finally came to bed, "one caught a good husband by *not* putting rats under his pillow. How times have changed!"

"I know," said Juliet, changing into her nightgown under the cover of darkness. "I can't think why he puts up with me, actually. Since the moment we met, I have done him nothing but wrong. I've publicly accused him of underhanded perfidy. I threw yarn at him.

Then I made him go after my worthless French trollop of a maid. When I hurt my leg, he came to the Vicarage every day to inquire after my health, and I wouldn't even see him. Then he comes here."

She slid into the bed beside her aunt.

"I put him in Hastings. Pickering scalped him. I fed him cheese for dinner. I put a rat under his pillow. When I found out he was engaged to Serena, I told him to hire men with sandwich boards to announce the match to the whole world by strutting around Hyde Park! And tonight, I nearly got him thrown out of the house. Tomorrow will be even worse. Tomorrow the announcement appears in the paper, and we will see how Serena likes it."

"Well, for heaven's sake, keep it up," said her aunt, who was nearly asleep. "He seems to like it."

"In fact," Juliet whispered, slipping out of bed, "I'd better go apologize in advance for tomorrow."

"Yes, do," murmured Lady Elkins, rolling over. "He seems to like that too."

Chapter 19

While not without considerable advantages, being a rake certainly was a stressful business, Swale decided. The part where lovely maidens slipped into one's bed smelling like the Garden of Eden was all well and good, but in the cold light of day, one felt rather guilty.

Marriage, one hoped, would be different. For one thing, the lovely maiden would not disappear in the morning like a wraith, and for another, one would not have to face the lovely maiden's brothers in the breakfast room.

Swale cautiously looked into the room before entering, rejoicing to observe no brothers grazing among the chafing dishes on the sideboard. The room was full of food and devoid of humanity, exactly what he wished for. Thinking himself safe, he picked up a plate, murmuring happily to himself, "Delenda est Cathago."

Why the immortal words of Cato the Elder should have such a remarkable effect on his Juliet he did not know, but for him, they were now forever associated with the most exquisite of all carnal delights. "Delenda est

Cathago," he told the muffins on the sideboard. They seemed to quiver at his approach, reminding him of Juliet.

Too late, he made the discovery that Cary Wayborn was seated on the floor in the corner of the room, his head on his knees. The sideboard had obscured him before, but now, he overflowed the eye.

Awkward, to say the least. It gave one pause.

Swale instantly retreated, the floor creaked, and Cary looked up. The Wayborn gray eyes were not flaying. Rather, they were bloodshot. His skin was pasty, and he evidently had slept in his clothes, ample proof of a royal hangover.

"H-hullo," said Swale, trying to be civil.

Cary winced in pain.

Swale lowered his voice to a whisper. "Listen, Cary, about those newts—"

"Hang the newts," said Cary in a surprisingly strong voice. "Bugger the newts!"

"Actually I returned them to the lake," said Swale, a little surprised that Cary held such strong views on semiaquatic salamanders. "Not their fault, after all. Mere pawns."

"Prawns?" Cary squinted up at him dully. "I thought they were newts."

"They *were* newts," Swale clarified. "But they were also *pawns* in a sort of chess match I was playing. If you see what I mean."

"No, I don't."

"No?"

"No."

"I see your point. What I mean to say, old man, is that *I* put the newts in your room. Heartily sorry and all that, but it was a case of mistaken identity. I ought to have put them in Julie's bed."

"Damn the newts," said Cary, expanding on his central theme. "Bugger the newts."

"Full circle," Swale remarked as the other man climbed laboriously to his feet. There was a piece of paper crowded with peacock blue ink in his hand, and as he stood up, an envelope with a broken seal fell to the floor.

Cary swayed dangerously and clutched at the edge of the sideboard, causing the mountain of muffins to wobble. Swale was able to catch a few with his plate, but some were lost forever.

Cary appeared to be fighting nausea. Sweat rolled down his face, though it was a cool morning. His lips were almost white. "Sir, will you do me the honor of reading this letter? I have just now read it, though I think it came for me yesterday. It contains news that may be of interest to you."

"Thank you," Swale replied, "but I don't, as a rule, read letters addressed to other people, particularly when they are written in peacock blue ink."

Cary blinked at him. "I'll read it to you."

"I—I just wanted a muffin," said Swale, desperately wishing he could get away.

Cary stared at the letter in his hand for a long moment, then solemnly turned it around. "Upside down," he explained in a hoarse whisper. "It is from Mr. Eustace Calverstock."

"Oh?" said Swale. "My father has already paid him for his nose. He can have nothing more to say that will be of interest to me."

Cary clutched at the other man's arm, jeopardizing the muffins on his lordship's plate. "It was him, Swale. He did this to me. He broke my arm. It wasn't you after all."

Swale pulled out a chair and put Juliet's brother in it before seating himself. "Do you know, I never thought it *was* me, old man. I always thought it was someone else. It just doesn't seem like my style, somehow. My *modus operandi*, if you will."

"I never suspected," Cary said bitterly, resting his head on the cool tablecloth. "I knew his debts were pressing, but . . . *this* . . . this betrayal. I called him my friend, the lying Judas."

Swale took a bite of muffin. Still warm and oozing with butter, just the way he liked it. "A moneymaking scheme then," he grunted. "But how? Calverstock bet on you to win."

Cary moistened his lips laboriously. "Redfylde. Redfylde would not pay Stacy's debts out of his own purse, but he agreed to place a dishonest bet for ten thousand pounds. Stacy was to be given half that amount, more than enough to cover the monkey he bet Mr. Devize."

"So it was Redfylde after all."

"Stacy convinced him that I had agreed to let you win the race." Cary threw back his head and howled, making Swale pause in the act of taking another bite of his muffin.

Awkward.

"As though I should ever do such a shameful thing!" cried Cary. "That is what I can never forgive, his telling Redfylde *that*. He has written to Redfylde as well, exonerating me—if that matters!"

Swale poured out a cup of coffee. "And my name? How did my name enter into it?"

Cary listlessly plucked at the tablecloth. "He claims *that* was completely the original idea of his partners in the crime. But then, he also claims that I was only ever to be kidnapped, then released after the race unharmed. His partners—to whom he was indebted for untold sums of money—thought kidnapping too risky and too bothersome. They opted merely to disable me. It is to be supposed that they profited from modest little wagers of their own amongst their own kind," he added bitterly.

"Pretty sordid," Swale observed. "I took an instant dislike to Calverstock."

"My friend! He might have sent it express," said Cary, tossing the letter aside. "But that might have jeopardized his escape. This was written before his departure for France, where your father's money has made it possible for him to go. He speaks of going to America."

"He will never see England again," said Swale. "That is punishment enough."

"The thing is," Cary said reluctantly, "I owe you an apology, old man."

"I consider the matter closed," said Swale. "Just don't shoot me when I marry Julie. That is all I ask."

Cary shook his head. "Sorry, old man, but I was telling the truth when I said she's going to marry Horatio. I told him I'd sell him Tanglewood Manor if he married her. Julie's always been keen on the place. He's made her an offer. She's probably giving him her answer now."

"He's here?"

"Yes, I saw him. It was he who brought my attention to this letter. He saw the London mark and thought it must contain the news of his elevation to the knighthood."

"He's with Julie now?"

"I sent him out to her," Cary replied. "Benedict has forbidden her to ride today. She was walking in the vicinity of the lake, if you wish to try and stop it—"

Swale shuddered. "No, no. He's bound to cry when she tells him she's already engaged to me. Coffee, old man? I don't mean to criticize, but you look as though you might need it."

"Will you shake my hand, sir?" asked Cary. "And I do believe that you must forfeit the race."

"On no account will I forfeit," said Swale. "You shall forfeit."

"But if I forfeit, Redfylde will be enriched by ten thousand pounds!" Cary objected.

"Can't be helped," Swale responded. "My dear fellow, if you had heard the disgusting comments that Dulwich made about your sister after the race, you would know at once why *you* must forfeit the race. I'll be damned before I let Dulwich walk away with ten thousand pounds!"

"Dulwich insulted Julie, did he?"

"So we are agreed? When the time comes, you shall forfeit."

They were shaking hands when Benedict came into the room, a newspaper folded under his arm.

"I see you have taken all our muffins . . . again, my lord."

A pair of flaying gray eyes regarded Swale from the doorway. The baronet set the paper down next to his plate at his customary place at the table. He picked up his plate and, wandering over to the sideboard, began rooting around in the various chafing dishes.

Swale waited in triumph, but Cary seemed lost in his thoughts. It was necessary to nudge him in the ribs.

"Benedict, I've had the most shocking letter from London. Stacy Calverstock has confessed."

Benedict sat down with his breakfast and listened without comment as Cary related the substance of Stacy's letter. "Hm-m. I confess I never suspected him for a moment. I'd make a poor magistrate."

Swale tapped the table. "The point is, Sir Benedict, there is now no impediment to my marrying your sister."

"There is one insurmountable obstacle, my lord,"

Benedict replied, taking a bite of ham. "My sister does not wish to marry you. It may seem a little thing to you, but I attach some importance to it."

"Don't be absurd. Of course, she wants to marry me."

"No, she doesn't."

"Julie loves me. Ask her."

"She put a rat under your pillow, my lord. Was that affection?"

"She thought it was Calverstock's pillow."

"And yet . . . she still put you in Hastings, did she not? Knowing there was a rat under the pillow? *After* I told her to put you in Runnymede?"

Swale frowned. "The important thing is that I am in Runnymede *now*, Sir Benedict."

Benedict appeared smug. "I spoke to my sister last night, my lord. I asked her if she were engaged to you. She told me in no uncertain terms that she had no intention of marrying you, she does not love you, and neither your riches nor your title are enough to tempt her, and she has promised me she intends to refuse your offer of marriage . . . today, as a matter of fact."

Swale flung down his napkin and stood up, his face spattered liberally with nettlerash. "She said all that, did she?"

"She also said you had a face that belongs in a grotto."

"I already heard that one," Swale said with chilly dignity. "May I inquire if that is today's newspaper, Sir Benedict?"

"As a matter of fact," Benedict affirmed. "Captain Cary brought along several copies. Apparently, the news that the Regent tapped him on the shoulder is contained within. Perhaps that explains why it seems unusually thick today."

"You might want to take a look in the society section," Swale said, his face turning red. "When you are ready to apologize to me, I shall be down by the lake, wringing your sister's neck!"

After fifteen minutes in her cousin's company without ever once being given the opportunity to speak, Juliet might have welcomed even such an unpleasant interruption as that proposed by Swale before he quit the house.

". . . and His Royal Highness the Prince Regent turned to the Admiral and paid me the very great compliment of saying I was very gentlemanlike and he wished he could offer me a baronetcy! Imagine that, my dear Juliet. But I was presented with the Order of the Garter, which I thought pretty well, though I did think the Order of the Bath would have looked better against my coat. What do you think?"

"I think—" Juliet began, sitting up straight on the little rustic bench near the water's edge where she had been sitting while glumly skipping pebbles across the water.

"I think so too," said Horatio, accepting her answer without actually pausing to hear it. "But of course, I did not say so at the time. His Royal Highness keeps his rooms unnaturally hot," he went on. "You would have been most uncomfortable, though he did ask after you."

Juliet was startled. "Did he?"

Horatio put his booted foot on the bench perilously close to Juliet's battered straw hat, which she had placed on the bench beside her to prevent him from sitting down. "Remember his Highness's little joke that he would marry you when his divorce from the Princess was finalized by Parliament? I was able to tell His Highness that you were to be happily married to me, and he was gracious enough to wish me joy."

"You had no right to do that!" Juliet cried angrily.

"There is not the least reason to be coy," Horatio assured her. "I had it in my power to amuse my sovereign lord. He was delighted beyond anything to know that I was going to marry the famous Miss Wayborn that everyone calls Miss Whip. To be sure, it was only after I told him our little news that he mentioned the baronetcy. He expressed an earnest and very flattering desire to be acquainted with you. I invited him to our wedding."

"Ugh!"

Never having heard that word before, Horatio chose to ignore it. "He also gave me this little snuff box to give to you."

He leaned over her to present a small green and gold enameled box, and Juliet defensively drew her shawl tightly around her shoulders. "See? It has a pretty little racehorse painted on the lid."

Her disgust overflowing, Juliet refused even to look at it. What sort of man accepted gifts from the Prince Regent on behalf of his betrothed, even when the betrothal was wholly presumptive and not at all real? Was she supposed to be flattered by the Regent's insulting interest in her? Pretty little racehorse indeed! She'd had quite enough of the race-themed innuendo from Budgie and his nasty friend Lord Dulwich.

"I don't take snuff," she said coldly. "I think snuff is disgusting. And you had no right to invite him to my wedding. Indeed, I don't recall inviting *you* to my wedding."

Chuckling, Horatio tossed the enameled box into the air and caught it. "I hardly think I need to be invited to my own wedding, Juliet! I had the opportunity to offer the civility to my sovereign, and I did so very creditably, and, I might add, in a manner highly flattering to yourself."

"You are quite mistaken if you think you do not need to be invited to your own wedding, sir!" Juliet snapped. "If the *bride* don't ask you to put in an appearance, then it ain't very likely that the wedding will proceed, is it? Not *your* wedding anyway."

"That is just the sort of clever repartee that appeals to His Highness!" said Horatio, opening and closing the lid of his treasure. "That baronetcy is as good as ours."

"No," said Juliet, rising from the bench and taking up her hat. "That snuff box is as good as yours." With her head high, she began walking back toward the house, leaving the deep shade of the spreading oak.

"That is very handsome of you, my dear," Horatio said, falling into step with her. "I confess I was loath to let it leave my possession. I was with His Highness as he was passing the little table where it was among many other fine ornaments when he suddenly picked it up and gave it to me, with an expression of the most earnest desire that I present it to my future wife. My hand, Juliet—my hand actually trembled as he gave it to me. I was actually touched—*physically touched*—by His Royal Highness. This little box passed from his hand to my hand with no intermediary."

Juliet tossed him a contemptuous glance, which he misunderstood.

"You are amazed. So was I! People remarked at the time the splendid condescension His Royal Highness showed me on that occasion, and more than one fellow cast me a jealous glance, I can tell you. I will keep this little snuff box, Cousin, as much as a reminder of your regard as of His Highness's, for he really meant you to have it."

"No," said Juliet, summoning a reserve of patience, "he meant it for your future wife. *Decidedly* not me." She stopped and gently closed his fingers over the box. "You must save the box, Horatio; treasure it up, along with the Regent's best wishes, until you have met her."

He frowned, and she thought with a glimmer of hope that her refusal had begun to impress itself on his stubborn arrogance, but she was mistaken. "I say, Juliet, did you hear something?"

"I was speaking just now," she said tartly. "Perhaps you heard me?"

"No, that's not it. There it is again! Hark!"

"Crickets," said Juliet crossly. Then she heard it— the faint, distant scream of a woman.

"Someone is in trouble!" Horatio pointed to the other side of the lake. Juliet squinted, but the sun dazzled on the water and made it impossible for her to make out anything on that side of the lake. "A woman! I think she is drowning." Hastily, he pulled out his handkerchief and wrapped the little green snuffbox in it before placing it in her hand. Then he removed his coat and dove into the lake.

Juliet ran along the bank, past the rustic bench and the overspreading oak tree, through a little woodland plantation, and over a manmade hill covered in primroses. From there, she could see Horatio swimming across the lake in firm, even strokes, but the trees overhanging the lake obscured her view of his destination. She ran down the hill, almost tumbling head over ears, and arrived out of breath in time to see two figures, one male and one female, wringing wet and intertwined, resting on the bank. The man was actually crouched over the woman, who was lying flat on her back, her pale muslin dress clinging provocatively to her body. Various articles of clothing were strewn in the vicinity, including, she noted automatically, the lady's hat and slippers and the gentleman's coat.

"Thank you, my lord," gasped Serena Calverstock. "I thank you with all my heart! I am in your debt!

Indeed, I do not know how to thank you." In tears, she clung to her rescuer's neck.

"My dear girl," said Swale, picking up his coat from the grass. "Wrap up in this. You will catch cold. Shall I carry you up to the house?"

His voice was full of tender concern. He had not yet observed Juliet standing just a few feet away in the shade of a tree, and he remained oblivious, likewise, of Horatio's approach.

"Captain Cary!" Serena saw Horatio first as he emerged from the shallow water, and she sprang to her feet, pulling Swale's coat around her.

Horatio stared at her, water dripping from his hair into his eyes. "Madam," he said stiffly, offering a curt bow. "May I congratulate you on your conquest? You have made fully as handsome a match as your own sister. You need not now envy her so much."

"You!" said Swale, turning on him. "Where is Julie?"

"My future wife is none of your concern," Horatio replied coldly, coming out of the water and striding past Serena, who was shivering violently. "It seems to me you have your hands full with her ladyship! I wish you joy of her, my lord. You are exceedingly well-matched."

"How can you say such a thing?" cried Serena.

"The man's a silly ass," said Swale. "He thinks he's engaged to Miss Wayborn."

"I *am* engaged to Miss Wayborn," said Horatio. "Who's the silly ass now?"

"Still you," snorted Swale.

"Very sensibly, Miss Wayborn refused your lordship in Hertfordshire," said Horatio. "But I see you have allowed Serena to *console* you. You must know you have compromised her ladyship beyond anything. But then, that seems to be your chosen method of getting a wife."

"Should I have allowed her to drown?" Swale asked.

"I saw you lying on top of her with all your parts lined up with her parts, my lord. Lord Redfylde, I promise you, will not be as forgiving as Sir Benedict Wayborn. You will marry Lady Serena whether you wish to or not!"

Juliet sat down under the tree and took a deep breath. She hadn't the least idea what to do. It was all so horribly tangled. The announcement of Swale's engagement to Serena had already been printed in the *Post*, and now this! It would be exceedingly difficult for Ginger to get out of marrying Serena now. And after observing him with the lady, she could not be certain he wished to get out of it!

It would be so much simpler for him to marry Serena, thus foregoing the doubtful joys of being sued for breach of promise and being forced to elope and live in Canada or Ireland like the meanest criminal. He could not possibly love her that much.

"I cannot possibly marry Serena," said Swale. "I am engaged to Julie. Why in hell's name would I want to marry a woman who can't even walk upright? Do you think I wish to spend the rest of my life picking up things that have fallen off my wife? Shoes and hats and whatnot? Or fishing her out of lakes into which she has fallen? No, thank you."

Serena sat down hard on the ground and began to cry.

"You cannot be engaged to Miss Wayborn, my lord," said Horatio. "I have just told you that *I* am engaged to her."

"No!" cried Serena, startling everyone. "You cannot marry her! I forbid it!"

Horatio ignored her, and Serena dissolved again into tears. "There you are, Juliet!" he called to his cousin anxiously. "Do you have the snuff box? Is it quite safe?" He ran up to her and snatched it from her hand. "Here is my proof," he told Swale, unwrapping his treasure. "A wedding gift from His Royal Highness the Prince Regent!"

Swale regarded Juliet with his brows drawn together. "Is this true, Juliet?"

"You can't marry him, Miss Wayborn!" cried Serena at the same moment, lifting her tear-stained face. "He is engaged to me!"

"Do you think I don't know that?" Juliet shouted, dearly wanting to scratch out the other woman's eyes. She could not help but observe that Serena's vulnerability had only enhanced her beauty. With her dark hair clinging to her cheeks, her enormous violet eyes filled with tears, and her muslin dress plastered to her pretty figure, she looked like an artist's conception of a water nymph.

"Please, I beg of you, don't take him from me," wept Serena on her knees with her hands clasped. "Miss Wayborn, my fate—my whole life—is in your hands!"

"Oh, stop crying, you silly peagoose!" Juliet snapped. "You've won. The whole world knows he is engaged to you! There is nothing I can do now. Congratulations on your victory!"

"I am no longer engaged to this woman," Horatio said coldly. "My dear Juliet, there is not a shred of truth in what she is saying. Pray, don't allow her to distress you with this unseemly display of emotions."

Juliet's mouth fell open. She, of course, had supposed Serena to be speaking of her engagement to Lord Swale. "What do you mean you are *no longer* engaged to her?" she demanded of Horatio. "When *were* you engaged to her? I never saw an item in the newspaper. Benedict certainly would have called it to my attention!"

"Pity me, Miss Wayborn," said Serena. "I have been

secretly engaged to your cousin these seven years while he was away fighting."

"Good God," said Swale, recoiling in disgust. "Secret engagements as far as the eye can see! Does no one remember what happened to Chuck and Macbeth? Heads on poles, by God!"

"It was a foolish promise," said Horatio, quickly seizing Juliet's hands. "She released me from it six months ago. For that deliverance, I am sincerely grateful."

"You so clearly wanted to be released!" wailed Serena. "Seven years I waited for you, not knowing if you would ever come back to me. And when you did, all you could think of was that wretched cow byre in Hertfordshire! You're too cruel, Horatio!"

"Sir Horatio," he corrected her.

"Good God," Swale muttered again, turning a little away from this sordid scene.

"Tanglewood ought to have been left to me," said Horatio. "Cary has run it into the ground. Naturally, I felt it was my duty to rescue the old place."

"He wanted to buy it, Miss Wayborn," said Serena, wiping her eyes. "I told him I could never live among the hayseeds of Hertfordshire. I wanted an establishment in London, a home of my own, not some moldy old Elizabethan pile! We quarreled. Your brother told him he would only sell Tanglewood to Horatio if he married you. I told Horatio to go ahead and do it—marry you—but I never thought he would!" She covered her face with her hands and sank to the ground, weeping.

Swale surreptitiously passed her a handkerchief.

"Is this true, Horatio?" Juliet demanded. "Were you prepared to marry me simply to get your paws on Tanglewood?"

"It ought to have been left to me," he said stubbornly. "My grandmother promised it to me."

"She also promised it to me on more than one occasion," said Juliet, "but when she died and we opened her will, we discovered she had left it to my brother. It was hers to dispose of as she pleased."

"I don't dispute that," he said. "But Cary had let it go to rack and ruin. My parents live in that neighborhood. It reflected badly on all of us. I was willing to marry you and purchase the property for the handy sum of ten thousand pounds."

"Which just happens to be the amount of my dowry!"

"Well, something had to be done." He glared at Serena. "Are you pleased with yourself, madam? You cannot be happy, so you attempt to make everyone else miserable! 'Hell hath no fury like a woman scorned!'"

Serena choked. "I do not deny my present misery. I am miserable indeed. But hear me out, Miss Wayborn—"

"Miss Wayborn cannot possibly be interested in the demented ravings of a lunatic!"

"For this, I waited seven years. Seven years! This is how you repay my devotion!"

"May I remind you, madam, you released me. Indeed, you were kind enough to release me from that obligation into which I foolishly entered seven years ago and which has become so decidedly repugnant to us both. For that, I thank you."

"I was angry, Miss Wayborn," said Serena, struggling to keep her voice steady. "I was jealous of you. I told Horatio I would marry Mr. Wayborn myself and become mistress of Tanglewood. And you see the result."

"The result is this display of madness," scoffed Horatio, his disgust for his former love evident in every syllable. "You did your best to seduce Mr. Wayborn, didn't you? Only Miss Wayborn saw through you and put a stop to your sordid plan."

"Hateful man!" cried Serena. *"He* was responsible for the attack on your brother, Miss Wayborn!"

Juliet stared at her, shocked to the very core of her being.

"You accuse me?" Horatio's lip curled.

"He was jealous," Serena continued tearfully. "He wanted Mr. Wayborn out of the way."

"Is this true, Horatio?" Juliet asked, pale-faced.

"You cannot possibly believe this nonsense," Horatio cried, horrified. "The woman is clearly out of her senses. You know I am incapable of acting with dishonor."

"I don't call a seven-year secret engagement precisely honorable," said Juliet.

Horatio attempted to explain. "Lord Redfylde was my patron. He would scarcely have rejoiced in his sister-in-law's engagement to a penniless lieutenant, which I was then. I was forced into secrecy."

Juliet looked at him intently. "Do you swear you had nothing to do with the attack on my brother? Swear to me now, Horatio, or I shall never speak to you again."

"Certainly I swear," said Horatio. "It is all the absurd fantasy of a demented young woman. I? Employ criminals to harm my own cousin? For the sake of a woman whom I no longer admire?"

"Did you ever love me?" Serena wanted to know. "Horry?"

"Horry!" exclaimed Swale and Juliet at once.

Horatio looked at Serena's tear-stained face contemptuously. "It is difficult to believe I ever did love you, madam," he said coolly. "You are making a disgusting display of yourself, you know. I thought you had more pride, more conduct."

"How could you be so cruel!" Juliet rebuked him.

He blinked at her in astonishment. "My dear cousin, you cannot possibly believe her ridiculous assertions!

Upon my honor, I am blameless! Your brother's attack had nothing to do with me."

"I meant how could you be so cruel to *Serena*," Juliet replied ferociously, walking over to the lady and wrapping her own shawl around Serena's shaking shoulders. "How could you treat her so?"

Horatio gaped at her. "It was she who was cruel to me! She broke the engagement in a fit of pique because I said I did not want to live in London! She broke my heart. You—you have mended it, dear Juliet. Do not regard her in the least. I don't."

"That is what I mean, *Horry*," said Juliet coldly. "You once loved her, but now you do not regard her in the least! As for your word of honor . . . I do not know that I believe you. Perhaps you *did* want my brother out of the way. I know you were angry that he inherited Tanglewood, and you did not!"

Horatio turned white.

Swale's conscience prompted him to speak in Horatio's defense. "As to that, Julie," he said with a cough of embarrassment, "I have information clearing your cousin completely of the deed. Cary has received a letter from Stacy Calverstock. He confesses to everything, and he has fled England forever."

"Stacy!" Juliet shook her head in disbelief.

"You might have spoken on my behalf sooner, my lord," sniffed Horatio.

"You're not my favorite person at the moment," Swale told him bluntly.

"My cousin would never do such a thing," cried Serena. "Mr. Wayborn is his particular friend."

"Then . . . Redfylde was innocent all along?" Juliet asked Swale.

Swale snorted. "Hardly! His lordship entered into a scheme with Calverstock. He placed his bet against

Cary in the full knowledge that Cary would be forfeiting the race."

"Good God! I must thank you again, madam, for releasing me," Horatio told Serena, suppressing a shudder. "I would not care to have my name associated with that of Calverstock. I don't even care to have my name associated with Lord Redfylde after what I have just heard!"

"That is ungrateful, Horatio," Serena gasped. "If it were not for my brother-in-law's patronage, you would still be a lieutenant and very far from a command of your own."

Juliet was aghast. "Abominable crime! Cary must be devastated."

"When he learns we are to be married, my dear Juliet," Horatio said quickly, "he will be consoled. The fate of Tanglewood must weigh heavily on his mind. We can reassure him on that score, at least." He took her arm, attempting to detach her from Serena. "Let us return to the house now. Lord Swale will look after Lady Serena."

Swale scowled. "I told you, Cary . . . I'm engaged to Julie. I will escort the ladies to the house, and you will quit the neighborhood!"

"I asked Miss Wayborn to marry me three days ago," Horatio argued. "I believe that gives *me* the prior claim. And I am properly addressed as Sir Horatio!"

"Juliet, is this true?" Swale's face was black with fury.

"No, I believe he is properly addressed as Cad!" she retorted.

"I say!" Horatio protested, but Swale drowned him out.

"Have you been engaged to this pompous ass for three days? *Three days*, Juliet? I need hardly remind you of certain events that have taken place in the last *two* days!"

"How dare you!" said Juliet, turning bright pink.

"Juliet, I am growing angry," he told her. "Either you tell this insolent puppy that you are engaged to me, or I shall let slip the dogs of war!"

Horatio drew himself up to his full height. "If you persist in insulting my betrothed with your bizarre and unwelcome claims, honor will force me to issue a challenge!"

"Do you think I would gratify your pretensions to rank and gentility by condescending to shoot you?" Swale replied contemptuously. "You are the sort of thing I scrape off my boot, sir. I am the Marquess of Swale, you a mere cypher."

"I am a knight of the Order of the Garter," said Horatio furiously. "I hold the rank of Captain in His Majesty's Navy."

"Piffle!"

"I consider you to have been used very ill by both these disreputable characters," Juliet told Serena, turning away. "You had better come to the house with me and get into some dry clothes, my dear."

"Disreputable?" Horatio was bewildered. "What have I done? Juliet? Juliet!" he called after her. "What about the Prince Regent? What about the snuff box? What about the pretty little racehorse?"

"Give me that!" Swale snatched the little green box and threw it as hard as he could.

It arced across the sky, sparkling in the sunlight, green and gold, and then it was gone, vanishing beneath the surface of the lake like the mighty sword Excalibur.

Horatio screamed as though Excalibur had been driven through his body and, in the next moment, he dove into the lake after the Regent's gift.

"Pompous ass," Swale muttered, hurrying over to

Serena. In one easy movement, he swept her off her feet into his arms. "You're better off without him, you know. Coming, Julie?"

Julie threw up her hands. "I'll get her ladyship's shoes and hat!"

As she scooped them up, she saw Horatio break the surface of the water and then dive back down, almost as if he were trying to rescue a drowning child.

"If you want him, Julie," Swale jeered, swinging around with Serena in his arms, "go and fish him out!"

Chapter 20

"I really am quite able to walk, my lord," Serena murmured in embarrassment as Swale carried her up the path.

"Nonsense," he replied. "You are light as a feather. Not like some people—eh, Julie?"

Juliet trudged behind them, rolling her eyes.

"You saved my life, my lord," she heard Serena say.

"You were very fortunate I happened to be there," Swale replied. "I was looking for Julie, and I thought you were her. Not that you bear the least resemblance to Julie, but from a distance, any two females bear certain—er—charming similarities. Up close, of course, there is no mistaking you for Julie. I saw you take off your hat and your shoes, and I asked myself, What the devil is Julie up to now? Thought you might be gathering more newts." This last remark he tossed over his shoulder to Juliet. "I was going to advise against it. Then you went in," he went on to Serena. "It must have been deeper than you thought, old girl. You sank like a stone. Fortunately, I got to you in time."

"Yes, very fortunate, my lord," Serena whispered. "I

am so grateful to you. When I think that I might be dead right now . . . when my sister is in such a fragile state . . . Miss Wayborn!" Blindly, she stretched out her hands to Juliet. "Please do not alarm my sister with reports of my accident."

"Of course not," said Juliet.

"They will be so worried about me at Silvercombe. You see, I left without telling anyone where I was going. I did not mean to go so far . . ."

"I shall send a message at once," said Juliet, increasing her pace. "And as soon as you are dry, Benedict will send you home in his carriage. Your sister need not be alarmed at all."

"Thank you, Miss Wayborn. My lord, I think you must put me down now. I don't wish Sir Benedict's servants to see me like this. I assure you I can walk."

Juliet put the lady's slippers on her feet, and Swale reluctantly set her down. He would have kept his arm around the lady's waist, but Juliet took this office upon herself, handing him Serena's hat instead. "You're very kind, Miss Wayborn," Serena murmured.

As they entered the garden near the terrace, servants came out of the house to help. Juliet was informed that Sir Benedict wanted her to appear before him in his study the instant she returned to the house. It was not an interview she anticipated with any pleasure.

Swale answered for her. "Please inform Sir Benedict that Lady Serena has met with a slight accident in his lake and that Miss Wayborn and I will attend him as soon as she is made comfortable." He cast a sidelong glance at Juliet. "Agincourt?"

She nodded, and he barked out the order to make Agincourt ready for Serena.

Juliet ran to her own room and brought her best

nightdress and dressing gown for Serena to wear while her clothes dried. Benedict found her in the hall.

"Not now, Benedict! Serena needs my attention."

"Yes, what has happened?" he demanded. "Is she injured? Shall I send for the doctor?"

"She walked here under her own power," Juliet replied. "She is in danger of catching cold—I will know better her condition when she is warm and dry. She fell into the lake and was nearly drowned."

"Good Lord," breathed Benedict, deeply distressed. "I must know the exact spot where she fell in! There should be no place near the bank where the water is deep enough to be a danger."

"Lord Swale saved her," said Juliet quickly. "You must not blame yourself, Benedict! I believe there has been no permanent harm. I must go to her now."

"Of course," said Benedict. "I would not detain you. But when she is comfortable, you will come to me in my study. I must speak to you on a very important matter."

Juliet nodded. "Will you send word to Silvercombe and, without alarming Lady Redfylde, let them know that Lady Serena is in our care?"

"Of course."

In Agincourt, Swale had taken the coal scuttle from the maidservant and was building the fire himself. "Out," Juliet told him. "Betsy can certainly manage, and it is of the utmost importance that Serena change out of her wet clothes as soon as possible."

"You are in very good hands," Swale told Serena before closing the door.

As Betsy started a good blaze in the hearth, Juliet helped Serena peel off her damp muslin and put on the nightdress and quilted robe she had brought from her room. Overriding the lady's protests, she made her climb into the big red and gold bed and pulled the heavy coverlet up to her chin. "Sir Benedict will never forgive himself if you catch cold, you know. He is already threatening to send to the doctor."

She dismissed the servant and found a towel to dry Serena's long, dark hair.

"The tea will be here soon," she said gently, "and a little brandy."

"You're very good. I'm sure I don't deserve it." Serena's violet eyes filled with tears. "Oh, Miss Wayborn, can you ever forgive me?"

Juliet stiffened. "I am sure I was quite as horrid to you as you have been to me," she said guiltily. "I never liked you. You know that."

"But you were right not to like me," said Serena. "I never cared for your brother at all. I only wanted to hurt Horatio. Is Mr. Wayborn's heart very much broken?"

"His heart . . ." Juliet scoffed. "Cary doesn't really have a heart, you know. His pride was hurt, but he's much more worried about his arm than his heart, I promise you."

Serena grimaced. "Yes, I've never really been able to give a man a lasting passion for me." Her face crumpled, and she began to sob.

Juliet could not help but feel sorry for her. It must be bitter indeed to be jilted not merely once but twice within six months! Seating herself on the bed, she began brushing out Serena's hair in an attempt to soothe her. "You did not really fall into the lake, did you?" she asked gently.

Serena turned her face away. "Please do not tell anyone, Miss Wayborn. I'm so ashamed. How selfish of me! I thought only of my own misery. My death almost certainly would have caused my poor sister to miscarry. And I never considered that Sir Benedict would feel responsible if I—if I died on his property. I only knew that I was wretched! In my despair, it seemed the only way to end my suffering."

Juliet listened silently.

"I knew that Horatio was returning today to hear your answer. I did not mean to come here, but somehow, I found myself at the lake . . ."

"How did you know that?" Juliet asked curiously. "I told no one he had proposed to me."

"He told me so himself when he came to Silvercombe to pay his respects."

"Insufferable conceit!" Juliet declared stoutly. "Why, he visited Silvercombe *before* he solicited my hand!"

"He gave me to understand you were very eager to accept him, Miss Wayborn, particularly after being scorned by everyone in the village. He thought you would accept him gratefully."

"He may have come to hear my answer," Juliet said dryly, "but I promise you, he did not listen to it! I never meant to accept him, and I would have told him so three days ago, but he begged me—insisted—that I take the time to consider the matter very carefully."

Serena wiped her eyes. "And are you seriously contemplating a marriage with Lord Swale?"

Juliet stiffened. "Yes, I am. We are very deeply in love, and if you do not love him—and I suspect you don't—I insist that you break your engagement to him at once!"

"Miss Wayborn, I am not engaged to Lord Swale," Serena replied with an expression of astonishment.

"Of course you are," said Juliet. "He came to Surrey for the express purpose of making himself agreeable to you."

"Then he has failed rather spectacularly!" said

Serena with an abrupt laugh. "I can think of no one I have ever met in my life who is *less* agreeable, except, of course, Horatio."

"Don't you like him at all?" cried Juliet, her own partiality for Swale making Serena's indifference difficult to accept.

"Lord Swale smells of cheese," said Serena. "And he's so clumsy—! Yesterday, when we were walking to the village, he *kicked* me some eleven times!" She became increasingly animated as she recalled the experience. "Kicked my shoe from my foot and then had the gall to pretend *I* was the clumsy one! And he *would* insist that I was some sort of weakling—that I could scarcely walk without his assistance. Assistance, he called it! Shoving me along the path with his beastly hand at the small of my back. I grew sick to death hearing myself compared so unfavorably to yourself. Miss Wayborn could walk to Scotland without so much as a blister on her toe! Miss Wayborn is so brown and healthy! Forgive me, but how I hated Miss Wayborn!"

"Please call me Juliet," said the delighted young lady.

"As I knew—as I *thought*—you were shortly to become engaged to Horatio, I heartily wished you to the devil! I was so eager to get away from Lord Swale that I pretended to faint." She sighed. "Unfortunately, his lordship's chivalry was aroused, and he saw it as his duty to see me safely home. On the way, he told me everything Miss Wayborn did to keep herself so healthy and that I would soon be dead if I did not follow her excellent example of a hearty diet and daily exercise!"

"But if you were never engaged to him . . ." Juliet bit her lip in confusion. "Why would he tell me he was engaged to you if it isn't true? Why would he make such a point of asking my permission to place the notice in the newspapers?"

Serena shook her head. "Oh, Miss Wayborn!" she cried softly. "I am very sorry for you because I can see that you really care for the brute. But I can tell you something about Lord Swale that will cure you of that."

"You are mistaken," Juliet said coldly. "I will be sick forever!"

"I wish for your sake I were mistaken," Serena replied sadly. "I'm afraid it is the talk of London. When you beat him in the race, his lordship vowed revenge."

"That is all in the past," Juliet scoffed. "That was before he met me."

"Indeed! He vowed to follow you into Hertfordshire and make you love him, ruin you if he could, and then abandon you. I am sorry to pain you, Miss Wayborn, but I heard it from Mr. Alexander Devize with my own ears. They are taking bets in London as to whether or not he will succeed in seducing you."

"I don't believe you," Juliet whispered, fighting off a horrible feeling of dizziness. "He loves me! I know it. He would never abandon me. You heard him say he was engaged to me! So did Horatio!"

"But has he ever actually *asked* you to marry him?"

Juliet felt her blood run cold. The hairbrush fell into her lap. "No," she admitted in a hollow voice that exactly matched the hollow feeling in her chest.

"Has he ever declared his love for you?"

She shook her head. "He has never said it. Not even in Latin," she added bitterly.

"If he has told you that he is engaged to me, it could only have been to make you jealous, Miss Wayborn. There is no truth to it. He never sought my hand, and

I certainly would never have bestowed it upon him. I don't know if I will ever recover completely from my attachment to Horatio."

"Then it was all a lie," whispered Juliet, tears spilling from her eyes. "He told me he was your betrothed to make me jealous. And it worked. I was horribly, insanely jealous. Oh God, what a fool I have been! I daresay he kicked off your shoe so that I would have the pleasure of watching him restore it to your pretty foot! The fiend!"

She struggled to breathe. "Why do we let them do this to us?" she groaned.

"They use us however they please," said Serena bitterly. "They use us against one another. They use us for their pleasure. They use us as broodmares like my poor sister! From this day on, I am no more a romantic, Miss Wayborn. The facts are too much against it. You are fortunate to discover his perfidy now. It took me seven years to realize the truth about Horatio."

Juliet covered her face with her hands. "It does me no good. It is too late for me now. He's done it! He's done everything he set out to do. He has seduced me. He has broken my heart. He's ruined me. And if I sue for breach of promise, he will make my disgrace public. How could I be so stupid? He isn't even handsome!"

Serena shook her head. "I'm very sorry for you, Miss Wayborn. One thing I have learned though—they are not worth drowning ourselves over!"

She smiled through her tears, but Juliet could not smile back. "They may be worth being hanged for murder for!" she answered, jumping to her feet. "Please excuse me!"

She went directly to her brother's study.

Benedict was seated behind his desk. Swale was

sitting in the armchair on the other side of it, cracking his knuckles. Both gentlemen rose as Juliet entered the room, and Benedict started forward. "How is Lady Serena?" he asked his sister. "Is she quite well? Does she require anything? Should I summon the doctor?"

Juliet ignored the barrage of questions; strode past him to Swale, who was *grinning* at her; and cracked him across the face as hard as she could with the back of her hand.

"Julie!" he spluttered. "What—"

Mercilessly, she struck him again, then doubled over in pain, nursing her hand.

Benedict was too shocked to speak.

"You . . . *serpent!*" she hissed at Swale, her face livid in some parts and white in others. "I have just had the most interesting conversation with Lady Serena, my lord." Wincing as excruciating pain traveled through her hand, she paused to rub it. Beyond an expression of surprise, Swale seemed undisturbed by the two blows he had received.

"What did the silly cow tell you that made you want to hit me?" he demanded. "Whatever it is, it's a lie!"

"Is it?" she shrieked at him. "Is it a lie?"

"Calm yourself, Julie. You'll burst a blood vessel," Swale murmured, his face turning pale, except for a pink mark her hand had left on his cheek.

She shook off his hand. "Is it a lie that you vowed to seduce me, to make me fall in love with you and then abandon me? Is that a lie, sir? Because, you know, they are making book on it in London! Did you come here to ruin me? Has it all been a game?"

"Oh, that," he said roughly. "Damn it!"

"Oh, that! Is that all you can say to me?" she cried, shaking out her hand.

"Here." He clawed at his neckcloth until it came free, then offered it to her. "Wrap up your hand, you silly girl!"

She struck out at him wildly and missed.

"For heaven's sake," he said, sidestepping her easily. "I will not let you hit me again until you have learned how to do it without breaking your own hand!"

Juliet collapsed into a chair, weeping bitterly. "I should have let Benedict throw you out when he wanted to!"

"I daresay," he murmured. "I'd give you my handkerchief to cry on, but I seem to have already given it to some other weeping female."

Benedict stepped forward with his. "Calm yourself, my dear," he said gently as she blew her nose. "Now that I know absolutely, beyond a shadow of a doubt that you are not engaged to him—"

"Engaged to him!" cried Juliet, flinging up her head. "I had rather marry an organ grinder's monkey. Indeed, he is the last man on earth whom I would ever marry! I loathe him! Make him go away, Benedict! I never want to see him again."

"For God's sake, Julie," shouted Swale. "I didn't come *here* to seduce you. I went to Hertfordshire to seduce you!"

"Oh!"

"I think you had better go, my lord," said Benedict coldly. "You have upset my sister. You are no longer welcome in my house. I will contact the *Post* and have the announcement universally contradicted. Good morning, sir."

Juliet sniffed loudly. "What announcement?"

"Never mind," her brother said gently. "I will deal with the matter myself. Try not to worry, Juliet. Why not go to your room and lie down?"

"What announcement?" she repeated.

"She gave me permission," said Swale, starting forward. "Julie, you know you gave me permission to put that in! I dare you to deny it."

"You don't mean to say—" cried Juliet. "You don't mean to say you actually did it?"

"Certainly I did."

"But you can't have done! You couldn't! Ginger, you can't go about the place announcing you are engaged to people you are not, in fact, engaged to!"

"Not in fact engaged to! I like that, miss!"

Benedict hastily folded up the newspaper on his desk. "My sister has told me in no uncertain terms that she is not engaged to you. This announcement is meaningless, and the *Post* will be forced to print a retraction or suffer a lawsuit! Juliet is a minor, and I never gave my permission to print any such announcement."

"Let me see that!" Juliet demanded, jumping to her feet.

"It will only distress you, my dear," said Benedict.

He tried to keep it from her, but Juliet succeeded in wresting the newspaper from his grasp. She gasped in shock, and all the color drained from her face. "It says . . . it says that you are engaged to *me*," she panted. "Oh, Ginger!"

"Indeed," said Benedict, shaking his head, "printed one thousand times!"

"That cost a pretty penny, let me tell you!" said Swale.

"Not half as much as my lawsuit will cost you," Benedict snapped. "You can't go about the place, wil you nil you, putting announcements in the paper . . ."

Juliet, meanwhile, had fallen back into her chair. She looked at Swale shyly. "And the sandwich boards too?"

"Sandwich boards!" Benedict's eyes started from his head. "What sandwich boards?"

"Two dozen," Swale confirmed, "walking up and down Hyde Park at the fashionable hour between five and six every evening for a month. 'Geoffrey Ambler, Lord Swale, is pleased to announce his engagement to Miss Juliet Wayborn,' printed fore and aft. I think I shall add the words *Amor vincit omnia*, my love. 'Love conquers all.'"

Juliet pressed her hand to her breast. "But—*my* name, Ginger? My name in giant letters on the sandwich boards?"

"Absolutely!"

"Oh, dear God!" Benedict whispered, turning on Swale with fury. "How could you do such a thing? Are you perfectly insane? Have you no regard for the feelings of other people at all?"

"It was her idea!"

"And the commemorative plates?" Juliet inquired, her eyes shining.

Swale shrugged. "Ready in six months."

Benedict watched in helpless astonishment as his sister threw herself into Swale's arms and began to kiss him passionately. "Juliet!" he cried, shocked. "Juliet, stop that at once!"

Neither Juliet nor Ginger paid him the slightest attention.